## BY JOSH MALERMAN

# Spin a Black Yarn

# Spin a Black Yarn

NOVELLAS

## Josh Malerman

NEW YORK

A Del Rey Paperback Original

Copyright © 2023 by Josh Malerman

Published in the United States by Del Rey, an imprint of Random House, a division of Penguin Random House LLC, New York.

Del Rey and the Circle colophon are registered trademarks of Penguin Random House LLC.

ISBN 978-0-593-23786-1
Ebook ISBN 978-0-593-23787-8

Printed in the United States of America on acid-free paper

randomhousebooks.com

2 4 6 8 9 7 5 3

First Edition

Book design by Caroline Cunningham
Frontispiece: AdobeStock/Xunantunich: Woman Spinning Thread

*For Ryan Lewis*

*and*

*Marty Feldman*

# CONTENTS

# Half
# the
# House
# Is
# Haunted

# PART ONE

# 8 AND 6

Half the house is haunted, Robin. Don't ask me which half! Don't you ever ask that again! I'll tell Mommy about the rat if you do. You think I won't, little brother? Didn't I tell Daddy about the fight? Didn't I tell him you roughed up that ninny at school? I didn't leave any of it out, either. Nope. The way you moved that ninny's nose. The way you made him sob. So don't fiddle with me, Robin! And don't you dare demand. Half the house is haunted, I say, and so haunted half the house is!

\* \* \*

Stephanie is trying to scare me again. It's all she does. Daddy says it's getting worse. He said that very thing at dinner. He said, *Stephanie is so hard on Robin.* She is! Mommy asked for an example. Daddy didn't have one and I was too scared to raise my hand. I could have told them she used to hide under the bed. I could have told them how later she placed that dead kid under the bed, dressed as her, so that I thought it was Stephanie down there. Then the real Stephanie leapt from out of the closet. She laughed so hard it made her look different. Then she demanded I help bury the kid again in the East Kent cemetery. I refused and she told me it was phony anyway and then she told Daddy about the fight I got in at school. I fight a lot at school. And I'm darn good at it too! If Stephanie isn't careful, I'm gonna fight her next. But what if what she says is true? What if half the house is haunted? And what if she knows which half?

What would I do without her?

* * *

You always think in such simple terms, Robin. You're such a simpleton. Do you know that word? You should. You are that word. You hear "half" and you say front or back, side or side. You don't even consider top or bottom. You don't consider it's every other step. Follow me. *Right now, dammit.* This step? Maybe haunted. This step? Maybe not. What's wrong? Are you really leaving me up here alone? Are you really going to run downstairs where there's nobody, when that might be the haunted half? Oh, Robin. You are much too simple for a puzzle like this. You think in lines. I think in depth. Yes, *in depth.* Maybe it's the outline of the house that's haunted and not the inner house, you see? Maybe you should find the center of the house and wait there while the haunting goes on, for the rest of your life, wait in the center of the house, Robin, where it might be safe, and . . . and it might not!

* * *

Stephanie is so terrible! She leads me around the house like a little dog. Mommy and Daddy are off doctoring and Stephanie is supposed to take care of me. I can take care of myself! Just not in every way. I can't make lunch, I know. I'm not allowed to use the stove. The oven is so big, Stephanie and me could squeeze inside together. The cupboards are too high. Even Stephanie steps on chairs to get the oatmeal down. I can get up on my bed, of course, but Stephanie has made me so scared I don't even want to take a nap. She tells me my bedroom might be part of the haunted half. I ask her if it is. Does she know? She won't tell! She's terrible. All she wants to do is scare me. That's all!

Where is she hiding now? Every curtain is a hiding place. She told me that once. She said even the middle of the hall is a hiding place for some things.

I want to go outside. I can't stand it inside anymore. I'm always just waiting for Stephanie to scare me.

I can't stand how terrible she is!

\* \* \*

You think the outside is safe, Robin? Why? Because there are no walls? No ceiling? No floor? Do you see how simple this is? You think the sun will help you? You think the open air is your friend?

I was in the library, Robin. I searched Mommy and Daddy's thesaurus for *simple*. I found many words and they all apply to you just perfectly, just perfectly so!

*Ordinary, common, plain, artless.* Just four there, already a biography. *Homely, average, feeble.* But my favorite? Oh, Robin, my favorite word for you is *credent*.

Now, get back inside, credent! Who said the outside isn't the haunted half?

\* \* \*

Mommy and Daddy are back and they asked Stephanie how I was. She told them I was *tolerable*. Mommy patted her on the head when she used that word and Daddy said,

I see you've been in the library, Steph. Continue to do that.

They encourage her. Always. And they asked me if I was feeling well, and Daddy placed his hand on my forehead and told me I should get some rest because I was "running hot." But I didn't want to be upstairs alone, I don't want to be anywhere alone in the house!

But Mommy and Daddy made me. They tucked me in. They turned the bedroom light off but left the light on in the hall.

I want it off.

But I don't want it off.

I want it off.

But I don't.

Is this what Stephanie means when she says half the house is haunted?

*　*　*

Robin, can you hear me? I'll stand watch in the hall. I'll tell you if something is coming. Can you see my shadow on the wall? Good. That's me. If you see any other shadow on the wall, it's not me. So don't speak to any shadow you see on the hall wall unless it's mine. Don't cry, Robin. Rest, like Daddy said. And don't be such a drama! We have a roof over our heads. Some do not. Some people sleep outside, under bridges, in cars, in graveyards.

Oh, they most certainly *do*!

They're called lamias and they like the smell of graves. Some of them wear it like cologne.

Yes. Just like Daddy's, only it smells of the grave, Robin.

That sweet ol' scent of the grave!

*　*　*

I can see Stephanie's shadow in the hall. It's longer than her, but I know it's her. She's trying to scare me again. She's making shapes with her fingers. Mommy calls them shadow puppets. She's trying to make birds or bugs and sometimes horns.

Stop it, Stephanie!

But I don't want her to leave me, I don't want to be alone up here! I told Daddy I didn't want to be alone, and he looked at me angry. He made a clucking sound with his tongue and shook his head no. Daddy does that and it's the end of the talk. So I stopped talking. And he left. And Stephanie is all I have.

She makes horns. And she raises her hands so her fingers look longer and the horns stretch up the whole wall.

I want to say I hate Stephanie, but Mommy and Daddy told us there's one word we're never allowed to use and it's that one. They told us there's "no coming back from hate." As if hate is a place! Mommy said someone could visit there and get stuck without a ride home.

So maybe I don't hate Stephanie. But I hate the shapes she's making in the hall, and I hate what she says and does. One night I counted and I think Stephanie has tried to scare me in every single room in the house. All nineteen of them. She calls me a liar when I say this, tells me she hasn't even used half of them, but there were some times I heard her before she had a chance to scare me. One time on the third floor, I heard her in the last room, heard her breathing real hard and I stopped and listened and I almost hated her then.

Oh, look!

She's stopped making shadows. She's gone.

Is she in the room with me now? Did I miss that? Is Stephanie hiding in my room?

Is she waiting for me to fall asleep?

Is she standing next to my bed?

\* \* \*

Boo, credent!

You're so easy! All you had to do was watch my shadow to know where I was. But that's too simple for you, isn't it? You think you're so smart, so you take your eye off things, thinking they'll be the same when you look back.

Don't tell me what to do. I'm your big sister and I can scare you all I want.

Remember the snake I found in the garden and drowned in the pool? That snake is still growing, Robin. It's ten times the size it was when it died, and it grows twice as big each day. Pretty soon you'll be able to see it sticking out of the water because it'll be too big to fit. And when it gets huge, it'll come back here for you. Because you're the one who was scared of the snake in the garden. *You're* the one who pointed it out to me.

The snake knows you now, Robin. Knows you're the reason it drowned.

* * *

Mommy heard us yelling and came in to tell Stephanie to leave me alone. Mommy asked me what's wrong so I told her Stephanie is trying to scare me. It's the same thing I always say because I don't want to say any more than that because I don't want Mommy to separate Stephanie and me.

I don't want to be alone.

I can't tell Mommy everything. No. Mommy and Daddy are doctors and they think Stephanie is big enough to watch me on her own even though she's not. They trust Stephanie with everything and they don't think I can do anything at all.

Can I?

I asked Mommy if there's a snake growing in the pool, and she told me there are many snakes outside and that I should be careful.

Is Mommy trying to scare me too?

* * *

Good morning, Robin. You fell asleep, after all. Didn't think you could after our talk. Mommy and Daddy are downstairs with breakfast. But they aren't alone. Don't look at me that way, I'm your sister. Your *conventual.* Even your *mother superior.* So, be glad I'm here to tell you the truth, to warn you of the ways of the world.

There's a woman sitting at the breakfast table with Mommy and Daddy. They can't see her, but you and I can. Well, I *think* you can. I can for sure. And this woman does not look nice. She watched me walk into the room and watched me set the table and watched me walk out. She sat there the whole time, her mossy fingers upon the table, and her eyes rolled like falling cherries in her mossy head.

What's her name? How should I know her name? You think I asked?

Don't worry about Mommy and Daddy. They can take care of themselves. And if they can't? Well, I can take care of you.

I'm your mother superior, after all.

Your conventual.

Your *sister.*

* * *

There was no woman at the breakfast table and Stephanie is the worst. I was so hungry I didn't even care about her stupid story. I wasn't even scared! One day she'll learn it's a lot harder to scare me in the morning than it is at night! Mommy and Daddy were busy with what they had to do, but they said they're with us today. I'm glad for that. I can sit in Mommy's office while she works so long as I keep quiet, and I like having Daddy in the house. I could tell Stephanie was disappointed, even though she didn't say so.

She would never admit something like that. Mommy once said some people can't admit when they lose something and when she said it, we all looked to Stephanie and even then, even *then* she nodded like she'd won.

After Mommy and Daddy left the table, Stephanie got up, picked up her plate, made sure I was watching, then looked to one of the empty chairs for a long time. Just looked at it. Then she looked back to me like she was scared and she fled the breakfast room, leaving me alone at the table.

She didn't win.

No.

I can plainly see the chair is empty.

No.

Stephanie did not win.

No.

\* \* \*

Robin, walk the halls with me. This storm is terrible and Mommy doesn't need you sulking about all afternoon in her office.

I know she doesn't hate it. I didn't say that.

I just think it's best for a boy to move about, to get some exercise, while his parents work.

See? Mommy agrees.

Come, Robin. We'll walk one half of the house.

Then we'll walk the other.

\* \* \*

Stephanie can make Mommy agree with anything. Anything she says, Mommy says yes, that's a good idea. They think she's so smart. And they think I'm not! And so I walk the house with Stephanie even though I know the only reason she wants me to come with her is so she can scare me. She never teaches me anything, other than the mean words she looks up, mean things to call me. And every few steps we take, she asks,

Do you think this spot here is haunted?

Then, another step.

How about this one?

In the kitchen she picked up so many things and asked me about each one!

Is this knife haunted, Robin? How about this one? Is this plate, this cup, this chair, this tile, this fork, this crumb?

Is this crumb haunted, Robin?

How about half this crumb?

She's trying to drive me crazy. She heard that people can do that; they can drive each other crazy and so she's set out to do it.

It's in her head. That's what she told me once without meaning to. She said:

I hear things and they must be real.

Well, who told her this is true? I don't know. But someone told Stephanie she can drive me crazy.

And so it must be true.

* * *

Now, here's a real test for you, Robin. Are you so simple as to believe the basement *must* be haunted? Or not? The former? The *former* means the first option: that the basement is haunted. Do you believe all hauntings must take place in the dark? In the corners? At night?

You do! I can tell you do, no matter what you tell me now. Your problem is you feel safe in the light and unsafe in the dark. But why would anything care about that other than you? Why can't there be something standing in the middle of the hall in the middle of the day, any old day?

No, I am *not* trying to scare you, Robin. I am trying to teach you.

We live here, yes? We must *know* the place we live in.

So? Is the basement haunted? Is half the basement haunted? And if so . . . is it the far half, the half farthest from the basement steps?

Yes?

Ah! You failed the first part of the test, Robin. You admitted you believe the dark places are the haunted places, and if you keep thinking this way, you'll never figure out which half it is.

Now, go on. *Go this minute.* Go down into the basement or I will tell Mommy and Daddy that you shit the bed.

Don't tell me not to cuss! You're younger than I am by *two years,* Robin. That's a long time. Do you know what I did for those first two years I lived without you? I *got to know the house.* I introduced myself to the house. I once walked these halls alone, as Mommy and Daddy worked. You've heard them say so. You don't believe it? You think they lie when they say it? Mommy found me in every room in this house, alone. Because even as a baby I knew to study the house, even then.

Now, go on into the basement or I'll tell Mommy what you did in the bed. What? You think she won't believe me? But Robin! Do you really think I washed the bedding like I said I did? Oh, credent, I kept those sheets under a rock outside! Yes, the black rock. And I can easily bring them back *inside* to show Mommy *and* Daddy just how big their little boy really is.

The basement, Robin.

Go.

Now.

Let's test your theory on whether or not the darkest places in the house are haunted.

\* \* \*

I can't stand it! Nobody should have to. Alone in the basement where the light doesn't go! Me, by myself, where Mommy and

Daddy tell us not to go! I'm as smart as Stephanie, if not smarter! And if she thinks I'm going to the far side of the basement, where the sheet hangs to stop anyone from going any farther in the dark, she's wrong.

I'll stop here. Where the light reaches. And I'll wait until Stephanie shouts. She'll be so happy to think of me losing my mind in the dark end of the basement, but she'll never know the truth.

Hear that? She's up at the top of the stairs now, listening to hear me walk. So I walk, but I walk in place! And I make my steps grow quieter without going deeper into the dark because I won't play her games and I won't let her do this to me.

And because Mommy and Daddy told us not to go back there. Not ever.

And I never would!

* * *

Oh, Robin! Oh, Robin! Have you tested your theory? Have you found anything in the dark? Only answer my voice, Robin.

If anybody talks to you down there, it's not me.

Okay?

Go all the way back now, Robin. All the way to the back of the basement.

* * *

Ridiculous! And I hate being made the fool! But it's all she does. Stephanie needs to make friends. Needs to play outside. Needs to *grow up*. Mommy and Daddy go all over town helping people, telling them what they need, but they forget about their own two children. They never say, *What Stephanie needs is to get out of the house and what Robin needs is for Stephanie to get out of the house.*

Ridiculous. *Half the house is haunted.* So dumb! I've never heard a more stupid thing in my life. Stephanie thinks she's being clever (she always thinks she is). She thinks she knows what's scary. Meanwhile, I'm the brave boy in the basement while she's up there giggling about *me*.

Stephanie? Come on. I went to the far end. I didn't find anything. I'm coming back up now.

But she's not responding. Of course not. She's up there thinking of the next way to scare me. She's got a hand over her mouth, I bet she does, so she doesn't call out to me, and she's giggling and thinking, *I'll scare Robin with this or that next!* Really, it's all she does!

Stephanie?

The worst. How much time does she spend thinking of ways to scare me? How much of her life does she waste on me?

Stephanie?

Oh . . .

I think she's down here now. She thinks I don't know about the second way into the basement, through the walk-in pantry in the kitchen. She thinks because I'm only six and she's already eight that Mommy and Daddy don't want me going down into the basement alone, she thinks I don't know about the other stairs.

But I hear her past the sheet, at the dark back of the basement.

I'm smiling, because this is the first time I can scare *her*. She's moving slow because she wants to scare me. But I'm not back there! I'm still near the stairs where the light still shines! And see, Stephanie stopped talking because she went to the kitchen and through the pantry and now she's down here with me and I'm going to scare *her*.

I'm going to step into the dark right here and wait for her to come to the steps. Because she will! She won't find me back there and she'll wonder where I am.

Oh, Stephanie, you're in trouble now. It's your turn to be scared, as I wait in the dark, listening to you coming this way.

Stephanie? Where did you go? Are you still there?

I know she's still there because she hasn't made another sound since she stopped sliding her slippers. She didn't go back up the steps or I would've heard her.

Stephanie?

I see you in the dark.

Stephanie?

I'm not saying a word. I'm waiting for her to step into the light so I can leap out of the dark. So I can scare her.

Here she comes. Yes. Stephanie. Stepping into the light.

Stepping—

\* \* \*

Robin! Calm down! Calm down this instant! I've been up here the whole time just like I said I would! Why do you yell at me? Why are you screaming? Mommy and Daddy are coming now, and they are *not* going to be happy. They need to work so that you and I have food and a place to live! You must stop screaming.

What's that? Me? No, I did not do that. And how could I have done that? I can't be two places at once!

Robin, get back here. Oh, it's too late. Mommy and Daddy are coming and . . . and here they are.

No, Mommy. No, Daddy. I have no idea why Robin is doing this. Why was he in the basement? No, I didn't tell him to go into the basement. No.

Robin! Stop yelling like that!

*Stop yelling!*

\* \* \*

Mommy and Daddy won't leave me alone, and thank God for that. They take turns watching me on the couch in Mommy's office because I scared them good. That's what Daddy says, *You scared us good.* But I tell him there is no good way to be scared, Daddy.

Stephanie was in the basement with me. She says she wasn't, but she also says she didn't tell me to go down there. She's all lies and scaring. That's all she does.

She was in the basement with me. The whole world heard her. Sliding her slippers across the floor.

Wait, Daddy! Don't leave. Please. I'm still shaken. That's your word. Shaken. I'm still shaken, and I don't want to be alone. No, I know it was Stephanie trying to scare me, but it worked. No, I know nobody else is in the basement. What? Mommy is down there now? Making sure? To prove it for me?

Daddy!

Don't tell me to stay on the couch! Mommy shouldn't be down there. It's scary down there, Daddy. And what if Stephanie tries to scare Mommy too?

No, no, you're right. Stephanie can't scare Mommy. You're right. Mommy isn't afraid of basements. Mommy is big.

But still, Daddy, still . . . Stephanie seemed bigger down there.

\* \* \*

Mommy? Did you find anything in the basement? No. I didn't think you would. No! It wasn't me. I haven't been in the basement in a long time. Robin wanted to prove to me that it wasn't scary down there. I know it's not. But he wanted to prove it. Yes, I know. Boys want to look strong for their sisters. They do stupid things like dares. Only, Robin dared himself, I guess you could say. He's silly and simple like that. All boys are. Yes. Except Daddy. What's that? Daddy too? Ha. Well, all boys then.

But so long as you didn't find anything down there, Robin can feel better about it. He was so frightened. I've never seen him like that. You haven't either, I know. It was like he was someone else. Like someone had taken the front half of him away and all we saw was the second half and that half was so scared . . .

So crazy and afraid!

* * *

Mommy and Daddy have taken us into town. They say we need to calm down. They say they treat people for nerves all the time and they've never seen two people as nervous as us. They argued with us about it at home, and they argued with us about it on the drive. Mommy drove and the whole time Daddy talked to Stephanie and me. He told us we had to change our ways. That's how he said it. Now we're in the park in the city. Daddy is pushing Stephanie on a swing and Mommy is kicking a ball with me. She's asking me about making friends. She's saying people can get nervous when they're in a house for so long, they can start getting mad at each other. She keeps talking about Stephanie and me like we're both to blame for the thing that happened, but I'm not to blame. Anybody can see that. Stephanie is just a liar. So, Mommy thinks she's a good girl.

She's not! Not even now as she's smiling and Daddy pushes her on the swing. Look! She's looking at me, right at me. And I know what she's thinking, she's thinking: *When we get home, I'm going to scare you, Robin, scare you so bad you shit the bed.*

What, Mommy? Nothing. I'm not thinking about anything. Here, let me kick the ball back to you.

Stephanie is still looking at me. She can do this all day. Mommy once said: *If a person is mean to you, they are mean to everybody, including themselves.*

That makes me feel better. Maybe Stephanie is mean to herself too.

That makes me feel better. That makes me feel like maybe we're even after all.

* * *

You need to really *think*, Robin. You can't just ask for any gift and bring it back into the house because what if you place your gift on the haunted half of the house and then it's used for bad things?

What do I mean? Oh, come, credent. Mommy and Daddy said we each get one thing from the store, but if you ask for a pocket-knife, that could be dangerous. Why? Are you really this *thick*? Robin. Ask for something that can't hurt you. Like a stuffed animal. Like a shirt. But I guess anything could be used to hurt you if it's in the haunted half of the house.

Oh, *stop* it. What are you going to do? Yell for Mommy and Daddy in a store? Come now, credent. Come now, thick brother of mine. Mommy and Daddy needed to get out of the house, too, and you don't wanna ruin the day for *them*. You know what that's called? A person who ruins the day for other people? That's called a *nincompoop*. I swear I did not make that up. It's in the thesaurus in the library. You really need to read once in a while, credent. Then maybe you'd stop thinking of things in equal halves and realize that one half of a thing can be very small and one half very big so long as the small one means as much as the big.

* * *

I got the pocketknife. Because Stephanie *sucks*. Yeah, I won't say that word out loud, not to Mommy and Daddy and not even to her, but she *sucks*. It's summer now, but during school I have a friend who said his big brother sucks and guess what? So does my sister. Benny told me what it meant, he said for someone to suck it means they aren't nice and don't care about anything but their hair. Stephanie sucks. It feels good to say it. Even as we're driving back home, even as we're heading back to the very place where she will try to scare me all over again, it feels good to say to myself that she sucks.

Daddy drives now and Mommy is talking funny and Daddy is laughing and they sound like they are in love. Mommy is loud and making jokes and once she turned to Stephanie and she said, *You two need to learn how to relax.*

But the way she said it made me turn red. Because she sounded right. Like she knows and I don't and I *do* need to relax. But then Mommy said Stephanie's name funny. She said, *Stepafie.* And Daddy started laughing and they told us we needed to *occupy ourselves* when we get home because they had work to do. Well, that sucks too. Because that means Stephanie is going to feel like she's the boss of me again and she's going to make me do something I don't want to do and if she tells me to go into the basement again, I'm going to tell her she *sucks.*

That would feel so good. Just to say it.

What I really need to do is figure out a way to scare *her.* What I really need to do is plan like she plans. So that I don't spend all my time being afraid of her and instead I feel glad about being alone with her.

I think maybe it has to do with my pocketknife. Yes. I think maybe I'll scare her with the knife.

But how?

Oh, look at her, planning! Looking out the window at the woods we pass! She's thinking of ways to scare me right now. She's smiling like she knows exactly what she's going to do to me when we get home.

Mommy? Daddy? Can I sleep with you two tonight?

They yell NO together so loud and so fast it nearly breaks the windows and now they laugh so hard they sound like funny little dogs.

* * *

Come, Robin, come quick. I can show you what I'm talking about. No, I'm not trying to scare you. And stop saying that! Read the thesaurus, come up with new words. *Shock, panic, startle, affray, daunt, curl my hair.* All good substitutions.

Oh my! Did you see that? The whole sky lit up! This is a *squall.* I guess the sky forgave us while we were in town. No, Mommy and Daddy are asleep. Snoring so loud you're mistaking it as part of the thunder.

Come, Robin. I can show you what I'm talking about.

I can show you something that's happening in the haunted half of the house.

* * *

Oh, *why* do I go with her? *Why* do I listen? *Why* can't I simply say, *No, Stephanie, no, I'm not going with you! No, Stephanie, no, half the house is not haunted!*

* * *

I'm not taking you to the basement, don't worry. And Mommy and Daddy won't hear us where we're going. We're going to the top, Robin. Yes, the attic. Oh, stop it. It's hardly a crawl space when it's a walk-in, credent. Don't give me that and do *not* look at me like that. But, then again, things do happen up there. How do I know? Because I make it a point to know these things. I actually do the work so you don't have to.

Here. Help me. I just need you to get to one knee so I can stand on your knee and pull down the rope. Yes. Just do it, Robin. And stop pretending like you're not interested in what I'm about to show you. Stop pretending this is all me.

Okay. Good. On your knee. And . . .

I got it!

Watch out, Robin! No, I don't think Mommy and Daddy heard the ladder come down. They're really sleeping. Okay. I'll go first. But get right behind me because we're not going up there, we're just going to peek inside. Yes. I mean it.

Come.

\* \* \*

Nothing! We climbed the ladder and we saw nothing. The attic looked like it always does and Stephanie seemed happy for that, but then she also said that half the house must've moved.

What?

We got the ladder back up and we're walking the hall of the second floor now. Mommy and Daddy sleep on the third floor because there's a room up there so big it's like a whole house in one place. Stephanie and I sleep up there, too, and the second floor is always a little scary to me because we don't use it very much. Daddy calls it "house sandwich," meaning the first and third floors are the bread and the second floor is the meat, I think.

Stephanie told me to be quiet and so I am but I also wanna yell in her ear to scare her. Maybe that's how I'll do it. Only, I don't wanna ruin it. I don't want her thinking I'm always going to scare her like she always scares me because then she won't be scared when I have a really good scare in mind.

Stephanie?

Fine. I'll be quiet. She's pointing to the window at the end of the hall.

She puts her lips to my ear and I back away and she pulls me closer and puts her lips to my ear and she says, *There.*

Where?

She does it again: *There.*

Her breath is hot and her whisper feels like a potato bug crawling into my ear.

But ... where? There's nothing at the end of the hall. Just the window. Just—

\* \* \*

*Robin, oh my God. Oh my God, did you see that? Stop it, stop asking what, stop asking. I'll tell you. But you gotta stop. Why did I pull you in this room? Because of what was at the end of the hall, you dummy! No! Not at the window. Is that where you were looking? The window? Oh my God, Robin. You missed it. It was right there, flat to the wall. On the left! No, no, no, on the right. I mean it, Robin. Well, it doesn't matter if you believe me or not. We're not leaving this room till I'm sure it's no longer in the hall. Stop breathing so loud. And no! We are not turning on the light in here!*

*Oh my God, Robin.*

*You really didn't see it?*

*I'll explain it to you later but right now just be quiet. Please. We need to be smart. Not simple. We need to think about the house and think about which half of the house we're standing in,* right now. Yes, this *room. It's not so easy to keep track of, Robin! Stop talking so loud. Stop it. It's going to hear you.*

*Oh God, Robin. It heard you. It's—*

\* \* \*

Stephanie had the door open a crack and I closed my eyes.

I'm never following her again on one of her dares through the house.

I'll never say yes again.

Tell Mommy and Daddy I get in fights at school, tell them about the rat I hurt, tell them about the accident I had in bed.

I don't care anymore, Stephanie.

I won't follow you anymore.

Never.

Never again!

* * *

Robin, are you okay? No, I mean it. And I'm glad you closed your eyes when you did. And I'm sorry you felt you had to close them the whole way back to your room. I'm really not trying to scare you. We're in your bedroom. It's better in here.

I'll sleep with you tonight if you want me to.

I'm really just looking out for you, Robin. You're my brother. And you're my friend. And maybe I just wanted to share it with you, the experience I'm having.

But I won't do that again.

I'm sorry. Here. Let me climb into bed with you.

I'm so glad you closed your eyes.

I mean it. I love you, Robin. I really do.

I'm so glad you closed your eyes exactly when you did!

Here, let me pet your head. I'm so sorry. You're only six years old and I'm already eight and I should've known that you weren't ready. I mean it. I care about you very much.

I love you, Robin.

Thank God you closed your eyes.

What?

No. Sleep now. I'll not tell you what I saw.

No need.

You're only six. What was I thinking . . .

Sleep.

I love you.

I'm so glad you closed your eyes.

So glad.

Brother. Friend.

Sleep.

* * *

Stephanie is not in my bedroom anymore. The sun is up. Mommy came in and she looked funny. Her eyes were puffy and her voice was scratchy but she smiled and said she must've missed a real storm because the lawn is really wet. Daddy came in after and hugged her around the waist and they kissed and talked about having headaches.

Stephanie is not in my bedroom.

So . . . where?

This is it. This is my chance to scare her.

Mommy helps me get dressed now, even though I don't need her to do that anymore. I can tell she feels bad about something. Not with Daddy. But like she didn't mean to fall asleep so early.

She asks me how Stephanie and my night was last night. Did we listen to the storm? Did we count the time between the lightning and the thunder?

I tell her yeah, we counted. Because I don't feel like telling her Stephanie was mean and tried to scare me with phony stories about things flat to the wall and things looking through a crack in a door, looking back at us.

She's happy to hear that. She hugs me and says her head hurts and when I ask why she laughs and says because sometimes adults drink more than water.

Stephanie hasn't made a peep.

Where is she? Where is she in the house?

When Mommy leaves my bedroom, I go straight to my desk and pull out the pocketknife. Here's what I'm going to do to scare her: I'm going to carve her name into a doorjamb and pretend I didn't do it and when she says I did I'm going to say, hey, you were the one who said a ghost might do something with my knife, not me!

Down at breakfast, no Stephanie. No Mommy either and I'm with Daddy as he drinks a lot of water and eats slowly and asks me about the storm. I tell him we counted. But then I also say not for long, so I don't feel like I'm lying all the way. Just halfway.

Mommy's back in bed, he says. Then he smiles and says he might do the same. He talks about headaches and the best thing for them and then the phone rings and Daddy is up and I'm alone in the breakfast room and I can hear him when he realizes he's needed on a house call, both Mommy and him, and then Daddy's calling up the stairs for Mommy to get back up because they have to go to work.

Where's Stephanie? He asks me. I tell him I don't know. You have no idea? He asks me and I say no. You can't narrow it down for me, he asks, you don't even know which half of the house she's in?

I watch him close as he leaves and heads upstairs to get ready. Mommy and him move fast when they get calls and the same Mommy who looked so puffy this morning doesn't look puffy anymore. She looks wide-awake like she does when she goes to work and Daddy is wearing his suit and the two of them pause at the front door and they both look at me and ask:

Where's your sister?

Stephanie! They call. Both of them together. Well, she can't be far, Mommy says, but they look at each other like maybe they're worried she might be far. Daddy starts to walk toward the stairs and Mommy says hang on. She crouches in front of me and says,

Your sister is somewhere in the house. Find her. We have to go save a man's life. A very old man who needs saving. Okay, Robin? Can you be really, really good so Mommy and Daddy don't have to worry about you, and we can save this man who needs saving?

I say yes, but I'm also a little scared because . . . where is Stephanie? I can't reach the cupboards and I don't wanna be alone in the house.

Thank you, Mommy says. And Mommy and Daddy look at each other like they're making a decision and then they are out the door and I'm alone in the foyer with my pocketknife, all of the house to search for Stephanie.

I start on the first floor and go to the kitchen and the pantry, but the sacks of flour are on top of the floor door that leads to the basement stairs, so I know she didn't go this way if she's down there. Then back through the breakfast room and down the hall to the library, where I really do expect to find her and so I move quiet and slow because I just wanna know where she is so I can go carve her name somewhere she isn't. But Stephanie isn't in the library. She's not in the music room or what Daddy likes to call the parlor, and so I go upstairs all the way to the third floor and I see the attic door is still closed and I take the hall to Stephanie's room and she's not there. She's not in my room either. I look out the windows and don't see her outside. Mommy and Daddy's room is empty, too, and I'm starting to whisper, *Where is she?* She's not in any of the bathrooms or the extra bedrooms and so I take the hall back to the stairs and down to the second floor.

All these rooms are mostly empty. Mommy and Daddy tried to do something with them, to make one a "sitting room" and another for "entertaining" but everybody sits downstairs and so that never happened. There are some chairs in some, and one has a bed, and I still don't hear Stephanie and now I want to call her name because I really am alone without her, and I've never been alone in the house before. I think of Mommy crouching in front of me and saying Daddy and her need to help someone and I try to feel brave about it because it's a good thing what they do and the least I can do is be okay when they go do it. When the second-floor-room thing didn't happen up here, Mommy said let's at least paint them each a different color so that we could have something to call them, some purpose (she said), and so one room is blue and one is green and one is brown and one is pink.

I find Stephanie in the pink room.

I'm fingering the pocketknife in my pocket, thinking of all the places in the house I can go to carve her name and then show her because she's all the way here at the end of the second-floor hall in the pink room and it's my big chance. But when I see her, I'm charged up about her, it's the first thought I have, the way she's sitting on the chair and facing the pink corner of the room.

Stephanie, I say, why aren't you wearing any clothes?

And I feel roly-poly bugs crawling up my arms and I'm hot and cold like I'm sick and dizzy and I step into the room and I say again, Stephanie, why aren't you wearing any clothes before I see, Oh, this isn't Stephanie in this chair without any clothes, staring at the corner of the pink room and she's not young like Stephanie at all.

Robin!

Stephanie scares me, it's all she does, calling my name from the door to the pink room, calling from behind me as I'm about to tap who I thought was Stephanie on the shoulder, as the woman who is not young coughs and Stephanie says: Robin, close your eyes, oh Robin, close your eyes, and I think to myself, Mommy once said the mind can play tricks on itself and sometimes those tricks are good, good tricks, so you don't feel so much pain and also so you don't go crazy if you see something that could make you crazy and I think, as the woman who is not young coughs again (not a cough, a laugh), and I realize she's *not* facing the corner, she never was, I think maybe I thought this was Stephanie when I came into the pink room because my mind was playing a good trick on me and so it told me, hey, there's Stephanie, hey, there she is, sitting in the pink room, hey there's your sister, Stephanie.

Robin! Close your eyes!

And then Stephanie's hand is on my wrist and she's pulling me from the pink room just as the woman who is not Stephanie is standing up, lifting a naked arm toward me, as I realize I wasn't looking at the back of someone's head, no, I wasn't about to tap someone on the back of the shoulder but the front.

Hurry! Stephanie says.

And I do hurry, but I feel like I'm made of something soft and I can't move like I normally do and I can't stop looking back up the hall to the pink room, to the doorjamb where I was going to carve Stephanie's name, thinking that what I saw in there is about to step out of the room, about to hurry up the hall too.

Then we're on the stairs and Stephanie is telling me to close my eyes, she's screaming it, and she's pulling me so hard, and when we get down to the bottom, I fall for a second and Stephanie picks me back up and drags me to the front door and she holds me there and we face the stairs and we just breathe really hard and wait.

Keep your eyes closed, Stephanie says. That was the haunted half, Robin.

And I do close my eyes. But I still see the woman standing up. I still see her naked arm. And I think, with Stephanie's arms around me, I think:

Yes, that's what my mind did for me, it played a trick for me, a good trick, to protect me from losing my mind.

# PART TWO

# 42 AND 40

The older I get (and I'm forty now, goodness), the more I think, *You know what would be* really *scary? A haunted condo.* No more of the big, garish house. No more gothic castles and stone corridors and secret stairways to the basement. Scare me in a condo in the middle of the day, you cowards!

Ha.

Yeah. Sometimes I think I'd give anything to hear a haunted-house story that doesn't at least partially resemble the home I grew up in.

Still . . .

I live in Samhattan now. A whopping ninety minutes (with traffic) from the gaudy abode I grew up in and have only seen a handful of times since high school. I got out of there as fast as I could, which was saying something, because in those days I could move pretty fast. But I wasn't the only one. Mom and Dad got out, too, moved south to do their doctoring for warmer patients. They still own the place. By the time I graduated college (I came close, truth be told; a semester short; seems I've been on the move a lot since growing up in that place) they'd left East Kent. But just because Mom, Dad, and I don't call that place home anymore certainly doesn't mean our family isn't represented in the flesh.

Stephanie . . .

Stephanie still lives there. And has for close to twenty years.

All alone.

Does she date? I don't know. I wish I did. Does she entertain? I don't know. I wish I did. Does she sit alone in the library and stare at the floor all day, telling it it's haunted? Probably. Truth is, I know little to nothing about Stephanie aside from the few times we speak on the phone a year. She's as short with me as Mom and Dad say she is with them. She's quick and distracted and yet, I try. I joke, I tell her stories about my life, I ask her about her own. From what I can tell, Stephanie is a shut-in. It's not an easy thing to accept; your sister is someone you care a lot about, and you can't help but think a night or two of tequila and live music might change her life. I've tried that, too, inviting her to Samhattan, inviting myself to East Kent. But, no matter how wily I might think I am, conversations with Stephanie always turn to grease; you can feel them slip out of your hands long before you both hang up.

I worry. As a brother. As a friend. As someone who grew up with her.

I worry about Stephanie.

So why haven't I been home more often? Well, that's hard to say. Time is like grease, too, of course. In college I took up music, almost accidentally, as my close friends were all super proficient and (as the logic of twenty-year-olds goes) they goaded me into doing the same. This took on a life of its own, in a sense: no, we didn't play stadiums, but we did tour the country, and parts of the world, for the better part of two years, me and my best friends, playing our own songs sometimes for twenty people, sometimes for two, and one glorious night when we opened for the Shambas and played for over a thousand people and I thought we'd reached the mountaintop of life. Which we had. But there are many mountaintops, I like to think.

I played the synth. I was put in charge of the spooky mood, the background glue ambience, a thing I turned out to be very good at and, to be honest, cared a lot more about than I ever thought I would. Mom and Dad didn't mind. In fact, they came to see me play at a bar in Samhattan I'd booked for us myself and they even once drove all the way to the Woodruff in Goblin, where we played a wedding of all things (incredibly, mercifully, we were asked to play no covers). They loved it. And the more they called and asked me about my life and my music, the more I realized how cool my parents actually are and always were. And the more I realized how cool *they* were, the clearer it became that they couldn't be (and aren't) responsible for the horrible low hum that accompanies all recollections I have, at random now, about growing up in that house.

So, the elephant in the room.

The pink room.

Obviously, it was Stephanie. I mean, the girl once made a dead dummy and put it under my bed. My entire childhood was my sister trying to scare the living shit out of me, and often succeeding. I don't think of anything else when I think of growing up: only Stephanie around a corner, Stephanie beneath a sheet, Stephanie at the side of my bed, demanding I come with her, travel the halls of that bloated gothic monster, that I *better* go with her and *had* to go with her because Mommy and Daddy were out doctoring and I was too little to survive even a bedroom on my own. Jesus, I just called them Mommy and Daddy. See? Things, phrases, ideas, get wedged into us, don't they? And believe me, those memories are *wedged* so deep that honestly, I can hardly remember any other times we had.

I see:

The back of Stephanie in a hall (I'm following her; always).

Stephanie daring me, taunting me, calling me some name she'd fished out of the old thesaurus in the library.

Stephanie exerting some weird prepubescent peer pressure.

Stephanie saying *half the house is haunted*.

Hard to explain how much that phrase has messed me up through the years. I'm a forty-year-old man, and while that might not be what it used to be, it's still old enough to get over childhood fears. Yet, how many parties have I been to, drinking, laughing, when suddenly Stephanie's phrase crossed my mind, and then a friend waved a hand in front of my face, asking where I went? How many times have I walked city streets across America, cities around the world, stopping to wonder at a cool house, when that phrase arrived with knives out?

*Half the house is haunted.*

And what the *fuck* did she mean?

Oh, I've thought about it. I've really, really thought about it. I've wondered if she meant *she* was haunted and I was not. Maybe she thought she was sick? In the head? Or maybe she meant *I* was haunted and she wasn't? Or Mom and Dad were and we weren't? Or we were, and ... you get the point. Maybe Stephanie meant to say the second floor and the basement were haunted. Those were the places I'd had my own "encounters," which were of course nothing more than Stephanie fucking with me. But maybe that's how she saw it. Third floor? No. Second floor? Yes. First floor? No. Basement? Yes.

Half.

The house.

I really try to put myself in Stephanie's eight-year-old head, but it always results in me telling myself: *You know how kids are.* But despite this universal truth, it just doesn't feel like a good enough explanation. Not in this case. And whenever I try to dismiss those days, and my gullible part in it, whenever I tell myself to forget about it, I'm immediately hit with a sense of *no*.

No. It wasn't just kids.

No.

There was a feeling too. That Stephanie was speaking at least some truth.

*Half the house is haunted.*

Did she mean the front half, the back half, the upper half, the lower half, the left, the right, outside? Did she believe every other step, every other tile, was haunted? Maybe she meant half the house was in disrepair? And maybe (and this is a thing I've learned about kids from watching my former bandmates raise theirs), maybe she'd just heard the phrase on the radio and gobbled it all up as her own.

Half the house is haunted.

Well, the *whole* thing feels haunted to me now. I literally don't have one memory that doesn't include Stephanie's face, her eyes dead serious, her mouth open, pouring forth crazy madwoman shit about half the house this, half the house that, this step, that step, the ceiling, the basement, the walls, the yard, the floor, her bed, my bed, this pillow, that pillow, the car, Mommy and Daddy.

You'd think a guy like me, with parents like the ones I have, would cherish memories of warm evenings in front of the fire, Christmas dinners, laughter at the breakfast table in the breakfast room. But I don't. And, instead, I find myself embarrassed I even *had* a breakfast room at all. Most the time I don't even tell people how big my childhood home truly was. Six-thousand square feet of too many rooms to use, so Mom decided one day to make one blue, one green, one brown, and one . . .

There was one time in Oxford, Mississippi, when we played an amazing show on the town square and slept on the floor of the after-party house and my bandmates woke me up, telling me I was asking Stephanie why she wasn't wearing any clothes, and I looked at them like they were crazy and made up a story about a dream I never had. You know what crosses my mind a lot? The time Stephanie said something about how people think the daytime is safe and the night is not and how the dark part of the basement wasn't haunted just because it's the scarier part. For whatever reason, *that* stuck with me. And so, is that what she meant by half? That the house was haunted during the day but not at night?

I try *not* to think about it. Or . . . I've *tried*. Over the years. Over time. But that little phrase has stuck in my head like a thirty-third tooth. I got by it in my twenties. I went off to school. Traveled the world. Lived. And my thirties weren't bad either. Had a string of jobs that had me traveling again, seeing the world, never in the area long enough to let it rule me. But recently, the last few years, yeah, well, Samhattan so close to East Kent, and my childhood home with Stephanie still in it.

Earlier I said the elephant in the room, but I should've said the elephant in the *car*.

Because I'm driving. Right now. Driving those miles home. I'm driving to see my sister for the first time in a long time, and I don't think I've ever been quite this nervous about it.

And why should I be? Weren't we just kids? And don't little kids scare one another? And don't they say the batshit-crazy things they learn from TV and hear on the radio? And doesn't every man and woman my age have mixed feelings about their childhood, their family, their childhood home?

As someone who grew up with Stephanie, I owe it to her. That's what I tell myself. Someone needs to go check on her. *I* need to check on her. I need to say hello. But the closer I get, the less this feels like my reason.

What I really wanna do is ask her what she meant.

*Half the house is haunted.*

Because the more I think about it, the more I feel like I've been forever living whatever dream my bandmates woke me from that night in Mississippi.

And the closer I get to that huge, showy home, the more I feel terrible about it, like I'm totally unprepared, until I'm about half worried sick.

\* \* \*

Robin? Is it you? Oh, Robin. You shouldn't have come here. You shouldn't have come here at all!

\* \* \*

This is madness. I haven't even made it into the house yet and Stephanie is acting exactly like she did when we were kids. Like, *exactly*. She's looking out the side window, her eyes set and cold, shaking her head no. Yet, honestly, I can't believe how okay she looks. The images that have come to mind through the years, oh boy: a constant flipping between her at eight, then her now, pale as a vampire, thin and sickly, a blouse covered in soup, some haunted witch of a woman who still lives in the big, bad house.

Stephanie! Hello. Yes. It's me. Let me in?

I honestly don't know at this moment if she's going to let me in or not. I mean, if things are still the same around here, then I know other ways to enter. But still. Is she seriously *not* going to come to the door? Is she really going to stand there at the glass, mouthing words I can't hear, shaking her head no like she's warning me, trying to scare me, all over again?

Fuck. I'm getting cold. Like, I feel cold inside. This is exactly like my childhood but playacted by forty-year-olds. Come on!

Stephanie. I drove into town to see you. I would love to talk. Let me in?

I don't think she's going to. She's no longer at the glass and she's not at the door. Where is she? Does she think I'll just drive off if she waits long enough? She's gotta know I saw her, right?

So, okay. I'm just gonna keep knocking until she lets me in. That's what I'm going to do. Because now I'm getting a little pissed. Now I'm feeling like she's somehow twisted our childhood into a knot where *I* was the one who tried to scare *her* all the time. I'm even feeling guilty, for fuck's sake. Guilty for planning to scare her that day with the pocketknife. Yeah, wow. I haven't thought about that pocketknife and the stupid little plan I'd had since . . . since *that day*. Whatever prank she pulled on me completely wiped that idea clean. Gone from my memory until . . . until right now.

Stephanie? It's been a long time. It's just me, Robin. Your brother. I'm just here to say hello, to check in. I know I could've called, but I missed you and I wanted to make sure you weren't sitting alone in a big, empty house all day and so, please, for me, for you, just open the door, let's hug, let's talk, I won't even leave the foyer if you don't want me to. I don't even have to step any farther into the house.

Oh, hey. It worked. I hear her now. Footsteps on the other side of the door. Sliding slippers. I recognize the sound from our childhood. Didn't Stephanie shuffle her slippers when we were kids? And isn't it amazing how a smell or a sound, one little sound, can bring back an entire scene from decades ago? As if that one sound is a seed and your life is one of those moments in nature documentaries when they speed up the—

Stephanie. Hi. I'm so glad to see you. You actually look amazing. May I come in?

* * *

Robin. Oh my God, Robin. You don't look a day over forty. Was that a bad joke? I thought it rather spot-on. And what's the difference? Jokes today are either about making fun of yourself or making fun of other people and anyways it's all making fun. Fun! Why are you looking at me like you're surprised? It hasn't been *that* long since we last saw each other. You seem stunned that I'm not an old cat lady by now. No, no cats. No dogs either. Can you imagine searching these halls and rooms for a pet? Or for pet shit? That made you laugh. What's that? No. I haven't been totally alone for all this time. I do have friends, Robin. You're not the only one, Mr. Musician Rockstar. Oh, really? You stopped doing that? Why? It makes me sad when people stop doing stuff like that. Like it was all some childish thing they thought they were supposed to outgrow. If there's one thing I'd like you to leave here with, it's the inspiration to start making music again. I bet I can make that happen. I've always had a way with you. I can see clearly how to make you feel a certain way. No! I love that. I think that's a sign of a good relationship. The worst is when you have no influence, no *say* in the matter. What? Why are we still standing in the foyer? Well, you said yourself that you'd like to come in and just hang out in the foyer, so I figured you meant what you said.

Robin . . .

No, I don't mind. Why would I mind? You want to go to the kitchen? Are you hungry? Let's go to the kitchen. Yes, I have food. Really, what do you think I do here? You think I eat the doorjambs? Come. But come quick. No reason to stop and fuss over every room we pass. No, it's not that they're dirty, it's just that they're *unused*. Who wants to hang out in an unused room? Not me. What's that? Scared? Do I get scared living in this huge place all by myself? Oh, Robin. This is our childhood home. This is the most special place in the world to me. This is the one place in all the world where I feel entirely like myself. No. I don't get scared staying here. I stick to my half of the house and let the unused rooms remain exactly that: *empty*.

* * *

Christ, she's like someone who hasn't seen a person in ten years trying to use the monologue of a late-night talk-show host. Stephanie's moving a mile a minute. But I gotta say, she seems okay. In a weird way. Hard to explain. She isn't mopey and her eyes are bright and she looks fit and alive. Well, who's to say what the right way to live is, right? Here I am, I've been the world over, gone on five hundred dates, and I'm not any more married than she is. In fact, Stephanie almost seems better adapted than I am. Has it always been this way? I think maybe it has. Unreal. Here we are, brother and sister in our forties, and I'm still a deer in headlights every time she gets going.

Salad would be great, Stephanie. Whatever, really, just glad to be here. Do you have anything to drink? Well, if I have too many, I guess I could just stay here.

Why am I testing her like this? I don't want to stay in this house, yet I want her to ask me to stay. Why? What am I proving to myself? That she's hiding something? But why do I think she is?

Oh, yeah, beer would be amazing. Is that what you drink? Beer? All alone out here?

She tells me to stop talking about how alone she is out here. She tells me again she has friends. She rolls her eyes. How is it possible that I've traveled ninety miles to see my sister who lives like a hermit yet *I'm* the one coming off as socially inept?

Thank you, Stephanie. And . . . cheers.

* * *

I'll have one, too, but not too many or else I start to feel heavy and tired. Some people are like that, you know. One beer is like a loaf of bread for some people. Why do you keep looking at me like that? Do I look that good? Well, good. I do take care of myself.

Just like I take care of the house. Half of it, anyway. What do you mean, what do I mean? You try taking care of a place this big! I have no idea how Mommy and Daddy used to do it. Yes, I still call them that. Live with it. And they like it! But they like everything. Every time I talk to them they sound like they're on vacation. I guess, in a way, they are. Living south, where it's warm. It's hard to keep a place like this warm. The best I can do is half.

What? What do I keep saying that you keep looking at me like that?

\* \* \*

But seriously, she's gotta be doing this on purpose. All this "half" stuff. There's just no way this is a coincidence. I've never heard of a verbal tic like it in my life. Is Stephanie trying to scare me? Even now? At age forty? Does she still see me as her little brother, someone she has some *say* about?

I'm not looking at you like anything, Stephanie. Only a brother who is really, really happy to see his sister.

But okay, not *only* like that because in a way, she's acting weirder than I could have anticipated. Old cat lady sounds normal now. She's vague about everything, has the energy of five people, and slips in these "halves" like I'm not supposed to notice. Or, I don't know. Maybe I'm not. Maybe it's a phrase she latched on to as a kid and I took it too seriously and here I've obsessed my whole life over nothing. One way to find out:

Stephanie, when we were kids, you used to say—

\* \* \*

Kids say a lot, don't they, Robin? Sorry to interrupt you, but the truth is, I've been thinking about those days myself. I can practically see us in the halls, now, when I turn in for the night, as I turn the house off. What do I mean? The lights, of course. Someone has to do it, right? To be honest, it's my two favorite times of day: when I turn the house on and when I turn the house off. Both feel like something coming to life for me. Of course I don't illuminate the *whole* house all day. Just . . . a lot of it. Maybe half. I don't like the idea of certain rooms remaining dark forever. You know how people say plants respond to voices? I think rooms do too. When I leave a room, I say goodbye to it. Sometimes I thank it too. Don't laugh at me! I say, *Thank you for having me.* Because really, it's in the rooms and in the halls where we have all our meaningful realizations, right? When's the last time something unexpectedly true struck you in the middle of a meadow? No. You were in your bedroom. Or your car. Or your kitchen. So, why not thank the space for having you? And for maybe even inspiring you? Like when you decided you were done with music (which is, of course, ridiculous, and you'll need to change that thinking), where were you? Do you remember?

See! You do! You were where? In the bedroom of your Samhattan apartment! Ha. I told you. Well, next time you see that apartment, tell it to go fuck itself. And then maybe the room will be nicer to you after that. Sometimes you gotta put your foot down, Robin. I mean it. It's not just people that influence us. A cracked step on the way into a house implies a cracked home. Cracked in half? Why are you asking me that? You want a second beer? Already? No problem. Maybe I want one too. And watch me now. Ready?

Here's the beer and . . . thank you for giving us beer, Mr. Refrigerator!

* * *

Yeah, I have no doubt now she's using some kind of subliminal language about "halves." I'm to the point where I kinda want her to keep doing it. Like I'm keeping score of a basketball game. Or like it's a set she's playing, song after song, each having something to do with halves. Christ, it's like Stephanie's been singing a concept album our entire lives.

*Half the House Is Haunted.*

I'm already feeling a little drunk. I'm starting to look over my shoulder, starting to think about the rest of the house. You'd think a couple beers would dull the idea, but nope. I'm starting to feel a little shut-in. But the kitchen is one of the biggest rooms in the house. Well, maybe it's because Stephanie hasn't made a single change to the place. Like, not one. It feels like I'm six years old again and Mommy and Daddy are out doctoring and Stephanie is talking about halves again, trying to freak me out, and it's working. My friends, my bandmates, they talk about certain people who get under their skin. I guess everybody has someone like that in their lives. And a sister is a prime candidate for the role. But still, it's never been like *that*. It's never felt like Stephanie *bothers* me. It's just not the right word. I'm trying to think back to those days on the road, traveling the country, studying the synth, trying to actually get good at it: How did I describe Stephanie to the people I met? Did I mention I had a sister in passing? Did I tell people what she was like, what I *thought* she was like? Did I ever actually break down and tell anybody how much she fucked me up as a little boy, how she used to walk me through the house, pointing to the wall and saying this one isn't haunted but the other one is? A real vague memory is coming to mind . . . me in a woman's bedroom after a show, a hilarious woman named Didi who I got real high with, and Didi is asking me about Stephanie and I'm not really giving her much and she's pressing a little bit and she's saying stuff like, *Sounds to me like something needs to be worked out there.* Did I tell Didi my sister told me she drowned a snake in the pool? That my sister told me it was growing out there, that it would soon get big enough to swallow the house? Holy shit, I haven't thought about this stuff in a really long time. Stephanie hiding in cupboards. Stephanie hiding behind doors. Stephanie hiding under my bed, and *in* my bed, waiting for me to brush my teeth and climb in before she pressed a cold foot to my leg, sending me shrieking into the hall, where she'd catch up to me before I got to Mommy and Daddy and she'd threaten to ruin my life if I said anything.

What's that, Stephanie? What do you mean? Did I *look* like I was thinking of the past?

* * *

Sometimes I worry it's all we think about, Robin. Like, literally every decision we make is based on the past. I don't mean it in a Freudian way (a lot of Freud in the library, did you know?), but more like we build this character of who we are, and we do it at a real young age, and then you either get encouragement or discouragement for it and spend the rest of your life reacting to *those reactions* and so who the hell are you really? But whatever. Think of the past all you want. You weren't? Great. What were you thinking about then? The rest of the house? Really? And you wanna walk around? Well, of course you can walk around the rest of the house, Robin. Imagine if I said no to that. Yes. Let's grab another beer each and go walk around the house. But not all of it. What? Why are you laughing? Listen, some of it's never used. I mean, I'm not going to stop you from going anywhere, I'm just saying every other room is nicer than the ones between them these days, but if you want to spend some time in every inch of this house, I can't stop you. Or ... *or* ... you can let me give you the tour I would give anybody stopping in. Because I live here alone, you know? And just like any house of any size, there are places you don't want others to see. No, I know you're not just anybody, of course not, you grew up here (the past!), but still.

Well, either way. Come on then. Let's go walk around the house. But stay close. I wouldn't want you to get hurt, we're drinking, wouldn't want you to take the wrong steps on the stairs, if you know what I mean.

Come on, Robin! You were so serious about it a moment ago. Now you look white as milk. It's fine. I didn't mean to imply a walk around the house wasn't fine. But if we're going to go do this, you actually have to stand up.

There you go! Look at us. Two forty-year-olds, taking twenty minutes to get up off our chairs to go take a walk around the house.

Then again, it *is* a big house. And sometimes by the end of it, I feel beat.

* * *

Stephanie is talking like I've never been here before. Is she doing that for me? To make me feel at ease? She definitely senses I'm a little messed up about it. But she hasn't asked why. That means something. That means she *knows* why. Right? If someone comes to your house and they get sweaty and clammy about the tour, you'd stop to ask why, right? Well, okay. So she knows. But what does she know? Does she know how many times I've seen this very scene play out in my head? Me, following Stephanie out of the kitchen, into the enormous, endless first-floor hall? Does she wonder if I'm seeing her as a kid right now? Because I am. Yet, I'm not. I'm seeing both, I guess, and I don't mean it's from the beers. I feel almost exactly the same at forty as I did at, say, six. I feel like I don't want to be alone, but I also don't want to be with Stephanie. And I wish Mommy and Daddy were home. Though, I do want to be with Stephanie. She's my sister and I haven't seen her in years and you know what? She's acting a lot cooler than I am right now. Is it possible that after all this time, and all the fucked-up vibes, that somehow *I'm* the one who's weird? If I didn't know better (and I'm starting to feel I don't), I'd say Stephanie is the well-adjusted adult, taking care of a huge old home, but no worse for the wear. I'd say

Stephanie is a goddamn queen, stalking the halls of her manor; focused, frank, unafraid. Look at her, walking the exact center of the hall like there's a line painted there. I actually looked to see if there was! This side and that side, half and half, half the house is haunted.

It looks good, Stephanie. Looks like it hasn't changed at all since the last time I saw it. When's the last time I saw this hall? Well, I don't know. Oh, that's right. Last time I was here I actually didn't leave the foyer, did I. I'd totally forgotten about that. Really? The time before that too? Well, let's not embarrass me about it. People all over the world struggle with returning home. I mean it! Ask one of your friends. No, I wasn't mocking you; you said you have friends. Did I really stick to the foyer the last two times? *What?* One time I didn't enter at all? Well, um, I refuse to believe *that.* Except, yeah. You're right. You're right! But still, it's literally impossible that I haven't walked these halls since high school. Even before then you're saying? No, no. Whatever this is, stop. It's like you're fucking with a drunk guy. Did you draw a penis on my face too? No. It hasn't been that long since I took a tour of the whole house.

But it has been. She's right. I just haven't thought about it in these terms in a long time. I'm not sure I ever have.

* * *

You were a fearful kid, Robin. I'm not saying that's bad. Most kids are. Hell, most adults are. People are scared of everything. Not just the usuals like spiders and snakes and flying. People are afraid of being wrong, looking dumb, telling bad jokes, losing, winning, getting a story right, remembering a word, pulling prickly weeds, long staircases, long hallways, empty rooms. I can't remember the last person I met who didn't express fear of *something* an hour or so into hanging out.

You remember these doors? These rooms? Of course you do.

You were raised here. Mommy and Daddy gave us an incredible life. And you and me? We shared stuff not even a mother shares with a child. *We met the world at the same time.* Sure, I was a little older than you, but looking back, it was close to a tie. You know what I did those first couple of years I had alone without you? I got to know the house. Mommy and Daddy found me in almost every room, that's what they still say; *Stephanie, we lost you so many times in that house, and we found you in every room.* Mommy claims she saw me up on a shelf in the basement. And Daddy says he found me before I could walk, up in the attic like I'd crawled up the ladder myself. They're getting a little older now, nothing to freak out about, but they *do* get some things wrong. You've noticed that too? Yeah. That's what parents do. How are you on that beer? Wish we brought the whole fridge with us? It shoulda just come, the way I thanked it! Look at me, making friends with the appliances. Remember this room? Yeah, this was where we had warm fires on Christmas and whenever else East Kent froze to hell. Do I still make fires now? I do. Yeah. It's kinda amazing, turning the house off, every light in every room, then coming down here and sitting in front of the fire, just staring into the flames. If you take pictures you capture faces so horrible they're impossible to describe. Bent mouths. Half-open eyes. Mommy and Daddy raised us well though. Taught us how to tend to a house this big and how to follow our dreams, too, our ambitions. You traveled the world playing music, Robin! I mean, *holy shit!* Who does that? Well, they just loved it. You know that. They would call me up and tell me they were coming in to see you play and then they'd spend the night here after seeing you play in Samhattan. You didn't know that? Yeah. They slept in their old bedroom because it's not like I ever made that one into mine. Something weird about that, right? I'll tell you, there were stretches I didn't step foot in their old bedroom for months. Which one is mine? Which room?

Second floor. The pink one.

I found a use for the second floor after all.

Hey, come here, let's sit down in the library for a minute. I don't think you did much of this as a kid, and speaking of being grateful for spaces, you gotta just *feel* this room for a minute.

Come on. I'll get the doors.

Here . . .

* * *

I can barely respond. Stephanie's opening the library doors and smiling over her shoulder. She's like she was at eight, zealous about the house, eager to talk about every part of it. I really didn't know Mommy and Daddy slept here after they came to see us play in Samhattan. Am I calling them Mommy and Daddy again? How long have I been doing that? Jesus. This place. But it's not just the halls; that was fucking eerie enough. And it's not just the way Stephanie glides through this place like she could do it blind-folded. It's not even the idea of her alone, staring into a fire, sur-rounded by what feels like unfathomable darkness:

Stephanie said she's been living in the pink room.

Why? Is she fucking with me? If I went up there right now, would I find her bed there? A dresser? Clothes strewn about? Why don't I believe this? Because, honestly, I don't. You're telling me that, out of all the rooms in this goliath, she chose the last room on the second floor, a space half the size of the old master bedroom, one-third the size of some others? Why? Why would anybody do that?

Oh, really, Stephanie? That's the exact thesaurus you used to read when we were kids? Yeah, of course I remember. Only the finest words for me. Oh, I'm just kidding. Who cares? What kind of sister would you be if you didn't call me names?

I think of the word *credent* for the first time in what feels like forever. Holy fuck have I suppressed a lot of memories from this place. It's like I've been living in a sketch; all outlines and no de-tails. But still, some color.

Pink, for example.

Did she really pick that room? And why can't I get out of the way from the anxiety she kickstarted when she said that? Come on. I'm on beer three, and instead of making me fearless, it's work-ing like a magnifying glass, making me crazier than ever.

Definitely, Stephanie. This room is magnificent. And you're right, I didn't spend a ton of time here as a kid. Me? No, don't worry. I'm fine. What do you mean I look freaked out? Well, if you keep saying that, I might be! No, no. Beers, books, my sister, my home. I'm good. In fact, if I can't be good here, where can I be?

But I'm not good and she knows it. And now she's telling me to say something to the space. To talk to the room. She's thanking it for having us and (her words) for providing so much. She's asking me to talk to the room. Tell it how I feel.

Well, uh, Mr. Library . . . it's been a long time and I, uh . . . it's good to see you. I'm sorry we didn't hang out more when we had the chance.

Stephanie rolls her eyes and she's trying to be good-natured about it, but she holds the roll a beat too long and her eyes are just white, and I've just about had enough of the house.

Goodbye, Mr. Library. Thank you for having us. Stephanie is going to walk me to the front door now.

She looks confused. I don't blame her. She's telling me there's no way I'm leaving right after finishing my third beer.

Okay. Then let's go outside, right?

\* \* \*

Robin, how is the outside any better than the inside?

\* \* \*

Okay, know what, Stephanie? This is all feeling a little too much like a game. No, just hear me out. Everything's so vague and ethereal with you. I'm not trying to offend you. It's just . . . I don't know how much you remember about our childhood, but it wasn't all nice, you know? This house has always been a little much for me.

She's saying she knows. She's saying she gets it. And she's also thanking the library for having us and is now leading me out the doors, closing them behind her. So we're in the hall again, heading toward the stairs, and all I can think about is how the first floor leads to the second. I don't want to go up there. I just don't. I'd rather we grab a fourth beer and hang out in the driveway. Shoot the shit. Talk about dates and sports and music. Why do we always have to talk about the house? That's what she's talking about now as I follow her toward the stairs and as her voice dances from word to word and she looks up the stairs like she's winking to the second floor, saying hello again, and look what I have for *you*, Second Floor, a surprise, someone you haven't seen in a real long time, an old friend! And just like that I'm following her up the steps, sweating, trying to sip what remains of the beer because the fucking bottle has become like a buoy for me, literally the only thing I feel good about, protected by. Fuck. Stephanie takes the stairs like it's filmed in reverse; that unnatural quality, but elegant, like she knows exactly how many steps there are and, actually, *actually*, she's taking every other one, bounding a bit, as I sludge up behind, saying yeah and wow to everything she says, trying hard to come off like a grown man visiting his childhood home rather than a sudden shell of a person who is on the verge of a breakdown, wanting her to say we're going all the way to the third, let's just go to the third floor.

Stephanie? The second floor was always boring.

Just a quick look, she says, because of course she does, because of course I'm not going to get away with *not* revisiting the core scenes that haunt me still, and so, like a dutiful younger brother

(Mommy and Daddy aren't home, remember), I follow her to the top, and then to the right, as she walks what really looks like the dead center of the hall, herself a roll of painter's tape, a house divided, Stephanie passing the green room, then I pass it, the blue room, then I pass it, the brown room, then me.

Stephanie? You in there?

Well, of course she is. I literally just saw her step into the pink room and I haven't sweated this much in years and I'm telling myself to shut up, to follow your sister, to take the tour, tell her you love her, invite her to Samhattan, and move on.

Coming. I'm coming.

Because I'm a little behind and because it takes all I have to make the turn into the pink room, the color of the walls hitting me in a much more thorough way than memory, and would you look at this? There *is* a bed and there *is* a dresser and there *are* clothes. Stephanie does sleep in this room, of all this house, this one little room, like somehow she made hugely uneven parts (this room and the rest of the house) equal halves.

What's the chair for?

I have that memory of someone sitting there. Naked. I don't look at it long.

Just a memory. Yeah?

I sit on the bed. Actually, I practically fall onto my back on it, three beers deep and not a little tired from the fear and Stephanie looks to the chair I just asked about, the chair that sits facing the far corner of the room. And Stephanie is looking at me like I'm missing something, like I'm supposed to get something, like she said something I was supposed to get about the chair.

So I look to the chair. I look a little longer this time.

And no. It's not a memory I saw. It's no memory I see.

\* \* \*

This is incredibly brave of you, Robin. I cannot express how much this means to me. You just walked right in and sat right down on the bed. And *that's* the way to do it. You didn't say a word about her when you entered.

What? Oh, Robin. Come on. Really? You don't want to see her? But you saw her last time. Yes, she showed herself to you. No, it wasn't something I did. You saw her last time. Well, okay. Just relax. Okay? Robin? Your mind is playing a good trick on you is all. It's trying to hide her. But it's fine. Yes, she's there. Sitting in the chair. She's either facing the corner or facing us, I can never tell.

Robin?

It's okay.

Seriously.

Robin?

No.

Don't get up, Robin.

No.

Don't leave.

Robin. Come on.

*Robin!*

Be careful on the stairs!

Oh my God.

Don't run!

Jesus, Robin! *Be careful!*

Don't be afraid! You'll upset her, Robin!

Please! Robin! Don't run!

*Don't run through the house!*

# PART THREE

# GONE AND 80

After a long battle with a rare blood disease, my sister Stephanie is gone. It was a wretched, emotional affair and the conflicting feelings I have are overwhelming. Of course I visited her as she struggled to hang on, and I was there the day she passed. But by then she wasn't alone in a big, mean house anymore, she was in a hospital, and seeing her out of context was striking. The first thing I felt was how little I truly knew her. I'd always (and justifiably) conflated her with the house itself, as if our childhood home were a limb of hers, an extension of her hair, her mind. For eighty years it's been near impossible to imagine my sister *without* also seeing the house, huge and gloomy, half-lit, turned on and turned off, Stephanie at the helm like a fierce captain of a luxury liner at sea. Yet, the woman I encountered in the hospital carried herself the way people do who had long ago set out to accomplish major goals in life, and then did. The last thing I was expecting was this *peace* in her eyes, her countenance, her voice. No, she didn't want to die but also she didn't seem afraid of it. I, of course, couldn't help but wonder if her ease had something to do with ghosts, and her believing she'd seen them: is there anything more optimistic, after all, than seeing a ghost? But the more I talked to her, the more I believed this strength came from within, by way of accomplishment, from years of working on a hidden goal. If you don't know the type, you ought to. There are few things more inspiring than people who never give up on themselves.

But Stephanie? My Stephanie? The same person who, at age eight, was terrorizing her brother with the glee of a psychopath? The same woman who, at age forty, still clung to her childhood home, and who, by age sixty, owned that very home due to the deaths of our parents, dear Mom and Dad, having died only six days apart? To say I was surprised to find Stephanie *owning the hospital room* is an understatement, indeed. The doctors and nurses deferred to her, approached her with their hands folded, their voices level, as if in the presence of . . . well, the presence of a queen. They sensed it too. And who's more worthy of that title than those who have dug as far into themselves as they go and returned with handfuls of gold?

Stephanie, I said, at her bedside, when she was still propped up and still had ferocity in her eyes. Stephanie, when we were kids, there's a phrase you used to say . . .

I had to ask about it because, I'm almost embarrassed to say, it never left me alone. That phrase, and the confidence with which she said it, clung to me like clothes in the rain, and no matter what phase of my life I endured, it was upon me.

I started making music again after fleeing my childhood home the last time I properly visited Stephanie. I was so rattled by the experience that the moment I got back, I dusted off my synth and phoned some former bandmates and eventually we started playing again. And it was good. And it was good for me. And we even recorded an album, one I daresay was twice any album we made while touring the country so many years before. Yet, even as the days got brighter, and the distance between me and the house increased, I recalled that phrase. And when I met Eileen, and we were swept up into the gorgeous storms of real love, I recalled that phrase. And when Eileen and I bought our first place together, a small but perfect-for-us home just outside Samhattan, I couldn't stop myself from asking the realtor:

*Is either half of the house haunted?*

Eileen and I would divorce four years later, and I would recall the words again as I was handed the papers. But the appearance of Stephanie's riddle wouldn't only show up at landmark moments: sipping a coffee at a diner on Fifth Street, late-night and alone, I would hear it in the music that played softly through the speakers. On the bus, heading downtown, I'd hear it in the wheels. One time I heard it in the darkness of my own apartment and I woke, aged sixty-six then, to stare so long at the open bedroom door that I pulled a back muscle in the process.

But when I made to ask her on her deathbed, Stephanie eyed me with such inner peace, I felt horrible for even thinking of bringing it up.

After all, was it because she was no longer in the house that she looked so . . . independent? Mom and Dad had left her the house, of course, because, by then, it *was* Stephanie's, more so than it ever was anybody else's. But no. It couldn't have been the distance from the house that gave her such a shine because, if I admitted it (and I did, freely), I realized Stephanie had *always* looked this strong. That last time I was there, following her up the stairs . . . I wasn't following a meek shell of a haunted woman. Christ, no. I was the dog on a leash, being *walked* by the master of the house. Stephanie didn't just lord over that house, she'd seemingly trained it.

But still . . . even after allowing the question to fall to pieces between us, it bothered me. It was close to my last chance to ask her, to find out why she spoke so often of halves. And at my age, you no longer discover chances after last chances, and I found myself with only one more. Yet . . . I wish I hadn't. Because that question is now the last words exchanged between us before she passed. Yes, I'd been visiting her regularly in the hospital and I knew the nurses and doctors by name. They knew me, too, and notified me when they thought it might be *the day.* And so I hurried there, not entirely loaded with altruistic motives, as I wanted badly a little more time to ask her. I entered the hospital, I hurried to the elevators as best an eighty-year-old man can, and nearly killed myself running the hall to her bed.

There, breathless, I knelt beside her.

Stephanie, I said. I love you. I've always loved you.

Robin, she said. She was smiling. But she knew, too, that this was the day.

Stephanie, I said, what did you mean when you said half the house is haunted? What did you mean?

But she didn't answer. And I understood that, despite the fact we were holding hands, despite the fact she was still facing me, her eyes upon mine, Stephanie had passed.

No more words.

And no answers. Certainly not to the last question I asked.

My God.

This was three days ago and I've run the gamut of emotions since. I've alternately felt terrible for her, and mad at myself for not doing more to get her out of the house. Yet wasn't she happy? And strong? And strong-willed? And aren't I still living in the little apartments I've rented across Samhattan, listening to music to calm the nerves, scared of my own shadow?

Still . . . the question haunts.

And, in her way, Stephanie does, too, as earlier today I received a letter from a lawyer, a letter I was expecting, one that reveals to whom Stephanie left her things. Now, that house had *many* things in it, and more than once through the years I'd wondered if I might ask her for a table, a chair, a bed. The cabinet from the kitchen might've come in handy, though I've never rented anywhere with the space for it. The clocks, the silverware, the pillowcases . . . still, I never asked. Not for one thing. And not because I'm too proud and never was, no: it was because I couldn't be sure from which half any item would come.

Yet, now, the letter. Stephanie's will.

I'm holding it, of course. Fingering the envelope, reading my name, which Stephanie did not write. I'm examining the wax seal as if it might be the very lips speaking the phrase:

*Half the house is haunted.*

Do I really want to know what was left to me? What if it's the sacks of flour stacked upon that walk-in pantry door in the floor? What if it's the rug runners leading to the second floor? What if it's a chair that always faced the corner of a room painted pink?

I'm opening it. Because if there's one thing you learn by eighty, it's that it's best to get right to it.

I almost cut my finger as I tear it open. Maybe Stephanie left me a letter opener. From Mommy and Daddy's office. Wouldn't that be nice?

I'm sweating. Haven't felt quite this way in some time.

And I see it. A letter, after all. But not written by a lawyer.

I recognize the hand right away. And the spirit within.

It's a letter from Stephanie herself, written for me. And the phrase I think of is not the one that's rattled me for decades but a far more customary kind:

*Last words.*

Stephanie's last words to me.

And so . . . I read:

*Robin,*

*I'm two years older than you, I always have been, and, despite what's inevitable, always will be. And while I've told you before what I did for those first two years when I was without you, some things bear repeating. Just like when we listen to a song for the hundredth time, we hear new things:*

*I got to know the house. For a long time this was something I was vaguely proud of. Mommy and Daddy spoke of those days with awe, and I, like most kids, gobbled that awe like candy. I was proud for being what? The kind of child who explored? Sure, that, except something bigger than that too. It took me a long time to understand* why *I felt compelled to explore our house rather than sit tight in my crib or remain as close to Mommy and Daddy as I could. The truth is: I* sensed *something. Yes, even then, as a toddler, I sensed "another" in our home. I've read countless books on the matter since, but back then I had intuition alone. And something much more powerful than that: fear.*

*How much time did you spend in the library growing up? Not much, I know, but perhaps enough that you might remember a particular spine in that wonderful room, a title made up of a single word, that same word I just used:* FEAR.

*It's the first book I took off the shelf. The very first book I read. I was no doubt attracted to it because I'd already lived a number of years (you were born by then, obviously), years of unease, of vague anxiety, of fear. And so the spine spoke to me and I spoke back, sitting in that amazing leather chair by the room's one window, reading it from cover to cover, a half-scientific, half-spiritual look at the concept of fear and what it does to us. And within those pages I discovered truths well beyond any a girl of seven ought to know. Yet, just like I knew something other than our family lived in the house, I understood these pages were delivering me a lifelong lesson, perhaps the very meaning of life itself.*

*I was right.*

*The book was about facing your fears, Robin. And how entire lives are wasted, cowering, sheltering ourselves, doing all we can to avoid the things that scare us. Here's a phrase from the book that stuck with me (hundreds have stuck, but this one I particularly adore): <u>everything you want is on the other side of fear.</u> This made more sense to me at seven than anything Mommy or Daddy could ever teach me. Wash my hands? Sure, of course. Brush my teeth? Okay. Be good to strangers? Absolutely. But who is actually doing the washing of their hands, the brushing of their teeth, and bestowing kindness upon strangers if that person is riddled with fear, and therefore <u>changed</u> by it? Indeed: who are you if you can't be yourself? I think of the phrase "half-mast" often, and how so many people are at half-mast. So many people are afraid to pursue their dreams, to speak their minds, to believe in themselves, and all for reasons they can't put their fingers on. People make excuses, often good ones, citing a lack of time, a lack of energy, a lack of funds. But this book spoke of these sentiments as the very fingers of fear, the things we do and say that get in our own way, the excuses we make, that stop us from becoming our full selves. And when you take away someone's ambitions, and the joy they would receive from accomplishing these goals, what are you left with if not a half person billowing at half-mast?*

*How much do you know about momentum, Robin? How often have you thought about how one moment in life leads to another, how one encouragement inspires another? You experienced unrivaled joy playing music once your friends (good friends at that) encouraged you to play. Now try to see all of life like that. Moment to moment. The build of it. Brick by brick, board by board, until you're actually standing on top of all you accomplished in life.*

*That's you in full.*

*Yes, that book didn't only change my life, it shaped me entirely. And so when I finally did encounter the other that lived in our childhood home, I was not only terrified; I was equipped.*

*To face it.*

*Oh, Robin. I was such a bully, wasn't I? I'm sorry for that. When I think back to our childhood, I struggle. On the one hand, we were just children, and that's a fine excuse. But on the other, I overcompensated in a rotten way. I wanted to scare you. I sure did. I wanted you to be so scared you had no choice but to face it. To stand up like I'd stood up, to find it within yourself to co-exist in a house you knew was haunted. What you heard in the basement was not me. What you saw twice in the pink room was not my doing. And I was so glad for you to encounter these things, to see what I'd seen, to be given the chance to overcome your own fears, so that you, too, might live a life devoid of fear, so that you, too, might achieve everything you set out to do.*

*But I went about it wrong. I went at you with the zealotry of a fanatic, or, on the days when I'm easier on myself, as a child.*

*When you left for college is when the truth of that started to sink in. You'd seen the sights, yes, but you hadn't read the book, you didn't have the same formative education I did regarding fear and facing it. When Mommy and Daddy decided to move south, I saw it as an ultimate opportunity to face my own fears. Because, believe me, in those days, bully or not, I was scared out of my mind. And so, my work wasn't complete. The work I was doing on myself. I chose to stay, an option afforded me by our parents, partially because they didn't want to part with the place they'd raised their kids, but also partially because I believe they sensed I was working on <u>something</u>. Imagine me as the vaccine in a house of disease. Imagine me as the one chance of bravery existing in a place of shaking darkness.*

*As I grew older, I was glad to know you hadn't seen everything that called that place home. It wasn't just "another." But "others."*

*Yet, if I wasn't ready to face these things, then I wasn't anything at all. Do you see? I stayed in our childhood home because I didn't want to run from the horrible sights and sounds, the unbelievably frightening experiences I had in the attic, the basement, the second floor, and really, at times, every other room in the house. And while you were traveling* *a wonderful world in a wonderful band, I was sitting alone in the dark, allowing these things to approach me, to speak to me, once to even touch me. And what did I do? I breathed. I steadied my breathing. And I faced my fears. And in doing so, I grew, day by day, into the kind of woman my childhood self would've been amazed by. A woman who could've written the book called <u>FEAR</u>.*

*By the time Mommy and Daddy passed, I had mastered our childhood home. I was no longer afraid of the woman in the pink room, the thing in the basement, and (the one that took the longest to face), the woman in the breakfast room who told me every day she would wait for me to fall asleep before she took the stairs up to find me. I faced these fears, Robin, and the joy I found in my evolving inner strength is a joy I don't find in most books, in most films, in most music. Yes, by the time the house became mine, legally mine, I had everything I wanted, and I'd found it on the other side of fear.*

*I was at full-mast.*

*So . . .*

*I'm sorry. For how I bullied you. And I'm sorry if my preoccupation with myself created real distance, as I have no doubt it did. But, at the same time, there was never anything more important than self-confidence to me, nothing as meaningful as inner peace. Some might call me an optimist, the way I walked those halls and approached those spaces where I knew evil lurked, where I knew things existed that man and woman should not have to see. And I suppose I am an optimist. But I reckon I'm more of a worker. I've spent my life working on myself, my inner self, from the day I sensed others in our home to the day I read the book, even to now, as I lay dying, feeling more proud than scared, proud for having dedicated a life to overcoming not only my own fears, but <u>fear</u> in all its forms, all its ways.*

*I said goodbye to the house as I left it for the last time, Robin. And I thanked it for having me and for all I found in it, for all it gave me.*

*It wasn't easy. But I wasn't afraid.*

*Death is here. Death I know. And so . . .*

*I love you, Robin.*

*To you . . . I leave the house. The house and everything in it. Every object, every inch, every corner, every door. I leave you the house and I hope you may enter with a mind to head to the library, where the book still sits on the shelf, where you might find a journey of your own, an inner climb, optimism in the face of such fears.*

*It is never too late for a goal, an accomplishment, of any kind.*

*Because if half the house is haunted, as indeed this one is, that must also mean half the house is not.*

*Stephanie.*

# Argyle

The father, Shawn Hasbro, on his back in bed, his deathbed, dying, close now, on the edge of the end of it all, chose now to tell his family the truth about himself.

He'd kept it hidden for a lifetime. A thing he couldn't have called a success, until now.

The immediate family were present; Andrew, son, Margaret, daughter, and Sheila, wife of twenty-seven years. Shawn's sister Ethel pattered about downstairs, having just this morning verbalized her sense that today was the day. As with many such visions of her brother, she was close. Day had passed. It was evening.

And so, evening it would be.

"Oh my God," Shawn said. "Oh my *God*."

There was some light in his eyes, half-light, a degree of vitality the family hadn't seen in days. They'd already begun accepting they would never see it again.

"Rest, Shawn," Sheila said, coming to his bedside, taking his hand in her own. She reached for a glass of water on the nightstand.

Her husband shook his head no, looked to her, looked to their two children, both grown now, late-twenties, yes, and both looking at their phones beyond the foot of his bed.

He looked to the closed wooden door.

"Is it just us then?" he asked. As if emerging from a mist. Taking stock of the room that would be his last.

"Yes," Sheila said. "Did you want me to get Ethel?"

Because, while his eyes revealed a gladness for the intimacy, there was a pound of disappointment there too.

"An audience," Shawn said. And the word was both fearful and proud.

A sheen appeared on his cheeks. Days prior, Andrew and Margaret both confided in Sheila they couldn't stand to see the sweat there. As if an expression, any, were tiring.

*He looks like someone constantly working to look normal,* Margaret had said. And Sheila and Ethel exchanged a look when she did.

"Us?" Sheila asked. "Yes, I suppose we make up an audience."

Shawn looked to the window, as if more faces might be seen there, people standing on nothing outside the second-story glass.

He adjusted himself on the bed. Andrew and Margaret looked up from their phones. It was the most Dad had exerted himself in quite some time.

Shawn smiled, and it was a nasty smile; the eyes and the mouth did not match. Two people sharing one face.

Then, something new in his visage, something the others hadn't only not seen in weeks, but ever before.

"I'm so *fucking* relieved," Shawn said.

Those gathered stayed quiet. This was, indeed, new.

Shawn laughed, and while it wasn't the laugh of the healthy, it was that of the earnest. He shouted:

"I'm so fucking relieved!"

Ethel's footsteps ceased a floor below.

"That's great," Sheila said. She was trying. No matter what she did here, he was dying. What else could she say?

"No," Shawn said. He tried to sit up, moaned, remained supine. "You don't understand, Sheila. You couldn't. But you will." Then, a little lighter again: "Yes! You will."

"Dad?" Margaret asked. "Are you okay?"

"He's literally saying he's okay," Andrew said, eyes still on his father, the mask of his father, wide new eyes glowing above those sweating cheeks.

"I'm worried," Margaret said.

"Relieved," Shawn said. "That's what you should be, Mar. *Relieved.*" He looked to the ceiling; spoke as if addressing someone there. "It's the end of my life. I've made it to the end of my life, guys. And I am so . . . *solaced.*"

"Are you?" Margaret asked. "Oh, please, I hope you mean that, Dad."

"I'm a good man," Shawn said. "*I'm a good man!*"

Something shrill in him. Something hysterical, yet . . . in check. Sheila put a little distance between herself and whatever was suddenly showing in her husband.

"Yes, Shawn," she said. "You are a good man."

*Encourage him,* that's what more than one doctor had told the three members of the immediate family. Encourage, praise, do whatever it took to remove any stress. Be aware of how natural it is to express negativity when one speaks. One doctor, Dr. Minchin, described a scene in which she witnessed a woman expiring mid-argument with her husband. *Whatever bygones make it all the way to the deathbed,* the doctor said, *should probably get no closer.*

"I couldn't be sure this would happen until right now," Shawn said. "How can someone know if they'll make it to the end before they actually do?" Vitality. Something like it. "But here I am," he said. "I made it to the end a good man!"

"Made it where?" Margaret asked.

Andrew shifted uneasily beside her. Like he might say something to dismiss her question. But nobody spoke. All waited. All wanted to know.

Shawn did something then that would've been unthinkable even a day before. He reached his bony hands to the pillow, adjusted it against the headboard, and rose, just enough, to be close to a sitting position. Now, cheeks covered in sweat, hair so thin numerous bald patches showed beneath the ceiling light, he looked less like someone dying and more like a man who already had: a skull, set upon the pillow. A warning, perhaps, or the thing one had been warned about.

"Guys," Shawn said. "You three: my closest." He laughed, a single trebly bark. "Hell, I couldn't even hurt you if I tried now. Look at my hands." He raised them. Ten weak, bony digits. "Even if I caved, right now, with almost no time remaining . . . I couldn't do a thing about it."

"What are you talking about, Dad?" Andrew asked.

"I'm talking about *urges,* Andrew," Shawn said. "I'm talking about being sick in an unseen way. The kind that doesn't show up on the X-rays."

"Shawn," Sheila said. But no more.

Shawn kept his eyes on his son, but he spoke to everyone in the room and, it felt, many more beyond it.

"Have you ever had a really dark thought, Andrew? One so bad you had to convince yourself it's natural, for fear of going mad? And then you start looking for that kind of thinking in other people, whether it's in conversations, essays, speeches, psychology, even fiction? You ever read a really cold book or news story and feel like you were going to be okay because the person writing it must've have had bad urges too? The desire to do bad things? It doesn't matter if it's true or not. That's not even the point. It's about how badly you, you as the person with the bad urges, need something to hang on to. It's about how badly you need to know you're not alone. In your thinking. Your feelings. Your *wanting*."

"Dad?" Margaret asked.

"I looked for it everywhere," Shawn said. Already this was the most he'd talked in weeks. The least they'd heard wheezing between his words. "And I found it. Over and over, I found it. In the least likely of places. Birds of a feather. Like-minded urges. People who had to have known what I wanted to do, doing it their own way." He tried to sit up a little more, failed, remained as he was. "There was a lot of it in the true-crime section of the bookstores, of course. People who had actually acted on those urges, people who had hurt others, many. People who had given in to their urges, those who let their urges rule. Sheila"—he turned to his wife—"do you ever thank your lucky stars for what you're *not* into?"

"What do you mean?"

"Think about it. You think bad men and bad women *chose* to be the people they are? You think a pedophile *chooses* to want little kids?"

"Jesus, Dad," Margaret said.

"Shawn," Sheila said. "I think you might want to relax a little."

"Oh, for fuck's sake. This is the most relaxed I've ever been. I literally can't do anything about the urges anymore. For the first time in my life, I don't have to resist who I am."

Silence then. An uneven quiet that was one part respect for the dying and ten parts confusion.

Yet, not all quiet in the house: Ethel paced again below. The creaking of the wood floors in the living room, the kitchen, the halls.

"What do you mean . . . 'hurt,' Dad?" Andrew asked.

Shawn cleared his throat and said:

"I've wanted to kill the three of you for as long as I've known you. And not just you guys. Oh God, no. So many. And for so many years. An entire lifetime, for as long as I can remember. I've wanted to hurt people, Andrew. I've wanted to kill. I've wanted to take people apart, to open them up, to remove the guts from one and put them in another. Do you understand? It's what I've *wanted* to do. I've wanted to strangle, to stab, to shoot. I've wanted to use my bare hands and use whatever was *at* hand too. You guys, yes, but strangers too. So many people I've passed on so many streets. Not all of them at night. Hotels we've stayed in, us, as a family, I've wanted to sneak out, head down to the lobby, murder the young man working the desk. I've wanted to kill every man, woman, and child I've found myself alone in a room with for my entire life. I wanted to kill Mom, my own mom. Dad, my own dad. Guys, it's nearly impossible to express how hard this has been, how *close* I've come. And, really, if you don't count the one instance . . . which I don't . . . then I've made it through an entire life *without* acting on these urges. This is the end. I'm at the end. Without harming a soul." Shawn, his eyes deep pools of relief and pride, blinked and held his lids tight long enough to express ecstasy. "And what's more noble than *that*?" He opened his eyes again. Lights in the sockets of a skull. "What's more noble? The man who never thinks to hurt another and so doesn't? Or the man who constantly *does* think about it, yet uses every ounce of willpower to resist?" He sank deeper into the pillow. Exhaled with resolve. "I'm so fucking relieved, you guys. I am . . . elated."

Below, Ethel had come to a stop again.

"Dad," Margaret asked.

"Yes, dear?"

"What do you mean by . . . the one instance?"

"No," Sheila suddenly said, cutting the air before her with a flat hand. The other three were familiar with her way of attempting to put a stop to a conversation she believed had gone too far. "No, no, *no*. Shawn . . . I think you're a little delirious right now. And I don't blame you. But this isn't right for the kids to hear. You don't know what you're saying. Andrew and Margaret, please don't take anything your father is saying to heart."

But the kids weren't even looking at Sheila. And Margaret's question still hung in the air.

Shawn eyed the question, too, then allowed his gaze to travel to the window. As if the incident under discussion, and others, too, played upon the glass like they would a television.

"Dad?" Margaret asked again.

"Margaret," Sheila said. But there was simply no strength to it. This moment was Shawn's. By rights and by wrongs.

"Ethel knows," Shawn said, still eyeing the window. "She had to. We were kids, you know, when it all started." It was obvious he wasn't answering his daughter's question. Not directly. Not yet. His face lit up with a partial smile, then sank into unseen sand. The others felt chilled by the quick changes in his face. Yet, the man was dying. And didn't anything go? Weren't all rules and regulations moot upon and beside the deathbed? "I have vague memories of Ethel eyeing me in the house. Always watching me. Whether I was in my bedroom or the basement. At some point in the day I'd see my sister peering around the corner. It used to scare the shit out of me. But I got used to it." A deep inhale, then: "She knew. Even then."

"Knew what?" Andrew said. Because, despite having just been told the *what*, it was near impossible to process.

"She could tell her brother wanted to kill things, Andrew. She could tell her brother was a killer."

This time the siblings did not exchange looks. Instead, Margaret leaned back in her chair, making the wood creak. Andrew sat as stiff as stone. Sheila glanced once their way and, it seemed, determined they weren't children anymore. As if, in this very moment, in the thick air of Shawn's sudden and frightening confession, she'd finally decided to accept they had grown.

"Just like you two know things about each other," Shawn said. He pointed at Andrew, then Margaret, the thin finger like a proctor's pointer, the scope of family and all urges mapped out on unseen paper between them. "Just like you know what Andrew wanted to do with your friends, Margaret."

"Dad," Andrew said.

Shawn fanned a weak hand dismissively.

"Come on, Andrew. Not all urges are as bad as mine. And nobody should be embarrassed of any. If that's what you got in you, that's what you got in you. What brother doesn't fantasize about his sibling's friends? We're made up of a lot of stuff, aren't we? Not all of it clean. But some of us, we're doomed to wander the outer rim, if you know what I mean. Some of us, like me, we're sentenced to a life unfulfilled or, if we act, one spent in prison."

"I don't understand," Margaret said. And the room felt hotter then. "Are you serious, Dad? You wanted to hurt people?"

"This is insane," Sheila said. "Everybody thinks of doing bad things now and again. Everybody imagines hurting someone else at some point in their lives."

Shawn no longer looked like a vacant skull, but like something vampiric, and hungry, slunk within it.

"Don't downplay what I've done," he said. "It's unfair. It's mean. Ask Ethel what she sensed when we were children. That time on the mountain. Ask her what she saw."

"The mountain?" Margaret asked. "What did you do there, Dad?"

"I followed an elderly couple on the trail, to the top of Sprake Mountain."

"Where you grew up," his daughter said.

"Yep. You've been there twice. On the very same trail. I chose older people because I figured they were so close to death. And when you're ten years old, you think forty looks like ninety. So, what did seventy look like but already dead? I didn't tell Mom or Dad what I was doing. Shit, I didn't even tell myself. I'd been at the kitchen sink, washing blueberries for lunch, when I saw them enter the base of the trail. There was a dark sky above. Hadn't seen anybody else on the mountain all morning. They would be alone up there. I knew."

"Okay," Sheila said. "But really, this has gone far enough. Out. Everyone out. We'll leave your father alone. Obviously, you have some newfound strength, Shawn. This is good. Okay? I'll let the doctors know. But . . . I can't stand here and listen to any more of this hogwash."

Andrew and Margaret remained motionless, expressionless, still.

"You didn't hurt any old couple on a mountain trail, Shawn," Sheila said. "For fuck's sake, why are you doing this right now?"

"Doing this?" he said. "Sheila, this is the proudest moment of my life. And you're absolutely right! I didn't hurt them. I didn't touch them. But I wanted to. And I wonder what I might've done had Ethel not shown up, peering at me from behind a boulder."

Sheila looked to the bedroom door. Ethel was quiet downstairs. Should she go get her? Put an end to whatever the hell this was?

"What did you wanna do to them, Dad?" Andrew asked.

Shawn smiled and nodded his son's way.

"This is good," he said. "Let's talk about it. *Finally*. Listen, I was too young to know what I wanted to do. I wanted to see them fall. Tumble. I wanted to see their old bones crack against the rocks on the side of the mountain. Most of all I wanted to hear them grunt, helpless, as they went over the edge. I wanted to see the old lady's skull split open; wanted to see the man's nose break against a flat stone. I wanted to be the last to touch them, before they died, to *feel* the power of being the *reason* they died. I followed about thirty feet behind them, going at their elderly pace, routinely checking the drop over the path's edge. I might've survived it. But there was no way they could've. I told myself nobody would know, and I believed it." He barked a syllable of angry laughter. "Would you believe I still wish I had? Even now? I still wish I'd shoved them. Even now, knowing what I know, knowing what's right, and priding myself on having *lived* right, even now I feel like I robbed myself of something. A joy none of you can fathom. Something better than good, if that makes sense to you. Something so much better than all the things you think feel good."

"Is this what you meant by the one instance that might count?" Margaret asked.

"No," Shawn said. "And there's no question I did the right thing on Sprake Mountain. Like a good little kid, I looked both ways before crossing the street. I got within ten feet of the couple (I can still see his plaid pants, her white cotton slacks), and I looked ahead and saw no one and I looked back and saw Ethel's outline, *just* in view, watching me. Because she knew. That's why she'd followed me. Because how could she not?"

"*Shawn!*" Sheila suddenly yelled. "What the *fuck* are you talking about?"

"Sheila, I'm telling you—"

"You're making it sound like you were a serial killer! Jesus Christ, Shawn! You sold latex gloves to hospitals for a living! What are you *doing* right now?"

The war within her was obvious. Here: a wife, a mate, prepared to grieve, to console, to encourage. And nothing more.

"That's exactly what I'm saying," Shawn said. Excitement in his eyes. The thrill of speaking it for the first time: "I *am* a serial killer, honey. Only, one who has not killed."

"I'm out," Sheila said.

And she left. Her footsteps were fury on the wood floor and were echoed by Ethel's below as Shawn's sister headed for what sounded like the foot of the stairs.

Sheila slammed the door behind her.

A stronger, cooler summer wind came through the bedroom's open window and blew the drapes like long, bony fingers of their own. They reached for Shawn, still on his back on the bed.

"I don't blame her," Shawn said. "After all, it wasn't just myself I was keeping it from all these years."

His two children remained seated. But both had a little more color in their faces. They looked more alert than they had in days too.

"I mean, Dad," Andrew said, "this is crazy. Like, really crazy. You're telling us you wanted to kill old people."

"Not just old people, Andrew. *Many* people. I might've been one of the greatest serial killers of all time. There was no pattern to my urges. No easy way for me to get caught."

"You said you wanted to hurt us," Margaret said.

Voices from below. Sheila and Ethel, discussing. Then, the back door opening and closing down there. Outside then, for privacy.

"I did," Shawn said, smiling. "But I didn't act on it! Is there any greater sign of a father's love than *not* drowning his children in the tub? *Not* smothering them with the palm of his hand? *Not* cutting off their toes just to see their small faces scrunch up in pain, horror, distrust?"

"What happened to you?" Andrew suddenly asked.

"To me? It was hell. Like being hungry and not eating when you're alone in a room full of cooked food."

"No . . . I mean . . . to make you this way."

"Wait," Margaret said. To Andrew: "You're just buying all this? That fast?"

Shawn looked from one to the other.

"It's a shock, isn't it."

"We're shocked," the siblings said at the same time.

Then, Margaret: "What about the one instance . . ."

Shawn's eyes widened. Had he experienced some pain just then? Another finger of Death gripping what he had left, so close to pulling him from the bed and into a dark forever?

"You keep asking about that," Shawn said. "I understand."

"Well?" Andrew said.

"It doesn't count," Shawn said. "I made my peace with that a long time ago."

"Can we, uh," Margaret said, "can we hear that story too?"

Silence. But no refutation either.

"I'm gonna talk," Shawn said. "For an audience of two."

No voices from below. No hushed conversation outside the open second-story window. No creaking below.

Only Shawn Hasbro's voice, his story, and just enough strength to tell it.

"Things got worse after the Sprake Mountain thing," he said. "Much worse. In fact, looking back, that day was easy. But it didn't feel easy at the time. Do either of you remember the first time you fell in love? Not the real thing. Not you with Laurel now, Margaret. And not your disastrous time with Grace, Andrew. I mean long before then. When you were kids. In grade school. Do you remember the first time you felt a real longing for someone else?"

"Yeah," Andrew said. "Katie McCain. Red-haired. She was a grade higher than I was and she still feels like an older woman to me now."

"Even though you remember her as she was, as a fifth grader."

"Right."

"That's how I remember that old couple on the mountain. The

experience was just as vague and innocent from my end as your feelings for Katie McCain were on yours."

"I think I'm gonna be sick," Margaret said.

Andrew turned to her, shook his head no. Whatever was happening here, as outlandish as their father's sudden confession was, they couldn't leave like Mom had. Someone had to hear his last words.

"And," Shawn said, seemingly missing what his daughter just said, "just like you moved on to much more complicated relationships, it wasn't long before I encountered the same. Only, rather than wanting to buy flowers for the person, I wanted to feel the life leave their body. I wanted to witness the moment they understood they were dying."

There was a sense then that, if Shawn were strong enough, even just a little stronger, he would've broken into a crawl across the bed, carried out those fantasies at last.

"I was never capable of love," he said. "Not in the way you know it."

"But you love us," Margaret said.

Shawn, a man alone on a small, dark stage, shrugged his bony shoulders.

"I don't know love," he said. "I know urges. That's my love. That's my overwhelming, life-defining emotion."

Outside, a car parking. A door opening and closing.

"Dad," Margaret said, "don't forget: Mom and I told some people to stop by, that they only had today to see you. That you might be ..."

She couldn't finish the sentence. Tears welled. Yet they were incomplete, cut by the yarn Shawn was spinning.

Who was she actually grieving here?

Below: many voices now.

Andrew stood up and stepped to the window.

"I can't see 'em," he said.

From the bed, Shawn said:

"My first best friend was a girl named Argyle. Well, that's what Ethel and I called her. Because she always wore argyle, of course. I can't be sure what Argyle's real name was. Lucy? God, that's terrible of me. I'll have to ask Ethel. Either way, she was Argyle to us. And she was so open, so kind, I found it nearly impossible not to tell her about my urges. So, I did. In a way. But she saw it on her own first."

"You told someone?" Margaret asked. "But never told us?"

Shawn ignored this.

"Argyle and I palled around Samhattan all the time in those days. It really was just the two of us, in theory, despite Ethel always lurking. My sister like a frumpy Jiminy Cricket. Always." He shook his head. But was he happy for his sister's intervention? Or angry? "Ethel never spoke. And I wasn't sure if Argyle knew she was there. Still, *I* knew. We were getting milkshakes at Sam's Hat on a Sunday, and we were sitting in a booth when we found ourselves alone in the place with a little kid. He was maybe eight years old, and his dad had told him to sit still while he ran to the restroom. Now, in those days you could do that kind of thing. Even when you two were little I felt safe turning my back on you for a minute here, a minute there. Nowadays that father would be arrested for negligence. And maybe he should be. How could he know a serial killer shaped like a teenager was giggling with a friend, one booth over from his child? Argyle caught me staring, asked me why, asked me if I wanted kids of my own." Shawn laughed and it came from a place so deep there could be no mistaking the fact that no, he didn't want kids then and, no, he'd never wanted them at all.

Andrew looked to Margaret and there seemed an unspoken sentence in the air:

*We were Dad's dark glasses, we were Dad's disguise.*

"I told her *no thank you,* I most definitely did not want kids. And this turned out to be a lesson for me: I'd been personal, honest with Argyle. And for that, I'd opened up other honest doors. We didn't just talk about movies or other kids at school. We didn't gossip. We talked about *who we were.* And so . . . how to explain to her I wanted to see this kid's head hit the tiled malt-shop floor? How to explain to Argyle, her so warm, so nice, that, just like she wanted, so badly, the vanilla shake she slurped through a straw, just like she wanted the comic book she'd bought on the way to Sam's Hat, *I* wanted to watch this little kid realize the moment he was dying, by my hands, beneath my hands; I wanted to witness his absolute innocence revoked: the moment someone who is alive and should remain so realizes they're not going to stay that way." Shawn sat up a little, moaned as he did. But neither Andrew nor Margaret moved to help. He struggled to find a new position, sitting up an inch higher in the end. "I cannot begin to express how *good* this feels, getting this off my chest. Thank you, guys."

Below, the back door opened and closed. The floorboards creaked. Three sets of shoes? Four? Five? People, anyway. Come to see Shawn Hasbro off. To pay their final respects. Goodbye to a good person, a kind face, a devoted family man.

"It wasn't about power," Shawn said, seemingly oblivious to the new noises. "Though you'll read that's what it is in every book you can find on the subject. Believe me, I've read most of 'em. The idea thrilled me as much as roller coasters thrilled you guys when you were thirteen. I was as excited about the prospect of grabbing that little shit by the wrist and twisting his arm as you two were about driving when you turned sixteen. You can't blame me. I didn't *ask* for this and I definitely did not choose it." He paused, stared un-blinking into the space between him and Margaret. "I slid out of the booth, went one over, and did take the kid by the arm. Argyle waited, watched. I placed both hands on his tiny arm and twisted his skin in opposite directions, and he cried out, his face morphing from happy to horror. *Where's Dad?* his eyes screamed! Ha! That little face suddenly so wrinkled, his fat cheeks wet with tears. Then, just when I felt like going a little farther, Argyle asked what I thought I was doing. I tell you, I'd nearly forgotten she was there. Just me and that kid, in all the world. It was something like being caught naked. Like I'd left my pants in the booth. And I hurried back, red-faced, as the kid screamed for his dad, as Argyle stared at me, studying me, as the father came quickly out of the bathroom and went to his child's side. 'What's the matter, Kenny?' he asked. 'I wasn't gonna leave you!' I looked to the young man behind the counter just as he looked away, and for the first time in my life I considered the word *witness* the way it was intended to be used. I couldn't look at Argyle, not again. Not when I wanted just as badly to grip her knee beneath the table and dislocate it. How dare she ask me what I was doing? Did I ask her why she liked her shake? But that word, *witness,* had me looking over my shoulder, to the store's front glass, where I saw her, yes, my Jiminy Cricket in a housedress, your always-intervening aunt Ethel. She was looking through the glass. Watching. She wasn't hiding. Yet, the situation in hand, she stepped away. You get it? Ethel didn't want to stick around any longer than she had to. She didn't want too many peo-ple witnessing her witnessing me. Because then . . . then *she'd* feel compelled to say something. *Shawn wants to hurt people.* Can't you hear her saying it to Grandpa and Grandma, who lived just long enough to meet you because of my benevolence, my resistance, my will? Remove the word *power* from your minds. I realize how all this sounds. But I swear to you, as your father, as the man who raised you well, it was never about control. It was always one hundred, one thousand percent urge."

"Shawn?"

A voice from the hall. A man.

Shawn ignored it.

"I believed the guy behind the counter knew. It's something you learn to see, when you're someone like me. And while I had already accepted Ethel as a witness to who I really was, I didn't feel comfortable about the teen who worked there. He was in high school. Three years older than me. And his name was Peter Barry. And I know this because I became fixated on him. That's another thing you learn. And it was all I could do *not* to find him alone, to get him alone, to kill him."

The bedroom door opened. A man Shawn's age with thick black hair stood in the doorway.

"Shawn," he said, smiling sadly. "I came to say goodbye."

Andrew and Margaret sat up straighter on their chairs. As if the man, William Gathers, had caught them doing drugs.

"I could come back," William said. "If this isn't a good time."

*Good time.* The phrase sounded insane.

"This is the best moment of my life," Shawn said, and Margaret reached out as if to quiet him, as if to say, *Dad, whatever you do, don't tell your boss of ten years you're a serial killer.*

"Well, that's really nice to hear," William said.

He entered the room, leaving the door open as he did. He carried his hat, a white derby, in both hands at his beltline.

"Hello, Andrew," he said. "Hello, Margaret."

"I've made it to the end a good man," Shawn said, his eyes no less vampiric than they'd been moments ago. "It's something I couldn't have been sure of pulling off until now."

"Really?" William said. He smiled kindly. "I think we all determined you were a good man a long time ago, Shawn. Everyone who's ever met you."

Shawn didn't hesitate.

"There's a letter opener in the top drawer of your desk, Will. I know it very well, its contours, its weight, how the office overhead reflects off its tip. I've cut myself with it before, testing its efficiency."

William looked to Andrew and Margaret, the sad smile now mixed with some confusion.

"I'd planned to stick you in the stomach with it a dozen, two dozen times," Shawn said. "More than once I'd eyed the soft tissue between your thumb and pointer finger, considering whether I'd cook it before eating or just have it raw. I told myself you had two hands; I could sample both ways."

"Shawn?" William said. He'd lost a considerable amount of his sympathetic deathbed visage. Now he stood as a boss, prepared to scold.

"That's enough," Sheila said, entering the room quickly, taking William by the elbow. The man recoiled, the littlest bit, at her sudden movement. As if he'd thought, for a second, it was Shawn himself who had erupted through the door, come to stick him, come to eat him too. "Shawn isn't himself," Sheila said. "I'm sure you understand."

"I've never been more myself in my life."

But William took a moment before following Sheila out the door. He squinted Shawn's way and Shawn smiled, acknowledging that, yes, maybe William Gathers had always suspected Shawn Hasbro wasn't to be trusted.

"They can tell," Shawn told his kids. "The people in the life of a serial killer. Mom, Dad, Will . . . they knew *something*."

Sheila had William out in the hall, the door closed again. The man didn't lower his voice out there and he told Sheila what he thought, even as Shawn continued his tale.

"I didn't like that one bit," William said. "Not one little bit!"

"Come downstairs," Sheila said.

Shawn continued. It was his moment, after all. In full.

"It wasn't until we had you two that I realized how obvious I must've been as a child. I can only guess what Mom and Dad saw. Because it's the little things, you see. It's not like they caught me torturing a cow, which I didn't, I never *did* that. And it's not like they found blood on my clothes. There was no blood to find, no more than any other kid gets blood on his clothes. But still, they had to have seen it in my eyes, the dark fantasizing, the television shows I gravitated toward, the images that interested me, my interests, the way I eyed men and women who were alone, whether driving in cars or walking the streets of Samhattan, day or night. What did other kids talk about during dinner? What excited kids my age? One afternoon, Argyle and I were deep in the woods, a place she called Two Stumps. Just two trees chopped down to chairs in the middle of the woods. Buggy as can be out there. She suggested we draw our 'greatest fantasies' on paper, then exchange them without a word. It would be our secret, she said, only we would know what could be found in the deepest places we had. I loved the idea. I'd been salivating for the chance to tell someone, in any way I could. I'd instinctively hid brutal visions from Mom and Dad and Ethel, hid them even better from schoolteachers and friends of the family. We had no pets. Did I mention that? Did Mom and Dad do that on purpose? And if they did, did they *know* they did it on purpose? Kept them away from me, I'd bet. But the truth is, you don't know someone's a killer until they become one. That's why people always express shock when a person they know, a neighbor, a workmate, snaps and kills. It's not because that person actually didn't fit the profile, but because they simply *hadn't ever done it before.* This is true of all things. You're not the kind of person to drive across the country until you do it. Then? Then people talk about you forever as a free spirit, a wanderlust god. Same thing here. Mom and Dad must've suspected but not *known.* Best to make it easier for everyone and keep any potential temptations at bay. Hell, they didn't even like it when I slept over at a friend's house. It's not that they over-worried about me, it was that (and in hindsight this is clear as day) they sensed their son might harm someone or *something* if left unsupervised in someone else's home. Still, they didn't seem to worry about Argyle, as she and I were together often. From malt shops to movies, weekends to the woods. And it was in those woods that I revealed to Argyle my true nature, by way of a hideous illustration of a young man cutting the breasts off an old man while a beheaded child looked on. Had I more time, I would've added more heads, shelves of them, dozens of blue faces watching me as I worked, as I lusted, as I prepped the stove for the parts I'd removed. There was an oven in the drawing. A black fiery box. I remember that. I remember the look on Argyle's face, too, when we exchanged drawings, as I looked down to see hers; a bright rendering of Argyle atop an office building, next to a sign that said THE BOSS, indicating she never wanted to work for someone else, she wanted to find success, to run her own business, to lead. When I looked up from hers, she was still studying mine. Then, she folded the paper up, tucked it in her pocket, and reached out to place a soft but strong hand upon my own. She smiled, sympathetically, a tear in her eye. But she said nothing about it, only gave my hand a little squeeze, stood up, and said, 'Wanna head into town?' I folded hers up, too, and said I'd love to. More than anything in the world I wanted to head into town, walking side by side with someone who knew the real me."

Outside, the car door opened and closed again. The engine

revved. William Gathers left in what sounded like anger. But just as his car squealed away, a fresh engine arrived. And soon, another door opened and closed out of sight below the second-story window.

"Who is it?" Margaret asked.

"Still can't see," Andrew said. He looked to his dad. "Does it matter?"

"To me?" Shawn asked. But he didn't wait for an answer. "Things got worse. That's the *thing*. Just like the two of you became exaggerations of yourselves about the time you learned to drive, I'll never forget getting my own license and the horrifying reality it presented me: if I could drive myself, and if I had a car of my own, well, I could go anywhere at any time. I'd no longer be tied to Samhattan and the familiar streets and the concerns about encountering familiar faces upon them. It's a lot easier to shed guilt and embarrassment if you do your business in front of strangers. And I must've said something to this effect in driver's training, as the instructor asked me to repeat something I'd said and eventually asked me to pull over when I wouldn't. To be honest, I couldn't remember what it was. I was concentrating on the pedals. And it worried me: could my true nature come out, unwillingly, if my focus was somewhere else? Might I accidentally let my slip show if I was, say, taking an exam? Fixing a roof? Was there more to keeping this secret than simply not speaking it? I had a vision then of locking who I was in a crate and drowning it. Once I pulled over, the instructor said, 'What do you think cars are for? Do you really see them as a means to that end?' But I couldn't recall what led to him saying this and I still can't. He half threatened me, told me he was going to tell my parents, even the police. Then, he seemed to shake it off, called me a 'punk kid,' and demanded we swap places. He drove back to the Secretary of State parking lot. And me? I added chains to that crate, even as I enjoyed fantasies of driving to unknown places, finding strangers alone in their cars, their towns, their homes, their lives. I got that license, barely, but thank God I didn't yet have a car of my own. I might've gone hunting that *day*."

"Hunting?" Margaret asked.

"It's obvious what he means," Andrew said.

"Jesus, Andrew. I know that. And I suppose you're fine with it?"

"I didn't say that."

"Well, maybe allow me to process what the fuck my dad is telling me on his deathbed."

At the word, Shawn's eyes lit up again. A reminder, perhaps, that he'd "made it."

"I started dressing like other people. I had to. Started wearing T-shirts with stupid slogans like I NEVER ARGUE, I JUST EXPLAIN WHY I'M RIGHT and I'M A FUNGI, with a drawing of a mushroom. Oh, just terrible, tacky shit I would never choose for myself, but which I knew would not only help me blend in, it might play a part in fooling myself that I could. I wore baseball caps for sports teams I didn't care about, laughed at the jokes everyone laughed at, frequented the same malls. Meanwhile, the actual me scoffed inside, rolled his eyes, fumed. A kid in a leather coat would pass in the high school hall and I'd think, *That's me, that's more my style*, but I was terrified, rightfully so, about opening any personally revelatory door at all. I understood, implicitly, that if I let any of me out, all of me could come tumbling. The same kid whose leather jacket I admired spent time in my head, of course, his arms and legs removed, kept in newspaper in my closet, such delicious fantasies of peeling the skin from his chest and back. What could I do but distance myself? And if you think a leather jacket isn't enough for two people to bond over, you don't remember high school very well."

"Dad," Andrew said. "You wore baseball caps all the time. When we were kids, on trips, around town. You wear T-shirts with stupid slogans now."

Shawn looked to him and the momentary, loaded silence was broken by fresh voices below.

"What was the one instance, Dad?" Margaret said.

Creaks from below. A burst of false laughter from Sheila.

"I started reading up on what I was around then. I wouldn't be caught dead checking out the stuff I really wanted from the high school library, and there was no way I was going to let greater Samhattan get a sense of who I was at the Samhattan Public, so I started borrowing Dad's car, driving to small towns, never repeating myself. As if the simple act of investigating was the same as committing the crimes I already wanted so badly to commit. I left no trace. I read abnormal-psychology books in Chowder, true crime in Goblin. Horror in East Kent. I didn't check any book out and I made sure not to read too much of any one subject. No cross-references, either. I couldn't have a librarian wondering why someone would read about a serial killer *and* a book titled *Who Am I?* on the same day. All this hiding, already, all while wearing those T-shirts and hats. It was, in a word, exhausting."

Footsteps on the stairs. More than a couple people. Andrew stepped from the window and took his seat beside Margaret.

"Ethel followed me," Shawn said. "All over. I'd see her unmistakable reddish-brown hair at the very edge of an aisle of books. Then she'd be across the library at the card catalogue, no doubt looking for what was missing off the shelf, what I had in my hands. How she got to these places? I never asked. I had the car."

The door opened. Sheila stepped in.

"Shawn?"

The way she said it, silently asking if the conversation she'd left had finally come to an end.

"She took the bus," Shawn said. "That's the only explanation. She was more fixated than I was, in her way."

"Shawn?"

"Sometimes I think I owe everything to Ethel."

"The Millers are here," Sheila said.

This, spoken more like a demand. Like it better be a good time. The Millers were Shawn and Sheila's best friends. The couples had done everything together, from catching movies to a still-talked-about vacation to Mexico. Shawn had worn many silly shirts on that trip.

"Hey, buddy," Quinn Miller said, peering into the room around Sheila. "Hi, Andrew. Hey, Margaret."

Nicole peered in beside him, her eyes red from crying. Quinn didn't look much better. He put his arm around his wife.

Margaret looked to her dad, but Shawn still seemed to be staring at an unseen biography, hanging between them.

"Kids," Sheila said, "give the Millers your chairs."

"Oh no," Nicole said, fanning a handkerchief. "They don't have to move."

But they did. After eyeing each other and their dad once more, seemingly deciding to allow what would be to be, they got up and stepped aside, making room for the Millers.

"Well, thank you, guys," Quinn said.

Shawn breathed heavy from the bed.

"I would like to say I would never have killed you two," Shawn said. "I would like to say I would never have hurt anybody in this room. Because, after all, you five were my disguise just as much as those shirts and hats were. You five made me look like a regular man. So, I'd love to pretend I didn't think, no, *plan,* to keep you in our basement, Quinn, when Nicole and Sheila went to Florida together, when the kids were already away at school."

Quinn didn't look surprised.

"Sheila told us you were saying some pretty wild stuff up here, Shawn."

"The plan was to ask you over for the game. A game I didn't care a thing about."

"I came over for the game."

"Yes. It remains one of the most confusing evenings I've ever had. I understood clearly that, if I hurt you, I would get caught. Yet, I had you alone. Drunk. Innocent. You were easier to take than a child."

"Oh, Shawn," Nicole said.

"Still, I found a way. I had methods for resisting my urges. Some uglier than others. The night you came over, I was in the bathroom for a long period of time."

"I remember."

"You called out to me. Told me what I missing on TV."

"Yeah, I did. I asked if you'd fallen in."

Shawn smiled.

"Like one of my shirts, that phrase you said helped. It's the kind of thing regular people say to one another. Made me feel like there was a possibility you might get out of the night alive. Only, you couldn't have known that on the other side of the bathroom door I was dipping Q-tips into the tip of my penis, crying out silently, raging against the pain."

"Okay," Sheila said, exasperated. "I'm sorry, Nicole and Quinn. I warned you it might not be pretty and here we are."

"It's okay," Quinn said. "It can't be easy."

"Easy?" Shawn said. "Denying the *actual* you your entire life? No, not easy."

"I meant . . . well, I meant dying."

"This is the most peace I've ever known."

"Well, that's nice," Nicole said. Then she started crying again.

"Don't cry for me, Nicole," Shawn said. "This is the time of my life. I learned what I was in the libraries of the surrounding towns and counties and I took that knowledge and kept it close. Like when the doctor says your problem might be X and you know, immediately, he or she is right. Only, I was sixteen, without anybody to talk about it with. Argyle and I had started drifting apart, naturally, as kids who are friends tend to do when they reach high school. Like you and Malcolm, Andrew. But I saw her, here and there, in the halls, on the streets of Samhattan. And once, she may have even stopped me from going too far."

"Too far?" Margaret asked.

"The night we graduated high school was a bad one for me. By then I'd been honing my resistance in a semi-informed manner for two years, yes, but believe me when I say that didn't make it an easy thing to do. I don't think anybody could become an expert in *that*. You simply had to say *no*, a dozen, two dozen, times a day every day. It felt like holding down a button that stretched the word *no* over all of time and space, so that you weren't hearing it on repeat, you were just under the weight of one endless word. At all times, all day, every day, even on the good ones, even when you smiled or laughed or thought you had, perhaps, no bad thoughts, even then you would hear the elongated *no* and you'd be reminded of what you were *really* doing, which was, always, resisting your true nature. I wasn't fully present at a single thing we ever did together, guys, not the real me, no, and I sure as hell wasn't prepared for high school to end, to have the security of a daily routine taken away, so that now I could go anywhere in the world I pleased, now I was eighteen and capable of traveling to Europe if I wanted, Scandinavia, where I might rent a small apartment, tell nobody my name, and stake out my first victim, the first man or woman, boy or girl, to die by my hand. God, it sounded *good*. Like the world was made of orgasms and I'd spent my first eighteen years in a convent. The gate was opening. But to get through it, I had to pass through some rituals, the ceremonies we all take part in. Like graduation night, the actual send-off. But when it came, I couldn't go anywhere near the school. I borrowed Dad's car and drove far, feeling not only the horrible possibilities that lay ahead but also the loss of all the peers I'd fantasized about strangling for the four years prior. While Amberly Motley lamented the end of her run as student president and Blake Hein cried for what he assumed would be the best years of his life, I, too, cried, for not having acted on my urges. Because, I thought that night, who cared? I hadn't chosen this. I didn't ask to be this way. And so why should I have to resist when nobody else did? Send me to jail, who cared? At least then I'd have done something about who I am and not felt like a shell of a man, dressed in somebody else's clothes, driving fast out of town, cutting the dark like a night chicken, running from any and all temptation. I drove to East Kent that night. I parked under the shadows of a maple tree downtown and waited for the first loner I saw."

"Shawn . . ." Sheila said.

"It's okay, buddy," Quinn said. "No harm, no foul, right?"

The floor creaked downstairs. Or possibly it was just outside the bedroom door.

"Sure," Shawn said. "But potential harm, my friend. This to a man not much older than I was then. I don't know if I was thinking provincially, if I didn't believe I could handle someone much older than myself, in some fear-of-the-father sense (my head is still stuffed with so many theories from all the books I read about people like me), but his slight figure, his youth, attracted me."

The words were so foreign to the five people in the room that the communal uncomfortable feeling added a thickness to the air, rivaling that of being in the presence of a dying man.

"Are you sure you want these to be your last words?" Sheila asked.

The question, reasonable as it would have been an hour prior, fell flat then. There was no question Shawn Hasbro was talking about exactly what he wanted to be talking about. And how to accept that? How to process that the most shocking conversation was also the right one to have?

He didn't respond directly. He answered by carrying on. And as he did, the exhaustion that had flattened him the last few weeks, the depletion of energy and life, fought to show itself amongst the newfound enthusiasm that propelled him.

"The first thing I thought of was his brain. What I could do with such a thing. How I could take it apart. How I might knead it between my fingers, cover myself in his thoughts and memories. Bathe in his gray matter. Horrid, no? Well . . . no. However, I worried I might be overcompensating. Here I had resisted my urges for years, my whole life, and possibly I wanted to make up for it all at once. The *brain*. Wouldn't strangling him be enough? Wasn't so long ago I wanted to shove the old people off Sprake Mountain. Now I longed for this young man's brain? It's all I could think about. Having it out of his skull and on the passenger seat of the car. I wanted to touch it, taste it, shove pieces of it up my nose. *Look*, I thought, watching him wide-eyed as he passed close to the driver's-side window, no idea someone like me ogled from within, *that brain owns him, tells him what to do.* And: *That brain will warn him of a predator too.* Is that what I was? Jesus, it didn't feel like that at all. It was the sexiest I'd ever felt. I was a svelte, intelligent, virile young man. It was graduation night! Everybody I'd ever known was dancing in the Samhattan High School gymnasium while I was in East Kent, parked, fogging up the window with my lust for the cells in this stranger's brain."

"No more," Sheila said.

"Mom," Andrew said. "Just go downstairs."

"Everybody out," Sheila said.

The Millers sat rapt. But the redness in their eyes had faded some. They watched now with fascination.

Shawn Hasbro wasn't just delivering his last words. He was *confessing*.

But to what?

"I would discover I had no pattern," he said. "At no point in my life did I find myself desiring the same thing twice. The only through-line here was the desire itself, the unbearable hurt of it. And I knew, then, that the young man walking East Kent alone could satiate this for me. I ran through a dozen rationalizations behind the wheel of Dad's car. I was out of town. It would be just this once. I needed it. I deserved it. I was young and I would have years to atone. That last one worked." Shawn smiled, as though recalling an idealistic viewpoint, formerly held. "I got out, closed the door quiet behind me. Followed the man on foot."

"I can't listen to this," Nicole said. "I'm sorry, Shawn. I'm so sorry you're dying. I just . . . I can't handle both. You passing and . . . your story."

Shawn looked Nicole in the eye as he said:

"There was nobody else in sight. East Kent is good like that. Of course, I didn't know that at the time, but I discovered it to be true over time. If you're ever looking for a ghost town after midnight, where it's truly rare to encounter more than a handful of people, and most of them drunk at that, East Kent is an oasis for the stalker in you. The kid (I call him a kid now, but I was a kid then too) walked quickly, like he could sense someone tracking him. And I . . . I really was. I felt like an animal under the streetlights, silent up the sidewalks, staying close to the buildings, trying my best to appear aloof at the same time. I can only imagine how much I failed at that. It's a good thing I can't re-watch how I did it in those days. Like the early lovemaking of a young couple; I knew nothing of how it was done."

"You've stalked people on the streets of East Kent since then?" Margaret asked.

"Too much," Nicole said. "I need to leave. I'm sorry."

Quinn made to rise with her, but Sheila beat him to it. She took Nicole by the elbow.

"Shawn," she said. "Your good friend Nicole Miller is leaving the room now. Would you like to say goodbye?"

"Goodbye, Nicole," Shawn said. "We'll always have Mexico."

Nicole smiled, sadly, and Sheila escorted her out of the room. Quinn watched them go.

"I'll be joining her soon," he said. "But I wanted to say goodbye, Shawn. I'm not sure what to make of all this, but I understand this moment isn't about me."

"I followed that kid for fifteen blocks. As you all know, East Kent doesn't really even have fifteen blocks. It felt like five hundred. The rush, the blood pumping in me, it was the most alive I'd ever felt. I'm getting a rush thinking of it now, despite discovering much bigger, stronger ones, later in life." Shawn brought a bony hand to his chest. His face was covered in sweat. "It turned out he had a not-so-gentlemanly reason to be walking alone himself. The young man entered an Irish pub, a thing I'd never done, was too young to do, and knew he was too young to do the same. Still, he went in and I went to the glass and watched him cross the length of the dark-brown wood bar till he vanished into a shadowy hall in the back. Gone then? But I was already locked in. Like cheetahs must be in the plains. There was very little that could cut the rope that had formed between us. All those fools I'd gone to school with, *dancing*, as I, Shawn Hasbro, quiet, average, the ultimate blender, entered my first bar, smelled for the first time the decay of beer, smoke, vomit. I didn't look right and I didn't look left, and I certainly didn't eye the bartender, for fear he'd spot my youth and stop me. I heard the murmuring voices of the clientele, people drinking, their words warring with the music I would one day come to recognize as the Pogues, a thing I later looked into because I would never forget the song that played as I crossed the bar just as my first victim-to-be had done, me without a plan, without knowing what I would do, me at eighteen, no idea, no knowledge, only knowing that I *had* to at least reach him, *had* to satiate what grew within me, that I deserved a bone. I entered the same back hall unscathed and, for what I knew, unnoticed. I paused in the dark. And there I attempted to steady my breathing. I imagine it was tenfold as frightening as finally, after four years of waiting, asking a girl to dance. I heard someone near, behind me, but was distracted, no, *held* by the opening of a door at the end of the hall, light spilling forth, the silhouette of my young man, placing a small bag of powder in his pocket. The word *drugs* crossed my mind, of course, but it was erased from my head by another, much more powerful word, spoken, mere feet behind me. It was, of course, my name. Shawn. Spoken by my first friend, the only person in the world who knew the real me."

"Argyle," Andrew said.

"I spun. I saw the length of the pub span out behind her, saw the older man who sat alone at the two-top, waiting for her, no doubt believing she was just going to use the restroom as she had no doubt told him she was. 'Shawn,' she'd said. My young man made to squeeze past me in the hall, or, at least I thought he was, until he stopped, level with me, and said, 'Hey, you. Stop following me.' Then he made to punch me, and I flinched, but he was only trying to scare me. Which he did. Me. A man who had fantasized of tearing open his head. Then he was off, and Argyle stepped aside to make room for him, leaving then only her and me. 'Argyle,' I said. 'What are you doing in East Kent?' I could just make out her expression as the men's-room door at the end of the hall slowly swung closed, could see it didn't matter to her what *she* was doing in a pub in East Kent. No, if there's such a thing as an elevator within us, a box that rises with the intensities we experience in life, then Argyle's had gone a floor higher than it had when we exchanged drawings in the woods at Two Stumps. 'It's graduation night,' I said. As if that should make her feel bad for being here and not *me*, no, *I* shouldn't feel bad, as if *I* were *her* Jiminy Cricket. Well, I was so focused on her that I hadn't noticed her older companion coming up behind her, having no doubt seen the odd way she'd stopped at the entrance to the dark hall, and no doubt seen me, too, perhaps suspecting something dark in me, a thing that was becoming more obvious every day. 'Everything all right?' he asked. The door closed behind me and they were swathed in mostly darkness, but I'd caught the false smile Argyle sported just prior to turning to him and saying, 'All good, Ted. I've run into an old friend. I'm going to need to have some time alone with him. Shawn, meet Ted. Ted, Shawn.' A head nod and a hand coming toward me in the darkness. I shook it, thought of the fleshy soft spot between his thumb and forefinger. 'Good to meet you, Shawn,' Ted said. Then Argyle said, 'Shawn's going to take me back to Samhattan. Is that okay? I don't want you feeling like I'm bailing on you. It's meaningful is all.' Not even a beat of silence when older Ted said, 'Absolutely. Do what you need to do. I fully understand.' He kissed her cheek and left us. And there, suddenly, I was alone with Argyle on the night of our graduation, neither of us in our accustomed context, yet both of us having some idea what the other was up to. Yes"—Shawn smiled, a mix of recalled embarrassment and warm nostalgia—"I'd been noticed after all."

"Do you think she stopped you?" Margaret asked. There was a hint of hysteria in her voice.

"But what would I have done to him in the bathroom of a public place?" Shawn said. "I had no weapons. I had no plan. I had no real idea of his size, his strength, nothing. I think I just needed to follow him, to prove to myself that I was allowed *some* luxuries, *some* tastes of the life I wanted to be living."

"Argyle sounds like a good friend," Quinn said.

"I did drive her back to Samhattan that night. I had the radio on quietly and she didn't ask me to turn it off and I think it gave us a hint of the night we'd missed in the gymnasium back home. I'd heard Argyle was seeing an older man and now I had my proof. It was shocking: seeing someone I knew in such a different way. It was a lesson, too, I think; I wasn't the only one whose true self went unseen, no matter how gentle or vicious that self might be. The mere sight of Argyle in a bar, a place I'd never been, in a town I'd rarely been, at a time of night I wasn't yet familiar with, was enough to rattle me. And how did she feel about what she'd witnessed with me?" Shawn laughed but it was strained. Another sign of that death, so close, seemingly staved off by way of revelation, advancing again. "When we were halfway home, Argyle said, 'That was a close call.' I gripped the wheel tighter. 'Maybe,' I said. She nodded. We watched the front of the car swallow the road. 'It's going to be a hard life for you, Shawn,' she said. We sat in the dark, the near quiet. I started to cry. She didn't look at me as she continued: 'You're going to have to live with it, Shawn, without allowing it.' I couldn't respond, I just cried. I wiped tears from my eyes so I could see the road. I drove ten under. 'It's not fair,' Argyle said, her voice firm. 'Nobody would choose it. Nobody would ask for it.' I felt like she was speaking to the very center of me. To a place not even I had seen before. 'It's cruel, what's been done to you. What you've been given.' She didn't reach over and give my hand a squeeze like she did at Two Stumps so long ago. Through my blurred vision I thought she looked more like a woman, after all, someone old enough to date the man back in the Irish East Kent pub. And this underscored, horribly, the fact I was now a man. No longer a child with dangerous fantasies. No longer endearing if something wrong were to happen. I had a vision of myself in prison. I cried harder. 'If I hear of anything that resembles what almost happened tonight,' Argyle said, 'I will have to say something. I will have to say, yes, I did, I saw this coming.' It was all I could do not to pull over, to beg her never to say that. *Please, Argyle, no!* This was the first person to whom I'd revealed who I really was, and the first to suggest turning me in. The weight of this moment was insufferable. We crossed back into Samhattan, the silence between us woven into the thoughts and feelings we both had. We drove through our dark town, no other car in sight, as if we alone lived here, we alone owned it. At the foot of her drive, the car idling, I told her, 'I want to make it, Argyle.' And she understood what I meant. I told her I *could* make it, all the way to the end. She nodded, but there was a meanness there, not presented by her, not consciously, a cruel, silent voice that said, *I won't be there to stop you next time, Shawn. Without someone like me . . . will you make it after all?* The words that actually came from her mouth were these: 'I love you, Shawn.' Then? She walked the drive to her front door before I understood we'd said goodbye to our youth. I've never felt as cold as I did then, leaving Argyle's house, driving back across town alone, no more school, no more rules, no more merciful and maddening chains. I had my whole life ahead of me, yes, just like every other senior at Samhattan High. Only, mine felt more like a sentence. As the doors to the rest of my life opened, I heard bigger ones close. And I suddenly felt like the whole wide world, without any guarantee of a guardian angel, was a much smaller place than the tiny one I was leaving. Upon pulling into our driveway, I saw the curtains of the second-floor bedroom nearest the garage close. And I thought, *Ethel's been up all night waiting.*"

"You still had her," Andrew said. "You still had your sister."

There was yearning in his voice, the sound of someone hoping one character in a story will be another's salvation.

"That cold feeling didn't go away for the next six years," Shawn said. "As everyone I knew entered what they called 'the real world,' things grew icier for me in Samhattan. I found myself in a wasteland I could not see the boundaries of, a world with rules only I had to follow. Imagine beginning a life, venturing into adulthood, already knowing none of your desires can be fulfilled. The things that propel other people are not allowed to propel you! No wants for *you*. No satisfaction for *you*. Your tastes are wrong. Your dreams are wrong. Your very DNA. Undoubtedly so, even I knew that. All color, all vibrancy, all impetus had been revoked the day I was born; I suppose you could say I was born *in check*, had to be in check, or there would follow a trail of dead bodies and my own rotting in a cell. I considered it, every morning, afternoon, every night. Would I trade my 'freedom' for the thrill of touching my greatest fantasies? Would I be willing to kill for death row? Believe me, there were times it felt worth it. As I took odd jobs about Samhattan, as I enrolled in college, I imagined myself alone in that cell, my eyes closed, at peace for having the memory of that kill. It didn't matter to me who it was, how old, how young, male, female, whether they were a good person or not. I'd elevated the status of that scenario's reward to such a place, I truly believed it would deliver me nirvana, place me forever on a plateau where I would no longer be required to shove back on who I was. Who I *am*. Because it takes a lot of strength, too much strength, to constantly resist. I could see my own release in every face I saw. These people, they didn't know how good they had it! Once I told a woman, as we both sat waiting for a bus on Benson, I said, 'How can you complain? You're free to wrangle your desires.' She looked at me like I was mad. She'd been talking about how late the bus always was, how her daughter and her no longer got along. When the bus came, I sat in the row behind her, and she got up and moved five rows back. You see? Even briefly expressing envy for what you all have is frightening, exposes something I cannot see."

"You've had a wonderful life," Quinn said. "Sheila and the kids. Come on, Shawn."

"It was six years of tundra for the soul," Shawn said. "I intentionally looked away if I saw someone walking alone. I exited shops and any place of business in which I found myself alone with another person. I began relishing self-pity, happy to be angry at the world, fully embracing the poor-me of it all. And was it ever poor me. I held no job for more than a couple months because each invariably led to fantasies of following my co-workers home. I declined all parties and get-togethers. I avoided our five-year high school reunion. I asked no women on dates, never entered bars where there might be less than a handful of people and tried to go to bed before the sun went down in the summer months. I'd become my own keeper. The warden of my own prison. It's a wonder my mind didn't split into multiples; what was I if not one person refusing another?"

"We all have secrets," Quinn said.

"Not like mine," Shawn said.

Outside, another car pulled close to the house. Andrew rose and went to the window, quickly, hoping to catch a glimpse before they pulled out of sight.

"It's Grandma Dee," Margaret said.

Andrew looked below.

"How do you know?"

"I'd recognize that uneven engine anywhere."

The bedroom door opened. Sheila.

"Quinn," she said. "Nicole is asking for you."

"Tell her I'll be down shortly," he said. "Saying goodbye to a dear friend."

"Go," Shawn said. "The story only gets much worse from here."

"I don't mind," Quinn said.

"Did Ethel come up here?" Sheila asked.

Shawn smiled, but he looked worse than he had when he'd started talking.

"I guess that means she's not down there," he said. "Which means yes, she's up here."

He looked around the room, as if she might be found hiding behind the corner plant, huddled beneath the bed, lying flat to the ceiling.

"Where'd she'd go?" Margaret asked.

"Quinn?" Sheila said, attempting to bring the subject back to why she came upstairs.

"Please," Quinn said. "Another few minutes."

"Fine," Sheila said. "That's fine."

Then she was out the door again.

"I feel bad for Mom," Margaret said to no one.

"I met your mother at the cessation of those six years," Shawn said. "And I saw in her an immediate opportunity to weld myself to 'the real world.' She was a bright thing to me, a person so practical, so focused . . . she expected people to *be* who they said they were. That's not to say she is or was gullible. No. On the contrary, she was so present and real in herself, it was inconceivable anyone would be otherwise. I understood. I was living that betrayal, that daily, by-the-minute deceit, so alone in a desert of ice. I was dazzled by her straight stare, the way she leaned forward in life and didn't stop to examine what she considered to be superfluous philosophical hurdles. Sheila was Sheila. From day one. And while I was not Shawn, I was someone who respected her and thought I might learn from her too. Still, those early days made me very nervous. A woman meant dates. And dates meant alone time." He looked to Andrew, Margaret. "I almost killed your mother the first time I went to her apartment on Walnut."

"Dad," Andrew said.

"It was the first time I was entirely alone with another person for as long as I could remember."

"Shawn," Quinn said. "This part might be too much for the kids. Your kids. Sheila's kids."

"It was like I had no say in the matter. The moment her apartment door closed behind me, something that had been sleeping in my basement came upstairs, stunk up the first floor before I saw it was there. Your mom's place was nice. Clean, orderly, with bottles of wine and good food and good books. Even then she was focused on the future, her future, and, I can only assume, her date that night, that being me, a man she'd met at the Donna O' Art Gallery on Eighth as I'd entered the space both confident that a full house (witnesses) ensured I wouldn't follow one home with a mind to strangle and interested in the dark artwork itself. I wore a T-shirt that said IF YOU HAVE AN OPINION OF ME, PLEASE RAISE YOUR HAND AND PUT IT OVER YOUR MOUTH. Should I have refused Sheila's offer for dinner? Maybe. I certainly thought so as that door to her apartment closed behind me, as she greeted me and told me this was 'unlike' her, that she hadn't told her friends or family because they would think it meant 'marriage,' as she laughed about this and led me deeper into her home, and as I realized that nobody in the world knew that I, Shawn Hasbro, was inside this space with this woman. If what she'd said was true (and I had no reason then or now to think otherwise with anything Sheila has ever said), then some terrible twist of temptation had occurred, and I was not only going to face the usual, unbearable resistance but a force much larger than what I was accustomed to. Possibly I wouldn't be strong enough to do it." He smiled but he did not look good. As if he'd lost pounds in the last hour, here in this bed. "It's amazing how many weapons people keep around the house. How suddenly *everything* is a weapon if you're looking to kill."

"But you *didn't* kill Sheila," Quinn said. He nodded, as if to say, *All settled, then.*

"I was worried about that wine too. I didn't have much experience with alcohol and even less experience being alone with people. What might I say? More than once I'd scared strangers off, unwittingly, hardly recalling what I'd done to offend. Surely I couldn't get through this night without at least scaring the hell out of her. But like I said, and as you know, Sheila has a way about her. A calming effect. It's almost like she says (without saying it), *Whoever you are, be it. Broadcasting would be dramatic.* That's right. She has a way of making internal struggle sound silly, of rendering a panic attack small (just one of many in a lifetime), of revealing the embarrassment of being entirely self-absorbed. Why couldn't we talk about Samhattan? Politics? Sports? Art? Life? Why not leave examination behind and actually have conversations about the world outside ourselves? However she does this, she does. And it worked on me. *For* me. From the start. And so, that first night went well enough. We drank two bottles of wine. We talked. We laughed. And it was only when I was leaving that I reached for a quartz stone cut in half, resting upon the hall table, where she kept her keys and mail. How easy, I thought, to bring it down against the side of her head. How thrilling to watch her expression change at the realization of who she'd invited in. But that was not to be for Sheila. She said, 'You wanna steal my key bowl? Go on. Take it. And then maybe you'll come back and let yourself in.' There was a moment of silence, I was shocked, she wanted a second date. Then, happily, we laughed. For different reasons, perhaps, but together nonetheless. I set the quartz down and we kissed, and I think we both understood this would be the first of many dates. Marriage, after all."

Below, doors opened and closed, voices rose.

"Your mom's here, Dad," Andrew said.

"Probably good to end there, then," Quinn said.

"They were easier days, at first. Married. But soon after, kids. It got harder when Sheila was pregnant because it was a tailor-made situation for a man like me. I was sent out on late night errands regularly. I could take as long as I wanted and make up whatever story for why. I had a wife, which helped me blend in, but my wife was currently stuck at home, which gave me the freedom to prowl. I was out at night again, eyeing loners, men or women stumbling home drunk, the occasional homeless man, night-shift workers at the gas stations, outside in the heat on their phones. As you all know, Hi-Fi Grocery is open till midnight, but it used to be open till two A.M., like the bars, and you wouldn't believe how empty a place like that could get. Often, it felt like it was just me and the check-out man, me eyeing his fingers as he scanned the pickles and milk Sheila had sent me for."

"What stopped you?" Margaret asked.

Shawn coughed. It was the most forceful reminder yet that he was dying. He sank deeper into the bed, closer to supine again, though his sweating, thin face was still propped at a slight angle by the deathbed pillow.

"I was wrapped up in the idea of kids," Shawn said. "I felt close to a clean life. Not that I saw you two, Andrew and Margaret, as salvation for what haunted me, but I wondered how distracted I might become. This was exciting, in a curious, cold way. With kids, I would have more leeway to say and possibly even do strange things. Meaning, if I were to slip up, the effect wouldn't resonate as loud as it would if I were a single man, living in a small house at the outskirts of town. It's ironic, no? The louder I got, a wife and kids, the wider I got, a family, the less likely someone might see me. I was constantly worried about that. Even as recently as today the thought crossed my mind: *Somebody saw it, someone who can do something about it, and now they are coming for you.* Well, when your mother was pregnant with you, Margaret, someone *did* see it. But nobody who would take this knowledge to the authorities. This was someone like me."

"Like you how?" Margaret asked.

Shawn hesitated. But not for long.

"A fellow serial killer."

"Oh shit," Margaret said. "This is it then, isn't it."

"Is Grandma coming up here?" Andrew said.

It'd been many minutes since she arrived.

"Your aunt Ethel's probably talking to her," Quinn said.

"Ethel is in the room next door," Shawn said. "Her ear to the wall."

"Maybe someone should go check on your grandmother," Quinn said to Margaret.

Both kids looked to the closed door, then back to Shawn.

"I was delivering flowers for Happenstance Florists at the time. I drove a big van all across town, delivering arrangements to office buildings, funeral parlors, husbands and wives. The exactitude of the scenario was not lost on me: a serial killer driving a van, after all."

"But not a serial killer," Margaret said.

"Yeah," Andrew said. "*Not.*"

"He was a mail carrier," Shawn said. "Slight of stature, wore glasses, had a wiry strength to him. We passed one another all the time, he in his mail truck, me in the van. We drove the same streets, going opposite ways on the main roads. Often, we were stopped at the same lights. Eventually, we got to nodding acknowledgment. City workers in the field. Soldiers in the shit. But soon I saw he was studying me as we drove, a little something more than hello, recognition in his gaze. One day he winked. Letting me know he knew. And to my surprise, I could tell just as easily what he was too. His name was—"

"Randy Scotts," Quinn said. "Are you serious right now, Shawn? You didn't hang out with Randy Scotts ... did you?"

"Randy Scotts has long been buried (dug up more than once, including a time when a different kind of psychopath exhumed his body to film it), but back when Margaret hadn't said Mama to the world yet, he was already well into the work he'd begun. We arrived at the same red light on Baskins Boulevard one afternoon. He gestured for me to roll down the window."

"I don't believe this," Quinn said. "It's just ... Shawn, it's too much. He's the Samhattan Boogeyman."

"Not yet he wasn't. Nobody's a boogeyman until someone finds out that he is."

"We spent years afraid of Randy Scotts," Quinn said.

"And a summer afraid of Daphne," Margaret said.

But this was recent. And Andrew and Margaret still felt the fear of the recency and said no more.

But Shawn did:

"I rolled down the van window. He wasted no time. 'Hey, killer,' he said. 'You wanna get some lunch?' I went as red as the light we waited for. I felt if I pretended not to understand what he meant, he would laugh and drive off and I would be left with a new sort of shame. Next-level self-denial. I wanted to talk to him. Wanted to break bread with someone who experienced the world the way I did. 'Sure,' I said. 'You lead the way.' He smiled. 'Planned on it,' he said. You don't read much about people like us getting together in the books. I suppose it has something to do with staunchly accepting our status, by necessity, as loners. But here I'd been given the opportunity and here I said yes."

"You went to lunch with Randy Scotts," Quinn said. "The most infamous, vile man in the history of Samhattan."

"Not yet he wasn't."

"But Shawn ..."

"Don't you lunch with fellow investors, Quinn? Don't you drink scotch with like-minded men?"

"Yeah, but!" Exasperated. "Shawn!"

"I followed his mail truck to what is now Kuznetsov Hardware but what used to be the original location of the Wild Stallion Bar and Grill over in Little Russia. Not a terribly dirty place but never intended for family dinners either. City workers ate there, drank beers on their breaks, played pool after their shifts. I'm surprised they didn't serve salt of the Earth. Scotts parked the mail truck and headed in before I parked beside him. I noted that. Like he wanted to enter separately, not because I would've exposed him but because he wanted to be in control of the situation. If he entered first, he owned the place. For him, it *was* power. And after I entered, I found he'd already ordered us beers. Double control. He was telling me what to drink. He signaled me to come sit with him in a booth at the center of the far wall, far as we could get from any windows."

Sheila's voice rose from downstairs. It sounded like an argument. Nicole said something about it being crazy upstairs. Quinn kept his eyes on Shawn. How could he leave now?

"Being so close to someone like myself was beyond fascinating," Shawn said. "I had proof that you *could* keep a job, *could* invite people out for lunch, despite who we were. Randy didn't care. He wasn't hiding his true nature, only the terrible things he'd done. So what if the world thought he was evil? So what if small children and old people eyed him the way pets did, their hackles up, rightly sensing something very bad? Randy didn't wear T-shirts with silly slogans and didn't marry and have kids so that he might look tethered to a life he had nothing in common with. As I got to know him, I grew more envious of this."

"Wait," Quinn said. "You *regularly* got together with Randy Scotts?"

"Randy became something of a model for me."

"Oh no," Margaret said. "Dad. What did you do . . ."

"That first afternoon, in that booth, he looked to my hands and said, 'You got married. That's insane, man.' And of course I knew what he meant. I also understood this wasn't going to be easy. I had to be prepared to take whatever he doled out. There was no pretending around him. 'Obviously this means you're resisting,' he said. I eyed the rest of the bar. People watched the TVs. People ate. None the wiser that two psychopathic killers lunched forty feet away. 'I haven't done it,' I said. 'In how long?' he asked. I looked to the tabletop and he nearly leapt from the booth. 'Oh, come on,' he said. 'That's impossible. *Never?*' Then he laughed and people did look at us. The mail carrier and the flower man, getting drunk on the job. 'That's the scariest thing I've ever heard,' he said. 'And I've heard some scary stuff.' He eyed me. 'You'll go mad. It's pointless. Useless. You'll end up doing it one day. Might as well be now.' He talked fast, direct, sipped his beer between declarations, wiped his mouth with his work-shirt sleeve. 'I'm not a killer if I haven't killed,' I said. He thought about this. Or maybe he just waited for effect. 'Bullshit,' he said. 'Are you not a man if you don't eat? Bullshit. You're punishing yourself for no reason. There is no God and the law is man-made. What does that leave you with?' 'Right and wrong,' I said. 'Oh,' he said. '*That.* And how many people are there on this planet and how many die from worse ways than me?' I thought about killing him then. I thought I might listen to him, act like I was awed, angle to get him alone. Surely, I could live with killing *this* man. 'How many times have you done it?' I asked. But he shook his head no. 'None of that talk,' he said. 'Besides, I don't keep count. I'm not into art-by-numbers. No more than I'm into guilt.' Then, without planning to and with no buildup at all, I said, 'Maybe my first could be one of yours.' He leaned back. Stared at me. In that moment I saw what people saw just before he hurt them. I was so ashamed. Embarrassed. I'd asked a man to do all the work. More than that: I'd asked a stranger to live the life for me. How bad off was I that, five minutes in, I was begging him for scraps? 'Not a chance,' he said. 'And if you ask for something like that again, you *will* be one of mine.' No humor there. No sip of beer. Just the metal lock of his eyes upon mine. 'Sorry,' I said. He reached across the table and gripped my wrist, pulled my wedding band from my finger. 'Stop saying sorry,' he said. He dropped the ring into my beer. 'The minute you stop apologizing is the minute you start doing what you were born to do. You have no idea what you've been missing, brother. You have *no idea* what good is. You know a good meal. Good weather. A good night's sleep. But this? This is better than sex. Better than respect from your peers. Better than inner peace.' I felt tears building up, but I didn't want to cry in front of him. Yet, why not? We'd already destroyed all norms of the day; why not show myself in full? 'You gotta kill soon,' he said. 'There's no way off this flight.' I went to fish the ring out of my beer, then drank it instead."

"Jesus," Andrew said.

"You told Mom you lost it," Margaret said. "We've heard that story a thousand times. You got a new one."

"I wasn't afraid of him," Shawn said. "What scared me was the mirror effect, the way I saw who I could be, in him. I didn't like what I looked like. What he looked like. I didn't like how easy he made it sound, the glory he found in killing. I know now that by the time I met him, by the time we drank our first beers, he'd already removed the mouths of six people. I also know he was holding a man captive as we spoke, a man with no lips. Scotts worked with scissors."

"Fuck this," Andrew said. He headed for the door.

"Andrew," Margaret said. "Dad is *dying*."

"I don't care if Dad is rising from the ashes," Andrew said. "I can't do this anymore. I'm going to check on Grandma."

He opened the door.

"The second time we went to an establishment it was out of town. East Kent, of all places. The site of my near first kill. It had been two weeks since the Wild Stallion, two weeks since I swallowed my wedding ring. I was about to knock on a door on Canyon here in Samhattan, a fist full of flowers, when I heard the mail truck pull up on the street behind my van. Randy had come to tell me about a "good club" in East Kent. He said Samhattan naturally attracted attention, the cemetery in the center of downtown, the silly tourist names for all the shops. Little Russia. He said some places, like some people, caught everybody's eye, whether they shined or not. East Kent, he said, naturally hid. He spoke of a club there as plain as a country feed store, and he suggested we'd eat. Our way, understand. Well, shocked as I was to see him, scared as I was to say yes, I didn't knock on that door, I didn't deliver those flowers. I quit that job on the spot, drove the van to Hi-Fi Grocery, and applied for a job stocking at night. My strategy was small: if they hired me, I could tell Sheila I had to work nights, including whatever night Randy wanted me to visit this East Kent club. It's amazing how convoluted lies can get. Hi-Fi didn't immediately hire me, so I convinced myself they were going to. I told myself I *would* eventually work nights. So, when I told Sheila I'd got the job . . . I wasn't technically lying. She believed me because she would never present herself as anything other than the truth. It's one of the many perks of marrying a good person. They expect you to be the same."

"This is awful," Margaret said. "Please say you didn't . . . you didn't . . ."

Andrew hadn't left after all. He closed the door and remained standing, as far as he could from Shawn.

"I understood what Randy was trying to do, of course. It didn't take much deduction to distill his intention, what he hoped to accomplish at a hidden club in East Kent. Yet, lies . . . I lied to myself, too, didn't I? Because, for days, I pretended I'd been invited for a night out and nothing more. But some lies are told to help us, to get us through an event we might not otherwise attend. Randy wanted me to break my seal. My first kill. And this place, this club, was where it was going to happen."

"Shawn," Quinn started. He slumped in the chair.

"The club was mostly dark except for glow-light poles," Shawn said. "I thought of Argyle and how she appeared, suddenly, in the last East Kent bar I'd been to. I think I even looked for her. The bar itself was lit from below so that everyone looked like they were haunted. Randy sat at that bar, no longer wearing his mail-carrier clothes, now with a collared shirt unbuttoned to show a naked chest, tight slacks, and no glasses. He could've been wearing a snowsuit and I would've recognized him. Birds of a feather, I suppose."

"Don't say that," Quinn said. "I don't think it's healthy to compare yourself to Randy Scotts on your deathbed, Shawn. Do you really want these to be your final thoughts? Your final words?"

"These are the truest words I've ever spoken," Shawn said.

"But still," Quinn said, "if you didn't kill anyone . . . then you aren't like him. I mean, this would be like someone saying they cheated because they thought of other people. It's just not true. It's not fair, really. You should be listening to words of love, how much you meant to Andrew, Margaret, Sheila. Your wife is downstairs, arguing with your mom that right now isn't a good time to come up because her son is going on about these morbid fantasies he never fulfilled. Don't you see how this is hurting people you don't mean to hurt?"

"I do love you, Dad," Margaret said. "But I need to know."

"I joined him at the bar and saw he had two shots already lined up," Shawn said. "George Washingtons, they were called. I can taste that shot now. He lifted his glass to mine and said, 'Tonight is your night.' It struck me that I hadn't given him my name. Nor did I know his. I don't think it was out of secrecy, though I can understand if someone else does. I think it was more that, when we were together, there was no denying who we really were, simply no pretending, and so neither of us cared for the societal names we'd been given, names that were meant to be used for navigating someone else's world. 'Tonight is your night,' he said, and so we drank to that. People danced in the heavy mist of a fog machine, silhouettes like soft noodles, all of them so virile, so alive. That only made it worse, harder; if it was shock I wanted to see in a victim's eyes, what greater distance was there to travel than from dancing to dying? I felt it in my groin, an arousal, not sexual, but like I was a child, standing in line for what promised to be the greatest adventure of my life. It struck me how perfect the place was Randy had picked: it was dark enough that nobody would remember our faces, it was crowded enough for us to get lost in the numbers, but not so packed we couldn't make contact, inroads, with a single person. The drinks were flowing, everything was loose, carefree, and, for the others, horribly unsafe. I didn't yet know what made Randy tick. I didn't know he had six bodies near his home and seven pairs of lips in the trunk of his car. I only knew he was like-minded."

Shawn coughed, tried to take a deep breath, and struggled with it. With his bony fingers gripping the blanket, he looked momentarily like a skull sinking in quicksand.

Andrew and Margaret went to his bedside.

"This is it," Margaret said.

"But he was just talking a second ago," Quinn said. "Come on, Shawn!"

Shawn coughed again and tried to sit up but failed. Someone moved downstairs and voices rose, and Shawn flailed a moment like a dying fish on the bed.

"Dad!" Andrew said.

Quinn was up now, all three at his bedside, able to smell it, the scent of the grave already upon him.

But Shawn seemed to stabilize, to remain still without coughing. His eyes wide, his face drenched, his breathing somewhat regular.

He gathered himself enough to go on.

"We got dangerously drunk that night," he said, his voice a bit hoarser. "I think we were both relieved to talk freely, but Randy would never have put it that way. Still, I saw it in him just as I imagine he saw it in me. For a little while it felt like we were normal men, a night out on the town, drinks at a club, just living. It got foggier, darker, the lit-up poles got brighter. A wave of people came, another wave left. Randy said, 'I could kill anybody here in the men's room. The door locks.' 'But someone might see you exit alone,' I said. He looked at me like I was crazy. 'So what?' he said. 'You overestimate how shocking it is, what you want to do. You underestimate people's ability to assimilate, to put one and one together. If someone saw me, then saw the body, the first thing they'd do is scramble to tell me. To ask for my help. Tell me to call 911. Don't you get it? You can do *anything,* and you choose to do nothing.' The insult hit me hard. But before I could respond we were heading outside, both of us tipsy, then crossing the street to a park bench perfectly situated in the dark. We wobbled there, we sat, and both our eyes fastened on the form of a woman who had just entered the far side of the park, her shoes like tiny hands clapping, a studio audience, happy to see the victim finally arrive."

"You do *not* need to say any more," Quinn said. "You are weak and your head isn't right. Enough of this, Shawn. Please."

"Randy then told me about the man he was already holding captive. Told me the man was asleep but would wake before he returned. Told me he wasn't worried about this because he had the man in a cement restroom in the park by his house. I looked around to see if this was the park by his house. The woman stepped into a shaft of lamplight, then into the dark again. She was far enough away that I felt I had time to decide. 'I should leave you here,' Randy said. 'I've already told you how good it is. If I left right now, you'd have the whole event to yourself.' I think I would have normally gotten shy then, in any other circumstance, but I was experiencing a freedom I'd never known before. Not even with Argyle at Two Stumps in the woods did I feel so *me*. And I could see the confidence brimming over in the woman, too, the way she walked, her head held high, her stride. Yes, she strode, into the dark, into the light, and I understood that, with the help of the liquid courage I'd swallowed, this might be the best chance I'd ever get. Yet I suppose I could've said that about any moment in my life. It's up to the killer if and when he kills." Shawn looked to Quinn's hand on the bedside and Quinn pulled it back quickly. Shawn said, "I thought about the potential look on this woman's face, the shock, the horror at my hands. I felt like I'd been told to enter a game I'd waited forever and worked forever to get into. I stood up, sat down, watched the woman walk, looked away, watched her again. And when I turned to Randy again, he was gone. Just like he said. Just me on the bench now. Was he there? Watching? I felt him then, *under* the bench, at the back of my shoes. The woman was close now. Close enough where I had to, absolutely *had* to decide. Everything felt right: the place, the weather, the dark, the moment. But everything also felt wrong; Randy waiting, for starters. And the fact I was being forced to do it before I was ready. I stood up. I sat down. I could hear him breathing from the woods. No, from under the bench. I couldn't tell. I still had the elements of his story in my head, the man in the stone restroom, the scissors, the lips. It was like I was on drugs, and I don't mean the drinks. It felt like I was surfing a fiery wave, and the woman, *she* was surfing in the same sea, and we were fated, heading for a collision, whether we'd asked for it or not. I felt something sharp at my side on the bench, reached to find a pair of scissors. Then Randy said something, but did his voice come from beneath the bench or from above me, in a park tree? I looked up. I stood up. The woman was ten feet away. She stopped walking. She said, 'I'm not looking for any trouble.' I didn't speak. I remained still. 'I'm just gonna walk by you now,' she said. But why had she stopped? Why was she saying these things? I felt I'd lost the most important part, to me, the shock, the surprise, the fracturing of what she deemed safe. She'd already counted me a threat. Where was the fun in that? 'Here I go,' she said. Still, I stayed quiet. I heard movement in a tree above and I looked up, thinking I'd see Randy fall upon her. But no. Randy leapt out from under the bench and roared at the woman and she swung once at him and he laughed and she ran and he laughed and he laughed until he turned to me and the coldness I saw there was not human, not man, not woman; it was *stone*."

"Jesus," Margaret said.

The door to the bedroom opened. Sheila's and Nicole's voices preceded them, but it was Shawn's mother who entered the room first.

Her black sweater and black slacks gave her face the pallor of floating skull as well. Here in solidarity for the dying.

"I don't like what I'm being told downstairs," she said. "And I don't care *what* you're talking about up here. You are my son. And I've come to say goodbye."

Shawn, exhausted from the thrill of speaking freely, weak from so many words, wiped saliva from his lips.

"You're just in time, Mom. I'm going to talk now about the one consistent variable in all this unbelievable life. I'm about to talk about Ethel."

Quinn rose and offered Shawn's mother his seat.

"Dee, please."

But Dee didn't look to the chair. She only watched her son.

Quinn sat back down, and Nicole took the chair beside him.

"What I didn't mention before," Shawn said, "is that after our conversation at the Wild Stallion, I saw Ethel peering over the end of the bar. She'd seen me talking with the mail carrier, though I don't suppose she knew what kind of person Randy Scotts was at the time. Still, I wouldn't put it past her. And in the park, after Scotts spit on me (yes, that was how he chose to exit) and left me alone to face my failed performance, I saw Ethel again, this time up in a tree. Not high, no, but her bare feet glowed white in the V of the tree and I knew, of course, it was her. Still, at the time, I was worried about the police. The woman Randy scared off must've called them. They'd be on their way. And while I didn't do anything wrong, it *felt* like I had. I dropped his scissors and fled, leaving everything, including Ethel, behind. I ran to a nearby twenty-four-hour burger joint called Studs. I slunk into a booth. I tried to calm down. It wasn't easy. How close had I come? And how much more of this could I take? I didn't choose this. I repeat this over and over for good reason, even as I repeat within myself, still. This horrible urge, it had been thrusted upon me. Don't you think I *wanted* to want the same things you all do? Don't you think I wanted to exist, to find satisfaction in the daily-do you take for granted? When I imagine your memories, I see clean scenery, good smells, a sun high in the sky. But mine ... there wasn't a day I lived without fiending, without longing, without nearly losing my mind with lust for a violence I could not have. What did the rules matter to a man born like me? Still, some voice, an unfathomable strength, had got me that far. Margaret was born soon after the failure in the park. I cried as I held her. Mom, you were there. Sheila and I now had two kids and I found a good job through Sheila's father. Suddenly I was selling medical gloves to hospitals in and around Samhattan. I was making ten times what I could at a place like Hi-Fi, and the kids were growing up. I stayed away from clubs and parks, alleys and late nights. I heard the news of Randy Scotts being caught just like everybody else heard it: on TV. Sheila and I were together. She was horrified. I was jealous. Because the man they showed in cuffs, carted off to prison, he didn't look as bad as I felt. He had experiences to bring with him to his cell. Memories of having satiated his needs. Even now, I see him with envy. People always say you can't bring possessions with you to the grave, you only bring memories. But where then were mine? I'd had good days with Sheila and the kids, even good times at work. But no matter how well I did and how happy my family was, the hole in me remained black. Nothing to fill it. I started walking hospital halls, medical-center halls, before and after pitching the new gloves. I noted who was closest to death. I thought of that old couple on Sprake Mountain, imagined their faces as they'd feel, *if* they had fallen, *if* I had found it in me to shove them. But what good would killing a person so close to death do? That'd be too close to mercy. Still, I went into hospital rooms, stood beside beds, eyed the patients, let them know, silently, I could kill them, that I *wanted* to. I told more than one person this very thing. And these slivers, these small satisfactions were like singular drops of water in a lifelong excursion through the desert. I went to funerals for people I didn't know. I wanted to see the grief on the faces of those who did. It wasn't what I was looking for, of course, it wasn't innocence lost, but it was an elongated version of it. I found some solace there. I followed more than one person in my car, out of town, all the way to Goblin and even back to East Kent, where I passed where the Irish Pub used to be. The years moved on, the kids became teens. I cried myself to sleep some nights, sat outside under the stars and quietly *resisted*. I thought of that night in the park often. Not only because I'd whiffed on a chance to kill but because I'd seen how easy it was to find a person alone. Randy and I had been in that park for seconds when that woman entered. And how many seconds are in each day? That woman . . . I saw her again in Samhattan years later. We were at Jenny Will's Pizza, Sheila, me, the kids. You were there, too, Quinn, Nicole. Nicole caught me looking at her but when I looked to you, Nicole, you played it off like you hadn't caught me. I had no doubt you thought I found the woman pretty. That made me sick inside. Thinking how little the world knew of me. Scotts was in jail, then buried. I lived this life alone, despite having a good job, a great family, friends. And it wasn't long after Jenny Will's Pizza, just when it seemed I'd reached my coldest temperature, that if I grew any harder inside I wouldn't be able to breathe, Sheila took the kids to Chicago, leaving me alone to work for the weekend, and I came home to find a young man tied to a chair in our kitchen."

"What?" Sheila said.

Everybody moved in their own way at once. Nicole stood up. Quinn turned away. Andrew and Margaret inched closer to the bed.

"Dad," Margaret said. It was all she needed to say.

"He was young," Shawn said. "Young as I was back on that day in the park. Blond hair, though you couldn't be sure for the blood from where he'd been knocked on the side of his head."

"Dad . . ."

"He had one shirtsleeve tied around his mouth and the other around his eyes. We couldn't hear him if he screamed. And he couldn't see us if we did."

"Shawn," Dee said. "Who was *us?*"

Shawn coughed and it sounded bad. His entire body shook with it and he flailed once again. His breathing got worse; the sweat on his face turned the color of cream.

"Ethel had got him for me," he said. "She'd already begun her own career by then, translating documents for the Samhattan Archives. I'd been fooled into thinking this meant she was living her own life. But . . . she'd waited for a weekend when Sheila and the kids would be out of town, and she kidnapped a man and bound him and brought him over."

Out in the hall, the floor creaked. All looked to see if Ethel would enter the room.

"Yes, Ethel. She'd witnessed my resistance from the start. She'd been there every time I said no. As the young man whimpered for his life, Ethel said, 'I can't stand it anymore. I can't stand to see you this way. It's driven me mad, Shawn. Just do it. *Do* what you want to do.' I couldn't believe what I was hearing. Ethel had broken before I did. She, my sister, Ethel, who couldn't bear the strife anymore, who cared enough about me to do what I could not. She who saw in me a tortured man living a tortured life, and it tortured *her.*"

Shawn's voice grew even hoarser. His breathing worse.

"I tried to leave the kitchen and she started shouting for me to stay, to do it, to get it out of me and over with. The man tried to break free from the chair, but he was tied too tight. Good on Ethel for that. And in the middle of this chaos, I thought, *Nothing can be fully repressed, it has to come out.* And this, *this* was how mine came out. Through *her.* My lifelong witness. She'd been there on Sprake

Mountain. She'd been there in the park. She was there the night I almost killed you, Quinn. She likely remembers more of the game we watched than I do. She stood outside this very home one midnight, looking up to the bedroom window where I held baby Margaret, attempting to calm her back to sleep, dark thoughts abounding. She'd seen ten thousand emotions I couldn't know I'd been expressing. Just as I existed in a freezer, she was buried in ice. '*Do it!*' she screamed. And I did not leave the kitchen. I could have! I could have run. I thought to, I tried to, I tried not to. Ethel crossed the kitchen and turned on all four stove burners and pointed to them and pointed to the blindfolded man and said, 'Do it.' Her eyes were animal, her voice wilderness. 'You do not deserve this torture,' she said. 'You need one. One to carry with you. You need *relief.* This is it.' What else could I do? I stood and gaped at the man, gaped at my sister, even as the burners turned bright orange. Ethel grabbed the man by the neck and dragged him and the chair to the stove. 'Do it,' she said. 'Hurt him.' I moved then, seeing here, *yes*, a chance to do it. An opportunity given me, after all that had been taken, the way it felt, for me, an entire life stolen by an indefatigable craving. All I had to do was hurt him. This man. This once. Ethel would no doubt help me get rid of him, Ethel who had initiated this, Ethel to blame. I felt the fever rising in me, the *urge;* unfathomable longing, every joint in my body pulling me toward the man, the stove. '*Now,*' Ethel said. I didn't refute, didn't think. I moved, took hold of both Ethel's wrists, shoved her back. The man, still blindfolded, shook his head *no* at the sudden commotion, and I reached for him, tore free the ropes that bound him. Ethel yelled, went for him, even as the man got free, even as he erupted out of the kitchen, screaming. To this day I wonder which neighbors heard him and what they thought of what they heard. I think, too, of what they thought of the second scream, a damned howl that came from a place as deep in Ethel as I'd found in myself; Ethel had lifted her dress and sat on the stove. Her skin melted to the burner. Her voice was Salem witch. I can smell her still. And the sound she made rendered me deaf, in that there is no other sound I hear. Even now, as I talk, I can hear Ethel screaming on that stove."

Shawn coughed. Hard. He reached for a nightstand that was out of reach. Andrew brought the glass of water to him, but Shawn dropped it and it shattered.

Grandma Dee looked to the door.

"Ethel!" she called.

Sheila went to Shawn's side. Quinn and Nicole held each other.

"Someone's here," Andrew said.

Shawn coughed. Turned onto his side. White bile spilled onto the pillow.

"Dad," Margaret said. "Did the young man turn you in?"

Shawn shook his head no, weakly, even as his eyes told her he wasn't sure why there was no repercussion for what happened that day.

Then he coughed up blood. And Sheila told Grandma Dee this was it. Shawn was dying. He'd spoken his piece. His last words.

Down below, a door opened and closed. Someone had entered the house.

Andrew looked through the window but could not see.

Quinn held Nicole closer.

Grandma Dee watched her son.

"Who's here?" Sheila asked.

Her voice harbored a madness of its own. Such an ordinary phrase, *Who's here*, rendered, here, insane.

Shawn gasped and all turned to face him, even as steady footsteps were heard creaking up the stairs beyond the open bedroom door.

"Dad!" Andrew said. But when he said it a second time, it was quiet, with reverence, respect, still, for the dying. "*Dad* . . ."

A woman entered the bedroom. A fresh visage amongst so much despair. Bright eyes like meaningful truth in a face that did not lie.

All looked.

"Who are you?" Sheila asked.

Shawn gasped for air. Found enough to say,

"You . . ."

The woman wore jeans and a beige blouse. She didn't have to ask if she'd arrived at a bad time; anything else would be unthinkable. Still, she carried herself with dignity, even as an enormous question worked its way up to her lips.

Above her black shoes, argyle socks. Across her right arm, an argyle coat.

"Hello, all. I'm an old friend of Shawn's. I happened to be in town. A brother-in-law told me the news."

Shawn wheezed as he reached for breath, his eyes upon hers.

And she stepped to him, between the rows of family and friends, before crouching beside his bed.

She wiped sweat from his brow.

She held his hand.

She inhaled deeply.

"Did you make it?" she asked.

Silence from the others. Silence outside.

Shawn nodded.

"I made it . . ."

Tears welled in Argyle's eyes as she leaned closer and whispered:

*"I knew you would."*

And then . . . Shawn Hasbro died.

A good man.

# Doug and Judy
## Buy the
## House Washer™

D oug and Judy Barman are assholes.

Everybody who knows them or has ever known them knows this. Everybody who works for them or has ever worked for them, or worked with them, knows this. Family knows this. Teammates from youth sports know this. Strangers who met them one time, tellers at the bank, countermen and -women at gas stations, retail-store workers, waiters, movie-theater ushers, car dealerships, home-furnishing employees, people who have driven beside them or behind them or in front of them on the highways, side streets, parking lots, they all know this. Valets, insurance companies, airline operators, tailors, tree cutters, lawn crews. Piano tuners, deliverymen and -women, people in the park, dogwalkers, door-to-door salespeople. CEOs, COOs, CFOs. Homeless men and women, dogs and cats, little children, old people, taxi drivers, furnace fixers, mirror hangers, roofers, mechanics, booksellers, deli owners, and neighbors. They all know Doug and Judy Barman are assholes.

Rita Cameron knows this too.

Rita, who sold them the House Washer™.

It's not the first she's sold, but the product is new, and it's hot, and only the wealthy can afford one. Rita, who considers herself levelheaded, was trained two full weeks on the roll-out; there's a lot to explain about a device that cleans your home and everything in it without anybody lifting a finger. And she did well with the Barmans, individuating the individual parts, specifying the specific steps, and, most important, of course, safely highlighting the safety features.

It's not every day a product requires its purchasers to remain in a Plexiglas tube as the appliance does its job.

Yet, no matter how well she did (*I could've been Groucho Marx and those two wouldn't have cared*, she later told her co-worker Ben), Doug and Judy Barman gave her paltry attention at best. And their behavior was noteworthy: the wife was impatient, dismissive, condescending. The husband bossy, ignorant, curt. It wasn't the first time Rita Cameron dealt with ornery customers, but it's the one she'll talk about at gatherings for years.

"You made the sale," Ben says. Ben who, like Rita, knows everything there is to know about the House Washer™ and has now sold two himself.

"I did," Rita says. "You're right. I'll try to hold on to that."

They fist-bump but Rita's still uneasy about the Barmans. The couple took at least some umbrage with every facet of the machine. When Rita told them the base of the tube is best placed in the center of the living room, the couple argued about rearranging the furniture and the wife, Judy, said to Rita, *Well, are you gonna move everything for us?*

And when Rita told them, yes, of course, Glasgow Inc. installs the House Washer™ and will assist in every facet of the process, the husband asked if any "dirty people" worked for Glasgow.

"You gonna celebrate tonight?" Ben asks.

Rita thought she might. Halfway through the sale, when she realized the couple were definitely status-oriented and therefore willing to buy the House Washer™ on its buzz alone, she started thinking of drinks at Egorov's in Little Russia. But there is something about this particular sale that has her wanting to go home tonight, to pet her dog, to appreciate the little things in life.

"I don't know," she says.

"Rita?" Ben says. "Rita! You know the commission on that sale!"

"I sure do."

Money. That was it, wasn't it? The fact the couple were dripping with it, from the Aston Martin they arrived in to the unfathomable ring on the wife's finger. Rita Cameron likes money, sure she does. But the Barmans made it feel so . . . dirty.

"Imagine the shit they have in their house," Ben says. He shakes his head and whistles, looking out the front windows of Glasgow Inc. as if those household items might be there on the streets of downtown Samhattan.

Rita is imagining those items. Things like that ring, rising up with the tide of the Glasgow Solution® as that magic fluid fills their entire home. If they'd been listening at all, Doug and Judy Barman will be safely situated in the tube as this happens.

"It's truly an amazing thing we're selling," Rita says.

It strikes her for the first time that it *is*. Every inch of a home filled with the soapy Solution®, every item cleaned in its own individual way, the homeowners able to relax or work behind glass for the duration.

Maybe it was the Barmans' communal disregard for everything that has Rita suddenly realizing the merit of the House Washer™.

"They'll definitely have enough space for the base," Ben says. "Bet on that."

The base, Rita explained to the Barmans, can be hidden under a rug, a table, or left to be viewed. It was certainly designed with aesthetics in mind; an ivory-white circle with a cool blue illuminated ring, light options and the holographic illusion of a waterfall, a plant, whatever the homeowner chooses. It's only when the House Washer™ is engaged that the base has to be cleared, the couple upon it, as the tube rises (at a slow and safe speed) flush to the ceiling, ensuring no Solution® will get in. And just as Rita was trained to do, she'd added:

*But if any Solution® ever does get on your clothes, they'd be all the cleaner for it!*

The Barmans didn't smile at this shop joke. Rita hadn't expected them to.

"Think they'll use it right away?" Ben asks.

Rita considers. It isn't her nature to gossip. Still . . .

"They strike me as the sort of couple who will want to show it off to their friends."

Ben laughs.

"Do you really think those two have friends?" Then he clamps a hand over his mouth. "That was mean, wasn't it."

Rita can't help but laugh. It's funny, in its way, imagining the cruel couple inviting friends onto the base, all of them watching the tube rise around them as the dozens of jets begin pumping the Solution® into the house.

"Maybe I will get a drink tonight," Rita says. Because the yuckiness of that couple seems to have washed off a little now. As if Rita herself took a dip in the Solution®.

"A whole house swirling with their possessions," Ben says. "All of it cleaned to mint. Even books. Even the pages of books!" Then, "You think those two read?"

And Rita, now feeling a little sassy for having decided to celebrate after all, says, "If it's a book about them, I suppose they might at least skim it."

* * *

"They'll be here at noon," Doug says, standing at the living-room window, hands on his hips, eyeing the street outside.

"You're acting like a child," Judy says. "Can you actually be this excited?"

"Excited? The crap you talking about, Jude? I'm staking out what kind of people they are before we let them into our house."

Judy stops mid-walk to the kitchen, looks to the window, shrugs her agreement.

"Any mess they make will be cleaned up by what they bring," she says.

But Doug isn't having any of that.

"Some things you can't wash out of a house."

"For what we paid for that thing, *nothing* should ever be dirty again."

Doug leans closer to the glass.

"What do you think the Slaters are gonna say about it?"

Judy is already in the kitchen now. Her voice echoes off the cold tiles, the high white ceiling.

"They'll hate us. Just like they hated us for the pool."

Doug smiles.

"You think it'll clean the pool? Did we ask that tart if it would?"

"Everything inside the house, Doug. Use your brain."

Doug shrugs.

"For the money we paid . . . it should clean the fucking yard."

He smiles again. It's one of his favorite phrases: *For the money we paid . . .*

A caravan of large white vans shows at the far end of the street. Vans like these have one purpose only in Model Ranch, Samhattan's wealthiest neighborhood: service men and women.

"They're here," Doug says.

Judy exits the kitchen. It's not until she's beside him at the glass that he sees she's wearing her bathrobe, green muck all over her face.

They watch the trio of vans park outside, watch the strong men and women in white overalls exit, watch the one wearing glasses approach their front door.

"Filthy," Judy says.

"They should use that thing inside their vans," Doug says.

The doorbell rings. The shimmering sound of clattering coins. Doug steps from the glass.

"Wash your fucking face," he says. "Don't make me handle this alone."

"Fuck you too," Judy says.

But she heads for the bedroom as Doug makes for the door. There, he peers outside once more through the glass bricks.

"The Slaters are gonna shit their pants," he says. "And we're not gonna help wash 'em when they do."

He opens the door.

"The House Washer™," he says. "It's about time."

* * *

Turns out the base can do a lot more than a holographic waterfall or a plant. Neither Doug nor Judy listened as the woman explained there were thousands of holograms to choose from. At first, this discovery was welcome, in that it squashed Judy's sudden disdain for waterfalls. But soon it became another hassle. Too many options, of course.

Doug spotted the choices screen, set near the thermostat in the living-room wall.

"Rock formations," he says. "Columns. People. This is nuts."

"People?" Judy asks. She's standing next to the base, where a glass table long stood. "The fuck does that mean?"

"Do I know?"

"Do a plant," she says.

Doug presses numbers. A large plant appears on the base; wide, green leaves.

"That's fine," Doug says.

"It's awful," Judy says. "Do a column."

"What's the difference?"

"This isn't a greenhouse."

"No, you're right, it's not."

He tries different combinations. One is a person, yes, but more of a mannequin in a plaid suit.

"Awful," Judy says.

"Is it supposed to be chic? Would Amy and Lou have one?"

"You and your Amy and Lou thing."

"I don't have an Amy and Lou thing. They just know cool."

"They most definitely do not."

"What about this?"

A faux-metal sculpture appears. The kind one might find outside a progressive university's library.

"I'm going to throw up," Judy says.

"I think I already did. Did you see the vent beneath the base?"

"Vent?"

"Yeah."

Doug leaves the panel, crouches by the base.

"Beneath this thing is where the dead things go. Bugs. Spiders."

"Dead things?" Judy says.

"Did you listen to the woman at all?"

"Doug, I had to remind you it was a woman at all."

"Whatever. I remember this part: there's hundreds of dead

things in every house. Bugs, I mean. And while the Solution®
cleans all our stuff? The dead things are shuffled beneath the base,
through the vent here."

Judy eyes the base.

"It's really something, isn't it," she says. "It knows how to clean
each item in the house, even if those items are cleaned in different
ways."

"Jesus, you trying to sell me a House Washer™, Jude?"

"Fuck you, Doug. You aren't smart enough to know that a *mal-
leable solution* is interesting. And groundbreaking. What we bought
is cutting-edge."

Doug is up and standing beside her.

"What'd you say? Not smart enough?"

"Right," Judy says.

"You wouldn't be anything without me, Jude. Don't forget that."

"Remember where you lived before we met, Doug?"

"Where *I* lived? Jude, you lived on Fifth Street."

A voice comes from the House Washer™:

*"Hello, Doug and Judy. Are you ready to try the House Washer™?"*

Doug and Judy stare at the cold blue-and-white circle in the
middle of the living-room floor.

"Not right now," Judy says. It feels odd, yet fresh, speaking to
the thing. "I have a meeting in forty-five minutes."

*"When you are ready, just let me know."*

"We'll let you know," Doug says. He brightens up. To Judy he
says: "Let's throw a party. Invite the hood. We'll use it beforehand,
have this place sparkling like the fucking brochures."

"If you're serious about arranging a get-together, do it yourself."

Both are moving now; Judy out of the room, Doug back to the
control panel to try different holograms on the base.

Judy stops at the archway to the master wing of their home.

"But I like the idea," she says.

"Of course you do," Doug says. "It's a chance to show off."

He presses some numbers. The sculpture becomes a white horse.

The Barmans eye it together.

"Awful," Judy says.

"The worst."

\* \* \*

They don't use the House Washer™ for two weeks. The tolerable hologram they've settled on is a column after all. They get used to it. They don't arrange a party for those two weeks. They forget about the idea as they work. As they make money. As they purchase other items, now decorating the glass cabinets, the mauve bookshelves, the windowsills and the yard. But on the fourteenth day after buying the House Washer™, Judy finalizes an enormous deal. Something big enough to talk about.

And one needs people to talk about it with.

"I was intentionally vague with the invite," Doug says. "Don't need to come off like desperate newborns."

"You better not have said anything about it at all."

"I didn't. I said, *You should come over.*"

"That implies something big will be waiting for them here. Big news."

"I don't think so, Jude."

"I know so."

"You should've sent the fucking email then."

"I did. Like we discussed. Now they've all received two invites. Classy, Doug."

Doug looks to the column in the middle of the living room.

"Let's use it," he says.

The voice, as if listening to their every word, as if it has for fourteen days, says for the second time:

*"Doug and Judy, are you ready to try the House Washer™?"*

Judy, in a white pantsuit, white heels, her dark hair done up, steps to the base.

"Fuck it," she says. "Doug?"

"Wait," Doug says.

They both eye the base like it might start prematurely because Judy gave it a sort of go-ahead.

"The windows," Doug says. "We gotta close all the windows, close all the doors. Otherwise, the shit seeps outside."

The two divvy up, Doug taking the master wing, Judy the offices. When they meet up again at the base, Judy says, "What if it ruins everything?"

"It won't."

"*The Glasgow Solution® improves everything,*" the base says.

"Does it, now . . ." Judy says. Doug's heard her use this tone with a thousand people at a thousand parties.

"We'll blow minds tonight," Doug says. "Make everyone else feel small as fuck. We got a House Washer™. Think, Jude: what are we gonna look like when they ask if we've tried it yet and we say no?"

"I'm the one who said let's do it," Judy says.

"The chairs are in the pantry," Doug says.

"Get 'em."

"Why do I have to get 'em?"

"Jesus, Doug."

Doug exits the living room, returns with the two plastic chairs that came with the base. Also included: the jets, the vent below the base, and the gallons of Solution® in the walls.

Doug, wearing a black suit and pink shirt with no tie, places the chairs on the base, breaking the mirage of the column as he does.

"*I see you've arranged for your seating,*" the House Washer™ says. "*Are you ready to try the House Washer™?*"

"How long does it run for?" Doug asks.

"Ninety minutes," Judy says.

"Do you have work to do?"

"Of course."

"Same."

They separate again, gather binders, pens, their phones. At the control panel, Doug turns the hologram off. Now the base is once again a cold white circle with an illuminated blue ring.

"We'll sue," Judy says.

"If that shit fucks up our stuff? We'll destroy them."

Judy eyes the base.

"But we really do need to use it before people come."

"Right."

"Because they'll ask."

"Right."

"And if we say we haven't used it, they'll know we buy things for no practical purpose."

*"Are you ready to step aboard the base?"* the House Washer™ asks.

Doug extends a hand to Judy. "Madame?"

Judy rolls her eyes and steps up onto the base. Doug joins her.

They stand, facing what suddenly feels like their entire house.

"Okay, House Washer™," Doug says. "We're ready now."

The base does not respond like they both imagined it would. Instead, the tube begins to rise, slowly, breaking the soft blue light at the circumference.

"We can breathe in here, yes?" Judy asks.

They look up to the ceiling, where the second rim was installed, where the tube will reach.

When the Plexiglas gets waist-high, Doug says,

"Fuck. Shoulda grabbed something to eat."

"It's ninety minutes."

"What if we have to piss?"

The base doesn't ask them if they want it to pause. Doesn't tell them they will be able to breathe, either.

Rather, when the tube reaches neck-high, the entire house reverberates with the sound of two dozen jets coming to life.

Doug and Judy step closer to the glass, watch the thick, translucent liquid pump out of the spouts, onto the floors, down the walls of their home.

It comes fast, loud.

But before either can express an opinion on the matter, the tube reaches the ceiling, turns an inch to the left, locking into place.

"Well, shit," Doug says. "You know what this means?"

"This means we're rich," Judy says.

"That's right, Jude."

And they watch the Solution® fill their home.

* * *

"How does it know?"

Doug's been standing at the glass, watching. Judy is already seated, glasses on, binder on her lap.

"It knows," Judy says.

But she watches too. Because it's impossible not to. Even before the Solution® reaches the height of the couch, it's cleaning everything in its path. The bottom of the drapes, the bases of end tables, the legs of chairs. It's hypnotic, in its way, how the liquid grows murky around whatever it cleans, so that now what looks like a flood is dotted with many murky pockets.

"Even the garage," Doug says. "This shit's even in the garage."

"Good. For the money we paid?"

Something dark and tiny slides beneath the base.

"A bug," Doug says.

Because both fly often, both sense oxygen being pumped into the tube. Both breathe it in, deep.

"This shit moves fast," Doug says. "A little less graceful than the brochure."

"Well, don't talk like that tonight," Judy says. "Last thing we want is to look like rubes."

"Who do you think you're talking to? Look at this stuff, Jude."

"Even the Ferrari's a little less something in person. You know this. It's the *Ferrari* that matters. Not the actual car."

"You talk so much crap."

But he knows. Nobody knows what Judy is talking about better than Doug Barman.

"Hey, wait," he says, his face still close to the glass.

Judy is up and beside him.

"What happened? Did it ruin something? Are we suing?"

"Look . . . it's pulling the art off the walls!"

"That's what it does," Judy says.

But there's some worry in her voice too. It's unsettling, watching all their possessions in anybody else's hands.

The doors of the glass cabinets swing open, as if by fingers of the Solution®, murky pockets form where each trinket usually rests, then the glass shelves themselves become opaqued.

The Solution® has reached eye level for Doug.

"I'm going to get some work done," Judy says. She sits again.

But Doug remains at the glass.

"It's all . . . floating. Jesus Christ. Everything we own is floating around the fucking living room."

"That's what it does, Douglas."

"Okay, *Judith*. But I thought maybe you'd care more about your egg than you're letting on."

Fabergé egg.

Judy is up again.

"Fuck. Fuckers. House Washer™! Do *not* touch that egg."

But the House Washer™ does not respond. And the darkness surrounds the egg, just as it surrounds dozens of other items throughout the house.

"Calm down," Doug says. He's laughing. "You care so much about that fucking egg."

"For what we paid for it?"

"There isn't a cheap thing in sight," Doug says.

The Solution® has almost reached the ceiling. It sloshes. Dark patches are starting to dominate the landscape. Like an inverse outer space, dark stars in a white sky. Still, when an item is wholly clean, the waters clear, and the object is back where it belongs.

Lamps now float in the living room. Pillows. The piano.

A book floats forth from the opacity, stays mostly motionless before the glass.

"Photo album," Doug says. "Jesus, I forgot that was even in the cupboards."

"It's yours," Judy says.

"I know it's mine. I'd recognize that pink puffy cover anywhere."

Judy opens the binder on her lap.

"Fuck," she says.

"What?"

"I brought the wrong one in."

She looks through the glass. As if she might still have time to grab the right one.

The photo album opens. Small, dark tendrils pull the photos out from behind the plastic, clean them.

"Are you shitting me?" Doug says. "Judy. This is unreal."

She's up again, clearly dispirited by the wrong binder. At the glass, she says, "It's thorough. As it should be. It's exactly what it should be."

A small, old photo, taken by a camera in a pre-cellphone world, floats toward the glass.

Doug's expression stiffens.

"Me and Alex," he says.

Judy leans closer to the glass. She hasn't seen this picture before.

"Brothers," she says. "Cute."

"Yeah," Doug says. "We were. I guess. Mom made us dress in those stupid striped shirts."

At the mention of his mother, Doug grows quiet. The dark tendrils clean the picture.

"Did that saleswoman describe it this way?" Judy asks.

"You looking for false advertisement? I like it."

But Doug is still eyeing the photo. A second one slips out from the plastic, floats forward.

"Alex and me again," he says. "I remember that day."

"Of course you do. You lived it."

"Fuck off, Jude. It was a good day. Alex caught a fish with his bare hands in that lake."

"I'm sure it was special."

"Yeah, well. If he wasn't such an idealistic moron, maybe he'd have a House Washer™ too."

"I doubt it," Judy says. "We can't all be success stories." Then, something Judy has said before: "If you're extraordinary, it's because you're surrounded by ordinary."

Doug studies the photo.

In it, two young boys smile so big their eyes vanish into the folds of their faces. The sun sprinkles light on every ripple in the water surrounding them.

Another book floats to the glass, a glossy white cover with embossed gold lettering.

"Oh, for fuck's sake," Judy says.

Because it's hers. A book she has no memory of storing either.

The black tendrils pull the book open even as it cleans the cover. A photo slips from the plastic.

Judy sits down again.

"Wow," Doug says, a fingertip against the glass. "When the fuck did you ever smile like that?"

"I don't have time to look back."

"Back is not a flattering angle," Doug says. Then, "You've gotta be . . . thirteen here? You're holding a little gold dog?"

Now Judy does look.

"Oh, wow. Copper. She was a good pet."

"Copper? You've never told me about Copper before. Did she shit all over the house?"

"I suppose when you're a child you don't notice those things."

Doug laughs.

"You sure as hell would now."

Two more photos float closer as they're cleaned.

On the right, Doug as a teenager with his father. On the left, Judy with a group of girlfriends on what looks like a trip out west, a mountain range as backdrop. They wear bandannas over their heads, baggy jeans.

Doug eyes his father.

Judy eyes her friends.

"Fuckin guy was such a pussy," Doug says. "Never heard him one time say he was worth anything."

"Those girls? Even worse. All moms now."

"I remember one time, at a roller rink, some guy elbowed Dad and knocked him over. Then the guy laughed at Dad. I said, aren't you gonna do something about this? Dad brushed himself off, told me something I'll never fucking forget, he said: however someone acts with you, that's how they act with everybody else. So, if someone's an asshole to you? They're just an asshole." He squints as the tendrils close in on his and his father's faces, cleaning the photo unseen. "I said, Dad, are you *seriously* not going to say something? But . . . naw. Not a word. He just started skating again like nothing ever happened. You know Arnie."

"It's a shame. A waste," Judy says, eyeing her childhood friends, even as the tendrils close in. "When your only function is to pro-create, what the fuck are you procreating for?"

Together, Doug and Judy say, "Rubes."

And the photos are swallowed up into the Solution®.

Two more emerge.

Doug turns his back on the glass, looks to the piano, spinning slowly, on the other side of the tube.

"Carla Cummings," Judy says behind him.

Doug knows the name well. Judy and Carla were best friends in high school. There was something of a major falling-out.

"Some people," Judy says. "They think they can maintain their immature philosophies for the rest of their lives. They live like hip-pies. And they expect everybody else to do the same. Carla actually followed the Grateful Dead. Can you imagine?"

The piano swirls in and out of dark patches. Black tendrils clean the keys like fingers playing a song.

"Didn't you follow them too?" Doug asks.

"No," Judy says, emphatically. "I went to a handful of shows. Whatever. I was young. They were fun. But to think you get to keep that feeling, that wanderlust. Come on. Carla refused to be-lieve there might be a way to monetize her interests. I remember her telling me once she wished there was a way to get paid for being a good person. Can you imagine?"

Doug still eyes the piano. Only one key shows now, the rest of the instrument in darkness. Getting clean.

"An entire drive home from Chicago we argued about this shit," Judy goes on. "For three hundred miles we debated moving on, embracing adulthood, the worth of money and making a living.

She had ideas, of course, quaint business ideas, wanting to help rescue animals from factory farms."

"Good grief."

"Oh, you have no idea."

"I bet she was coming at you hard with that shit."

But Judy is quiet at first before responding.

"Whatever. She actually wanted to free some pigs from a farm up near Chowder. Actually wanted us to pull some clandestine, special-ops deal. Get one of those huge animal trailers, coax the pigs into it, bring them somewhere safe. She spoke of opening her own farm. Rescuing animals from what she called *the meanest cruelty on Earth.* I told her, hey, Carla, if people wanna eat beef, they're gonna fucking eat beef. It was just . . . so stupid."

"Sounds like a tree-hugger."

"Worse. Because she was smart enough to do whatever she wanted. But she *chose* to latch on to these unrealistic tropes. For fuck's sake."

"And where is she now?"

The piano is clean. The darkness slowly slides from its enormous body, its black and white keys.

"Right now?" Judy says. "How the fuck should I know? I heard she sells fruit from a stand on the side of the road up north."

Doug laughs. "And how much money do you think she makes doing *that?*"

"None. Or . . . just enough to give her a roof, and a hole in the ground to shit in." Judy steps from the glass, eyes the binder on the chair. "She could've had it all. Carla could've had everything we have."

"Rubes," Doug says.

Something taps on the glass. Sounds loud enough to have been a hand.

But . . .

A notebook in the Solution®.

"Jesus," Judy says. "Scared me."

But her face and voice soften, momentarily, at the sight of the pages slowly flipping.

"What is this?" Doug says.

"I don't remember holding on to it," Judy says.

"Looks like a journal."

"Poetry," Judy says. Then she laughs at her answer. "In middle school, I think. Maybe even before then? Childhood, I suppose. And childish at that."

"You wrote poems, Jude? Jesus, I had no idea."

"Yeah, well . . . fuck it now. When Mom and Dad got divorced, I suppose . . ."

"So, wait," Doug says, squinting, trying to read the words. "You're telling me when your folks split up you kept a fucking diary?"

"Poems, Doug. I wrote poems, yes. Newsflash: we're all a lot stupider as kids."

"Yeah, but, come on, I *gotta* read this."

As if cued, the book floats closer to the glass. Doug nearly presses his nose to the tube.

"The fuck," Judy says.

She pulls him back by his shoulder.

"Hey, easy now," Doug says. But he's smiling. He recites:

"*When the love you observe falls apart . . . so does your knowledge of the heart . . .* Holy *shit,* Jude."

"Fuck you, Doug."

Dark tendrils form around the open page, obscuring it from view.

"And all this time," Doug says, "Judy Frost in the house."

"Hey, dick, it was a difficult time. Nobody saw it coming."

"I'm sure *somebody* did."

"No, really. Mom was blindsided."

"Well, she should've seen it coming. And someone should've taught her there ain't no such thing as happily ever after."

Judy clenches as if to argue this, but doesn't.

"Yes. She should've. And I should've too. It's clear as hell to me now. The way Dad didn't give a fuck what the rest of us did. The way Mom had to work to smile in public."

"When my parents split? I thanked them," Doug says. "I told them it was about time they got real and started acting like adults."

Judy's eyes are still on the notebook, despite it being mostly shrouded in shadow.

"You did not, Doug."

"Did too. And what do you know? You weren't there."

The tendrils shift, then split, giving Judy a clean view of the words. She reads them aloud without deciding to:

*Just people, Mom and Dad . . . but I thought they were mountains, beyond good and bad . . ."*

"Jesus," Doug says. He laughs.

Judy turns on him.

"I was a kid, Doug."

"Yeah? So was I once. And I never wrote garbage about it. You think the House Washer™ is cleaning your tears off that page?"

Judy looks to the pages again, her expression suggests, *I hope not.*

"You're right," she says. "It's bullshit now and it was bullshit then. Can you believe I bought into that? It's child abuse, the way parents deceive their children, present the family unit, love ever-lasting. They deliberately show you a bullshit reality, and when they grow too tired to maintain it, they take it from you. Who gets fucked by that? Not the parents. Mom and Dad were relieved for different reasons. I could tell. They got to move on, they got a second wind in life. But me? I turned into a fucking poet because of it."

"You think that's bad?" Doug says. "Arnie and Lori gave me a fuckin talk about the first girl I ever went on a date with. Told me how important it was to be a gentleman, how fucking much it mattered to say nice things to people, how to treat them well. And for what? For *show*. That's what. Because that's all family is and all it ever was. A *show*. And the second I realized *that* nugget was the same second I got a leg up on all these other dips in Samhattan. Nobody could stop me after that."

"I suppose I should thank Mom and Dad," Judy says.

"You should!"

"Without them showing me what the world's really like, I might still be living on Fifth Street."

"Yep."

"I have no idea where the House Washer™ found that notebook."

"Everybody's got a life in boxes, Jude. Who *really* checks all the boxes when they move from place to place? The past is in storage, where it belongs."

"Still . . ."

The soapy Solution® swirls about the glass tube, dozens of dark pockets spreading about the living room, the archways to the far halls, frame the windows, from floor to ceiling. And as each item is cleaned, it shows again.

"I want a drink," Judy says.

"No shit. Hey, House Washer™? You serve drinks?"

No response from the base. Just the sloshing sound.

Doug checks his watch.

"When did it start? How long we been in here?"

"I don't know, Doug. And don't start getting impatient on me. You're not the only one stuck in here."

*Stuck in here.*

Both recall the saleswoman spoke briefly about claustrophobia. But what did she say exactly?

Something bright blue emerges from a dark oval, two items it seems, connected by a cord.

"The fuck is that?" Judy asks.

"Oh, come the fuck on," Doug says.

It floats closer, even as the Solution® works at its edges.

Judy points at it. "Is that a . . . microphone and speaker, Doug?"

"It's a kid's toy."

"This is not Little Tikes, Doug."

"Hey, come on. Elementary school. High school. What's the difference?"

"No, no, wait. Wait. You used to *sing*?"

"For fuck's sake, Jude. No. I did not *sing*. Arnie got me that stupid thing and I never used it. Or . . . maybe once."

"Once? What did you sing that once?"

The dark fingers cover half the old speaker, slither up the length of cord toward the microphone.

"How would I know?"

But he does seem to know. As he gets close to the glass, eyeing the microphone, the Solution® swirls, rotating the speaker.

Doug hums.

"What's that?" Judy asks. "Are you humming your song?"

"Hey, fuck off, okay. I wanted to be a singer like the people on MTV. Sure, why not? They got to do whatever they wanted."

"What were you humming?"

Doug turns to her.

"I'm not singing for you, Jude, no matter how hard you poke." He looks to the base, as if there's someone other than Judy he's shy for.

"I don't think the House Washer™ will judge you," Judy says. "But I might. Was it a hit?"

"A hit? What are you talking about? It was something I came up with myself."

"Wait. *You* wrote a song, Doug? This I need to hear."

"Naw. And you won't. Never. And fuck the House Washer™ for opening all these ancient boxes. Gonna make the place dirtier than it's ever been."

They both watch as the speaker is swallowed into the darkness before that darkness parts, fades, revealing a cleaner, second glimpse. Then it's pulled back into the soap, delivered, no doubt, back into the box from which it came.

"Jesus Christ," Doug says. "Anything else I don't give a shit about lurking in this house?"

But his voice has less oomph than it normally does. And he watches the speaker fade until it can no longer be seen.

"Every house has its secrets," Judy says. "Even ours." Then: "Singer."

"Hey, watch it, Jude."

"Watch you sing? I'd love to."

Doug steps to the second chair, sits down. "Fuck if this thing doesn't take its time."

"What was it about?"

"Don't."

"Was it better than my poetry?"

"Yes."

"Prove it."

"Don't, Jude."

"Oh my God."

"What?"

"You remember it. Word for word. Don't you? How many times have you sung this little song to yourself over the years? Since we've met?"

Doug makes to argue but doesn't. He lowers his head. "It was about wanting to change the world."

"Oh my *God*."

"Yeah, yeah. Alex gave me shit for it too."

"Jesus, even your brother thought it sucked?"

"Did I say he thought it sucked? And who cares if he did? Alex only listened to hardcore metal."

"And what was this? Flower power?"

"Jude. Just don't."

"This seems to have struck a nerve."

"Oh yeah? And your stupid fucking poetry didn't?"

"At least mine was quiet."

"Yeah . . . well, mine wasn't. It was raging, to tell you the truth. And in its own awesome way it completely kicked ass. And I'm the asshole who stopped singing it."

They go silent a beat. What Doug just said means something more than either are willing to verbalize.

"Whatever," Doug says. "Probably would've cost me a thousand bucks to record it right, would've hated the way it was done, and would've broken up with the band. Who knows. I dodged the terrible life of a starving fucking artist because I was smart enough to quit when I was behind."

"The song, Doug."

"No, Jude."

"Now."

Doug looks up at her, opens his mouth like he might debate, might yell, might even sing. Then he hangs his head again.

"No, Jude. I've forgotten how it goes."

They listen to the sloshing, the at-times steady rhythm, at others uneven, a sense the House Washer™ is working too hard.

"My fuckin diploma," Judy says.

Doug looks up to see it flat to the glass, still in its yellow and orange, school-issued frame.

"Dipshit High," Judy says. "Where we were taught what matters when literally nobody knew what mattered. Not even the teachers."

"Especially not the teachers."

"I couldn't *wait* to get out of there."

"You ran for class president, Jude. How much could you have hated it?"

"That's just the thing . . . the idiots voted for Pollyanna Sarah Allen. She promised them communism, a veritable Marxist vision in which every student in the school had the same lot in life."

"Madness. Even then."

"Yes. I'm embarrassed I even ran. Had I known how easy it was to trick a student body into believing in drum circles, I might've spent my time more wisely."

"All of high school was a joke. What did we learn there? What do we actually use now that we learned in high school?" Doug stands up. Goes to the glass. Points at Judy's diploma as it's washed in a dark pocket. "Fuck textbooks. Fuck math too. Know what we shoulda learned?"

"I know what we shoulda learned. I taught myself in time."

"Damn straight you did. The school day shoulda gone like this: First period: money. Second period: who to trust and who not. Third: all of life is a race and you gotta get there before the other guy. Fourth: optics; they're all that matter. Fifth: how to sell yourself. And sixth: how to make a proper drink."

"Amen."

"Don't get religious on me now, honey."

"Amen as in the end of a sentence, of course."

"*Period.* They can keep all the books about the *human condition.* Don't worry, teachers! There's enough of that in real life. Enough of that coming down the pipes. Fuckin' teachers. Good thing we never had kids."

"Period."

"*Period.* Imagine being tasked with unraveling all *that.* 'No, Junior, what they told you is wrong! Money *is* everything, money *can* buy you happiness, because without money you have to worry about your goddamn house, your goddamn car payment, if you can afford a car at all.'"

"You didn't have one when we met."

"No shit, Jude."

She taps on the glass, meaning for him to look. Doug turns to see an old pair of shoes in the dark fingers of the Solution®.

"Wait," he says. But he doesn't go on, not yet.

The shoes are worn through, holes where the toes had long been jammed, a half size too small.

"You wore those when we met," Judy says. "You wore them everywhere. Wore them out."

"Yeah, but . . . what the fuck are they doing here?"

How should Judy know? But the condescension seems to have left her eyes. She says: "I'm kinda glad to see them, I think. These were on my apartment floor a hundred times and a hundred times I wondered when they were going to turn to dust."

"I walked everywhere in those shoes. Fuck, by the end of college they felt like slippers."

The Solution® cleans the shoes, exposing a green that wasn't there when it began.

"Jesus, this thing really does its job," Doug says.

"Good."

Together: "For what we paid for it."

Doug sighs. It's a real sigh; the sound of a man remembering times more complex than words like *good* or *bad* can define.

"Those things were like a fuckin' baby's blanket for me. The only security I had in the world. While my roommates were driving all over campus in their shitty sedans, I walked. When I didn't have

bus money, I walked. And I rarely had that money. In the winter, I
walked. In the rain. Those things got so wet one time I had to leave
them outside the classroom. No one noticed. I ran in those shoes.
Ran to a conference at Saturn Hall, too, where Nathan Albright
was speaking. Shit changed for me then."

"You were very taken by that man."

"Damn straight. His talk did *everything* for me. He talked like
how I felt. He said money *can* buy you happiness. He's the first
fucker who was honest about that."

"Why'd you keep the shoes?"

"Keep them? I didn't. I tossed them in a box and they ended up
here, years later, floating around in some crazy shit we bought because we're rich now."

"Period."

"I wore those shoes to every class, every party, and, when I wised
up and stopped going to parties, then it was every meeting, every
job, every chance I had to make enough money to put them in a
box for good."

"Good. They were disgusting."

Doug turns on her, hatred in his eyes. "Fuck you, Jude."

"Really? You're getting sentimental about a pair of shoes?"

But her voice doesn't have the same oomph it usually does.

"No, Jude. I'm not getting sentimental. I'm just waiting forever
for the maid to finish cleaning the fucking house."

The shoes rotate in the Solution®, the laces extend as if drawn
apart by unseen hands, someone standing in the thick soap, close
to the glass.

"Nathan Albright, Jude. In a way, we have him to thank for all
we have now. He got me caring about what mattered."

"Maybe he's responsible for what *you* brought to the table, but I
didn't go to any pep rally. I found the path on my own."

"Bullshit."

"Naw. And you know it."

The shoes are taken away, into the froth, and both sit in the chairs upon the base. The sloshing continues. It grows louder, softer, harder, gentler. Soap suds thud against the glass, slither up, around and around Doug and Judy. Dark pockets climb the drapes in the distance, the far side of the living room; they crawl across the floor, too, sometimes shooting dead bugs from the corners to the vent below.

"The Slaters are gonna shit," Doug says.

Judy eyes only the suds.

"How soon before they get one themselves?" Doug asks. "A week? Two? Two tops."

Judy eyes only the suds.

"And good," Doug says. "They can keep up with us for a change. *We're* the Joneses now, Jude."

"Yes."

"Damn right, yes. We're the trendsetters in this neighborhood. All of Samhattan. 'Bout time too."

Doug reaches out, plants a hand on the glass.

"Thanks to this baby."

A hand flattens against the other side of the glass.

"*FUCK!*" Doug yells.

He leaps from the chair.

"*What?*" Jude says.

"Did you see that? *Did you?*"

"See what, Doug? The fuck is going on?"

Doug breathes hard, too hard, stares where he saw the hand.

"There was a hand, Jude."

"What?"

"A *hand.* Out there. It touched the glass where I was touching it!"

Judy eyes the Solution®.

"No," she says. "There wasn't. You're insane."

"Jude, I swear on our 401 there was a fuckin hand."

"It was the reflection of your hand."

"But it wasn't. Mine was there first. Flat against it."

"Then it was . . . a glove." She nods. "If there's one thing we now know, the House Washer™ cleans it all. Sit down."

"Wasn't a glove, Jude."

Doug inches toward the glass again, gets close. Squints out into the soap.

"That was no glove . . ."

But a glove, yes, a glove, emerges, now two, about shoulder-high, floating hands in the Solution®.

"And there you go," Judy says.

But they go silent, as though waiting to see if arms show too.

"I'm telling you, Jude . . . it wasn't . . ."

The gloves rotate, fingers splayed, open hands spinning in slow circles.

Judy stands up.

"There's no way I kept this pair."

"I've never seen those," Doug says, anxiously eyeing the glass. "And I didn't see them a second ago."

His voice is smaller than it usually is, buried in the sloshing against the tube.

"It's an old pair of gloves I wore back when I lived on Fifth Street," Judy says.

Her voice is smaller too.

"Why'd you keep them?"

"I didn't. I didn't mean to. No more than you meant to keep your disgusting shoes."

Doug walks the circumference of the tube, eyeing the dark shapes beyond.

"But these," Judy says, "these are particularly memorable because Lauren Paul commented on them in a full staff meeting."

"Lauren Paul," Doug says. "That hag."

"She was younger than we are now."

"Yeah, well, hags had to be young once too."

Judy eyes the gloves as the fingertips go dark, then the palms, too.

"Lauren Paul . . ."Judy's voice gets softer. "My first real boss. The heat had gone out in my apartment on Fifth. I wore those things to sleep. I slept in them, Doug. And I wore them to work too. They didn't help, though. No matter how much I wore those gloves, my hands were still cold. It was like the cold had gotten into my heart. Do you know, right now, I can remember how that cold felt? I can feel it again, just looking at those gloves. And Lauren . . . in front of the whole office . . . I'd forgotten they were on . . . they'd become part of my living, my life . . . and she says, 'Judy, could you please not remind the rest of us how poor you are?'" Judy clucks her tongue. "I turned red, Doug. And I took them off and tucked them beside me on the conference-room chair. And the worst of it: I *smiled*."

"So what?"

"So what . . . So what. The woman humiliated me and my first instinct was to appease her."

The darkness ebbs from the gloves, they cease rotating but remain floating by the tube.

"Good for her," Doug says. "You needed a kick in the ass."

Judy turns to him, a fire blazing in her eyes. But then . . . it subsides.

"I did. Lauren Paul was my Nathan Albright, I suppose."

"Damn straight."

"I didn't sleep in them that night. I didn't have to. I went to the landlord's place and told her if she didn't fix my heat, I was going to the *Samhattan News* with a story about bugs, beds, and under-age sex."

"Wow."

"I made it up, of course. At first she said nobody would believe me. But I delivered the same speech I'd prepared for the news. I scared the shit out of that woman. She told me she had to make ends meet too. Told me she had someone coming in a couple days to fix the heat. I told her if there wasn't heat in my apartment by midnight, her building would be closed down and she could go to jail."

"You go, Judy."

"I went. That night. I went. And I never looked back again. And I never looked poor in front of Lauren Paul and her hag partners again. In fact—"

"You became one."

The gloves recede, taken back into the Solution®, returned to whence they came.

"*Hello, Doug and Judy,*" the base says. "*So far, there have been no problems with your cleaning.*"

"Better not have been," Doug says. "People coming over to-night."

"House Washer™?" Judy asks. "There's a binder in the bedroom I'm concerned with. I brought the wrong one with me in here and it's very important it does not get ruined."

The House Washer™ does not respond.

"Did the lady say it would respond to us?" Doug asks. "Anything we say?"

"I don't remember. She said it talks."

"Yeah, but does it listen?" Then: "What's in that binder?"

"The new deal."

"Already signed?"

She looks to the base. To the wrong binder.

"Jude," Doug says. "Don't worry about it. It's the future, don't you know? We're sitting in a fucking tube while every item we own is cleaned to mint. If something happens to the doc? Print off a new one."

"Right. I know. Thank you for the pep rally."

"Oh, fuck you, Jude. You're always so damn serious."

"Me? You thought someone was standing on the other side of the glass."

They both look to the glass.

"Yeah, well . . ."

"Yeah, well don't get on me." She stands up. "Serious is what got us here."

"You gotta be kidding me," Doug says. But he isn't talking to Judy.

He steps close to the glass again.

A restaurant menu, laminated, floats slowly in a circle around the tube.

"China King," Doug says.

"The #1," Judy says.

They look to each other, but before asking who saved it, they both laugh. The sound is a new one in the tube.

"The *number one*," Doug says. "Unreal."

"Our first date," Judy says.

"Don't get sentimental on me."

"It's a fact. Our first date. If the concept of sentimentality occurred to you, it might be you who is sentimental."

The menu comes closer, the paper yellowed despite the lamination.

"We both ordered the #1 because we'd been talking . . ."

"About being sick of not being number one."

"Yep. You remember that?"

"Of course."

"It was like we met at exactly the right time in our lives."

"We both wanted the exact same thing."

"Number one."

"Period."

"Fuck, we were driven, Jude."

"Yep. Both of us were ten steps beyond impatient. We were done with the lives we were living."

"And we wanted more."

"And we told each other so."

"And we got it."

The menu rotates, a slow full circle.

"What a dump," Doug says.

"I wouldn't step foot in there today."

"And I thought it was fancy at the time. Unfuckingreal. The night we ordered from this menu, I felt like we were dining on top of the world."

"It was expensive at the time."

"It crushed me."

"We split the bill."

"We did not."

"We did."

"Jude . . . I paid for that meal. You think I'd let you pay on our first date? I'm telling you, it crushed me. I was broke for two days after."

"No, Doug. We split the check. We've talked about this before. We've told this story before."

"Jude. I paid for that fucking bill."

"You did not."

"Hey, fuck you, okay? I didn't eat for two fucking days."

"That bad, yes, but from only half the bill. Plus, I tipped."

"Hey, why are you getting on me?"

"Doug, it's a fact."

"Really?"

"Doug . . ."

"You wanna go there?"

"Doug . . ."

"A fact, huh? You wanna tell me I don't carry my weight as we're standing in the House Washer™? This is only the most luxurious item on the market, Jude. Don't think you're gonna make me feel like shit because of some bill from nine hundred B.C."

"Oh, I'm sorry, did we not buy the House Washer™ together? We split this bill too."

"We didn't split that China King bill, Jude."

"We did."

Doug slams a hand against the glass. Beyond it, embedded in the Solution®, the pockets of darkness momentarily pause. As if they're worried about the state of the glass.

"*Jude*, I'm *sick* of this. All I do is work my *ass* off for shit like this fucking washing machine and you make it sound like I don't do fuck!"

"Doug? Guess what? Fuck you."

"What?"

"Fuck you. You're turning into a fucking cartoon of yourself."

"Okay, Jude. Let's roll. Okay. Gloves off. And not those shitty Lauren Paul gloves. *Off.* You wanna talk shares? You wanna talk *doing your part?*"

Judy moves quickly, is inches from his face. Beyond them the soapy water, and all their possessions, swirl.

"Yeah, *roll*, you big fuck. Roll away. Give it to me, Doug. Tell me all about *shares.*"

Doug looks to the glass like he might not go to the next level, like he might quit now.

But when he turns to face her again, there is fire in his eyes. "How about sharing in your family's trouble, Jude?"

"What the *fuck* does that have to do with anything?"

"Yeah, Jude. What about sharing when the chips got down with your mom and dad? Huh? You split half those bills too?"

"Fuck you, *dick*. What have you *ever* done for Alex, Arnie, and Lori other than whine like a bitch?"

"Here you go, high and mighty, for who the fuck tolls, and you're telling *me* I didn't pay my share in a fucking China King five hundred years ago?"

"I said we split it, you fucking *douche*."

"Okay, Jude. Okay. Because you're such the splitting type, right? Because you're *such a good person*."

"You have to pee or something, Doug? You need to eat, you fucking baby?"

*"You didn't even go say goodbye to your mom when she died, Judy!* YOU DIDN'T EVEN SPLIT THE COST OF THE CASKET."

Silence. Like every industrial contraption in the world has shut off at once. Like they can hear an entire world going dark.

Only, not true.

The sloshing continues, the steady rhythm of the House Washer™.

"All right," Judy says, breathless, the red leaving her face. "Okay."

She steps away from him, back to the chair, then passes it, steps to the far end of the tube, as far as she can get, eyes on the Glasgow Solution®.

But Doug isn't done yet.

"How long did it take her to die, Jude? A year? And how many times did you make it over to say goodbye? None. You didn't go once. So don't start acting like this is a life of give and take. You only take."

Judy eyes only the Solution®. In it, she sees multiple framed degrees, awards, honors. All with her name in perfect bold, black cursive.

The dark tendrils slink over the glass that covers these honors, then pulls the papers out of their frames. And as each goes momentarily dark, as each achievement is temporarily opaqued, it feels as if the moment never happened, the award never given.

"At least when Arnie died, I called," Doug says.

Between two rectangular accolades, an odd thing: recognizable, unmistakable even at a distance, so small as to be silly it was ever used at all, the pretense of pretending it was ever needed, when its only function was seduction, a thing no doubt already achieved.

It's a tiny pair of underwear, a G-string, rotating toward Judy in the Solution®.

She doesn't speak up, not yet, because the tiny writing upon the label will tell her more than Doug ever will.

*Bri Collins*

The brand. Yes. The very one Judy was expecting to find.

Doug has gone silent behind her and she knows he sees what she sees. Knows he sees the evidence of a mistress, once tucked into a box, a small garbage can that never made it outside, a proof he thought he'd disposed of but one that has been turned up, and over, and cleaned, by the House Washer™.

"I know one person who shops at Bri Collins," Judy says, her voice regaining a centimeter of steam with each syllable.

She turns to face Doug.

He stares beyond her, into the soap, at the rotating G-string.

"Jenny Slater," Judy says.

Doug, unable to come up with an excuse in time, still tries.

"Did she . . . she must've left it here after swimming . . . in the pool . . ."

"Are the Joneses supposed to fuck their lesser neighbors?" Judy says. "Is that where all the keeping up happens, Doug? In the bedroom?"

"Judy . . ."

But Judy holds up an open palm and steps to a chair and sits.

Doug steps past her, as if he might be able to retrieve the proof, to clean not only the underwear, but the history of them too.

"House Washer™," he says. "That's enough. We're ready to get out of here."

The base doesn't respond.

"House Washer™," he says again.

"Please," Judy says, "let the machine do exactly what it does. For what we paid for it . . ."

* * *

"Infidelity," Doug says, "is another hallmark of the successful. You know this."

It's the first either has spoken in five minutes. Maybe Doug broke the silence because he feels like speaking his mind or maybe it's because he, like Judy, can't stand the sloshing sound on its own.

"Yes," Judy says. "I do."

They both sit in their chairs, binders on their laps, though neither is doing any work.

"It's one of the apex freedoms," Doug continues. "Even as a scandal it's *rich*."

"I agree."

But she still hasn't looked him in the eye.

"Are yours any better than mine?" Doug says.

Framed artwork circles the tube. Farther in the murkiness, chairs float upside down, couch cushions are half covered in black mist.

"No," Judy says. "No better."

Doug looks at her long enough to give her a chance to return the look, but she doesn't.

"Public rows, affairs, drunken scenes, frivolous spending, driving fast, off-color jokes in the men's locker room," Doug says. "All part of the lifestyle."

"I agree."

Cold. A sadness in Judy's voice mirrored in Doug's.

Then, Judy says, "But what do you think about those things?"

Doug shakes his head.

"Christ, I'm not about to go through some self-evaluation, Jude. I was just sayin'."

They go quiet again.

Doug gets up. "Is it better than the maid?"

Judy doesn't answer. She only opens the binder she accidentally carried into the tube.

In it, old papers. Some newer too.

She closes it again.

"I think it's a hassle," Doug says. "Next time we use it, let's get the fuck out of the house first."

"Franklin," Judy says. "Franklin was one."

Doug doesn't turn to face her at first. Rather, he seems momentarily caught between what's real and what's not, as the name Judy just spoke emerges from the Solution®, beside Doug's own on a small business card.

Their first.

*Doug Barman and Franklin Barthow*

"Franklin?" he asks.

It sounds like he's asking for more than just verification from Judy. It sounds like he's asking Franklin himself.

"The Rise," Judy says. "Come on, we've talked about the Rise a thousand times. To get where we've gotten, there had to be people to step on."

"Jesus," Doug says. Then, "Look at the address on the card.

Franklin and me, working ten, twelve hours a day in that ratty fucking office on Fifth Street. Him and I, we got that place before you and I got serious."

"We got serious."

"Yes . . . and the day we moved in, we wore suits, me and Franklin, despite the rest of the building being mostly unoccupied and the few offices that were belonging to total scams. That building was shady as fuck. But Franklin hung our names on the office door like we were the CEOs of Glasgow. We bought that stupid little tray on wheels, to give the impression we could serve drinks to clients when they came. *If* they ever came, right? Jesus, those days. Yeah. There was one proper office and the other room was as small as this tube."

"Your desks faced one another."

"Yep. A work phone to the right of each of us. We could look each other in the eye as we worked out deals. That was the idea anyway."

"Yeah, well . . ."

"Were you fucking him then, Jude? Back in the Fifth Street office days?"

"The Rise," Judy repeats. "Franklin and I started when you two started to get big."

Doug eyes the spinning business card. Can still smell that small office, can feel the beating sun coming through the office's one window.

"We always talked about the Rise in those days," he says. "We joked at first."

"We were never joking."

"We'd get drunk and say things like, *You can't have success without a proper side fuck!*"

"You have to fuck people over."

"You have to say mean shit."

"You have to lie."

"Yes," Doug says. "But only to the people you're supposed to care about. Your spouse, your business partners, yourself." Then, "Jesus, Jude. Really? Franklin?"

Judy stands up, sets the binder on the seat.

"Yes. He was one of a dozen."

"Then why'd you bring him up first?"

Judy looks into the Solution®, sees the business card is cleaner already.

"Jude? Why him first? Were you trying to poke me? Trying to say something bigger by bringing him up?"

"Fuck you, Doug."

From the thick soap, something new: papers, dozens, and dozens of signatures upon them.

"The deed to Palm Street," Judy says. She laughs. Cold. "Why the fuck do we keep this crap?"

"Because no matter how smart we are, we're stupid," Doug says.

He steps beside her, the couple shoulder to shoulder, eyeing the deed as it's cleaned.

"That house coulda fit in this living room," Doug says.

"Yeah, but it was fucking *ours*."

"It was. You were a partner at Paul; Franklin and I were serving bottom-shelf bourbon to clients, after all." Then: "Were you with him, then?"

"On the *Rise,* Doug."

"Hey, that *was* the way up, Jude. That was the start of some serious shit. We once hired a maid to clean the living room of *that* house."

"We did. A dumb, simplistic couple. But not without ambition."

"Yep. And we've completely justified our way of living, our worldviews, since."

"Period."

The deed goes black, all the pages immersed in the Solution®, the dark fingers cleaning papers the couple had forgotten they'd held on to.

"We sold it for twice what we paid," Judy said.

"Not even two years later."

"By then you and Franklin had a new office, and Paul was no longer looking at me like I was poor, but like I was a threat."

Judy smiles but it's tempered.

"She was right to," Doug says. "You fucking sank her."

"Fuck Lauren Paul."

"No, thank you. Not even I could've done *that*."

They look to each other like they might laugh. But no laughter comes.

"How long have we been in here?" Judy asks.

Doug eyes his watch.

"Honestly, I didn't check it when we came in. House Washer™?"

But the base doesn't respond.

"Has to be close," Judy says.

"Why'd you bring him up first?" Doug asks. "If there were a dozen, why didn't you say someone else's name?"

"Fuck, Doug. Stop acting like a baby."

"No, hang on. I can't let this go. Did you bring him up because I brought up your mom?"

Judy turns on him.

"Shut up with the Mom bit, got it?"

"What are you gonna do about it, Jude? Hit me? Is that on our list of apex behaviors?"

"We're the Joneses now, Doug. Whatever we *do* makes the list."

"Go on then. Fuckin hit me. Let's see how long *that* fight lasts."

"Oh, fuck you, Doug. You're so out of shape, the paper boy could beat you down. When's the last time you *walked* anywhere?"

"Me? You're the one who sits in her leather fuckin chair all day, ear to her phone, making deals instead of salads, Jude."

"Doug, shut up."

"No, Jude, *you* shut up. You think you—"

"Doug, *shut up*."

"Fuck you, Jude, I'm not—"

"Doug"—she grabs his shoulders, she's looking past him. "*Shut up*. There's someone in the living room."

Doug spins to face the glass. The memory of the hand against his own clear upon his brow.

Out in the Solution®, a figure stands beneath the archway to the master wing.

Doug and Judy don't speak. Not at first. The sloshing continues, the hypnotic rhythm of the House Washer™, cleaning everything they own.

The figure steps into the living room. Doug and Judy instinctively back away from the glass.

The figure, cloaked in patches of darkness, obscured by thicker pockets of Solution®, crosses the living room, passing the floor-to-ceiling bookshelves, vanishing behind objects as they're cleaned.

"What's going on, Jude . . ." Doug asks. Quietest he's ever been.

"It's just something being cleaned," Judy says.

"What, Jude . . ." Doug near whispers. "What's being cleaned that looks like that?"

But there's no answer for this. No proper response. The Barmans don't own a dress form, a mannequin, anything that resembles what they see.

And what walks this way? Ambling across the room, its head seemingly turned in their direction. Arms at its sides. And what's able to breathe out there in the soap?

"Get out of our house," Doug says, but does not yell.

"House Washer™," Judy says, quiet, "there's someone in the house."

Surely this will bring the machine to a stop, to remove the liquid as fast as it can, to rescue whoever's out there?

But the House Washer™ does not stop. And their possessions continue to circle the tube.

"Guns," Doug says. "Our fucking guns are in the bedroom."

"Don't tell it that," Judy says.

The form stops mid-bookshelf.

Doug whispers: "I didn't think we'd need them in here. Jude . . . do you think the people who sold us this . . . do you think they're here?"

"They'd know when we were in the tube."

The figure steps toward them as black tendrils climb up its legs, extend from its fingers, curl around its neck.

Then it's all black, all shadows, all being cleaned, and Doug reaches for Judy's hand.

"Be ready," he says, sweating now.

"For what?"

The black swirling grows wider.

"I don't know for what. Just, be ready."

An eruption then, the darkness coming fast across the room, toward the tube, splitting the space between two lamps spinning in the Solution®.

Doug and Judy scream.

But when the darkness reaches the tube, it dissipates and fades back into the soap.

"*Fuck*," Doug says.

What shows is not a person, but a rotating cardboard box.

There's not even the suggestion of a face to haunt them.

Doug and Judy release the breaths they didn't realize they were holding.

"Jesus Christ," Judy says.

"It was just this box, getting cleaned."

"There's a lot of shapes out there. A lot of different colors."

"That's right. It's like looking at the clouds. You see people you know up there."

"Right. And none of it's real. Just approximations in the sky. The friends, the family, none of it real."

They catch their breath.

They turn to face each other and this time they do laugh. It's not hearty, it's not love, but it's relief.

"Jesus," Judy says. "We're a couple of pussies."

"I didn't know what the fuck to do," Doug says. "It was like we had a burglar!"

"I didn't either. I felt like a sitting duck."

"Like someone could've done anything to us."

"We were vulnerable."

Both go quiet again as they gaze out into the Solution®, as dark patches form other shapes, look like fingers and limbs, wrapping themselves around each item in the room.

The box continues to rotate near the tube.

The lid slowly opens.

"I don't wanna look," Doug says.

He turns his back to the glass.

"Let the thing do what it does," Judy says. But her voice is meek.

Both look away, out into the Solution® behind them, still shaken by the form they saw, both saw, crossing the room like a person.

The item from within the box begins circling the tube.

Judy turns when it flattens against the glass, when she can't help but look, when she sees what it is.

"Fucking hell," she says.

"What is it, Jude?"

"And fuck you, House Washer™."

"What is it, Jude? You're freaking me out."

"No, I'm not freaking you out, Doug. Our *things* are." Then, "It's a fucking receipt from the Samhattan Steak House."

"So? We've eaten there a hundred times."

"No, Doug. This is from when Franklin and I went alone one night."

"You and Franklin went on a fucking *date?*"

"What part of 'affair' don't you understand?"

"Yeah, but . . . *we* eat there."

Judy shakes her head.

"This wasn't a date. This was a night Franklin asked me to meet up because he had 'something important' to tell me."

Doug steps closer. Reads the itemized receipt.

"Told you over two bottles of wine."

"There was more wine than that."

"What happened, Jude? Why is this night fucking with you?"

Judy touches the glass, as if reaching for the receipt as it was handed to her by a waiter.

"Turned out Franklin was worried."

"About what?"

"About us."

"You and him."

"Me and *you,*" Judy says.

"So?"

"He chose this night, at the Samhattan Steak House, to tell me he believed we were approaching some . . . point of no return."

"You and me?"

"*Listen,* Doug. Yes. He said he was all about making money, but that the way you and I were going about it . . . it scared him."

"Yeah, well . . ."

"He said we were stepping into"—she searches her mind for the phrase, finds it quickly—"*the Dark Country*. Said we were blind to the lack of heart, the wasteland, the 'destitution' of the life we were beginning to lead."

"What a fucking drama."

But Judy doesn't share his scorn. "He told me he witnessed you playing a part in evicting a family of three on Fifth Street, only a year after you two moved your office from there."

"Yeah? And?"

"And he spoke about the wonders money could bring . . . the places we could all go . . . the travel, the experience, the joy, and the security of money."

"Was this while sucking on your fingers or not?"

"Fuck you, Doug."

"What the fuck, Jude?"

"I'll never forget the way he put it, he said, 'Judy, you and Doug are in danger of dropping your souls.'"

"Good grief."

"He said, 'There are certain things that, once you do them, you have no choice but to trick yourself into believing you had to.'"

"He felt himself slipping, falling behind me. He could see the bottom of my shoe, Jude."

"But he meant it. Every word. And he spoke like a man who had seen a ghost. Like a man who had smelled the fire before everyone else in the building."

"So what? He was weak, Jude."

"The Dark Country," Judy repeats. "Dropping our souls. I was a bottle of wine deep myself when he said it. And when I told him he had nothing to worry about, he warned me not to 'get dirty.' Said there was nothing but dirt, the direction we were heading."

"Rich, coming from a man who was sleeping with a married woman."

"He said there are differences between indiscretions and out-and-out cruelties. Of course, *I* had a lot to say in response. I told him to shut up, to enjoy his steak, the same steak he was able to afford because of the things you and he were doing and had already done. But he shook his head no, that ghost face fully upon him. He was a bit drunk himself, and I guessed he'd had some drinks before arriving, steeling himself for this talk. I reminded him that there is a ladder in life, and one must climb it or fall to the yard below. He told me he'd seen a line, a dark-red line, a line he never dreamed he'd approach. Yet, he had. With you. With you and me. And the way he spoke, it was as if the affair paled in comparison to the things you and I would soon, willingly, do. He spoke with confidence about us . . . dropping our souls."

"Fuck Franklin Barthow."

"He was scared for us that night."

She runs a finger down the glass, down the items she and Franklin ate and drank. Down to the total, the tip, and her own name signed at the bottom.

"He was afraid we'd kill for the lives we wanted," she said.

"Fuck him, Jude."

"Not murder, per se, but the same thing in the end. Franklin spoke of financial destitution, of depression, of how you and I were being seduced by something we couldn't see. He said the day would come, and it would come soon, when one of us would choose closing a deal over life."

"And what did you tell him, huh? What did you say to that?"

"I told him I would get the check. And I told him to fuck off. And I told him to stop acting like a child in a grown-up world."

"Good."

But there's something lacking in Doug's voice.

"Then I asked him to fuck me in the bathroom and he said no.

It ended there. He said, 'the only thing you'll own in the Dark Country is dirt.' And he got up. And he left."

"Jesus. What a fuck."

"And I paid the bill and ordered two more bottles for myself. And I sat at that same table, eyeing his empty seat, and I drank them. Laughing at everything he said. I even spoke to the empty seat, too, telling him all the things I'd come up with since he left, all the things I'd wished I'd come up with when he was there."

The receipt is clean. It floats back to the box.

"He sounded scared?" Doug asks, watching the box close.

"Oh, what does it matter," Judy says. "That's what we weren't, right? We weren't scared of anything."

"Damn right. We went for it. That isn't just some phrase, you know. Going for it means something."

"But what does it mean, Doug?"

Doug turns to her.

"Jude ... whatever this is? Stop it right now. You're getting fuckin pensive about the old days. Don't get bogged down."

"Not bogged ..." she says. But she says no more.

"Fuckin Franklin," Doug says. "There were flags from the start. He shook hands like a little boy and he couldn't look any clients in the eye. Do you remember he initially said no to the Delaware deal?"

"Let's not get bogged."

"Fuckin guy said no at first to the very deal that got us started, got us *really* started. I couldn't believe it then, and I don't believe it now. But I guess if he's asking you out to dinner to tell you I suck, then I should believe it."

"He didn't say *you* sucked, Doug. He said *we* were playing with fire. He said a lot more than that. But ... anyway."

"Anyway is right. It's complete madness. The Dark Country? And where the fuck was *he* going? Heaven?"

Judy looks to him fast and severe.

The heaviness between them suggests exactly what happened: heaven or not, Franklin is no longer alive.

"Okay," Judy says. "Enough. We need to get the fuck out of this tube."

"It's almost done," Doug says. But he eyes his watch with doubt. "I don't know if I'm talking about this goddamn machine tonight or not, truth be told. This thing is bullshit. Why isn't there a toilet in here?"

"Doug."

"I mean . . . this is longer than a lot of flights. What were we thinking?"

"We weren't. We never do."

"Really? You see a few receipts and photos from the past and now you think we're a couple of dumbasses? Don't be talking like that tonight, Jude."

"Doug, you're an asshole."

"That's fine. But I'm not going to apologize for it. And you? You're gonna say you're sorry for . . . stepping into the Dark Country?"

Doug laughs and Judy is up and in his face.

*"Franklin Barthow was a good fucking man who was warning his asshole friends of what they were becoming."*

"Rich, Jude. A row. Maybe if you kill me, we'll reach the mountaintop finally. That's the ultimate scandal, isn't it? Rich wife murders rich husband in state-of-the-art vacuum cleaner?"

Judy grabs the front of Doug's shirt. Doug slaps her hands away.

"Hey, Jude, get the fuck off me, okay? Get your shit under control. Sit the fuck down."

But Judy doesn't sit down. And she doesn't grab him again.

She cries.

It's just a little bit, but it's striking. Judy Barman hasn't cried in a long time.

"You're right," she says. "You're fucking right. We *are* assholes and that's *fine*."

"Jude, quit crying."

But Doug doesn't sound so stable himself.

"I can't stop thinking about him," she says. "Can't stop thinking about what he looked like that night at the Steak House, the look in his eyes, the *truth* he believed he was telling me. He wasn't looking for a leg up, Doug, he was *warning* us. The way friends fuckin' do."

"So now there are friends in business, Jude?"

"Franklin was different. He was there at the start. Before the Rise, you motherfucker. And if you wouldn't have done what you did to him, then *he* might not have—"

A woman's face flattens to the glass tube.

Doug leaps back and Judy cries out.

Wide, blue eyes. Bold, blond hair.

But they recognize who and what this is quickly.

"Holy shit," Doug says.

He steps toward the poster. A different look on his face now.

"Lauren Paul," he says. "How do you do?"

Beneath the woman's face, across her beige blouse, her name in block letters.

"House Washer™," Judy says. "Get rid of that poster, *now*."

Doug turns to her, smirks.

"Why, Jude . . . did you really think the conversation would end with what *I* did wrong?" He looks back to Lauren Paul's confident business face. It's the look of a woman about to achieve everything she's ever worked for. Doug says, "We're only getting started, baby."

"Don't *baby* me, you piece of shit. House Washer™, *now*."

Doug laughs.

"It doesn't listen to us, Jude. It only talks."

He looks back to the poster.

"This night," he says. "Oh, holy shit, *this* night."

"That's enough, Doug. We're both assholes. I said as much."

"No. No, that's most definitely *not* enough. You think you can install regrets in me, Jude? You came in here with a fuckin shovel and you're digging to plant regrets? In *me*? Naw. Sorry. They might be there, but *you*, Judy Barman, you're not allowed to dig. And you know exactly why."

He plants a finger firmly against the glass, as if poking Lauren Paul's shoulder hard.

"Remember how much this night meant to her, Jude? Remember the build-up to this night? Jesus Christ, she rented out the whole fuckin Holliday Ballroom. This was supposed to be Lauren Paul's coming out. Lauren Paul's *top of the ladder*. The apex of Lauren Paul's *Rise*. Remember how much we respect the Rise, Jude? It's our favorite thing, isn't it? The cutthroat nature, the dog eat dog, the climb up the razorblade ladder? Yeah, well Lauren Paul liked it too. And she was a few rungs ahead of us, wasn't she. But little Judy couldn't let *that* happen, could she? And who are you to decide who gets to rise and who doesn't? Isn't that what you're saying about Franklin, Jude? That the reason he offed himself is because he fell into *our* meat grinder?"

"Doug. Enough."

Lauren Paul is still plastered to the glass, looking into the tube, witnessing the fruits of that climb.

"She went all out," Doug says. "Gold tablecloths, red velvet centerpieces, a glory of a conservative's convention, everything screaming money and money to stay. Money not going anywhere. Money not getting any *smaller*, no way, certainly not *their* money, the donors who arrived in equally fine cloth, adorned, as it were, all dressed up but with somewhere, indeed somewhere, to go. There was a podium, remember that? Three microphones to give the appearance of a press conference, Lauren Paul announcing her new business venture in front of Samhattan's monetary epicenter, the men and women making that same climb, some of whom had already reached the top, some with weathervanes up there. This was supposed to be Lauren Paul's *night*."

"Fuck you, Doug."

"Except . . . *Except* Lauren Paul kinda fucked up, right? She had her eye on the future, reaching this next level, and she took her eye *off* her existing world, i.e., her own co-workers, her staff, each a blade of grass, and there, a snake in that grass, the snake's eye on those tablecloths and centerpieces and trays of Champagne like she thought they belonged to her. To *you*, Judy, you snake in the grass, who deliberately sank a woman for no other reason than she was higher up the ladder than we were at the time."

"Yeah, well . . ."

"Yeah, well, I say the same 'yeah, well' about Franklin, but mine doesn't cut the mustard. Yours is supposed to. When *Judith* says 'yeah, well,' we're all supposed to stop and say, 'right then, maybe it wasn't so bad, after all: it was just business.'"

"It was just business."

"Was it though? Does Franklin offing himself somehow rank higher on the scale of atrocities to you than Lauren Paul being forced out of town, to eventually sell all she owned, to try her desperate hand at a new start in another state because you, Judy Barman, spread lies about her on the biggest night of her business life?"

"They weren't lies."

"Were they not? Well, whatever they were, they certainly didn't need to be told *that* night, of all nights, *Lauren's* night to Rise."

"I worked with her, Doug. I knew her dirt."

"There's that word again. Only when you use it it's supposed to denote your righteousness but when Franklin does it spells doom for our souls."

The House Washer™ picks up speed. The sloshing increases. The murkier patches spin quicker throughout the room; the lamps, the cushions, the books, the odds and ends from boxes neither Doug nor Judy has any memory of ever packing, let alone allowing into their spectacular home.

They're both up now, at the center of the tube, a little afraid of the violence of the sudden swirl.

The tube rattles.

"House Washer™," Doug asks, then: "Never fucking mind."

Because he knows it won't answer. And receiving no answer to a worry is worse than the worry.

The objects move fast. The cords from the stereo whip through the Solution®, leaving tracers, creating lines in the thick soap, even as dark tendrils continue to wash what Doug and Judy have accumulated over a lifetime of Rising.

"Jude," Doug says. "Did the saleswoman describe this? Did she say this would happen?"

"I don't remember a word she said."

The dark pockets expand, then decrease; some seemingly explode, sending black dots throughout the rest of the soap and water, dots that elongate and become full lines, until what circles the glass tube begins to resemble the faces of sheer cliffs, the sediment visible now, only here, beneath the surface people walk upon.

"Something's going to break," Doug says. Deep concern in his voice. A tone that implies it isn't a lamp he's worried about but the tube itself.

"Doug," Judy says.

The way she says it, Doug senses a new problem, a scenario that will eclipse even those that have already occurred since they stepped into the House Washer™.

"Fuck. What is it?"

"Look . . ."

She points into the swirl, to the far side of the living room where the (now) clean drapes bob with the motion of the soapy Solution®.

A person stands behind the drapes.

"Jesus," Doug says. "Judy, what's going on?"

"That's no fucking face in the clouds, Doug."

"No. That's a person. In our house."

"In the soap, Doug. Able to breathe."

"Just be ready."

"I don't know what that means."

"Jude . . . I think I recognize who that is."

"Stop it."

"You see it, too. I know you do."

"Doug, it's impossible. Please. *Stop.*"

But Doug steps to the glass. He looks longingly into the swirls of white and black. Yes, Doug is sure.

"Franklin," he says.

As he says it, the figure steps out from behind the drapes. As if able to hear his name. As if summoned by Doug, a ritual of two syllables and no more.

"Franklin," Doug says again. And his voice is belief, disbelief, regret, and spite. But also, a change in him, a central shift: his voice is like it once was, back when he and Franklin first got the office on Fifth Street, a place that felt, at the time, like an elevator to the top. "Franklin! It's Doug and Judy! Hello!"

"*Doug,*" Judy says. "Are you losing your mind?"

"Honey, it's Franklin. He's okay!"

Judy is at his side, quickly.

"Doug, that isn't Franklin.

The figure is close enough that Doug can now see this for himself.

"Oh *God*, Judy. Look at his face!"

Is it a face? Or a group of smaller possessions combining to make dark-blue cheeks, cracked skin like dried paint on the walls of a very old home, a very old office, their first office, on Fifth Street?

A suit of yellowed paper, their first bills, crinkling even as it passes through the Solution®.

Judy pulls Doug from the glass, but it's too late. The thing is at the tube, soapy white eyes upon them both, as their possessions swirl behind him.

It raises a fist.

Is it a fist?

And pounds on the glass.

"Oh fuck, oh no," Judy says.

"Franklin!" Doug yells. "Don't do it!"

The thing pulls its cracked blue fist back, pounds the glass twice.

But is it a fist? Or a fruit bowl?

The thing pulls its arm back and the pair know this is it. This time its fist will crack the glass, this time the Solution® will come fast into the tube and they will have to swim through what they own to survive.

Judy grips Doug's wrist and closes her eyes.

Doug raises an arm in front of his face and braces himself.

But the pounding doesn't come. And when they open their eyes again, they see there is no fast swirl, no blur of possessions, and no Franklin Barthow, crusted like old walls and files. Only objects and possessions, gently floating in the soap.

Doug and Judy remain standing in the central tube of the

world's most exciting home-improvement product ever made: the House Washer™.

And the House Washer™ continues to do what it does.

"Jude," Doug says. "Are we?"

"Are we what, Doug?"

"Are we losing our minds?"

Judy lets go of his wrist and together they step to the glass. There is no evidence Franklin ever stood on the other side. There is nobody standing behind the curtains that sway in the Glasgow Solution®.

"Jesus Christ," Doug says. "Jude . . . what's happening?"

But Judy doesn't know any better than he does.

"Let's just wait for it to pass," she says, the way someone talks about a wild animal, close.

"But . . . he was . . ."

"Clothes," Judy says. "Everything we own is being cleaned. Clothes, gloves, paper. There are faces in everything, Doug. Paintings. Ads. Let's sit down."

"Paintings? Ads?"

"Let's sit down."

"Jude, I can barely move, let alone sit down."

Judy can barely move herself. So, the couple stand beside their chairs, eyes upon the Solution®, no longer like the two who paid for the machine but like tourists in the tall grass on a safari; ready for nature to overwhelm them.

"Paintings . . ." Doug says. "Ads . . ."

Then he laughs. Because he can't take any more seriousness. Because one more layer of seriousness will be one too much to bear.

"We were talking about him," he says. "And then? Then we saw him. Holy *shit*, Jude. This is a ride. Like tequila. Like cocaine. This is a *ride*."

"Let's sit," Judy says.

But she hasn't sat yet either. And her eyes are on the binder on her chair.

"What?" Doug asks. "What's in there?"

"Nothing," Judy says. But something. "I just brought in the wrong one."

"What's in there, Jude?"

Nervousness, even fear in his tone.

Judy, resigned, steps to the chair, takes up the binder.

"I'll show you," she says. "But I really think we should sit for this."

* * *

"It's a collection of letters from Carla," Judy says.

"Carla?"

"My friend from middle school, high school."

"The tree hugger?"

"Yeah."

Doug, wet from sweating, his black jacket on the back of the chair, waves a hand for her to get on with it.

"She sent me letters through the years, wherever she was living, whatever she was doing."

"I thought you said you didn't know what she was up to now."

"I lied."

"And you kept them? The letters? Why?"

Judy eyes the stack on her lap. "I don't know why."

Doug leans back in the chair, runs both his hands up through his sweating hairline. "I don't like this, Jude. None of this."

He looks to the glass.

"Same," Judy says. "But here . . ." She opens the first letter. "In the early days, years ago, she'd invite me to concerts, gatherings. I don't even know what to call them. Events. She described a life on the road, she was seeing the world. And she thought it would do me some good to come see a slice of it with her. She said things like, *God knows you can afford it* and *God knows you could use it too*."

"You coulda made that shit happen. If you wanted to."

"I know that. But I didn't. Didn't want to be anywhere near Carla and her moneyless, natural life. Nothing sparkled there, not for me."

"So what? We're different people. Do we really deserve to be punished for that?"

At the word *punished*, they both look to the glass; memories of figures moving, a cracked blue fist against the tube.

"In her most recent letter, she asked for a donation."

"Of course she did." Doug sounds emboldened again. He even creeps to the end of his chair, sits more erect. "Not a moneyless correspondence after all."

"But Doug . . . thing is . . . I wanted to donate."

"What was it for?"

"For a rescue farm."

Doug smiles but it's tempered. Nothing funny in the tube right now.

"You *what*?"

"It's hard to explain. It's not that she was asking for a donation . . . it's how *happy* she sounded. How unbelievably and obviously happy Carla has become."

"I don't wanna read the letter."

"I've never seen so much actual joy in written words before, Doug. It's like she was standing next to me when I read it."

"Okay. So you remember a bright-faced girl from middle school. You don't know anything about her now."

"But I do." She plants a hand on the stack of letters. "I know quite a bit."

"So . . . why didn't you donate?"

Judy's face tightens. "Because I was jealous of her fucking happiness, Doug."

"Okay. Big deal."

But there's no more oomph, not even enough to pretend, and he's a far cry from the man who stood on the sales floor where the House Washer™ is sold.

"Still," Judy says, "I couldn't stop myself from responding."

"What did you say?"

Judy looks to the glass. Looks anywhere but into Doug's eyes.

"Wait," Doug says. "No way, Jude. You didn't."

"Stop it, Doug."

"Jude, did you ruin this old friend like you ruined Lauren Paul?"

Judy stares at the letters without responding.

"What did you do?"

"I made some calls. Found out who she was working with. Told them stories from our youth."

"What kind of stories?"

"Stories that would make Carla look bad."

"Even if the stories weren't bad."

"That's right."

"Jesus, Jude. This woman"—he fans a hand to the letters—"she isn't on the ladder."

"Aren't we all?"

Doug slouches.

"She wasn't in your way," he says. Then, incredibly, "How could you?"

Judy's face tenses even more than it already has.

"Thing is, and I didn't realize this was a thing at all until now: I didn't feel bad about it. Not even a little bit. In fact, I had no more emotion attached to making those calls than I do to making the calls that are required of me every day. I doubt my pulse reached higher than a walking beat when I spoke to the people I needed to speak to in order to, as you say, ruin her. And I didn't think any-thing of those calls after I hung up either. All in a day's work, right?"

"Right. How long ago did you do this?"

"How long? Are you asking because you're wondering if there's time to fix what I did? If there's time to fund the project myself? If there's hope yet for someone like me?"

Doug makes a face like he didn't expect Judy to say this.

Judy goes on: "A year ago. At least. And while I've gone years at a time without getting a letter from Carla, I know she hasn't writ-ten since because she knows, somehow, what I did. And you know what's the worst part of that?"

"What?"

"That when I imagine her knowing, when I imagine her on a farm, and I cross her mind, and she thinks of the heinous shit I did . . . she isn't any less happy for it."

"Well, I'm sure you made her feel bad. Which was your aim."

"Right. But feeling bad isn't the same as being unhappy. A happy person can feel bad. But can an unhappy person feel good?"

"I don't know."

"No. I don't either. But I do know that Carla is happy. No mat-ter how hard I tried to take that away."

"What are you saying, Jude? What are you really saying?"

"I'm saying . . . at some point . . . you and I stopped worrying about whether or not we won . . . and we started needing everyone around us to *lose*."

"*Hello, Doug and Judy!*" the House Washer™ says, and the sud-denness of the voice brings Doug to get up quickly from his chair, to eye the Solution® swirling about the tube.

"*We've located an item we are unable to clean.*"

"That's fine," Doug says. "Don't clean it. We'd like to get out of here now."

*"We will bring the object to the glass for you to see it for yourself."*

"No, really," Doug says.

"Whatever it is," Judy says, "we don't need to see it."

*"That way you won't be surprised when you find it's still dirty when the job is complete."*

"Seriously," Doug says. "Whatever the fuck it is, we don't need to know. It's fine. Just, please, *end the session now.* The house is clean enough."

*"It's on its way. Thank you for understanding."*

"Come the *fuck* on!" Doug says.

"House Washer™," Judy says. "We will be returning the product, *you,* unless you end this process *right now.* We have had *enough.*"

But the House Washer™ does not respond.

"We're very powerful people," Doug says. "And one bad word from us can sink you."

The House Washer™ does not respond.

"We would like to speak to a manager," Judy says. "*This minute.*"

The House Washer™ does not respond.

Instead, an object slowly floats toward them from the archway to the master wing.

"Oh, Judy," Doug says. "What is it?"

"I don't know. I don't want to know."

It moves slowly, and the distance is still so great that neither can tell what it is. Dark ribbons swirl about it, cleaning other objects, even as the soap divides to make way for what comes.

"Is it big?" Doug asks.

"I can't tell."

Its size is indeterminate. So is its age, shape, its purpose, its value.

"Something from the offices," Judy says.

"Or the bedroom," Doug says.

They exchange a look.

"What's under the bed?" Doug asks.

"Could be anything."

"House Washer™!" Doug says. "Don't fucking show us! Whatever it is, *it's fine*. We don't care. And you can't make us look!"

"Just *end the wash*," Judy says. She looks to Doug. "The saleswoman. Did she mention a safe word?"

"No. I don't know. Maybe."

"Did she say anything about stopping the cleaning?"

"I don't *know*, Jude, or I'd have fuckin done that by now."

"I don't wanna see what's coming."

"I don't either."

"I don't wanna see what it is."

"What do you *think* it is?"

"I don't know, Doug."

"Something else you're hiding from me?"

"What the fuck, Doug? What do *you* think it is?"

"I don't know!"

"Is it something *you're* hiding from *me*?"

The object comes, floating, rotating.

Doug and Judy turn their backs to the glass.

"I've never hid a thing from you, Jude."

Sweat drips down the sides of his face.

"The fuck you haven't. You didn't tell me Franklin died for seven days after you found out."

"Jude, you didn't tell me about your father's death for a *year*."

"Yeah? Well, my mind was on other things."

"And mine? The fuck's wrong with you, Jude?"

Before them, in the Solution®, in view, a figure rises from the dark waves that clean their possessions.

"*Fuck*," Doug says.

"Clothes," Judy says.

"Paintings ... ads ..."

"Faces in the clouds. *House Washer*™! We're fucking done!"

A second figure now.

"We want out!" Doug yells.

A third.

Dead bugs are sucked up into the vent beneath them.

A tap on the glass behind them.

"Doug, don't look."

"Fuck no."

"I don't wanna see what can't be cleaned."

"Don't look, Jude. Don't fucking look."

But the tapping continues, even as the figures, a half dozen now, stand in the Solution®.

"Clothes," Judy says. But her voice is hysteria.

"Paintings. Ads."

Dead bugs get sucked into the vent beneath them.

Tapping at the glass.

"What could it be?" Doug asks. "What haven't you told me?"

"Fuck you, Doug. *Fuck you.*"

"What haven't we told ourselves?"

At this, they look to each other.

The tapping behind them. An object? The House Washer™ wanting to show them what cannot be cleaned.

"Jude, we're gonna die in here."

"Why would you say that? Why would you *say* that?"

"Jude, this is never gonna end."

Dead bugs get sucked into the vents below them.

"Doug . . ."

"Jude . . ."

Tapping.

"Are we happy?"

Doug looks to her, sweating, shaking his head no.

"No."

"Why *aren't* we happy?"

"Because it's not part of the Rise, Jude." Then, "We're gonna die in this fucking thing. *We're gonna die, Jude!*"

Sweat streams down their faces. Silhouettes sway in the swirl. Dead bugs get sucked into the vents. And the crisp, unmistakable sound of a possession knocking against the glass.

Judy grabs the binder. Returns with her back to the glass.

"Listen," she says.

"Fuck, Jude. *Help!*"

Tapping.

Forms in the froth.

"Jude, oh fuck, I think your mom's out there. Jude, I see your *mom!*"

"*Listen,* Doug. I'm going to read you something."

But her voice is hysteria.

"Oh God," Doug says. "I know these people, Jude. We passed all these people on the ladder."

"'Dearest Judy,'" Judy begins. She's shaking, crying. "'How the hell are you? My goodness I've missed you. And here I go, I keep sending letters, year after year. Because I love talking to you. I love your mind. Your humor, your drive. How is Doug? The two of you have to come out here. I know, I know, I say it every time, but you gotta know I mean it. We'd treat you like kings at our modest home in paradise.'"

"Jude, I can't take this. Can't take the tone of that letter."

"'Bob wants to meet Doug, wants to grill vegetables for you two, and says he even has a business idea, if you can believe that. I can't remember the last time I heard him say anything remotely related to business, but hey, who knows!'"

Something big and heavy brushes against the glass and Doug cries out.

"'I know time has passed and we haven't seen one another in

years, but hey, Judy, that's how it goes, and I won't let it stop me from trying. Nobody's ever made me laugh harder than you did. Nobody's ever got my jokes, either, like you did.'"

Suitcoats are plastered to the tube. Long-sleeved shirts and hats. Pants and shoes.

Dead bugs are sucked into the vents.

An object that cannot be cleaned continues to tap on the glass.

"'Lately I've been tending my own garden. Bob helped with the rows. It's truly incredible how much you can save by growing your own produce. And it's fun too!'"

"Jude, fuckin *stop*."

The tube is covered in sloshing clothes.

"'I do think there's something I can get for you, Judy, for the woman who has it all.'"

"Oh God," Doug says. "What's she going to offer? Can she save us? Can she get us *out of here*?"

"'I can offer you a joke. I can make you laugh. And whether or not you're laughing already these days, it will be a joke made by me, for you, to make you laugh a little more.'"

Tapping. Sloshing. The increasing darkness from the clothes against the glass.

"'I already wrote it for you,'" Judy reads. "'Wanna hear my joke? Here goes.'"

"Judy, we're going to die in here. *We're not going to get out of this tube alive.*"

"'Why did the Grim Reaper steal the gardener's shoes?'"

The tapping against the glass. The sloshing of arms and legs.

Bugs, sucked into the vents.

"Why?" Doug asks, urgent fury in his voice. "*Why did the Grim Reaper steal the gardener's shoes, Jude?!*"

"'They wear the same scythe.'"

A sudden BOOM.

And darkness. Complete.

*"Jude, the machine broke! The fucking lights went out!"*

"House Washer™, *STOP!*"

"Jude!"

But some light . . . enough to reveal fingers in the gloves, bodies in the clothes, faces beneath the hats. Faces they know.

*"Doug! It's Franklin!"*

*"It's Lauren Paul! It's Mom and Dad!"*

*"HOUSE WASHER™!"*

Franklin? Lauren?

*"Doug."*

"Oh, fuck, Jude. I feel it too. *Jude!*"

Solution®. In the tube. At their shoes.

Rising.

Doug and Judy hold each other in the dark.

Then Judy pounds on the glass. "*LET US OUT!*"

The Solution® is to their knees.

Doug kicks at the base, but the soapy liquid slows his foot. He tries to reach both sides of the tube, to climb above the rising Solution®.

"Jude . . . I can't make it."

"Doug . . ."

It's to their necks now. They tread in it.

*"HOUSE WASHER™!"*

A deeper darkness within the darkness: tendrils passing through the liquid in the tube, reaching for their ankles, their wrists.

Judy makes to scream, but the Solution® fills her throat. Doug makes to breathe but can't.

It's above their heads now, in the dark, the tube is filled with it. And Doug thrashes.

And Judy pounds on the glass.

And both feel the soft, dark fingers as the letters from Carla are cleaned, as the pages of those happy correspondences brush against their hands, their necks, their throats.

Then . . .

Another BOOM.

And there is light in the house again.

And the House Washer™ comes to a stop.

No more sloshing. No more tapping. No more to clean.

"*The job is complete,*" the base says.

And the Solution® throughout the house and the Solution® in the tube recede, lower, as quickly and as methodically as it came.

As the objects are returned to their proper places, as the liquid is sucked back up into the jets, as there is space again between the Solution® and the ceiling, the tube unlocks, spins, and slowly lowers back into the base.

Doug and Judy lower too.

And once they reach the base, their slack forms, still well-dressed, cleaned to mint, slide off the base, and into the vent beneath.

Even as the last of the Solution® returns safely up into the walls.

Silence then.

And the house, and everything in it, is clean.

"*Thank you for using the House Washer™,*" the base says. "*Please . . . tell your friends all about your experience. And why not? For what you paid?*"

# The
# Jupiter
# Drop

S teve Ringwald woke from dark dreams of swirling storms, bruise-purple gases threatening to choke him if he opened his mouth, and a surface with no support; his boots kept slipping through the ground and as dreams go, he had no real idea what held him up at all.

He was sweating, yes, and he was alone, yes, and his apartment felt too cold then too hot and oh damn he'd had a bad dream. Big deal. And to make it an even lesser deal, Steve knew just what had caused the dream in the first place.

It wasn't a nightmare necessarily, had nothing to do with his family or the accident *at all*. And the true root of it lay on his chest, visible by the light of the lamp he hadn't turned off before falling asleep.

An advertisement, card stock, originally found in the *Samhattan Daily News*, wedged now into the first third of the paperback that had put him to sleep. The book was a good one, if not a little slow-going, but the ad interrupted it cold.

THE JUPITER DROP!

Certainly they were outdoing themselves with this one. Whoever "they" were who moneyed experiences like this, the funds behind these insane interstellar joyrides; the people who were turning the solar system into a carnival. Steve hadn't even been to Mars yet, and here they were advertising a free-fall trip through Jupiter, the stormiest, most violent of all Earth's neighbors.

Free fall.

Steve let this idea sit a minute. Truth be told, it chilled him, and not just a little bit. He got up out of bed and went to the bathroom, but once there he realized he didn't have to go. What he *did* need to do was move. A little bit. Get the blood flowing. Get going. Standing impossibly on the gaseous surface of Jupiter wasn't so farfetched a thing, seeing as he had the means to do it. He had the money. Many people did.

Steve didn't bother looking at himself in the mirror. He didn't think of his family, either, his wife and two kids who had more than less vanished from his life in the haze of a particularly anxious period of his life. Amy was cold that way. In cold, out cold, and the only way that she wasn't cold was the fact that at one time she thought he was funny and Steve (like many people) guessed wrongly humor was enough to base forever upon. What would Amy say if she knew he was considering a yearlong flight to Jupiter just to be dropped through the planet like a pebble?

*Was* he? Was he considering that?

Steve turned on the overhead light and put on his socks. The clock told him it was only 5:40 in the morning, a fine time to get up, get out of the apartment, and get some coffee. Wake up. Begin the day. Possibly even get some work done.

But his thoughts of Amy and the kids, Jupiter and the solar system, followed him outside the same way vague anger follows a bad morning person. It would fade, Steve knew. The idea. The option.

The Jupiter Drop.

But beside his breakfast plate at the diner was a copy of the *Samhattan Daily* and on page three was another ad. The same purple block letters telling men like Steve Ringwald they could have the time of their lives if they had twenty-six months to kill.

Did Steve? Did Steve have twenty-six months to kill?

He read the ad. This time all the way through.


THE JUPITER DROP!

A TWO-YEAR FLIGHT ON DOWNEY AIRLINES, A TWO-MONTH

STAY INSIDE JUPITER!

A FULLY FURNISHED LUXURY APARTMENT.

STATE-OF-THE-ART VIRTUAL PARTNERS.

COMPLETE WITH A VIRTUAL MOM.

EAT, SLEEP, READ, EXERCISE, RELAX, DANCE, AND LOOK!

FOUR TRANSPARENT WALLS, TRANSPARENT CEILING AND FLOOR!

FALL, COMFORTABLY, FOR TWO MONTHS!

FALL BY . . .

THE JUPITER DROP!

(THE DOWNEY CO.)


"More coffee?"

The morning waitress. A nice woman. Maybe they could find some chemistry between them that didn't include a past.

"Look at this," he said, mouth half-full. He pointed at the ad with his fork. "What do you think this means? You literally just . . . *drop*?"

The waitress leaned over his table for a better look. She smiled.

"Yeah. They drop you from this huge crane connected to a space station. You're in an apartment and you get to—"

"Wait. You know about this? Does everybody know about this?"

"Sure. Or I do anyway. I know someone who went."

Steve wiped his mouth clean.

"For real? And so . . . what did they think?"

"Well, he's not back yet."

Steve didn't watch her walk away. He reread the ad. The phone number at the bottom looked too easy, like all he had to do was call, pack his bags, and he'd be traveling to Jupiter.

To then be dropped through the planet.

In a glass apartment.

He laughed, couldn't help it, and turned the page. The waitress returned.

"You gonna do it?"

She was smiling. It was a smile Steve knew well. The kind of smile from someone that implied, if you answered in the affirmative, they'd see you in a way you always wish you saw yourself.

Fearless.

Funny.

Fun.

Steve smiled.

"You know what," he said, looking to the newspaper as if he could see through to the flipped page. "I might. I really just might."

* * *

In training for motion sickness, sitting on the edge of the bed in the simulated apartment, Steve read the pamphlet Downey had issued, the rules and regulations of the ride. What to expect, what not; there being much more of the former than the latter.

Turns out it wasn't quite a free fall after all. And it was a tank of an apartment. The pressure, as you sink into Jupiter, is thousands of times the pressure of the Earth's oceans and . . . and Steve perused these facts with the same half-interested mind and intrinsic sense of trust people once adopted when strapping in to ride a roller coaster that went upside down. You trusted the people who built it. Downey wouldn't send anybody through a planet if they didn't know what they were doing, and that was (more *more* than less) enough for him. Besides, the apartment was equipped with jets that propelled it through the denser levels of Jupiter as well as steering it far wide of the planet's solid core. The pamphlet went on to detail the sun-level heat of Jupiter's core and to assure people (like Steve) that the apartment was built specially to withstand such conditions, being made almost entirely of Glasgow, the (thus far) indestructible and transparent material that revolutionized the theme-park industry as well as other, perhaps more practical, walks of life. Steve read through all this quickly. If they were going to send him into a scalding furnace of hell, so be it, he'd decided to go, and was indeed already upon the yearlong shuttle out.

It was the storms he was interested in, the Great Red Spot; to be surrounded by such cuckoo chaos, the natural angst and fervor, submerged wholly into the virulent landscape, Mother Nature Madness . . . *that* was interesting . . . *this* was something a man would remember, possibly even think about on his deathbed. As friends and family came to say goodbye, they just might see the violence of Jupiter repeated in his eyes.

It was just the sort of thing that could bring a man to accept his insignificance, even his death.

Or the death of others.

Steve wiped sweat from his hairline as the simulated apartment began to rock, experiencing faux turbulence, the worst (they said) he would meet out there.

*The death of others.*

"Ah, come on," Steve said.

The agent Rob responded, and his voice sounded tinny through the small silver speakers.

"All good, Steve?"

Steve waved a half-dismissive hand. Yes, all good. But no, *not* all good. And perhaps nothing had been all good since the silly accident; the day Steve had killed a man named Dennis Coleman. Coleman, a neighbor, had been raking his leaves by the curb in front of his house, back when Steve had neighbors, a house, a family.

"I barely touched him," Steve said, shaking his head in time with the turbulence. "I'd had nothing to drink and neither had he." He felt a little sick from the motion and the sudden recollection of Dennis and all the bad things that had fallen like dominoes since that day.

But were any thoughts of Dennis sudden?

"All good, Steve?"

"All good. I barely touched him. Slammed on the brakes, nicked him, just *touched* his knee. But then he . . . he fell back. Jesus, man, he was *smiling* when he fell. We both were! Smiling because we both thought how close we were to something much worse. But still, he fell, see? He stumbled back and nicked his head on the tree and . . . *Goddammit,* man, that was all it took."

The apartment came to a standstill, though never quite completely still, like being at sea. Rob had turned the turbulence off.

"Take a nap, Steve."

"All good," Steve said.

He recalled the one item in the Downey Preparation Pamphlet that he considered the most curious statement of all, the singular directive that interested Steve more than the reasons why the apartment wouldn't be crushed by pressure or go up in flames:

## THERE IS NO LIFE ON JUPITER. IF YOU THINK YOU SEE
## LIFE ON JUPITER, YOU ARE MISTAKEN!

No, there is no life on Jupiter and there is no life for Dennis Coleman anymore either. From a simple nick. A nick to the knee.

Then a nick upon a tree.

"Take a nap, Steve?"

Steve looked to the transparent wall, could see Rob sitting behind a big white desk, surrounded by wires and loops and blinking yellow lights. Rob wore the white jacket and slacks, another of the Downey "mood" effects, one that particularly worked, whether you knew it was for show or not.

Steve stood up.

"You're doing just fine," Rob said. "And you're going to *be* fine. These feelings pass."

Downey-speak. Steve had been warned about things like depression, cabin fever, and hallucinations. Would the two-month Drop be more intense than the yearlong shuttle out?

Steve tried to laugh but couldn't quite shake the idea of Dennis Coleman raking leaves, smiling as he fell, as if he were the one taking the Drop.

"Interested in a virtual friendly face?" Rob asked. Part virtual, part immediate 3-D print. Tactile.

Steve raised a hand to say no, then paused.

"Sure. Send one in?"

"No problem."

Nope. No problem at all; except Steve was still eight months from the Drop and two more from the bottom of Jupiter and another year home, and here Dennis was already smiling, looking him in the eye through the windshield, saying without saying, *That was a close one, ha!*

Steve blinked, and by the time his eyes were open again there was a dark-haired woman, kindly sitting at the white kitchen table in the simulated apartment. She was smiling warmly, yes, though Steve understood things like this could never quite be perfected, and an artificial smile will always make you smile the same.

Steve joined her at the table.

Outside the glass walls were digital renderings of sweeping colors, fervent electricity, and untamable storms.

Rob vanished like powder into the winds of a false Jupiter.

"Steve," the woman said.

"Yes?"

"Don't be anxious. This is an incredible, once-in-a-lifetime experience."

"I understand."

"Did you wanna take a nap? Lying down is good for the nerves."

"Hmmm. Maybe? Sure."

Steve blinked and the woman was now standing beside him, looking down into his eyes, smiling.

"Take a nap," she said, gesturing with her head back toward the bed, as if she were about to fall, smiling, backward forever.

* * *

Because Steve had never been on an interstellar thrill ride before, he imagined certain things being just like they were on Earth. A long line of sweating tourists waiting to board their apartments, the clanking of the chain that would raise the apartment above the planet (that "way up" feeling of dread and excitement banded together), bad music pumped through bad speakers, a carnival barker describing the exaggerated horrors of the ride and the mettle of those brave enough to try it.

But the launch site at New Jupiter Station 1 was nothing like this.

Steve should have known. This trip was *special*. He hadn't seen another rider (a *Dropper*, Rob said) since boarding the shuttle, though he knew others were on board. Sometimes, at night, he thought he could hear phony turbulence through the walls. Sometimes he even got up and pressed his face to the glass, looking for those people.

But despite the distant whisper of tinny voices, Steve never saw one. He wondered why. The pamphlet didn't explain the significance, though Steve could guess; if a man could handle a year of semi-isolation, surely he could withstand two months of the real thing. The view itself ought to occupy him, and he probably wouldn't have time to think about silly things like loneliness, solitary confinement, and the fact that he couldn't step outside the four glass walls for sixty days.

For the most part, Steve didn't think about other people at all. The virtual friends who appeared, suddenly, were so well timed it was as if Downey had a direct line to his brain. The moment Steve dipped below a certain level of happiness, someone to talk with would appear. Steve allowed these mysteries to belong to the men and women who built the ride. Who cared how it all worked? What difference did it make why the apartment wouldn't explode halfway through the planet? Who cared how Downey knew there was no life on Jupiter and said it would be a mistake to think otherwise?

Who cared?

On the day he arrived at New Jupiter Station 1, Steve thought again of the waitress from the diner near his Samhattan apartment back on Earth. As the men and women in white helped him out of his simulated apartment here and escorted him down a long, winding hall, Steve thought of her smiling when he told her he'd registered for the Drop. It excited him, knowing that when he returned home, he'd have the story of all stories for everyone he met.

Four agents escorted him, their tight jackets and pants showing off their athletic builds, and Steve did feel something like a celebrity, a special person, a person of great interest. His own form-fitting yellow suit was the only color to stand out in the tunnel and he couldn't help but imagine a daisy, himself as the potent pollen centerpiece, traveling confidently toward the real thing, the actual apartment, all simulations and getting-used-tos accounted for and over with.

"You did *wonderfully* in your training," one agent said quietly, then gently tugged on his elbow, steering Steve around a bend to a second long hall.

Only, this hall wasn't white.

This hall was as transparent as the walls of his apartment would be.

Steve stopped walking.

Below him, he saw it for the first time, horrifyingly massive, the colors and motion much more severe than anything he had been prepared to face.

Jupiter.

"Jesus."

He felt a tinge of embarrassment, as if the Downey men and women would be disappointed to discover their prized Dropper was actually, in the end, scared silly.

He crouched and planted a flat palm to the glass floor and stared into the chaos he had volunteered, no, *paid,* to experience.

"Jesus," he said again. And the planet seemed to respond, seemed to swirl into a lifeless, mean grin before the clouds and gases dispersed, creating new shapes, new illusions.

The agents helped him up.

Ahead he saw the leviathan metallic crane-arm and the empty transparent apartment—so out of place!—gripped in its claws.

"So," Steve said, a tremble in his voice. "So . . . it just . . . *falls* from there?"

"*Drops,*" one of the Downey men said. The others smiled brightly. "Welcome, Steve, to the Jupiter Drop."

* * *

It was an almost overwhelming sensation, standing beside the table, taking in the apartment (much nicer than the simulated one), noting the glass door, too, trying not to make eye contact with the men and women operating the crane, the agents standing on the platform, waving goodbye.

Either Jupiter was louder than billed, or the gears of the crane had Steve covering his ears. Would the next two months be just like this? Should he say he wanted off?

"All good?" a voice asked, stronger, less tinny in here.

Steve wondered when they were going to strap him in. Did the pamphlet talk about this? He recalled the word "equilibrium," saw it a hundred times on the pages. Homeostasis. Maybe he should've read more, trusted less?

Jupiter's surface moved, constantly, beneath him. Steve tried not to look down. *Don't look down.* But the pamphlet didn't say not to look down. The whole point of this was to look down.

So Steve looked down.

Shapes below, the size of countries, then colorful webbed fingers gripped the arc of the planet's surface, then reached, spread till they vanished over red horizons; golds and yellows swarmed as one new hue; fresh fingers rose, fresh countries, a sudden and improbable perfect circle, before its circumference melded into the heads of meeting storms.

*I want off.*

The Downey agents were waving goodbye; no barker here, no sale; Jupiter sold itself.

Numbers through the speakers. Decreasing. A countdown?

Steve gripped the edges of the tabletop, sat down in a chair. No seatbelt? No safety?

He thought of Dennis Coleman, nicked by the front bumper of Steve's car. One minute raking leaves, the next falling back, head hitting a tree . . .

"Hey," Steve said, rising, then sitting back down. "Hey, am I supposed to be strapped in?"

Waves from the staff. As if animatronic. Only the arms move. From the elbow.

Waving.

Goodbye.

Goodbye, Steve.

The numbers continued to decrease, and Steve tried to count down with them, but God damn the noise of the crane and the volume of the storming below obscured them. How close was he to falling, to dropping, to spending two months inside *that* madcappery beneath?

"Hey," Steve called again. "Is there a safety harness? A belt? Is there—"

He heard the number seven. All by itself. Not seventeen, not seventy-anything. Seven.

Steve rose.

He yelled.

"HEY! Hey, I want off! HEY! I WANT OFF!"

Waves from the staff, a purple mist rising about them on the enclosed platform, as if the planet below were counting down as well, reaching up to make an exchange, to take the apartment from the crane.

Hadn't seven seconds passed? Absolutely. Must have been seventy then. Steve went to the glass door and pushed, pulled, knowing of course the thing was locked, coded, from the outside.

Nobody ought to be able to open a glass door as they're falling through a planet. But he tried. Tried to open the door.

"Hey, I'm getting off now! Sorry, but I've had second thoughts!"

A tremble in his voice, then a hand upon his shoulder and Steve turned quickly, too quickly, and saw the slightly uneven face of an otherwise beaming dark-haired man. It was clear this visage was supposed to be calming. Another friendly face. This worried Steve. The purple mist rising behind him reflected black in his eyes and when he opened his mouth it was as if he were counting down the muffled numbers himself.

"What?" Steve asked. "What did you say?"

He smiled and shook his head *no, get away from the door, silly, you can't open it from the inside, silly, come sit down with me at the table, this is gonna be nothing, man, this is gonna be* great.

Steve turned back to the door, the glass, the platform, pounding now with both hands.

"*I WANT OFF, DAMMIT!*"

Fingers upon his chin, turning his face toward him, his dark eyes so close to his, his breathless artificial mouth open, relaying numbers, yes, no doubt, the number one, in fact, solitary, not one hundred, not one thousand, not one and one again.

Then—

—the drop.

And Steve screamed as the storms below rose to meet the floor of the apartment.

* * *

Immediate thoughts of Dennis Coleman. Thoughts of Amy, too, leaving him, taking the kids, telling him the kids can't watch their father lose his mind over an accident; he was teaching them the wrong things about guilt, the wrong way to get over something;

the way he was carrying on the kids were going to think it was okay to spend your whole adult life trying to change one silly moment, history, your own history, move it an inch or two to the left.

The kids were going to think they could move history, Amy said, she actually said.

Steve, standing with both hands against a glass wall, couldn't take his eyes off the scenery, the sights, the planet. The lights framing the apartment made it so no sun was necessary and even inside what should be the darkest, most dense areas of Jupiter, he *saw*.

And yet, he thought about Dennis. About Dennis Coleman never seeing anything so incredible, so absolutely horrifying and invigorating at once. If Steve had seen this before that autumn day on Miller Street, would he have nicked poor Dennis's knee? He didn't think so. He *knew* the answer was no. There was no way a man could be a part of such an infinitesimal oversight had he seen the depth of the cosmos in person. Steve was changing, right now, one day deep, would never be the same, would never see Earth the same way again, would never not notice a man raking leaves into a gutter one house before his own.

Dennis. Dennis Coleman should have got the chance to see this. Had he seen this he would never have raked leaves in the street to begin with. He'd have valued each and every cosmic second of his life and he would've let the leaves rot rather than stand in a street, a place where a car could come, could come nick a knee.

The view was . . .

There was no word for what the view was and no word for the darkness beyond the view, either, the infinite (no, there are boundaries, an end to this) chasm of ebony the apartment lights couldn't reach. Steve wanted to do more than tell his ex-wife, write his kids about it, call Dennis Coleman's grave. He wanted to *show* them. Show them the green fingertips that turned orange as they connected with the glass, then spread like something sentient across the ceiling, the floor, until Steve was completely entombed in an orange, then red, box, then seeing clearly again as the gases the mists the webbed fingers released the apartment and allowed it to fall, to drop; the beginning of a two-month descent into gorgeous improbability.

Eventually, thoughts of Dennis receded, and Steve stepped from the glass, stepped deeper into the apartment, took stock of the options afforded him. The small toilet and shower were sectioned off by a white curtain. The bed, white sheets, white headboard, was flush against a glass wall. No television in here. No computers. Nothing more entertaining than Jupiter itself, and the inside of Jupiter, and if a man or a woman needed something more than *this* . . .

Steve stepped to the kitchen nook and poured himself a glass of orange juice. He carried it with him to the bed, sat on the mattress edge, and stared. He watched the blues and greens and heard the howling of violent winds.

He lay back on the bed.

"I'd like a friendly face," Steve said, then blinked, and when he opened his eyes he saw a funny-looking man in glasses seated at the table. He wondered if Downey knew not to send the face from the Drop, the one who had held his chin as the apartment was released by the crane. He was grateful for this face instead.

"Pretty incredible, huh," Steve said. Because he had to say it to someone, even someone who wasn't alive.

*Alive.*

THERE IS NO LIFE ON JUPITER! IF YOU THINK YOU SEE LIFE ON JUPITER, YOU ARE MISTAKEN!

But Steve was alive. Wide-awake alive. Experiencing-the-apex-of-human-stimulation alive.

And Dennis Coleman was not.

"What do you think?" Steve said, and the man gave him a goofy thumbs-up and Steve wondered again if the apartment knew, was somehow wired to his brain, his nervous system, knew he wanted someone to say it was okay, as the walls and ceilings went blue then orange then white beyond him.

\* \* \*

The "virtual mom" pitch in the advertisement seemed unnecessary to Steve when he first read it. But a week into the Drop, "Mom" was as welcome as she'd been in childhood.

"Have you noticed you've entered the far north temperate zone, honey? You're still very far from the rings. You might not see them from here, but you know, it's nice to know they're *there*."

*There, there.* Mom always used to say "there, there."

"No," Steve said, fixing a sandwich at the marble counter. "I mean, yes, but I didn't know that's where we are."

A clucking of a tongue. Mom.

"You should've read the *brochure*, honey. It's all in there."

Steve smiled. Strange relief, so alone out here, to be nagged by Mom.

"I noticed the clouds," Steve said, knowing this vague statement wouldn't be enough for her.

"Counter-rotating cloud bands, dear."

Steve carried the sandwich to the glass wall, watched the fresh colors curl in and over one another, vibrant snakes in the mist.

"I also noticed the sound has picked up, Mom. It's gotten louder in here."

She sighed. "It's bad, yes. But you know what? It's the price you pay for the view."

She was right. And she was right-on, too, so exactly like his mother in tone and content that Steve had to wonder how extensive the interview process with her must have been.

"Steve, dear."

"Yes."

"No need to think about that nasty accident out here."

"I wasn't."

"But you were. And that's okay. But this isn't the place for guilt. This is a new journey. An experience all its own."

Steve ate his sandwich and observed Jupiter's colors overlapping; a bright flash of lightning so close to the apartment Steve actually recoiled.

Leave it to Mom to make him feel guilty for having felt guilt.

"I know it, Mom. But . . ."

"But what?"

"Do you think it could have been anybody, Mom? Anybody driving down Miller Street that day? If I hadn't nicked him . . . would somebody else have?"

Silence from Mom. Steve wondered if she were searching somehow for the right response.

"You're talking about fate," Mom said.

"Am I?"

"Yes, dear. You're talking about things happening no matter who is there to start or stop them."

Steve took another bite. "I guess I am."

"Oh, honey. Don't talk with your mouth full."

"Mom."

"No, I don't think it would've happened had you not been driving down Miller Street that day."

Steve smiled. Sadly. Now, this was as close to Mom as possible. She would never have gone for fate.

But she knew other ways to soothe. "But is it your fault that microbes are dying in your mouth as you eat? And who's to say we're any more important than them? And aren't you but a microbe here, a week into Jupiter, passing the north temperate zone?"

Steve rose from the table fast and stepped to the glass. He'd seen something outside.

"Mom, did you see that?"

"See what, dear?"

"I thought I saw ... I swear I thought I saw a ..."

"A what, Steve?"

"Nothing."

But he didn't take his eyes from the glass wall. Didn't stop staring into the motley abyss and wouldn't remember to take another bite of his sandwich for another five minutes.

* * *

Steve woke to a tapping on the glass.

He opened his eyes in the dark, the outer lights off for the "night," for sleeping. Tomb-like darkness hugged him close, wrapped its own opaque fingers around his ankles, his wrists, his neck, slunk down his throat as he opened his mouth to say something, then finally did, the one word in the dark, fracturing that opacity like a different kind of storm.

"Lights!"

And the lights came on and Steve hardly noticed the myriad hues, like stained water, swarming the walls of his apartment. All he noticed was that there was nothing to knock on the glass. Nothing by the walls. Nothing on the ceiling or beneath the bed either.

Nothing at the glass door.

* * *

Two weeks into the Drop and Steve was disinterested in the transmuting bands, the morphing paint, the way the world beyond the apartment constantly shifted, never to repeat its exact self again.

But he wasn't tired of the shapes he saw, the quick flashes, in strobe, a figure here, a configuration there. Sometimes, if you looked for too long, you could see a person out there, arms extended, as if falling, dropping, without an apartment, without the assistance of Downey.

Steve stared. He sat upon the edge of his bed and looked up, through the ceiling, into a wash of chromism, magnificent tincture and dye. Every now and then an eye would look back; not the dreaded red eye of Jupiter but an eye as small as his own, peering out from the vapor, the greasy luminosity, beseeching; the look of someone forlorn, worried, in need of help.

Shelter.

Steve got up.

"Mom."

"Yes, dear?" Never a sleepy take on her voice. As if Mom never slept.

"I saw something out there. And I believe it was a person."

A slight intake of air. Perhaps the sound of a smile.

"You most certainly did *not*. There is no life on Jupiter. And if you think you saw life on Jupiter? You are mistaken."

Steve mouthed the second half of her statement with her.

"I'm not convinced," he said, feeling emboldened by it, suddenly, as if having Mom to argue with was exactly what he needed in order to believe in what he was saying.

"Well, do. Do be convinced. Fixating on life out here is as silly as fixating on death at home."

But Steve brought his nose to the glass and stared deep into the miasma beyond. He pressed one hand against the wall and, for the first time, wanted to touch Jupiter, wanted to actually feel what the planet felt like, to smell it taste it hear it without the protection of the Glasgow walls.

He thought he could hear Mom breathing, through the speaker, or like she was in the room with him, behind him, so clear he turned to face her and found nobody, no Mom, and so he faced the wall again and thought maybe it was the sound of Jupiter breathing, the planet itself, and all this pigmentation, this iridescence, was the effluvium of a single intake held, then released, his apartment riding the living waves of something so large, he couldn't see it.

Mom told him he'd reached the equator, but Steve didn't need to hear her say it; it'd been a month in the apartment and the world outside his walls went solid white, solid blue, then colors too deep for his human eye to process. He knew the core of Jupiter was hot, sun-hot, and he knew, too, that it was larger than the Earth, much, but the jets had steered him far enough away from the ice and rock to be safe, leaving him momentarily in a sort of interstellar purgatory, a less interesting, less colorful limbo.

And yet . . .

It was here, level with the center of Jupiter, that Steve saw a form so complete, so perfectly *made,* that there was no way (to him, for him) to credit a random crisscrossing of mists.

It was a man, something like himself anyway, with two legs and two arms, no apartment to speak of, though Steve looked for one, thinking (perhaps crazily) it was a fellow Dropper. He asked that the lights be turned up, brighter, but was informed they were set at their maximum luminosity, and there was no greater vision to achieve.

That was okay. Steve believed he had seen it; swarmed by piebald worms, flashes of frightening gales, swallowed by a gob squall, an inhuman blizzard at Jupiter's equator.

Or below it now. Steve wasn't sure. As the colors began to re-semble the hues he'd seen days prior, still on his way *to* the equator, perhaps he was seeing their mirrored selves *from*.

*If you think you see life on Jupiter . . .*

A touch on his shoulder, cold fingers, and Steve turned to see a friendly face, a woman his age with large brown hair. He glanced once more through the wall, suspicious in that moment someone was trying to distract him.

"Well, hello," he finally said, grateful for the friendly face after all.

"Hello," she said, and Steve kissed her, held her close, and tried not to think of Amy driving away from the house, the silhouette of the kids in the backseat, their small heads, Amy driving up Miller, away from him, the same street he'd been driving when he struck (no, *nicked*) that poor man who was kind enough to smile after averting a much worse accident only to discover it hadn't been averted; still falling back, dropping, south of the equator now, toward a tree that would connect just hard enough to kill him.

How could Amy take *that* street to leave him? Of all the streets in the world to drive away on . . . how could she take *Miller*, the very street that had delivered all their problems to begin with?

"Well, that was fun," the woman said again, her voice a hair too tinny, *just* unreal, justifying perhaps the creed of the Jupiter Drop, the "you are mistaken" that rattled in Steve's mind like loose teeth, extra marbles, rolled for the noise of it, the roll of it, entertainment in place of television, a computer, even the cosmic masterpiece beyond.

Steve didn't answer her, though he didn't mean not to. He was looking up was all, to the ceiling, lit up, staring there indeed, be-cause something had moved, yes, something was crouched upon the glass ceiling and was peering into the apartment, at the life within.

"Look!" Steve cried. He gripped the friendly face by the wrist. His fingers sank into the rubber too far, unnaturally, and he pulled her aside. He stood flat to a wall, Jupiter like an open mouth behind him, but he wasn't (couldn't be) sure himself, as the colors shifted again, the tendrils of murky fog dispersed then returned in the form of a new shape. No. He couldn't be sure he'd seen anything at all, but as the woman spoke and as Steve stepped from the wall, racing for a different angle, a fresh view of the receding pattern above him, he couldn't shake the image of something crouched, followed by that something sucked up, vacuumed, into Jupiter's cruel sky above.

*  *  *

Steve wondered, is this what it's like, dying and being dead?

Six weeks deep and falling through a planet alone had gotten as lonely as advertised. And yet, Steve *did* have a hobby; the continuous staring through the walls, the ceiling, the floor. Most nights he'd wake, call for the lights, look under his bed, find a cluster of clouds approaching, maroon shapes that might have been larger than the Earth or as small as the mattress that held him. Sometimes he'd cry, from the sheer awesomeness of it all; other times he'd stare, waiting to see something staring in return.

Mom told him they were level with the Great Red Spot, though the apartment was much too far from it to see.

"I'm going to take a shower, Mom."

Up and out of bed, Steve couldn't be sure if it was night or day, and these terms didn't mean much to him now. He felt buried, buried alive, and wondered, with alarming regularity, if this was what death felt like; the dark colors, the emptiness that wasn't really an emptiness, the vast and brilliant existence he couldn't touch.

No more than Dennis Coleman could touch another tree.

"Go ahead, honey. Make sure to wash behind your ears."

Steve crossed the apartment and felt a slight tremor, turbulence, though it was never as bad here in Jupiter as it was in the simulated apartment on the flight through space. He paused, waited for it to pass, and continued to the corner bathroom. There he disrobed and ran the water, able to see the currents swirl down into the drain and leave the apartment immediately, falling into the abyss below, as if Steve were responsible for the tiniest raincloud in all this storm.

He closed the white curtain, though there was nobody to see him showering. It was all beginning to be too much for him; the onslaught of impossibly gorgeous images, the endless run of brilliance, zenith sights, the apex of human observation. Sometimes it felt good to draw the curtain on that.

He lowered his head under the hot water. He closed his eyes and opened them to see the bar of soap was down to a sliver; he'd need to open a new one soon, next shower. He ran shampoo through his hair and hummed a tune. He closed his eyes. He opened them, watched the water rain out through the floor as if there were no floor at all, as if Steve showered without an apartment, just a man standing above it all, falling, cleaning himself on the way.

He washed his face, rubbed his eyes, closed them, opened them, and saw a shadow, something obscuring the light beyond the white curtain that cocooned him.

"Mom?" it was the first word he thought to call.

Yes, he thought. It looked like the shadow of a person.

Steve held the edge of the curtain. All he had to do was pull it aside, fast, and see what was there, what was pressed to the glass, what blocked the light.

"Yes, dear?"

Mom's voice, Mom talking, asking after him, asking if he was okay.

Steve pulled the curtain aside and was sure, *sure,* he had seen it move, tear itself from the glass, allowing the atmosphere of Jupiter to reclaim it, to vacuum it back into obscurity.

But Steve saw nothing against the glass. Nothing remained.

"Mom," Steve said. "Did you see something, someone, outside?"

That smiling breath from the speakers.

"There is no life on Jupiter, honey. If you think you saw life on Jupiter, you are mistaken."

Steve turned off the water but did not step out from the shower. Instead, he stared long through the glass, imagining something capable of flying out there, something strong enough to withstand the storms.

And the isolation too.

* * *

Steve knew it was the worst thought he could allow himself to have:

*I wanna go home.*

It was a thought he'd had in Germany, when he and Amy had taken a trip, this before the kids and long before the accident on Miller Street. They'd scheduled three weeks, but Steve got the itch, the bug to leave, ten days deep. Almost involuntarily he'd voiced it. A fight ensued.

*I wanna go home.*

Bad thought to have while falling through Jupiter.

Sitting at the table, Steve laughed.

*Oh, Amy,* he thought, *if you could see me now. You thought Germany was a mindscrew?*

A glass of orange juice in hand, Steve rose and stepped to the kitchen counter.

On the way he saw a man tapping on the glass wall.

Steve dropped the orange juice. It shattered and pooled by his feet, clung to him, as if frightened of the storms below.

The man was alive, yes. Tapping on the glass.

He wore a suit. His hair flapped from the fall. Steve looked to his feet.

He was floating. Yes, nothing to support you out there.

Steve screamed. Like a child, like one of his own children, he screamed and he stepped on a piece of the broken glass and brought his foot to his hands but did not take his eyes off the man outside his apartment.

"Steve!"

A word? His name? Steve heard Mom's voice above, asking if he was all right, telling him no, he must be mistaken, there is no life on Jupiter.

Lightning flashed beyond the reach of the apartment lights and Steve saw the man in full. Thin enough to be skeletal.

In the flashing lightning, Steve approached the wall.

The man did not fly away.

Another tap on the glass.

Lightning; rash-pink clouds; green tendrils beyond the man—mindless, disorganized eels in the mist.

A tap. A tapping.

"Stevie, buddy. I'm coming in."

More assured now, and Steve, shaking his head no, no man could survive out there, no, this is mistaken *I* am mistaken no, Steve standing at the glass, his own nose only the width of the wall from the other's, only the glass between them.

Then a flash of lightning, bright enough to expose storms Steve hadn't known he was traveling through, dropping through, and in this new light the man blinked, Steve was sure of it, and his expression silently said, *I am life on Jupiter.*

"LIGHTS!" Steve shouted, and the lights went off and the world outside the apartment went dark and Steve, trembling, inched back from the glass, one hand out behind him, feeling for the bed, finding the bed, then crawling up and onto it, under the covers, where he could hide like his children used to, crying out for their parents in the night, Daddy! Mommy! Then running down the carpeted hall to knock on his and Amy's bedroom door.

*We're coming in!* They'd cry.

"NO!"

Steve screamed it, and he screamed it again and Mom came to him, Mom's voice as concerned and wise as the real thing.

"Steve, dear? Do you know we've passed the Great Red Spot? Did you know we're that deep into the planet now? Don't worry, dear. And don't cry. If you cry, you'll blur all these beautiful sights and won't see a thing."

And Steve in the dark, on the bed, clutching the bedsheet, shaking his head no as Mom carried on, in time with the tapping, the tapping of bone-thin fingers against the glass wall of the apartment.

\* \* \*

The bowels of Jupiter, storms, endless, but only the sounds now, only the music they made.

Steve in the dark. No lights on in the box.

*Do you remember when Amy told you you smelled different? Do you remember thinking it meant she'd fallen out of love with you? You were wrong. It was dying she smelled. You've been dying since you nicked the knee and the head nicked the tree. You've been falling back, dropping, like Dennis fell back, dropped. He was smiling. You remember that? You were smiling, too, when you told the waitress you might try it out, take the Jupiter Drop. You were smiling and she was smiling and Dennis was smiling, saying without words, That was close, thanks for* stopping, could have been a lot worse *until his expression changed, involuntary, contact with the tree, a sudden scrunching, the air sucked out of him.*

The air had been slowly vacuumed from Dennis Coleman since. Dehydrated flesh. Airless body. *Did you see that man, Steve? Did you see that life on Jupiter?*

No, no! No life on Jupiter.

*So is this death?*

"Steve, honey?"

Mom.

Mom's voice in the dark. How long had Steve been sitting in the dark? Falling? Dropping without an image beyond the glass walls, nothing to see, nothing seen? He'd eaten in the dark. Pissed and shit, trembling, in the dark. Slept and woke and waited and slept again.

"Yes, Mom?"

"We've reached the far south temperate zone. Not much longer to go. A shame, really."

Steve nodded in the dark. Wiped his nose in the dark.

No, this isn't death, he knew.

Right?

This was just the Drop. Surely if he'd read the pamphlet, he'd have been warned of mistaking life for death and vice versa.

Maybe there had been no man at the glass. No man in a suit. No man who said *Steve, I'm coming in Steve, are you ready Steve?*

"Mom?" Steve asked, his voice so vivid, physical in the dark.

"Yes, dear?"

"What do you know about cabin fever? About hallucinations?"

Trembling, shaking for days.

"Well, if you'd read the brochure you'd know hallucinations are very common, and they usually come in the form of things that do bother you in your everyday life."

"What do you mean?"

"Well, honey, a man who is worried about money may hallucinate open suitcases full of dollar bills falling through Jupiter. A
man worried about infidelity may hallucinate an affair in the
clouds out there. Strictly speaking it's called *cabin fever*, since you
asked."

Steve looked to the ceiling, saw lightning so far away, the quick
spread of purple veins in a blue thumb, then gone, swallowed by
the enormous blackness again.

"Mom."

"Yes, dear?"

"Let me know when it's the day we land."

"Sure, dear. But why? That's still another week away. You're not
planning on sitting in the dark all that time, are you, dear?"

Steve didn't answer. He kept his ear to the walls, to the ceiling,
to the floor, where he thought he heard something, a scratching, a
different sort of tapping, the sound, perhaps, of cold, hard fingertips pressing buttons, attempting to discern the code that unlocks
a door.

\* \* \*

"Steve, dear," Mom said, with no visible speaker to give the words
shape. "We land today."

Still, the dark. Still.

Steve sat up in bed. He'd been teetering on the steeple of sleep.

"Thank you," Steve said anxiously, swinging his legs over the
mattress side.

He crossed the apartment fast and felt for the coffee maker,
then made himself coffee in the dark.

"Thank you for everything."

He felt genuine gratitude for all Mom had done for him.

He was close, close to the catch pad, New Jupiter Station 2, close to exiting this apartment and boarding the shuttle back to Earth.

He knocked into a cupboard, and something fell inside, a glass perhaps, and the sound startled him. Sounded something like a closed fist on a glass wall.

He packed in the dark. Feeling for his shirts and pants scattered by the side of the bed. Outside the apartment, he could still hear the storms. Mad Jupiter wheezing.

The ride was almost over.

He latched his suitcase closed, sat on the bed, and waited.

And waited.

He fell asleep this way, sitting up, then woke to the sound of a voice.

"This isn't Dropping, Steve."

Steve leapt from the bed, away from the sound, and crashed against the glass wall.

*Lights,* he thought. *Tell Mom to turn on the lights.*

"Who's there?!" he screamed.

"This isn't Dropping," the voice repeated (*a man, a thin man in a suit, a man who can survive out there OUT THERE!!*). "Do you wanna Drop for real?"

Steve looked down, but down was the same as up, the same as side-to-side. All dark. The distant veins of red lightning in all directions.

"MOM!"

"Mom can't help you anymore, Steve."

Only a voice in the dark of the apartment.

"Who—"

"Let's Drop for real."

But Steve heard her, in the distance. Mom was talking to him. Telling him he was mistaken.

*Lights,* Steve thought again. But he didn't want to see this man, didn't want to see him seated at the kitchen table, his legs crossed, any expression on his unfriendly face at all.

"This isn't free fall," the man said. And his voice was the whistling of a cosmic wind over teeth. "If you wanna really Drop, you gotta step outside."

Steve shook his head no in the dark.

"No," he said. "No no no no—"

"Yes. Go on. Step outside the apartment. *Free fall.*"

Steve slumped against the wall. Fell to a fetal position on the glass floor. He looked through it, below, down, into the dark. And deep in there he thought he saw a light. Not the celestial light of another storm, but something more familiar. A bulb, perhaps. A man-made flicker in the abyss.

"How did you get in?" Steve asked, trembling.

"I know the code."

"How did you survive out there?"

The man coughed.

*Lights,* Steve thought. But no, not yet.

"They tell you you can't survive out there so that you don't try it," the man said.

Lightning flashed close to the apartment, and Steve saw him, the man, not sitting at the table, but crouched upon it.

Darkness again. Complete.

"Wanna get over the nerves? The guilt? Wanna . . . free fall?"

Steve looked down again. Saw that flicker die in a swirl of black sludge.

"Yes," he said.

Mom said something, far away.

Something about being mistaken.

"Go on, then. Step outside the apartment."

"The door is locked from the inside. So that nobody jumps out, so that nobody—"

White lightning again and Steve saw the man was now standing upon the bed and beyond him the door was open, a crack, just
enough for Steve to imagine his own palms upon it, opening it
wider, allowing himself to step outside.

Steve slid along the glass wall, toward the corner of the apartment, away from the bed.

But the man was moving too.

Motion. In the dark.

Shoes on a glass floor.

Mom talking about no life.

The steps closer.

Mom talking about mistakes.

No life.

Shoes.

Taps on glass.

Shoes.

Mom.

Life.

"LIGHTS!"

The lights came on inside and outside the apartment and Steve
saw no man coming, no man upon the bed, the table, or anywhere
else.

Wide-eyed, getting up, Steve searched everywhere. Under the
bed. Behind the shower curtain. In the cupboards. Outside.

"MOM!"

"Yes, dear?"

The door was still open. Just enough that he could pull it open
wider. Could step outside if he wanted to.

He looked down. He thought of Amy and the kids. How Amy
must have taught the kids that Dad was a nervous man, a wreck, a
shell, ever since nicking Dennis Coleman on Miller Street, ever
since Dennis Coleman nicked the tree.

"Yes, dear?"

"What do you know about . . . getting over things? Bad experiences . . ."

Steve was crossing the apartment, stepping toward the unlocked glass door.

"Getting over things? Well, for starters I'd guess a person needs to face their fears head-on. But that's what everybody says, and yet, most people don't get over things, do they? So then that's not the answer, is it?"

Steve was halfway across the apartment. The glass floor was cool against his bare feet and Steve realized, distantly, he'd spent most of his time in the dark without wearing socks or shoes.

"So it'd have to be something more like . . ." Mom was thinking. "Experiencing the thing for yourself, the thing to get over."

"Yes."

"What are you trying to get over, dear?"

"The top of it. The all of it."

"I'm not sure I understand. But yes, I imagine the only way to get over something is to go straight over it. Or possible, even through."

"Yes."

Steve was at the door. His lips curled into an imitation of the smile Dennis Coleman wore, the expression Steve saw through the windshield, as Coleman fell back toward the tree.

He felt for the edge of the open door. A flash of red lightning helped him find it.

"Now, dear. We'll be landing in less than an hour and I know you'll be happy about *that*. You'll be on the shuttle and headed back to your everyday life in no time."

*My everyday life,* Steve thought.

THERE IS NO LIFE ON JUPITER. IF YOU THINK YOU SEE
LIFE ON JUPITER, YOU ARE MISTAKEN!

Steve opened the door.

"Dear? Don't."

But Steve was already stepping outside. As Mom started to tell him to look down, that the lights of New Jupiter Station 2 were visible at last, Steve was already too far away to hear her, her voice sucked up and swallowed by the storms, unseen waves, and the astonishing volume of a planet with no apartment to hush it.

\* \* \*

Free fall.

Steve was falling. Steve was breathing. Steve was seeing too.

Below him, the propulsion jets on the top of the apartment glowed like distant cigars in the dark, four men playing cards perhaps, gambling, someone's life on the table.

The apartment was far below him, moving much faster than him, and beyond it was (*yes*) the catch pad, an enormous pentagon of elastic material (Glasgow, just like the walls of the apartment), and standing upon the catwalks and solid bridges were men and women in white, Downey agents, ready to escort Steve

(*Steve stepped outside*)

to the shuttle that would take him back . . .

Home.

It was impossible not to hold your arms out as far as they could go, to spread your fingers, your legs, to keep your eyes open, wide, as you fell. It wasn't just *wind* in your hair, Christ, no, it was the *storms of Jupiter* against your clothes, your face, your teeth. Steve felt rains he'd never felt before. Snow? Who knows. At times the current was so thick it felt like arms and legs against his own, at other times so thin as to be mere fingertips, tickling, and Steve smiled and laughed, an honest laughter that felt as free as advertised. The laughter of a man who wisely, calmly, knows it's okay to laugh, no matter what comes next in life.

*Life.*

Below him, at what appeared to be the bottom of Jupiter, the planet's very edge, nestled into the impossible, gaseous surface, was something that looked like . . .

"Amy's hair."

Steve laughed again, but it was clipped now. Not because he was saddened by the correlation but because the object (objects?) was so out of place as to be shocking, astonishing; a tangle of dark roots, unmoving, still despite the raging winds that shook the glass apartment below.

*Life.*

Steve, still alive, still falling, free falling, recognized the tangle as roots indeed, as though he were coming up from under the ground, as if he were digging rather than falling, rising, up up up, to the surface, and just below that surface were, yes, the roots that nourished life, that supported the whole song and dance to begin with.

Roots.

Life.

"A tree," Steve said, and blue winds toyed with the syllables, keeping them near, before they were sucked up into the cosmic tempest above.

**THERE IS NO LIFE ON JUPITER.**

Yes, a tree.

The apartment's jets sputtered, slowed as the glass box came level with the tree and in the apartment's lights Steve saw the bark in great detail, the branches like petrified lightning, the knots and the nicks . . .

"The nicks . . ."

Above that tree (Steve could see a crown now upon the tree, the green head in full bloom) New Jupiter Station 2 sat like a second sun, all man-made lights aflame, the pentagon catch pad ready for the coming apartment. The thought struck him he should be falling *into* Jupiter, there was no top or bottom.

And yet . . . falling . . . still. Following the apartment out.

The empty apartment reached the catch pad, the Downey agents waved hello, hello Steve Ringwald, you've been gone so long, you did it, you didn't lose your marbles in isolation, didn't go nuts and try to drown yourself in the sink, try to chop your fingers off with the bagel slicer, no blood, no mess, didn't try to open the door, didn't open the—

The door swung loose. Open.

Steve saw clearly their expressions as the apartment landed, as nobody waved back to them from within, the glass box empty, easily seen, all the way through.

A magic trick. The vanishing man.

But the agents knew where to look. The agents looked up. The leviathan ball storming above them, the Dropper Steve Ringwald dropping dangerously close to a tree.

(*up? down? There is no top or bottom to Jupiter . . .* )

Steve heard Mom, then. Heard her voice as though she were still beside him, no longer using one of the speakers, her tone clear and full, her syllables emerging and slipping back into the thick then thin winds, the blues, the oranges, the browns, the blacks, the—

"The tree," Steve said as he reached it, as his body careened hard against the roots, as he tumbled up the body of the bark.

Mom spoke.

"THERE IS NO LIFE ON JUPITER. IF YOU THINK YOU SEE LIFE ON JUPITER, YOU ARE MISTAKEN!"

Below, the agents were searching under the bed, in the shower, in the cupboards too.

Steve crashed hard against a thick branch, fell up to another, to another, thought:

*That wasn't Dennis Coleman.*

But it didn't matter who it was, who had advised him to step outside, to leave the safety of the apartment, to free fall through the center of a thing he couldn't get over.

"They're looking for you, dear," Mom said, her voice Jupiter's thunder, the sound a life cycle might make. "But they can't find you."

Steve crashed into another branch. Another.

"Where are you, dear? Steve? Where did you go? Are you hiding under the bed? Are you hiding in the shower?"

Steve connected with another branch.

His head this time.

"Are you hiding in the dark, Steve?" Mom's voice echoed through Jupiter. "Are you still there . . . being silly . . . hiding . . . in the dark?"

# Egorov

*Translated by Ethel Hasbro*
*from Galina Khanukov's* Notable History
of Little Russia, Samhattan
*with permission of the Samhattan Citywide Archives*

# ONE

The two surviving triplets stood across the pit, stared at each other, neither looking into the open grave of their third, each failing to blink, each seeing a man who looked identical to himself, each seeing only himself readying for revenge.

Both their wives had noted this: the quiet intensity had been escalating within Pavel and Barat like Russian bathhouse steam since the murder, and now mingled with the dew, the fog, the clouds so low they darkened the visages of everybody present. There was a considerable body in the grave and a considerable body of people attending, Mikhail being mostly liked but the triplets as a unit stone beloved, seen by most in Samhattan's Little Russia as a revelation, seen by their own family as divine.

Mother and father were present, Grigoriy and Kaarina, married still, despite poverty, temptation, miscommunication, coming into money, losing the money they'd come into, change, bigger change, children, new rules in a new country, breaking those rules, and now, the death of one of their four children, one of their triplet boys, their joy, their three: Pavel, Barat, and Mikhail. Grigoriy had long ago imagined and then discussed such possible futures, as both he and Kaarina took too much drink and smoked too much smoke and allowed their fears to tread into the least pleasing regions of the mind.

There, the death of a child. But more: the death of one of the boys, Grigoriy argued, was even worse than if something were to happen to Ekaterina, their sole daughter (and the youngest of the four). For death to come to all the triplets would be one thing, but for it to come to only one of the boys was wholly another.

In the past, Kaarina fanned these morbid topics away from her face just as she avoided exhaled smoke, but sometimes she did speak of the death of one of her sons and sometimes she agreed with their father. The death of a triplet would indeed be something of a death for them all. And now, Mikhail had been murdered, senselessly, without an obvious motive, by a man the police had yet to even partially identify.

Mikhail, so intelligent, so composed, and now in the ground.

Who did it? For Kaarina who did it mattered, but only to a point. How much of her could this senseless mystery occupy? There were the surviving brothers to tend to, Barat already encumbered by a dozen naturally poor dispositions, the sort of mindset some called "down" and others dubbed "sour" and yet others "blue." Barat, who looked no different on the outside from either Pavel or Mikhail but who seemed to possess a bodily strength transcending that of his size and the size of his arms, legs, and chest. Grigoriy called these "good genes," but Kaarina knew it had something to do with anger, an emotion no doubt galvanized in her son this day, the funeral of his and Pavel's third. If she could only get a clean look at Barat's face to confirm this.

Ah, but there was the expression! On the face of her other remaining son, on Pavel. And, perhaps, on the face of Mikhail in the grave. Still, who could get a good look at anything out here? What with the fog and the tears and the black worn by all, as if they'd been instructed to bring night with them to Raskoff Cemetery, the cemetery situated here in the very center of blooming Samhattan, this city with such big dreams here in the state of Michigan, the country of the United States of America, at the turn of the twentieth century.

"We will get through this," Ekaterina told her mother. She patted her mother's hand and repeated herself: *Everything will be okay.*

But Kaarina knew better: Grigoriy scoffed whenever Kaarina spoke of his sons as "pack animals," as "ants," as a communal organism split into three, but Kaarina believed it all the same. Pavel, Barat, and Mikhail were equals in a way other trios are not: each man contained a slice of a single personality. They balanced each other in a way that was traditionally provided for most people through marriage or friendships made in childhood, enduring well into old age. Mikhail's stoicism was necessary to Barat's ostentatiousness. And it was necessary for Pavel to be a blend of both.

But perhaps this horrible event would force the surviving brothers to evolve out of this symbiosis, or so Ekaterina seemed to suggest, as the pastor spoke of Mikhail in relation to his brothers, the only way anybody could ever speak of one of three. No islands unto themselves, no brother like the neighborhood they called home, Little Russia, here, an island in the sea of Samhattan.

But couldn't the pastor see he was underscoring the fact Pavel and Barat would never recover? Couldn't he see he was turning the knife in the remaining brothers' bellies just as the murderer had turned his in Mikhail's?

"I need to speak to Inspector Getz," Grigoriy said, his sudden declaration ending Kaarina's musing and Kaarina somewhat grateful for that.

But: "Not now," she said. Then: "When?"

Grigoriy, large, proud, his torso testing the seams of his brown overcoat, only stared into the hole in the earth, the hole his remaining sons refused to gaze upon.

Kaarina actually looked back, for Inspector Getz, thinking his thin, Russian face might shine in the river of black flowing about the grave. But the man was not near. Because the man was out looking for the killer of her son Mikhail.

"Have you had an idea?" she asked her husband.

Grigoriy nodded. "He said he was going to pick up a guitar, did he not?"

"He did. Inspector Getz knows this."

"So, the man must be musically inclined."

Kaarina exhaled steady. She had to tread lightly on most days, but lighter today. After all, Mikhail had got his even keel from his mother.

"Getz knows this," she whispered. "But it doesn't mean there ever was a guitar in the first place."

Grigoriy shook his head no, his way of telling his wife to keep her dead ends to herself. "No man claims to have a guitar that does not."

"And nary a man kills for no reason, whether it be passion or money."

Nothing was missing from Mikhail's person when he was, mercifully, found on, mercilessly, Fifth Street, bleeding, dead.

"Had he even made it to the man claiming to have a guitar, I might think it worth exploring," Kaarina said.

"He made it," Grigoriy said. "The murderer is that man. And that man carried our son far from his home and left him for dead in the street."

Ekaterina believed it, too, evidenced by the few words she spoke prior to the ceremony today:

*We* will *find the address in Mikhail's things,* Ekaterina said. *I have no doubt the numbers will lead us to more of Mikhail's blood. On the fingers, on the cuff, of a monster.*

And Ekaterina, now, still placating, patted her mother's hand while anger raged within Kaarina. Kaarina wanted this man found as much as anybody did, but she wanted all actors to be smart in this play. To not waste a day on making false assumptions.

The cold she felt within was Russian ice. And she sensed the anger in all those around her.

It burned hottest in Pavel and Barat.

As the pastor continued, slow and dreary, Kaarina returned to the dark shadows of her imagination. Her mind felt as if it had been turned over, spilling confusion and unwanted ideas at her feet.

What if, perhaps, in some hellish way, it had been *necessary* that her son had been killed? Had she known Mikhail as solely Mikhail at all, or just as one of the triplets? She turned to her memories of him as a child, his brothers in tow, racing the streets of Little Russia. She recalled how she couldn't always be sure which brother was which when they were still so small. She had even often wondered if she'd ever called one of the boys by the wrong brother's name, and had this error stuck, an error Grigoriy would no doubt have missed as he returned tired from a day of work and went straight to the cellar for vodka. Kaarina remembers the thoughts she would have:

*Who am I holding?*

*Which one is this?*

*Who is it that pulls on the drapes by the window?*

*Which son?*

All the trust in the world had been placed unto Kaarina, their mother, to protect the individual identities of her sons, the very same Kaarina, yes, who could not recall a time when she was certain which boy was which. Certainly not before they started speaking.

Were her memories of Mikhail's childhood perhaps actually memories of Pavel? And what befuddlement did she then bestow upon her triplets in adolescence, as she, the mother, resisted what she once mistook as Mikhail's nature, having long ago mistaken him for Pavel or Barat?

Might his death not clarify exactly who remained?

"Oy," Kaarina said.

Ugly thoughts in grief.

Yet, more to come:

What if Barat were to die next? Now? What if, instead of holding Pavel's eyes across the hole in the earth, what if Barat were to fall into it, headfirst, cracking his skull upon the timber? With only one triplet remaining, would Kaarina finally have closure? Would she finally know exactly who it was she gave birth to those twenty-four years ago?

Only Pavel. And why not? Barat the brute. Mikhail the level-headed. And Pavel . . . the blend, the slate upon which the others saw their own strengths, and what they lacked too. The other two triplets were always tugging on Pavel, as if to say: *With you I have numbers, an alliance that will serve me well into old age!*

But there were no sides, and Kaarina wondered if there ever could be with three. Certainly not *even* sides, and there was certainly no way two of the triplets would ever leave the third out in the cold. On anything. Pavel had always needed Mikhail in a different way than Barat needed Mikhail. And Pavel and Barat, alone now, needed each other in a whole new way altogether.

Because it had always been three.

"It's all right," Ekaterina said. She squeezed her mother's hand.

But it scared Kaarina deeply that neither Pavel nor Barat looked into the box. Neither was addressing the loss but rather the remainder of their troupe, their team, their trio.

What did this mean? Were they trying to change, here, at

Mikhail's funeral, to force themselves into a new dynamic they must get used to?

Or were they silently speaking to each other, as Kaarina believed the triplets often did?

She imagined Pavel in the box. Imagined Mikhail and Barat, and their relationship, the two of them staring into the hole. And suddenly she felt a bit ill. Had the wrong brother been murdered? If either of the surviving brothers were left to bleed in the gutter of a city street instead, would the two remaining be facing a more fruitful life than these two were going to? Was Mikhail, in the end, revealed now, in his end, to be the other brothers' rock? Had Mikhail perhaps carried more weight all along than she'd realized, her being confused and calling them by the wrong names so often she'd inadvertently switched her own children on herself? Could she even actually identify the son in the box?

And the two who were not?

She leaned forward, felt like standing. Ekaterina patted her hand.

"It's okay, Mother."

But Kaarina didn't believe it was. She wanted a peek at Barat, to see if she could glean anything from his glance, to know what unspoken words were traveling between the two sons who refused to sit with the rest of the family (without saying so, both, at the same time), who stood in the fog and shadows, their wives not at their sides but a step behind each, the pastor there, too, going on and on about a young man he, in truth, knew very little about.

And what did Kaarina know of Mikhail? Or any of them?

"What is it?" Grigoriy asked.

"What do you think it is?" Kaarina hissed back.

Grigoriy looked at her, finally. His eyes as firmly set as she'd ever seen them.

"Justice will be served."

But would it? Here in America, where immigrants were treated like rats? Would a local inspector even try to solve this case?

For as good as her husband's words were meant to make her feel, she was not able to say whether it was justice she wanted. She only wanted to truly know who her sons were.

"Mother?" Ekaterina said.

But Kaarina was already standing, not listening to the pastor, not listening to her husband's encouraging language as he suggested she sit. Kaarina wasn't even looking to the box or the grassy edge or the hole.

She saw only her remaining sons.

Identical to the point of uncanny, the trio had long been a living parlor game, learning to dance together on the cobblestone streets of Little Russia, always presenting themselves in a vaudevillian way, but never with drama or flair. Those elements were inherent! And did not need to be sold. And never for money. By the time of Mikhail's murder, the trio was poor as Grigoriy and Kaarina had been at their age. Barat the constant beggar, with a manner suggesting he begged for three. Pavel, the forlorn yet optimistic, suggesting to his brothers that a life among roaches and rats might actually be quite an adventure.

And Mikhail. Even-keel, level, always.

Level now in a box.

Kaarina sat down again.

"I'll see to them," Grigoriy said.

Kaarina knew what this meant. This meant vodka and fish. This meant barrel laughs and tears and her two sons and her husband sitting around the small wooden square table in their cellar. There, Grigoriy would miss all the signs of the boys transmitting silent information. There, Grigoriy would feel he had cured them of the sadness of this day.

But Kaarina would, of course, know better. Nothing Grigoriy had planned could stem the coming flood. The anger, the rage.

And what if the murderer were pinpointed after all? What would stop the two brothers of the slain triplet from arriving at the courthouse with knives of their own?

"It's all right, Mother," Ekaterina said.

Had the loss really reached Ekaterina yet? Could it have, to repeat such a platitude?

"It's a sad day when any family loses a member so young," the pastor said, and Grigoriy stood up.

"Please, pastor, be quiet now. No more."

There was no gasp amongst the family and friends. And no reddening of the face of the religious man. The pastor did as Grigoriy said. Grigoriy sat back down, and the ceremony continued in silence.

And so they remained, the Kuznetsovs. Their family and their friends. As two of the three triplets remained standing, facing each other still, unmoving, neither addressing the third in the box.

The elderly Yadira Popov said to his wife, "Did you see that, Lagina? They blinked at the same time!"

In the quiet, these words were heard by all.

And once again, Kaarina feared her remaining sons were exchanging information she would never be privy to. She only hoped they were grieving, in their new way. Accepting the ghost of their third. She only hoped they were working out feelings she had some history with herself, and were not, in contrast, blinking at the same time for having reached an understanding so buried in shadows and fog that they would not listen to reason, of any kind, if any were to show its face.

She only hoped they had not already agreed upon revenge.

# TWO

"Justice will be served!" Grigoriy said, and he sat, knocking the wood table with his knee and rattling the vodka and fish.

He handed a shot glass each to Pavel and Barat.

"They will find the man responsible for this crime. A musician, no doubt. Or a collector of musical antiques! Perhaps they will apprehend him mid-song. I can only hope he's singing of freedom as they do."

The three connected glasses and downed their first shot. Then they ate the fish. The remaining brothers stared at each other across the table.

The small cellar had long been a point of pride for Grigoriy Kuznetsov. While he hadn't achieved the monetary heights most men, and all fathers, dream of, their home was a good one, with space in all the right places. And here, in America, no less. Their own small piece of Mother Russia, though at the turn of the century, Little Russia constituted almost a third of all Samhattan. The triplets had been raised here, in the home above, almost never

wanting. Even Ekaterina, who, contrary to her behavior at the funeral of her brother, complained as often as the men and women
outside V's Pub, never had a bad word to say about the home she
grew up in. Grigoriy often told his wife this was because they had
chosen wisely. Too much space, Grigoriy said, led to space between
people. And the Kuznetsovs were forced to be in the presence of
one another, to speak of what was on their minds, to grow, together.

"Your mother is beside herself," Grigoriy said, though Grigoriy
himself seemed the more beside himself of the two. It was their
way, both mother and father, to be strong in front of their children
even in the face of severe distress. Still, neither attempted the folly
of hiding their grief entirely. One of their sons had been slain. The
fact they had two remaining, two who looked absolutely identical
to the lost Mikhail, did not matter. "I will speak with Getz tonight." He paused, as if perhaps one of the two sons might attempt
to talk him out of a late-night drunken rendezvous with the neighborhood police. When neither spoke, he said, "And I will tell him
everything I think about the case."

Tears then filled Grigoriy's eyes. His considerable, strong torso
pushed his white shirt and pinstriped gray suit vest against the
wooden table. He lined up three more shots and three more morsels of fish.

"Poor Mikhail," he said. He leaned back on his short stool and
gripped the table with both large hands. Grigoriy was a bigger
man than his three sons. They'd received their svelte statures from
Kaarina.

"To Mikhail," Barat and Pavel suddenly said, the first words
they'd spoken all day. It wasn't until both brothers raised their
glasses that Grigoriy realized both had spoken at once.

They downed their shots. They ate their fish.

Grigoriy slammed a hand on the table.

"It's inconceivable! A crime of this nature! Whoever this man was, he could not have known anything about our Mikhail! You two would've known if he did! But maybe we're overlooking something simple, eh? Did you two know someone who disliked our poor Mikhail so greatly that he might desire him dead? And not only dead! Gutted! In the street under the stars! Left in a gutter where the water is used to wash the blood of animals traveling red to the drain!"

Grigoriy loaded three more shots, three more morsels of fish.

"To Mikhail," the two brothers said.

They downed their shots, they ate their fish.

The cellar door opened, allowing scant light from a streetlamp to the cracked gray stone floor. The stains from spilt liquor past.

Ekaterina came down the wooden steps.

"Hey," she said. "But I could use a vodka myself."

Grigoriy eyed his daughter long and lovingly. "Ekaterina my dear, on a night like tonight, there is only justice. And it will be served."

He pulled up a stool for her to join them.

"Annushka and Vada are asleep upstairs," Ekaterina said to her brothers. "Your wives are as torn up as we are."

The brothers only stared at each other across the table.

"A guitar man!" Grigoriy said, slamming his hand on the table once more. Ekaterina grabbed hold of her glass, but the vodka spilled onto her wrist. Grigoriy refilled it.

"It wasn't a musician," Barat said. As if he and Pavel were alone down here, talking only to each other.

"Ah, but we don't know that," Pavel said. As if he and Barat were alone down here, talking only to each other.

Grigoriy's eyes lit up at the voices of his remaining sons. And with the prospect of playing detective.

"Who was it then?" Grigoriy asked Barat. "Mikhail went to purchase a guitar."

"No musician has such indifference to life," Barat said.

"Maybe he knew him," Pavel said.

"A guitar doesn't a musician make," Ekaterina said. She downed her shot. "He could've built instruments. That's a carpenter." She ate her fish.

"She's right," Grigoriy said. "And Getz will tell us what he knows."

"What does Inspector Getz know?" Ekaterina said. "How many murderers run free on the streets of Little Russia? How many did Mikhail pass as this one approached our Mikhail?"

Grigoriy poured another round, set out more fish.

From above, they heard the creaking of Kaarina pacing about the kitchen of their home.

"I want him dead," Ekaterina said. "And even if Getz finds him . . . to what end?"

"I want him dead too!" Grigoriy said. Then he eyed the two brothers eyeing each other across the table. "You know, I always thought the three of you kept each other's violence in check. Your mother never agreed with me, but I saw it. I've seen it many times through the years. The boiling rage in one, governed by the remaining reason in another, and the third giving credence to both options so that neither were fully achieved. Your mother told me Ekaterina has the most vinegar in her soul, but I know better." He leaned across the table, a fresh twinkle in his eyes. "Tell me you want him dead too?"

The brothers looked to Grigoriy at once.

"It was the person who put up the listing," Barat said. "This much I believe."

"But we don't know that," Pavel said.

"Like mormyshka on a hook," Barat said. "And our Mikhail, thinking he could buy the instrument and sell it for twice across town."

"Crime," Ekaterina said. "And no way of stopping it. Do you know that the police asked the city to hold off on crimes on Friday as it's to be too hot for them to investigate of sound mind? Do you understand what this means?"

"It means the police are talking to the criminals as if they are people," Grigoriy said. "It's disgusting."

"They aren't talking to criminals!" Ekaterina yelled. "They are talking directly to *crime!*"

"Like they are friendly with it," Grigoriy said. He punched the open air before him, swinging his arm so that his vest tore a few stitches at the seam.

"Like they have to ask its permission," Ekaterina said. She lifted her refilled glass. "Inspector Getz will get us nowhere. The American courts will do nothing. And the man who murdered our brother will be free to put his feet up on a barrel, hands behind his head, smiling at the news in the papers."

"Drink," Grigoriy said. "For the love of God, drink."

They did. And they ate their fish.

"No father wants to outlive his son," Grigoriy said. "It was my duty to outlive him. My one duty!"

"He wasn't a businessman," Barat said, looking directly into Pavel's eyes. "Mikhail would never have answered the post of a businessman. He would've recognized it as something he was unable to get the jump on."

"But we don't know that," Pavel said.

"The jump?" Grigoriy asked. "You speak as though your brother were a criminal himself!"

"Not a criminal," Ekaterina said. "Just trying to make money."

She took the bottle from Grigoriy's loose grip and refilled the glasses herself. She set out the fresh morsels of fish.

"For all we know the man was at the funeral," she said. "Laughing at us crying."

"Not all of us were crying," Grigoriy said. "Some of us were too busy being angry to find our tears."

"It is our turn to suffer," Ekaterina said. "We have a nice enough home and we have our health. But we're too poor to be as happy as we've been. And now Fate has come to collect. It's balance, our lot, our turn."

"There are no turns," Grigoriy said. "And I won't hear you speak of it as if there are again! Getz will catch this man and this man will be hung. Yes. *Hung!* Here in Little Russia like we would have done in *Mother* Russia! All under the American nose."

"And for what?" Ekaterina said. "So that he dies quicker than even Mikhail did?"

"Quick or slow," Grigoriy said. "Quick or slow! Rid the city of this vermin so no other family sits in their cellar demanding justice again!"

Ekaterina shook her head no. "That's not humanity, Father."

"Oh? And what is, daughter of mine?"

"Humanity is a single mind, Father. Just like that of your sons. And even you have dirty thoughts, Father. Wrong thoughts. Of death and decay. Of infidelity. Of murder. *That* is humanity and *that* is what is thought of in all cellars under all homes!"

"You be quiet this instant!" Grigoriy said.

"It's all right," Ekaterina said. "Mother has the same thoughts. And all the world is one mind. And our actions are those thoughts. You see? Some lives are like dreams. Others nightmares. Some toil steady. Like Mikhail. And Mikhail was taken by a whim. A bad thought the world had. You see, Father? There is no ridding the world of vermin any more than there is ridding your eyes of Mrs. Volkov across the street."

Here Grigoriy reddened. But he restrained himself and refilled the glasses.

"I like this idea, Ekaterina. Though it scares me."

"As it should."

"Because who's to say I won't be someone's nightmare soon?"

The door opened again before they could lift their fresh glasses to their mouths.

"Down here," they heard Kaarina say.

Grigoriy dried his eyes.

"Who's here?" he asked, rising to standing.

But he didn't have to wait for an answer. Following Kaarina to the cellar's stone floor was a man in a gray coat, gray hat, bearded and blue-eyed. His lithe features were the opposite of Grigoriy's and his visage approached the intensity of the remaining brothers.

"Grigoriy," Kaarina said. "Inspector Getz is here."

"You see?" Grigoriy said, drunk and attempting to sound sober. "I told you boys I'd be seeing the inspector later tonight."

Getz eyed the four but paused on the remaining brothers, as if seeing the undead having risen, twice over, the man whose murder he'd been examining for two days.

"And?" Grigoriy said.

"We found him," Getz said. "We found the man who murdered Mikhail."

# THREE

In the Little Russia station, all the remaining Kuznetsovs listened. Inspector Getz briefed them in a stone room with black
wood doors on either end. He sat half upon a splintered table, a
single light in the ceiling. Stains on the stone walls spoke of inter-
rogations past.

Getz's coat now lay upon the table. His sleeves rolled to the
elbows. His thick silver and black hair shone with his hat removed.

"He's in a cell just through that door. A thirty-four-year-old
man named Misha. That's the name and age he gave us. We found
him on the same street Mikhail was left to die."

"Excuse me," Kaarina said, stone-faced, "but isn't it rare for a
criminal to return to the scene of the crime?"

Getz's expression did not change as he responded. "How mad
does one have to be to kill for no reason at all? Or for whatever
small reason they perceive? Who murders that isn't mad?"

"We need to be sure," Kaarina said.

Getz nodded. "He was on his hands and knees. Sniffing the

very spot we found Mikhail. He had a spoon on him and seemed to be attempting to scoop some blood into a vial. Desirous, perhaps, for a keepsake of what he'd done. All this mere hours before I took a coach to your home. The sun was already down. And there are no streetlamps at that location."

"No light?" Pavel asked.

Getz eyed him closely.

"Almost none. Just the light of the moon."

"How did you see him clearly then?" Grigoriy asked.

"We've had three men on the street since Mikhail was found. First there was the cleanup crew. Then men to watch. Again, there is no explaining the disturbed mind. Misha fits that bill, as you will shortly see."

"What are we waiting for?" Barat asked.

"My men are readying the prisoner. He won't look very good to you, I'm sorry to say, as we had to use some force to gather information. At first. Now he sings freely."

"What information?" Kaarina asked.

"What he was doing on his hands and knees at the spot of a recent murder."

"And?" Grigoriy asked. "What was his reasoning?"

Getz appeared unhappy with the question. "He claims to worship crime. And I've no doubt he does, it being a hobby of his own. A passion, perhaps. He compared it to art. Spoke of the beauty of crime. We discovered a lengthy record on the man. Burglary. Assault. Theft. We found knives in his flat."

Grigoriy turned away and Kaarina held him.

"What sort of knives?" Barat asked.

"Do you know knives?" Getz asked Barat.

"I do not."

"Well, suffice it to say any of the ones we found would've done the deed. And all were spotted with fresh blood."

Ekaterina made a fist, her breathing intensified.

"Show us the man," Grigoriy said.

Getz stood in full and stepped to the room's far door. "Follow me then."

Beyond the door: a dark and wet cobblestone hall that smelled of sweat and urine. The Kuznetsovs followed.

"Never mind the other prisoners," Getz said. His inspector shoes clacked on the cobblestones. "And ignore what they say as we pass."

The first, a very old, thin man, only watched the procession with squinted eyes. Grigoriy paused at his cell, staring back into the gaze of the criminal.

"Why?" Grigoriy asked. "You didn't have to grow old in here. And now you do. Why? Is it religion? Do you believe a second life awaits? Do you believe this is not a waste of your precious first?"

Inspector Getz gently took Grigoriy at the elbow.

"This way," he said. "Up there where the light shines brightest."

The brothers arrived first, standing shoulder to shoulder, facing the lean, short man inside the filthy cell. The shadows played upon the man's clothes, giving them the appearance of having been torn, but a quick and closer inspection showed he wore bandages across his torso and shoulders. The police had worked him over, but had perhaps been more careful with his face.

"You see?" Getz asked. "This is the man who worships crime. The crime of murdering your brother included."

The man who called himself Misha spoke as the five Kuznetsovs faced his cell.

"In order to be an artist, you must *finish* works of art."

The two brothers stepped closer to the cell as one, where the light that illuminated the criminal shone brighter on them.

"Why?" Grigoriy asked the man. "Why Mikhail?"

"I would say it makes for a darker work of art if he was innocent," Misha said. "But who knows?"

"*You* should know," Kaarina said. "You murdering *scum*."

Misha looked surprised. "Are we all supposed to enjoy the same music? What kind of world is that?"

"And what were you going to do with a vial of my dead son's blood?" Grigoriy asked.

Misha's eyes lit up momentarily. "Keep it with the others!" He stepped closer to the uneven iron bars. "I have a collection! Crimes committed all over Samhattan!"

"Pig," Kaarina said. But she eyed the man uncertainly. As if the little thing in the cage couldn't possibly be responsible for such a large hole in her life.

Barat and Pavel suddenly appeared no longer interested. They started their walk back up the hall.

"Boys?" Grigoriy asked. "Whatever are you doing?"

"This is not the murderer," Pavel said.

"What's that?" Getz said.

The brothers stopped, ahead, in the dark. Barat said:

"There was no reaction from him when he saw the face of his victim twice over."

And Pavel said:

"He did not recognize Mikhail in us."

# FOUR

T he brothers stood in the doorway of their fallen third's apartment many minutes without speaking. Getz had already
been through the apartment, that much was clear from the muddy
footprints and open drawers. But the brothers were looking deeper.

"His books about sport," Pavel said, pointing to the shelves.

"I miss all that talk now," Barat said.

"Me too."

"His desk is clear as ever," Barat said, pointing to the small desk
by the small apartment's one window.

"He didn't have much use for it."

"No."

They went silent again. Barat entered, went to Mikhail's garbage can.

"Sardines," he said. He did not smile, though it was Mikhail's
favorite food. Most of the can was loaded with empty tins. He
removed the few papers within.

"Bills?" Pavel asked.

But Barat hadn't determined that yet. He unfolded a receipt for a pair of shoes. A piece of paper with a doodle on it of a man leaping from a cliff into an ocean. Pavel approached with a paper of his own.

"An address," Pavel said.

Barat eyed it. The address was nowhere near where Mikhail had been slain. But still?

Pavel folded the paper and placed it in his pocket.

A creaking in the hallway brought both of them to turn and look to the open door. There stood a little girl with a blanket.

"Mikhail?" she said.

She looked from one to the other, confused. Also: a little afraid.

"I'd heard you were killed. I'm so glad you weren't."

Still, she spoke to both.

"No," Barat said. "Not killed. Still here. Twice over now."

The little girl inched back into the hall.

"Are you . . . ghosts, then?"

"Go to sleep," Barat said. "And when you wake, this will have been a dream."

But the girl did not move. "I've already slept. I'm done with that now."

Pavel approached her.

"I am Mikhail," he said. "Do you remember me?"

The girl looked from him to Barat. "Who is he?"

"He is my brother. We look much alike, don't we?"

"Yes."

"Do you remember the last time you saw me?"

"Yes."

"Ah, good. And when was that?"

She held up a small fist, raised one finger, a second, a third. "Three days ago."

The brothers exchanged a look.

"That's really good," Pavel said. "And what was I doing when you saw me? It's very important that you let me know."

"You see," Barat said, now standing before the little girl, too, "my brother and I are fighting over what he did three days ago. And I want to win this fight. Do you have a brother?"

The girl nodded yes.

"Well," Barat said, "you understand."

"What was I doing when you saw me?" Pavel said.

She pointed down the hall. "You were laughing over there."

Pavel and Barat moved to the door and looked to where she'd indicated.

"Down there?" Pavel asked. "Do you know what I was laughing about?"

"You had a girl with you, silly. And she was laughing too. Mother said you had been . . ."

"Drinking?" Barat asked. "Did your mother say my brother had been drinking?"

The girl hesitated before nodding yes.

"Aha," Barat said, "I win. You were drinking."

Pavel sighed to play along.

"Can you tell me about the girl I was with?" he asked. "Just so I can ask her if this is true?"

"It's true!"

"I'm not saying you are lying," Pavel said. "But your mother could've be mistaken, and I want badly to win this argument with my brother."

The girl stepped farther into the hall and stared, as if retrieving the memory.

"She was tall! And big. And wore skimpy clothes!"

Barat and Pavel exchanged a look. Did they know this woman? Had Mikhail ever introduced them to a tall woman?

"She had paint on her face," the girl said. "And so did you!"

The girl made to run off. Barat grabbed her by the arm.

"Not quite yet," Barat said. "I have a bet to win, see?"

"Let go of my arm."

Pavel looked down the hall. Would she call for her mother?

"Call for your mother," Pavel said.

The girl did not hesitate. She cried out. She cried out again. A door opened two flats down and Barat let the girl go.

"What is it, Eva?" the woman asked. She saw Pavel alone in the hall. She squinted, as if unsure of what she was seeing. "*Mikhail?*"

"Yes. Hello."

The mother walked the short distance to him. Little Eva grabbed her mother by her legs.

"They were being mean to me," Eva said.

But when the mother looked, there was only Pavel.

Barat hid behind the door of Mikhail's flat.

"I'm sorry if I came off that way," Pavel said. "I just asked Eva if she could describe the woman I was with a few days ago. We were laughing in the hall? We'd had something to drink, of course, and I can't recall who I was with."

"We heard something had happened to you!" The mother said. "But I see this was only rumor. And since you are okay, you should be ashamed of yourself! Drinking to the point of not remembering! And here, in a family building!"

"I know. And I am sorry. Well?"

The mother looked down to her daughter. "Eva, go to our place for a moment."

"But Mother, there's two of them."

The mother looked to Pavel.

"Two Mikhails!"

"Shush. Go to your room. Do as I say."

The little girl looked once Pavel's way, then toward the open flat door. Through the crack in the hinges Barat eyed her back.

She slunk back, frightened, to her flat.

"You were *very* drunk, Mr. Kuznetsov," the mother said. "And I think it would be a good idea for you to keep that in mind in the future."

"Yes. The woman?"

"Your friend Toma. It was she."

Pavel smiled.

"Ah. *Thank* you." Then, "Did you happen to hear what we were laughing about?"

The mother reddened. "I will not repeat the joke, Mr. Kuznetsov! Good day."

She turned and moved quickly back to her flat. At her door she paused.

"I am glad it was only rumor," she said. She placed a hand to her heart. Then she frowned again. "But keep in mind this is a family building!"

She stepped into her apartment and closed the door.

Barat stepped out into the hall.

"Toma."

The brothers exchanged a long look. Neither, it seemed, knew of the woman the mother or little Eva spoke of.

On the way out of the building, Pavel said, "Do you think Inspector Getz really believes the culprit was that man Misha in the cell?"

"Yes. Because he confessed."

"And Mother and Father?"

"I think they will want to believe it. But we have sown doubt. And Father is determined."

"And Ekaterina?"

"I do not know."

Still at the apartment building door, a threshold they had passed with Mikhail many days, many nights, the brothers stood quiet. Thinking, it seemed, in tandem.

When Barat spoke, Pavel didn't appear surprised at the word.

"A ghost," Barat said.

Not surprised at all. In fact, Pavel echoed the word as if it had been in his head before his brother spoke it:

"Ghost . . ."

# FIVE

In V's Pub, the brothers sat at the chipped wood bar, facing the grizzled barkeep who couldn't get past how much they looked like his former regular, Mikhail.

"Triplets," the man, Luka, said. "He'd told me he was a triplet. But I didn't expect this. You even sit on a stool the same. Both of you, just like him."

"And today we will drink the same as him," Barat said. "So long as the conversation flows as freely."

Luka frowned. "Are you looking for information?"

"Isn't everybody?" Barat said.

"I suppose. Some people just like to sit at a bar and to speak and to be spoken to. Your brother was like that. Though I suppose you two know more what your brother was like than any two people in Little Russia."

"Any two," Pavel said. "And any two beers, please."

Luka poured them.

Behind the brothers, no tables were full, it being very early in the day.

"Have they not caught the man who killed your brother?" Luka asked.

Barat smiled. "They caught him, yes. A man who sniffs gutters."

"Oh."

"Indeed."

He and Pavel drank from their beers.

"Do you know a woman named Toma?" Pavel said.

Luka perked at the name.

"Here's the problem," he said. "I don't know either of you well enough to read your faces, and because there are two of them, nay, three, a third in my memory, I can't tell if my suspicions, the ones I am just now feeling, are unfounded or not."

"Eh?" Barat said. "And why not come clean with how you feel?"

Luka breathed deep. "It appears, to me, that you two are on the verge of doing something you should not do. It appears to me you two have decided to take matters into your own hands."

Barat and Pavel only stared back, sipped their beers, and set their glasses back on the bar together.

Music played. The distinct scents of urine and vomit clung tight.

"Am I wrong?" Luka said, his leather vest showing his bare arms. "I know criminals. And I know what the Americans call 'frontier justice.' Don't smirk. Although neither of you seem to reveal any expressions at all. I've poured drinks for men and women seeking revenge, you see. And it never works out to the satisfaction the men and women imagine it will as they drink what I've served them."

"Toma," Pavel asked. "Do you know her?"

Luka looked up the bar, as if perhaps the tall woman might be seated there that moment.

"Yes. I know Toma. And I know Toma and Mikhail were friends. They came in often, sometimes closing the bar. Once Toma slept here, as we couldn't get her to leave. A good woman. But a bad influence."

"A drunk?" Barat asked. "The sort to start fights?"

"Do you think she was with Mikhail when he was murdered?" Luka asked.

"Where does she live?" Barat asked without answering.

Luka shook his head no. "I wouldn't give that information out for all the money in Little Russia."

"Then we shall drink here every night," Pavel said.

"Until she returns," Barat said.

"That you can do," Luka said. "And . . . I said I wouldn't tell you where Toma lives, but that doesn't mean I won't tell you any more about Toma." He looked up and down the bar once more. "This isn't the only place the woman drinks, you know. Toma is legend in these parts. And rightfully so."

"Where else?" Pavel asked.

Luka smiled and shook his head. "Look out the window, friends, brothers of Mikhail. Any place you see! Toma drank everywhere at least once a day on Fifth Street and many places twice."

# SIX

"You look like him," Pavel said as the two sat in a booth at the far end of Rubles on Third.

"So do you," Barat said back.

But neither laughed. They eyed every man and woman who came through the door. And if the woman was on the taller side, neither even blinked.

This marked their sixth night in a row at a pub. Sitting, sipping, watching.

Where was this woman Toma? And would she give them any more information than they already had? And would that information be key?

The door opened. A large, sturdy figure filled the doorway. Neither brother spoke as the silhouette entered the establishment and the pub lamps made it evident this was their father, Grigoriy. Grigoriy surveyed the space once, quickly, before alighting on the four shining, familiar eyes in the back booth. Watching his sons, he leaned against the bar, in his way, which is to say, with power, and ordered a vodka without looking at the barkeep. When it came, he lifted it to his lips, took a sip, and ordered three shots, then pointed to the back booth and walked the planks of the bar to join his surviving sons.

"Out looking," Grigoriy said. "But for what?"

"Drinking off our grief, Father," Pavel said.

Grigoriy removed his suit coat and hung it on a rusted hook. "Neither of you are the type. You, like me, drink to celebrate. But this? And here? I would never suggest something is beneath your station, but I would make an exception here. What are my sons up to?"

"One of your sons is dead," Barat said.

The shots arrived and each took one.

"To Mikhail," Grigoriy said. "Who seems to have possessed you two, even the look in your eyes."

They cheered and downed the vodka.

"Now, tell me," Grigoriy said. "Do you plan to find the man who you believe murdered your brother, then murder him yourself?"

Silence did not follow, as a bearded man played a fiddle twenty paces off, but the absence of an immediate response was enough.

"No, Father," Barat said. "That's not the plan."

"Ah, but one like it? Listen to me. You do not want to become something you are not. Something you have proven you are not by abstaining from such behavior for two dozen years. You are not bad men. Neither was Mikhail. And while the American books glorify vigilantes, I cannot abide."

"That's not the plan," Barat repeated.

"Then what is it? Eh? Tell."

Pavel and Barat did not exchange a look. They only watched the door.

"And do you think the real murderer will walk through that door?" Grigoriy asked. "Or someone who knows who that is?"

Grigoriy leaned back in the booth.

"Boys, if you're hoping answers and truth will stumble through that door, the door from which you cannot remove your gazes, then want no more. Answers have come."

The brothers looked to their father at once.

"Your mother doesn't know I'm here. And of course she doesn't know I've been doing some investigating of my own."

He removed from his pocket a piece of paper. He eyed the length of the bar with suspicion and motioned for his two remaining sons to lean closer to read with him.

"Here is the name of the street Mikhail was taken from. He was not slain where they found his body. In fact, the darkness was done many blocks off."

Barat reddened. "How can you know this?"

Pavel spoke too. "Who did it?"

Grigoriy held up a palm to calm them.

"Now, I need confirmation from you two that you will not kill the man. If you discover he is indeed the murderer, you may find him, and hurt him, and bring him to me at the home you were raised in. The home Mikhail was raised in. But I will not permit you to know what I know until I have your word I will not lose all three sons for it."

The brothers only stared back at him. Grigoriy folded up the paper and made to place it back in his pocket.

"You have our word," Pavel said.

Grigoriy looked to Barat.

"Our word," Barat said.

"But how do I know this is true? How can I be sure what matters to you two now that your third has been taken? Any balance has been unbalanced; here you two are re-creating your brother both in character"—he pointed to Barat—"and in setting." He fanned a hand to the rest of the bar. "Perhaps your word doesn't mean what it used to mean? If a man loses his rocks, his roots, his reality, what's to keep him from losing also his dignity or his . . . word? And here, you have numbers. Most everybody would carry out a terrible deed if they had a second to encourage them to do so. And here, by way of birth and scenario, you two have built-in seconds. You were born with someone who agrees. You emerged from your mother's body with numbers. Most people stake their claim, fight all their lives, to find such help. So how? How can I be sure you mean what you say? What matters yet to my sons? Does justice? And if so . . . of what sort?"

"Father," Pavel said. "You're leaving us little choice. What can we do but tear from your pocket the paper and read it for ourselves?"

"Is there a description of the man on that paper?" Barat asked.

Grigoriy seemed to be making a final decision before he said, "Indeed, there is."

The fiddle played alone.

"Give it to us," Barat said. "Or suffer a torn pocket."

Grigoriy removed the paper a second time and gestured for his sons to get close again.

"He is an old man. But possesses a stubborn strength. His hair hangs to his shoulders, though it has thinned mightily on top. He sees with enormous eyes. He licks his lips as he walks the seedy streets, using a cane that costs more than some of the buildings he passes."

"He is rich?" Pavel asked.

"He wears robes," Grigoriy continued. "Shawls. I'm told he is covered from shoulder to toenail in cloth."

The remaining brothers sat back in the booth and pondered.

"Old," Barat said.

"And rich," Pavel said.

"Not a word of this to your mother or sister. And if you do find this cretin, you must bring him to me alive. And *I* will bring him to Getz."

"Do we have your word you won't hurt him?" Barat asked condescendingly.

"Easy, Barat. I am still your father and will always be stronger for it."

"How did you come by this information?" Pavel asked.

Grigoriy only shook his head. "I haven't barely kept us above the poverty line for this long without knowing who lives just under it and who might benefit from a handful of this very establishment's namesake. Seems someone recognized his 'work.' And meanwhile Getz still believes it's the man who would call something of this nature a 'work of art.'"

The brothers got up.

"Right now?" Grigoriy asked. "Not a second drink first?"

They made for the door as the door opened. As a tall woman with a painted face entered and someone cried out, "Toma!" from the bar.

But the brothers did not stop to look any closer her way. And they nearly knocked her over as they passed.

Still, she watched them. Wide-eyed.

As if she'd seen not one ghost, but two.

# SEVEN

P avel stood at one end of Peacock Street, Barat at the far end of the other. And if the street where Mikhail had been left to die had been considered seedy, this one was filth. Brothels lined the west side, as if, by coming together, they might share customers. Or perhaps they felt a strength in numbers, avoiding the harsher facets of both American and Little Russian law.

Pavel looked out for the sort of character his father had described but found himself distrusting the details. Whatever Grigoriy had been told, it didn't ring true with any sort of man Pavel had encountered before. At the far end of the street, Barat felt the same.

They looked for an approximation of these traits rather than an exact copy.

The sky was dark, but the street was lit with torches and lanterns, cigars and cigarettes, fires in cans every thirty feet. The people who called this street home seemed plucked from another world, characters the remaining brothers would have read about only in salacious books or heard loathingly described in finer places.

Here disease ran rampant. Pavel brushed his arms for fleas and lice and Barat checked his feet often to be sure he was not standing in urine.

Laughter ran rampant too. Men and women howled from balconies bloated with ferns and from the swinging saloon doors of the brothels.

In all the bustle, Pavel could not see Barat and Barat could not see Pavel, but they faced each other all the same. The few people who recalled seeing one brother at one end showed pleasant surprise at seeing the second at the other. As if the presence of the brothers were somehow planned, as if they were yet another of the street's attractions.

Pavel eyed the old men. Saw one in robes. Saw men with thin hair. Saw men who might be rich. But none, so far, with a cane, none who licked his lips. And Barat discovered the same, checking off boxes silently as he smoked against a brick wall, the corner of an empty storefront, eyeing the many windows above for a face close to the one Grigoriy had described.

Women shouted and men argued and bottles were broken and the loss of liquor was lamented. Money changed hands. But not in sums like the small fortune that might buy a murderer a cane.

After much time spent studying, Pavel walked the length of Peacock to Barat, where the brothers sat in uncertain silence.

"We'll find him," Barat said. "And we'll know if he did it."

"There's nothing else to be done," Pavel said.

They looked up the street, a street where everything, it seemed, was for sale. They watched, waiting. Every old man who appeared at the head of the promenade could potentially match Grigoriy's description, be Grigoriy's man.

"Whoever this is," Barat said, "he knows not to return to the scene of his crime."

"But Father spoke of someone who recognized his work. This means he has been seen. He is known."

"But here? That same someone could have seen his work a hundred miles away."

"All the way to Mother Russia."

They waited. They watched.

"It's only one night," Pavel said.

"And how many nights will it take?"

But they both knew this answer and so neither said, *all*.

# EIGHT

A t dinner with his wife, Vada, the truth came out.

Pavel never lied, not even about small things like sexual thoughts about a passing woman or a dislike for a meal his wife had prepared. He and Vada had long been more than partners, more than lovers; they were best friends. And their son, Little Alexander, seemed to take after Pavel, espousing his true feelings on every subject under the Little Russian moon.

"You've been looking for him on your own," Vada asked as they walked the river, Alexander in Pavel's arms for the time being.

"Yes."

"Do you know the man Misha is being painted as a killer?"

"He says he is. Let him live like one."

"But . . . he's not well."

"Well as anybody, I suppose."

"Is that really how you see it?"

The water lapped against the stone barriers; moonlight shone off the railing. People passed in both directions. Pavel had decided before taking the walk he would not reveal Grigoriy's description of the man, even if she asked for it.

She asked for it: "Do you even know who you are looking for?"

Pavel did have some maneuvers in the event he felt it unwise to be entirely truthful with Vada. One was, of course, not responding to her question. Here he pulled Alexander's small face from his shoulder and asked his son if he was enjoying himself.

"Yes," Alexander said sleepily.

But Vada was not deterred. "How do you know who you're even looking for? Do you have information? Pavel? Talk to me."

"No," Pavel said. And immediately following the lie he attempted, inwardly, to make sense of the word, to somehow rationalize it into a truth for himself.

"So then . . . what? What do you look for? A menacing man? Someone who looks the part?"

Pavel was surprised to feel Vada's hand on his arm.

"Pavel," she said. "Look at me. What's going on here? What do you and Barat plan to do?"

Pavel looked past her, out upon the river. The reflected moonlight rippled, and for a moment it felt like there was no Little Russia, no Samhattan at all. No horses or horse droppings. No people who might murder a man for reasons the rest of the world could not know.

"We have no plan," Pavel said. This much was true only insomuch as their plan had not yet been spoken.

But both knew.

"Truly?" Vada asked. Because even more than lovers, best friends know.

"Yes," Pavel said.

But best friends also know when to relent. Vada looked out upon the water herself.

"I suppose this is because of your grief," she said.

For what else was there to say? Who could know but triplets what it was like to lose one of three?

This was something Vada was well accustomed to living with: Pavel, Mikhail, and Barat shared a silent life of their own. From the day Vada met Pavel's brothers, she witnessed the change in Pavel's personality while around them. As if parts of who Pavel was when he was whole and solitary went into hibernation while his brothers instead presented those facets of himself on his behalf. It wasn't that Barat was better at talking or that Mikhail had a sharper sense of humor: it was as if the brothers had agreed long ago who would represent which of their personality traits when together.

Many times Vada had wondered what the real Barat and Mikhail were like, at home, the two of them no doubt leaving parts of themselves behind when the three were together, the only instances in which Vada spent any real time with the other two. Did Mikhail have a manic side she was never privy to? Did Barat have a ponderous side, was he quiet when home with Annushka? Often Vada wanted to ask Annushka about these things but almost never found herself alone with the woman. Often, still, she wanted to push. And now, walking the cobblestones along the river, her husband in the disorienting grip of grief, she wondered: should she push? This was no laughing matter, no gathering of relatives around a Christmas table, Barat making boisterous remarks as Grigoriy poured shots of vodka. This was not Kaarina espousing deeper observations than Vada expected to hear. This was not Mikhail and Pavel saying the same things at the same time, suggesting a nearly supernatural link amongst the triplets.

This was her husband, staying out late in pubs and dirty streets, determined to find the man who killed his brother, his third, as if that murderer were not the man Misha.

She put her arm through his.

"Whatever you do," she said, "do it with intelligence."

Ahead, the clacking of a cane upon stone steps. And the grumbling of the man who used it.

It took Vada a couple steps to realize Pavel had stopped walking. She looked back to the steps, which Pavel stood facing. There, an old man struggled to work his way down to the cobblestones. Vada took Alexander from Pavel's hands without a word. It felt, to her, as if her husband, given another few seconds, might've dropped their son where he stood.

A peddler approached the old man.

"Sir?"

But the old man, hidden mostly by a robe, shooed the poor beggar aside.

"Come any closer," the old man said, "I will strike you with my cane. I will lie to the police. I will tell them you struck first. And if I see you again on my evening walk, I will do more next time than refuse."

The beggar hurried off and the old man made it at last to the cobblestones.

"Pavel," Vada said. "What is it?"

But her husband had turned his back from the man, as if he did not want to be seen.

"Pavel?"

Pavel stood facing the river, his hands upon the rail.

The old man limped toward them. When he was a few steps short of being level with Vada, the moonlight reached him, a shaft just wide enough to show Vada half the old man's face. And in that half she saw enough to make her shudder. She wondered if perhaps he wore makeup, a disguise, for it was not possible any person could appear this way. His eye, the one she could see, was too wide open, she thought, as if perhaps it were made of glass, despite it locking momentarily on her own. And as it did, she felt a chill deeper than the one she'd felt as he'd mocked the beggar who asked for alms. His nose hung low to his lips, and his tongue, the half she could see, lolled out and licked the tip.

Vada looked away. She, too, faced the river.

"It's a shame," she said, trying suddenly to appear normal, as if by doing so she might avoid a man like this. "How the lanterns dull the starlight, the moonlight, the world."

Pavel did not speak. Long after the dragging leg of the old man could no longer be heard, long after the tip of his cane no longer clacked against stone within earshot, still he did not speak.

Then, at last, Pavel did turn to her. He took Alexander back into his arms and began walking the way they had originally been going, that is, toward home. Without a word as to why he had stopped.

And he spoke no more on the walk, despite the few questions Vada asked him. He looked back twice, and Vada saw Pavel looking the way a person does when they want a thing memorized; a person, a place, a thing.

She felt sure she'd caught her husband studying.

She thought of the old man's lips in that shaft of moonlight as she walked the stone steps to home. Above her and Pavel, on the first floor of their building, Mrs. Lavrov's drapes were parted about as wide as the moonlight had been, giving her the partial visage of the cruel old man. And Vada shivered again as Pavel set Alexander down and used his key to unlock the building door. For she imagined, momentarily, the man peering out from that same space, that face embedded somewhere in the dark of the flat belonging to Mrs. Lavrov.

As if this awful stranger had done more than pass by her in life but had now assumed occupancy of a space she would encounter again.

# NINE

Barat was drunk even before his family all sat down to dinner. He and Annushka had been invited over, without Pavel and Vada, as Kaarina wanted to encourage her two remaining sons to explore their individuality. She understood something deep had been stolen from both. Something much worse than a limb.

Grigoriy didn't seem to agree with her—though he seldom ever had when it came to her feelings about their sons—and meanwhile, these days he always seemed to be busy speaking with Inspector Getz. Grigoriy had visited the prison half a dozen times and each day returned home with the lack of news.

Lack of motive too. The man had long since admitted to the deed. He'd been found sniffing the bloodstain of the very spot Mikhail had been slain. He admittedly worshipped the macabre and his flat was filled with drawings of dead people, amongst other shadowy things, including, yes, vials of blood, supposedly from other crimes. Sensing an endless darkness, Kaarina didn't want to hear any more than she had to about the subject. Her son had been killed. A man had been caught. That same man had confessed. This was enough for her insomuch as it gave her the means to begin grieving rather than asking questions as her husband continued to do. But that was Grigoriy's way. She knew this about him, of course, had known it for decades. Grigoriy asked questions. Then he asked questions about those questions. And when you answered him, he liked to explain to you why you answered in the specific way you had.

Still, these visits with Inspector Getz were somehow different. It was clear Grigoriy was not convinced of Misha's guilt. Of course, Kaarina had heard of such things in the past: that somebody who was not quite right in the head might find glory in confessing to a crime he or she did not commit. And for some, even prison was a brighter option than living on the streets of Little Russia. And while Misha had a flat, Grigoriy's description of it was jarring. He spoke not of dirt, but of *filth*. Not just of cockroaches but of rats. Misha had no mattress and no furniture; to Grigoriy's eye, it appeared that Misha slept on a discarded suit, laid out on the floor as if someone had been wearing it and suddenly disappeared. Grigoriy told her of other things: small altars to death and decay, rodents preserved mid-rot, adorned with browning flower petals, and what looked like bloodstains on the walls but which Getz said was more likely wine and punch. Misha did not drink, Getz said, but he enjoyed the blood-red color of wine and he particularly liked bad smells. In one of his many monologues delivered in an attempt to fathom Misha's nature, Grigoriy spoke of how much the confessor thoroughly prized squalor. For this, the rats had run of the place. Even the dead ones. Flies occupied every corner and, Grigoriy said, when he first entered the flat and turned on the light, something larger than a greasy badger scurried out of sight, into what would've been called the bedroom had there been a bed. Neither he nor Getz ever saw the animal again.

Kaarina was upset her husband had spent any time at all in a place so described, but she also understood why he had done it. Where to find better closure than studying the actual details of the loss? Was Grigoriy expected to play cards? Drink and smoke with old friends? Host dinners with his daughter and remaining sons? What could possibly eclipse the fascination with exactly what happened between Misha and Mikhail?

Still, more than once, and after drinking in the cellar, Grigoriy had alluded to the possibility of a coming reveal. He mumbled about a "real" killer and whispered the words "old man" in his sleep.

Inspector Getz appeared bothered by Grigoriy's reluctance to accept Misha as the murderer. Yet, Grigoriy still spoke of Misha as if he were. Or, as if it were at least likely Misha was the culprit. Yet, the few times Kaarina saw the inspector in her husband's company, she felt a warmth, as if Getz had decided upon the exact correct profession; his fascinations were in tune with Grigoriy's, his passions just as bold. Yet, the man had no son in the story. So off they'd gone, a half dozen times, to the prison, to Misha's flat, to the street where Mikhail had been found, bled out. And with each return, Grigoriy would loosen his tie, remove his large suit coat, and sigh as he took a seat at the kitchen table. More than once Ekaterina met with Grigoriy in the cellar. Kaarina heard the muted thunder of the debates below.

Tonight, Barat and Annushka were coming over. Kaarina prepared for the meal and Grigoriy didn't speak much but she could see his words bubbling beneath his considerable jowls. She knew that, once the knock came at the door, Grigoriy's lips would part and Barat would be bombarded by all the same intel she herself had endured. But when the knock did come, and Grigoriy himself opened the door, it was an inebriated Barat who spoke first, deluging his parents with bizarre descriptions of seedy streets and places in the city Kaarina would never have imagined her son to visit.

"Can you believe these places exist?" Barat said, stumbling into the kitchen. "Door after door after door."

"Come eat," Kaarina said. "To soak up some of that wine."

Grigoriy took his son by the elbow. He nodded to Annushka and walked Barat farther back up the hall.

"Nothing about the old man," Grigoriy whispered to Barat. "They do not know of that possibility."

"Let's eat, Father."

They sat around the table and ate chicken and potatoes. Kaarina gave a nice big glass of water to her son.

"I've been back to the prison," Grigoriy told Barat.

"Yeah?" Barat said. "And did he confess again?"

"He did, indeed."

Barat sighed the way drunks do when suggesting the world has its way and there is no changing that way.

"Good for him," Barat said. "May he burn in hell. Or burn here on Earth first. I'd like to see that."

"Barat," Annushka said.

"He may do just that," Grigoriy said.

"And I suppose some other dedicated follower of filth will sniff the embers, sniff the ashes," Barat said.

Silence then as Barat forced chicken into his mouth while the others watched him. Why did it feel to Kaarina like Grigoriy and Barat were playacting? That they knew more than they said?

"Did you know, Mother, that there are streets in this city where people walk nude?"

"Barat," Annushka said.

"Oh, the *people* in such places!" Grigoriy said. He stood up the way he often did when speaking of a subject that so overpowered him he could not remain seated. "Old and young, rich and poor."

He eyed Barat in a way that confirmed for Kaarina an entire unspoken conversation between father and son.

Then: a knock at the door. All looked to the hall.

"I'll see to it," Kaarina said.

But Grigoriy was already barreling up the hall, speaking of Inspector Getz and new information.

He opened the door to reveal Pavel standing with his hands in his pockets, a serious look upon his face, the sober version of the drunk brother still seated at the kitchen table.

"Hello, Father," Pavel said. "I need to speak to Barat. And I need to do so alone. And I need to do so now."

# TEN

The brothers whispered in the cellar, their faces only inches apart. Grigoriy's steps could be heard outside. Kaarina's voice, pleading with him to let the brothers be, had quieted already.

"I found him," Pavel said.

"Oh?"

"He's a cruel man."

"Did he see you?"

"I made sure he did not."

Barat's features slowly sobered as Pavel's seemed to grow drunk with certainty.

"And you know where he lives?" Barat said.

"No."

"So we stand where you saw him."

"Yes. No more street parades, no more bars. We stand where I saw him. He spoke of an evening walk. A routine. We follow him home."

"Are you ready for this, brother?" Barat asked.

"Yes. And you?"

"Yes."

Pavel was the first to speak the word in this new context. It had power now: "A ghost."

Barat nodded immediately.

"Not death for him," he said.

"Not yet," Pavel said. "First: madness."

They held hands above the small wooden table.

"Ghost," Barat said.

"Haunt," Pavel said.

It was the first time their silent plan had been spoken so plainly.

And thus it was put into motion. Thus it began.

# ELEVEN

They stood by the river the next night, and for the two weeks following. They stood in the shadows, their backs to the stone walls. They listened for the clacking of a rich cane.

They did not turn at the sound of heels, young laughter, dogs, horses, carriage wheels, or debate.

The water lapped against the stone walls and the moon danced upon it. Always, these constant sights and sounds. The scrim for their waning patience.

"Perhaps he died," Barat said.

"Men like him don't die," Pavel said.

On the fourteenth night, with no sign of the old man, no "evening walk," the brothers entered a pub, an establishment neither had been to before. They ordered vodkas and sat in a booth and did not speak.

How to find the man in a city this size? And should they? What if Grigoriy's information was wrong? Surely a man such as the one Pavel witnessed had enemies, people who wanted to see him fail.

Was it possible Pavel and Barat were pawns in someone else's revenge?

The brothers drank.

"Remember, when we were children, when Mikhail asked to dye his hair a different color?" Barat asked.

The brothers almost never reminisced about Mikhail. It was akin to asking themselves if they remembered themselves.

"Of course," Pavel said. "That was when he wanted to separate himself from us."

"Well, he is separated now."

"But is he?"

The brothers rarely surprised each other with what they said or how they said it. It was difficult to make each other laugh or cry.

"I suppose it's still the three of us," Barat said.

"Always."

Two men argued at the bar. Punches were thrown. Neither man was removed. When they had tired each other out, they both rested against stools, breathing hard.

"We'll stand again tomorrow," Pavel said.

They rose and quietly exited the bar, subject to the stares of those they passed.

"Twins!" a woman cried. "Twins are good luck!"

"And triplets?" Barat asked. "Are they good luck too?"

But the woman's face went stony as she shook her head no.

The brothers exited the bar. Even though it was one of the nicer streets in Little Russia, the smells of horse droppings and alcohol dominated. Virile youth passed by the brothers. Even a set of twins, young girls, who eyed the grown brothers as if they were in on some kind of secret.

The brothers turned onto Tally Hall, a small street lined with shoe stores and an apothecary. They passed under a brick arch and came out alongside the river, on the other side from where they'd sat quiet for two weeks. They walked in tandem, and the bond Pavel and Barat felt was not a thing born of inspiration. It was born of being born as one, all at once, along with Mikhail, of having learned the rhythms of the world, their world, at exactly the same times and in exactly the same places. Barat did not ask after Pavel's son and Pavel did not ask after Barat's wife and neither spoke of their father, Grigoriy, and his amateur investigation nor their mother, Kaarina, and her keen sense of what truly mattered in all things.

They only walked.

And listened to the sounds of the water against the stones.

And heard the distant voices of the night.

And heard, embedded within the noises of Samhattan's Little Russia, the sound of a clacking cane, of rich jewels against ageless stone.

The brothers did not pause, did not change the pace of their steps. They looked left, across the river, and saw in the moonlight the silhouette of an old man with witch hair blown by the river wind, limping with the assistance of a bright, clacking cane.

"Out of my way," the man said to the very twin girls the brothers had passed not long before. "One of you is awful enough, but two of you makes me ill."

Pavel tugged gently on Barat's cuff, directing him to a row of hedges at the river's edge. From this cover they watched the man, draped in billowing robes, move in a manner neither had seen before.

"Does he touch the ground?" Barat whispered.

But it wasn't quite as if the man floated. It was more that he was moving through a world he utterly rejected.

Pavel and Barat came out from behind the bushes. They kept to the stone wall. The man had stepped out of sight.

The brothers listened for the clacking of the cane.

Barat led the way quietly toward the small cobblestone bridge at the head of Tally Hall, the only way across the dark blue, cold water. With some distance remaining, the brothers flattened themselves to the wall, draped in shadow, just as the old man was draped in many robes.

They heard the cane.

The cane was no doubt a Swarovski, a luxury stick, and the sound it made, its tip touching stone, was crystalline like rain upon glass. The man still unseen, the clacking seemed to go up stone steps, then back down again, until it sounded from all directions.

The old man could be anywhere.

The brothers listened. As people shouted from behind pub doors, as men and women ran fast up the streets, as old couples walked slowly and the fine heels of the rich clacked and the poor asked for alms. Threading through that cacophony, with its distinct, almost pleasurable clacking, came the sound of Swarovski and its unique beat that suggested no feet at all, as if the cane were only a tether to the earth, the stone, the street. As if a man in the shape of a balloon, buoyant, glided, the scraggles of his hair like weeds from the muck of the river. Both brothers caught a whiff of expensive cologne. Was it the old man's? Was the wind carrying the scent of him their way?

Zealous yet cautious of being seen, the brothers stepped from the shadows and to their side of the bridge. The sound of the crystal cane came from the far left, telling them the man had indeed passed the bridge on his end, which gave them the gumption to cross it, to go to his side, to go to him.

And so they did, bundled in their coats, faces down, keeping their features hidden. Halfway across, Pavel bumped into a woman and did not apologize, fearful of his own voice, it being like that of Mikhail's. Did this old man know Mikhail's voice? Was it possible? Was it tucked somewhere in his memory, his mind, to be plucked?

At the other side, both brothers turned in the opposite direction from which they'd last heard the cane. They did not speak of this. They moved in tandem. At the first sign of shadows, they flattened themselves once again to a wall, this time the side of a bicycle shop. As they hid, two men passed, eyeing them for hiding.

"And you two?" one of the men said. "You've got reason to be scarce?"

"Move on," Barat said with the rage of one whose brother had been slain.

"Or how about if I shout your whereabouts for the police to come find ye?" the same man said.

"Move on," Pavel said with the cold, hollow tenor of one whose brother had been slain.

The men moved on. The brothers, still in shadow, looked right, looked left, listening for the walking stick.

"There," Barat said.

On the other side of the river, one thick hand upon the rail, the old man leaned. Cloaked in night, moonlight dripped upon the man's bulbous features as his tongue slid over his lips and touched the tip of his nose, as if he were eyeing the river for fish, for garbage, for a drowned body to eat.

"We could kill him right now," Barat whispered.

But both knew this wasn't the plan. Yet, it was true. They could. Readily. Here, an old man with a cane, vulnerable to all varieties of American justice, even those found in Little Russia.

"Careful," Pavel said.

The old man lifted his gaze, seemed to look their way. At the same time, he appeared to look at nothing at all.

He spit into the river and the saliva hung long from the tip of his tongue. His round, milky eyes seemed fixed on the shadows where Pavel and Barat hid, as if he knew the shadows by name. Then the old man smiled and without speaking seemed to say: *No shadows can hide you if I can see in the dark.*

He slurped the remaining saliva, ran wrinkled, ringed fingers through his long, grassy hair. The moon shone off the top of his skull, which was the color of a rotting peach.

Pavel and Barat did not move.

The old man released the rail, turned, and the clacking started anew. He limped farther from the brothers, out of sight, into fresh shadows of buildings and bushes, vanished, swallowed by darkness; willingly he went.

The brothers quietly crossed the bridge with more urgency now, less afraid, more desirous of holding on to their catch. On the other side again, they tracked him. Far enough behind so as not to see him, and not to be seen, but close enough to follow the call of the cane. Passing men and women, late-night people, strays, dogs and chickens, one of those chickens dead, its chest caved in perhaps by the tip of a Swarovski.

The brothers moved steadily, their plan formulating with each step, their will galvanizing without speaking, the way they would treat this man, what they would do to him in lieu of death, too sudden, too soon, if indeed he killed Mikhail.

Over arches, under walkways, through Samhattan Park, where still the cane could be heard but the man not seen. How much longer would the man walk? How much longer could he, with the odd way he moved? Pavel and Barat followed, silent, smooth, until the tip of the cane touched the finer stones of a finer street, and the brothers knew themselves to be in the neighborhood of Hemkin, the jewel of Little Russia. They did not acknowledge this; Grigoriy had told them the man was wealthy. Ahead, dim lampposts without bushes, the moon uncluttered by the spires of new churches, an open black sky under which the old man strolled.

Under a lamp, a detail: the hem of his robes were stained burnt sienna with the filth he had stepped through this night and likely many others.

The color of blood.

The brothers followed, walking the center of the road, less gravel there for silence, both fixed to the lurid man who arrived at what must be his home.

Number 33 Vasiliev Court, where the front door was made of finer wood than the brothers had ever touched.

Here, two homes back, Pavel and Barat stopped. Fueled by a sense of potential justice beyond what they'd previously known, they watched as the old man huffed his way up stone steps, clasping the marble railing, the regal cane rendered momentarily useless.

And so the clacking went quiet.

The old man did not look back. He looked up, once, to the moon, at which he scoffed, a hate-filled spate of laughter that ascended into the black sky, making a shadow of its own, momentarily blotting the moon, it seemed, so that as he entered his home he went unseen by the brothers.

One moment the old man was there. The next he was not.

The brothers turned as one and began the long walk back, toward home, where their wives and their mother and their father and their sister were not waiting but continued with the lives they, Pavel and Barat, had taken leave of.

All but Mikhail.

Mikhail continued nothing. And it was possible the brothers had just found the man who manifested this brutal, grisly truth.

And paramount:

"We've found our setting," Barat said, quiet still. "Our theater, our stage."

And together the brothers said:

"His home."

# TWELVE

"His name is Egorov," Barat said, the brothers sitting in a café on Eighth. "He's more than rich. I don't know how, and I don't care to know."

"It could matter."

"How so?"

"You know how so. The more we know about him, the better."

"But first we need to make sure. Above all else."

"Of course."

"And we won't be sure until we're inside his home."

"You sound like Mikhail."

"Good. And you need to sound more like him yet."

"True."

"So we'll find out how he came by his money."

"Yes."

"And his age."

"He walks with a cane. Moves like a snail."

"But there was some power in him nevertheless."

"Hatred."

"Perhaps."

The brothers sipped their coffees.

Pavel pulled a sheet of paper from his pocket and unfolded it on the table. A cursory rendering of the large home they'd seen in the moonlight, down to the gate the old man, Egorov, passed through on his way to his stone steps and front door.

"That many windows?" Barat asked.

"We'll verify tonight."

They sipped. They studied the drawing.

"A lot of ways in," Barat said.

"Yes."

"Now to get haircuts."

Pavel unfolded a second sheet of paper. This one showed their slain brother as he was in the street. But it wasn't the blood or the death that Pavel had attempted to capture, it was the wardrobe and style of Mikhail's hair the day he was murdered. The only day they could be sure the old man, Egorov, had seen him.

Barat nodded.

They knew the shirt and pants. They knew the shoes. Both had bags beside them in the café with the same clothes already purchased.

"Are we overlooking anything?" Pavel asked.

They studied the drawings for many minutes.

Then, without speaking, the brothers got up. Pavel folded the papers and pocketed them. They took hold of their bags and left the café, on their way then to get haircuts, to look even more like their identical, slain third.

# THIRTEEN

At dinner, Pavel ate quietly. Alexander studied his father and Vada knew something was afoot. Whatever Pavel was doing, he'd gone deeper into it.

"You got a haircut," she said.

When he looked to her, it wasn't Pavel. It was Mikhail. Sitting at the table. And it wasn't only the hair. It was the set of the jaw. The slight flare of the nostrils. The cheeks that were sucked in a little bit more than Pavel's ever were. It was the slight pout. The wider eyes. The erect shoulders and the slightest tilt of the head.

"I did," Pavel said.

Vada almost asked, *And so did Barat?* But she wasn't sure why this question crossed her mind.

"Pavel, please."

"Not now," he said.

"But are you setting to do something dangerous?"

"Not now."

# FOURTEEN

The brothers stood outside Old Man Egorov's house at night. It was dark and the wind swished the few trees between the finer homes and grounds. Above them, the moon was nearly full. Through the glass of the first-floor window they saw an empty library. No books on the shelves of this library. Rather: glass jars, the contents of which neither Pavel nor Barat could discern. The door to this room was closed, affording them no deeper view into the house. Despite there being many windows, this was the only in which the drapes did not obscure the view.

The brothers studied. They wore the same plaid yellow short-sleeved shirts, blue pants, and black dress shoes. Their hair was cut the same, by the same person. Their faces were partially reflected in the glass as a small lamp burned in the library, and it looked to them like they were both Mikhail's ghost, come for vengeance.

When Barat spoke, he used his slain brother's cadence. "This one then."

But there was no need to speak. Pavel knew as well as he did this was the window they would enter. This was the way they would take the stage.

The brothers stepped to the glass together, crushing what might have been, in different hands, a garden, but was here, by Egorov, only weeds. At the window, a bit more of the room was revealed. A desk with a leather blotter. A vat for ink. No books. No papers. Only jars.

And a knife.

Barat tested the window first. He placed his palm, slowly, making certain all five fingers were equally flat to the surface before attempting to lift it open.

But Pavel tugged on Barat's identical shirt. He pointed to his ear.

The brothers stepped from the window, quietly back over the weeds, out onto the lawn again.

Pavel raised a finger, silently telling his brother to wait.

To listen.

A voice from inside the house. The cadence they'd heard by the river.

Pavel led the way around the house, to the side, where a stone path remained uncluttered by weeds, but where roots reached for the steps as if attempting to touch the brothers, to stop them from doing what they set out to do.

They stood before a side door, the door's single window blanketed by a purple cloth visible in the thick moonlight. They waited. For light. For movement. For sound. To track the old man through his home.

They heard no more of his disagreeable tones, his cruel intonation.

Barat signaled for Pavel to follow him back to the library. There he placed his hand to the glass again. Pavel joined this time. Together they pushed the window open.

The hinges squeaked almost imperceptibly, but still: noise.

A stuffiness from within escaped immediately. As if the old man hadn't opened a window for a year, perhaps two. It felt to both brothers as if something physical had exited the library, an unseen presence, something escaped, something let out.

Pavel lowered himself to one knee and knitted his hands together. Barat stepped onto his brother's palms.

Pavel lifted and Barat pulled himself up by the ledge and, hushed, crouched like a cat in the frame. He waited. He listened. Then he entered the room. Inside, he took his brother's two hands. Pavel put his shoes to the bricks as Barat pulled.

The two brothers stood inside Egorov's library, dressed the same as their third.

Barat lifted the knife. They inspected it for the blood of their brother.

A rat darted along the base of the window wall and both brothers remained icon-still.

"Eh?" The old man's voice came from beyond the closed door. Sudden. Close. "Rats in there?"

The brothers did not speak. They did not move.

The old man's voice only the width of one door away.

"Go to sleep, rats. And die in slumber. I will not share my house."

The wind flowed beyond the library's still-open glass.

"Or maybe you're not rats at all," the old man said. "Maybe you are the thoughts rattling my head."

He laughed and his laughter was a knife, unclean.

"Maybe you are memories in there, hmm? Memories of my deeds. If so, begone! Sleep! Kill thyselves with the knife upon my desk."

The Swarovski then, the clacking of the cane upon a wood floor. The sliding of the man's bare feet.

The brothers waited long. The silence of the room, the house, swelled. No sound confirmed the man had gone any farther from the door than the few steps they'd heard him go.

Barat moved to the window first, climbing to the ledge carefully. He lowered himself to the weeds below and stood ready for Pavel.

Pavel stepped to the window.

Behind him, the doorknob rattled.

"Are you my thoughts in there?" Egorov said, the door still closed. "If you are, begone! I have many thoughts and I need all rooms to think them!"

Pavel remained still, staring into the eyes of his brother. They did not speak, they did not move, they did not suggest anything but silence and stillness as the voice came again from the other side of the door.

"Memories or mice, memories or mice? You will find no crumbs in this house. You will find no bread at all!"

The knob rattled again, and Pavel made for the ledge. On it, he paused.

"Memories or mice, memories or mice . . ."

Pavel lowered himself to Barat's waiting arms. Once together, the brothers did not hesitate to close the window and step back from the house.

Without speaking, they went to the gate they'd entered by, and went out onto the street, just as, in the distance, both believed they heard the sound of an old door opening, a door that hadn't been opened in perhaps a year or two, the creaking hinges of a room never used, where even a knife lay long enough to have rusted.

## FIFTEEN

The brothers visited a man who claimed not to be a locksmith but boasted of "assisting people who lock themselves out of their homes." His "shop" in Little Russia sold items by which to break into other people's homes.

"You need to get through windows?" Fedorov said. "Why not just pick some rocks from the nearest garden?"

The brothers did not laugh at the joke.

"We'd like to hear into the house," Barat said.

Fedorov raised an eyebrow. "But what would you listen for in your own home?"

When neither Barat nor Pavel responded, the man burst into sudden bright laughter. He slapped a hand on Barat's shoulder.

"So serious, you two," Fedorov said, a strand of his slick blond hair falling from the top of his head, tickling the tip of his nose. "But are you wealthy?"

"We can afford what we came for," Pavel said.

"But you cannot afford the items you wish to have by way of my equipment?"

Pavel and Barat turned to leave the shop.

"No! I jest! I'm alone all day in this crowded hole. You think a few jokes are impractical? Imagine no audience at all."

The brothers stopped at the door.

"We're here to buy certain items," Barat said. "Then be on our way."

"Yes, yes. I realize now how serious you are! Come in. Again. Let's begin anew. I am Fedorov. I have the goods you seek. You are interested in the enhancement of sound . . . come, come."

Fedorov led them deeper into the shop, shallow as it was. The tools on the shelves made little sense to them. But some motivations were clear. Crowbars and thin cards. Gloves and padding for the shoes.

Pavel studied the slippers.

"Here, come," Fedorov said. "But get those slippers too. You want to hear them, but you do not want them to hear you!"

He laughed, not as heartily, and brought the brothers to the back wall. He raised a glass.

"Cheers, no? Nothing more than a drink, no? But indeed, here, always more! Let's test the device. You"—he pointed to Barat—"you go on the other side of that door." He pointed to an office door. Barat opened the door to find a stinking blackened toilet. "Never mind the mess!" Fedorov said. "Just go inside and close the door. It's not the nose we're worried about here. It's the noise."

Barat stepped into the room and closed the door. Fedorov handed Pavel the glass. "Now, place it to the wood like so."

He showed Pavel the trick, but Pavel had seen tricks like this before.

"I can tell you are not impressed," Fedorov said. "But this glass is especially designed to enhance the sound through a door."

Pavel placed the glass against the door and placed his ear to the glass.

"No," Fedorov said. "You do not need to put your ear against it. Only . . . listen."

Pavel listened. There was no sound.

"You need to whisper there in the washroom!" Fedorov called to Barat. "Whisper your deepest secrets!"

He winked at Pavel, smiling.

Then, a whisper through the glass. The voice of Barat. Pavel took the glass from the wood and was unable to hear his brother anymore.

Pavel nodded.

"Very good," Fedorov said.

Barat exited the washroom.

"Now," Fedorov said, "for sight!"

He walked the brothers deeper yet into the shop. And so went the next hour as the brothers' imaginations, and their thirst for revenge, grew with every item they were shown.

# SIXTEEN

The brothers walked the cobblestones at midnight, listening for the clear clacking of the Swarovski.

They finally heard the cane at quarter past, as the moon appeared bloated above them. They didn't need to see the man to know he was there. And this time they didn't wait for Egorov to limp home.

This time they went there first.

Using the tools from Fedorov, they easily entered the front door. Inside against the foyer wall they discovered a half dozen paintings and a coatrack strewn with loose threads from the old man's many robes.

Without lighting any lanterns, so as to be sure not to be seen from the street, the brothers went deeper into the house, dimensions they could no longer see once the front door was closed.

The windows were still draped, intentionally, as if Egorov were in hiding day and night. No lanterns burned. No scents of recently cooked food wafted throughout. The brothers were unable to name the rooms they found themselves in, unable to see any of the items inside. Pavel felt the corner of a table, Barat the side of a cabinet made of glass. Together they continued without speaking, determining the best places from which to begin.

They hurried through the house, often feeling lost, without voicing this concern, without needing to, as they bumped into things in the dark. More than once Barat knocked his shin against something hard, something steel, something wood. Pavel knocked his shoulders against low shelves, and more than once they found themselves in rooms in which the furniture was draped in heavy cloth. All this: getting to know their stage.

They counted eleven rooms on the first floor alone.

Barat found a secret passage, secret stairs. He discovered it without meaning to, as he felt along the wall, searching for places to hide. His elbow connected with the wood; enough to send hinges creaking, enough to allow a draft to come their way. The brothers covered their mouths as the cold, smelly air accosted them and both thought of the man Egorov breathing.

Up the stairs they went, spiraling, gripping the railing as the staircase groaned. At the top, a door.

Pavel lifted the Fedorov glass to the wood.

The brothers waited.

It was possible, of course, Egorov had come home without them knowing. The house was big enough, the darkness complete.

Pavel listened for the same canned sound he'd heard in Federov's shop. But here, searching for an old man wheezing. An old man snoring. An old man waiting on the other side of the door with a knife, possibly the same knife he'd used to murder their third.

Together they opened the door.

They were greeted with deeper darkness, no evidence of where they stood. Yet . . . signs, unseen, smells, the scent of sleep and old age, dirty blankets and pillows, drapes and old clothes, linen that had not been properly washed.

The brothers did not have to speak to tell each other they believed this was the master bedroom of Old Man Egorov.

Barat knelt in the dark, feeling for space and spaces to hide. Pavel went to the walls, searching for mirrors. Barat found the bed first and slid under, discovering there enough room for himself and Pavel to lie side by side.

Meeting again in the center of the room, the brothers stood silent for many seconds, listening for the crystal clacking of the Swarovski anywhere else in the house. Hearing none, they exited by the room's proper door and, if not for the railing, would have fallen down many steps, perhaps to their broken-necked ruin, below.

Still upstairs, they discovered six other rooms of similar size to that of the old man's master bedroom. None of these were furnished. They found no books. No clothes. No evidence that anyone other than the old man had ever called this house home.

At the head of the stairs, Pavel tugged on Barat's shirt. Barat knew what they had forgotten before Pavel spoke it and so the brothers traced their steps back through the dark, around the oval railing, feeling for doors, counting rooms, until they reached the master bedroom once more. Inside, they moved quicker for now knowing the space, and reached the door in the wall, the one they had opened and passed through, the one they had forgotten to close.

Below them, another door opened and closed. And the familiar clacking of the Swarovski resounded through the otherwise empty, un-insulated house.

Pavel and Barat stepped fully into the passage and closed the door softly behind them.

"Warm me bones, warm me bones," Egorov said, his voice familiar to them now, even through layers of stuffiness and wood.

Pavel and Barat breathed steady, quiet.

The cane did not sound for many minutes as the old man seemed to have stopped below, somewhere on the first floor, perhaps standing by the library door again, listening for rats within.

Then the clacking sounded again, the tip of the cane's call as unique as the nose upon its bearer's face.

Pavel and Barat did not cringe at the sound of a crash below, as if Egorov had swiped items from a shelf in search of something else.

"Where are you, eh?"

Knife laughter, followed by a string of shrill syllables, words impossible to make out from where the brothers hid.

Pavel closed his eyes. He thought of Mikhail, drunk in the cellar of their childhood home, as both Mikhail and Grigoriy rose to standing and challenged each other to a staring contest. Pavel recalled the look in Mikhail's eyes as his brother twisted his face into an expression both empty and full, as if Mikhail had been practicing the *Mona Lisa*, able to fool their father into thinking he was about to break character when in truth he was not. Mikhail was good for many things, but none so much as a good time. When Pavel opened his eyes again, he saw only the darkness of the hidden passage, the details of his slain brother, so vivid moments ago, now swallowed by the black of Egorov's home.

"*Me first*," he whispered, his lips to his brother's ear.

He turned and stepped through the door in the bedroom wall. Below, the clacking of the cane continued. But now Pavel, in the master bedroom, saw light. Light from the first floor, from a lantern, the item the old man had been looking for as he'd carelessly swiped other objects to the floor in whatever unknown dark room he'd been in below.

Pavel held his breath, opened his ears, and mimicked, as best he could, an exact facial expression he'd seen upon Mikhail one serious evening in the cellar at home.

The Swarovski reached the foot of the stairs a step before the muttering that followed it.

"They deserve it, they do, whatever they get they deserve . . ."

Pavel crossed the room, to the drapes cloaking the room's large windows. There he stood, partially hidden but just visible enough to show the shirt he wore, the pants, the shoes, the haircut, and the expression on his face.

It was not easy, even for someone who had spent so much time being mistaken for two other men, to play the role entirely. For Pavel, like Barat and Mikhail, had spent his entire life attempting to delineate between himself and the two men with whom he escaped Kaarina's womb twenty-four years ago. So much time spent pondering the differences between himself and his brothers, often acting against communal character in the name of claiming his own. But now, here, by the drapes, as the Swarovski clacked steadily up the steps, Pavel held fast to the power of being one with his two brothers. He recalled moments: walking the streets of Little Russia, he and Barat flanking Mikhail, the three of them a spectacle of nature; the spirit and life of three in one, so that the third was the same as the second the same as the first, all three: one, in heart, in soul, and most meaningfully, now, in appearance.

The Swarovski reached the top of the stairs, the light expanded, and the railing creaked as the old man used it as a second brace, to pull himself up the final step to the second floor. Pavel saw him now, saw his enormous, unfocused eyes; his nose; his tongue as it lapped the thick lines that were his mouth; the doorway to that dark throat from which the meanness within poured forth. Even now:

"Oh, the poor may die of hunger if asking what they want of me!"

As the flame in the lantern moved, his visage wavered, too, so that Pavel saw many expressions upon the face of the man walking the final hall to his master suite, including one that had the appearance of looking Pavel right in the eye, if only for a breath, before the large black pupils looked back to the wood floor upon which he moved.

Pavel stood, half cloaked in drape, as the old man entered the bedroom, moving shadows creating a hole in the top of his head.

"Death becoming, death bemoaning . . . What?"

Egorov's muttering ceased as he lifted his face, his eyes upon Pavel at the window.

"Christ, impossible," Egorov said. He brought a hand to his head, as if staving off madness, and Pavel knew then that Grigoriy's informant had been right. "Christ, not right, *not true!*"

Egorov turned then, to swipe the vision from his eyes, to run the sight from his head. And when he looked back, Pavel was no longer by the drapes; the ghost of the dead man was gone.

Egorov stormed across his bedroom, lantern held high. He swung the drapes wide, spilling moonlight like sour milk across the floor, across his robes and face.

Wide-eyed, Egorov looked through the glass, then spun to face his bedroom, searching for what he'd seen.

"Not true!" he echoed himself.

He brought his hand to his head again, as though attempting to block something much deeper than fancy, than whim.

Through the glass Pavel held on the other side of the secret door, Pavel and Barat heard the old man groan. They heard him moan, the sound an elongated thing, as though he were not sure he had been triumphant in pulling out the weeds, protecting himself from the roots of insanity before they could find space to thrive.

"Impossible . . ." he said once more.

Pavel put his lips to his brother's ear and whispered: "*He knew me.*"

And Barat said: "*For Mikhail. We have begun.*"

# SEVENTEEN

Misha was sentenced to death the next day. Inspector Getz received much praise throughout Little Russia for having apprehended Mikhail's murderer so quickly. Grigoriy asked Getz that no mention be made of the victim having been a triplet, at the behest of the two remaining brothers. Getz told Grigoriy of course he would respect the request, but he was curious: why? It seemed to him the brothers might enjoy the vindication. News like this, morbid as it was, could potentially help them down the road. Pavel and Barat were victims, too, after all, and there was no shortage of businesses that might hire them out of genuine sympathy. Grigoriy said he understood, of course, but who could know the bond of triplets? Not even the parents, Grigoriy said, not even them.

And: Grigoriy needed to speak to his sons. He was the one who tipped them off to the existence of the old, rich man who was, Grigoriy still considered, possibly the murderer, and he didn't want to feel responsible for the death of Misha, no matter how macabre the man had been.

*Do you think Misha capable of murder?* Grigoriy asked himself, dressing in front of the mirror, preparing for a dinner with the entire family. Kaarina was downstairs already, preparing. Ekaterina would be there soon. And the brothers and their wives and little Alexander would not be far behind. *Because if you do not, then you must do something! And even if you do, you must do something! And quickly.*

Because they had to be sure. *He* had to be sure.

And did his sons know any more now than he did?

Grigoriy did not like feeling this way. He did not like feeling any way that wasn't confident and at ease. Trouble troubled him greatly. It was the same reason he didn't enjoy traveling by ship; the unsteadiness fished its way into his mind and soul, and every time he was on a boat he found himself doubting all his life's decisions.

Now, eyeing himself in the glass, he saw not a rotund and powerful father but rather a middle-aged liar whose lies had added shiftiness to his eyes. He needed answers.

What to do about the man named Misha? For, surely, if Misha were innocent of the crime, the real killer would find himself at ease, hearing this news, and would therefore be most vulnerable *right now.* Surely Pavel and Barat would tell Getz the truth about who killed Mikhail if they discovered it was not Misha. Right? So how much time did they have? And should Grigoriy stay out of this so that, whatever the outcome, his guilt for having been involved might remain at a minimum?

He buttoned his top button and then undid it. Felt like a noose. Like the kind of thing Misha was going to feel if somebody didn't speak up and say hey it wasn't him, hey he may love the dark, he may worship crime, he may even want to die, but we can't be the ones to grant that request.

Can we?

Grigoriy left it unbuttoned and put on his vest. Felt too tight. Like a straitjacket. Like the kind of thing Misha might have to wear if he were transported from the stone cell to the gallows. Public hangings still went on in Little Russia, right under the American nose.

Grigoriy removed the vest. He put on his coat. Felt too formal. He looked a bit like the priest come to deliver the last rites to the sentenced man. He instinctively adjusted his features to look something like Pastor Sokolov, who had presided over the burial of Grigoriy's own son, Mikhail, one of three, now two, slain and left to bleed out in the gutter of a filthy street, killed yes, but maybe *not by this man*!

Grigoriy removed the jacket.

He bent at the waist and panted as he lifted his shoes. He carried them to the bed, sat down, and put them on. All a struggle. Still, they felt right. Felt like the correct footwear, no matter who was guilty and who was not.

Downstairs, Ekaterina had arrived. He could hear his wife and his daughter talking and he suddenly wished he'd had no sons. He remembered well the day in the hospital when Kaarina gave birth, how Barat slid out first, or maybe it was Mikhail, or possibly even Pavel. Grigoriy thought she was done. Why are you still screaming, dear? You've already had the child!

But then . . . twins! What an incredible day, and now nothing would ever be the same! Two sons in one morning, an hour ago, none! He would name them Mikhail and Pavel and they would become best friends! They would tease their sister mercilessly and they would team up to become Little Russia's greatest athletic duo! No . . . all of Samhattan!

But Kaarina's screams did not falter once the second son (Barat this time? Mikhail?) slid out and into the doctor's waiting hands. The doctor handed Grigoriy the second son. A nurse held the first.

*There is another,* the doctor said. And he turned to Grigoriy, his eyes wide enough to declare this rarity an occult surprise, as if twins might be predicted but a third could be nothing but the shadow of the first two, the space between the first two, a ghost in the womb, crawling out the passage, following the initial pair, prepared to haunt them.

Grigoriy remembered being a little frightened of the third. Or was he frightened of raising three sons? The money involved, the attention, the energy? And the fact that three was one more than two and two was already a lot to keep safe.

To keep safe from men like Misha.

Right?

Grigoriy stood before the mirror, his wife and daughter debating, preparing a family dinner, below.

Oh, he needed to talk to his boys, one of whom might be the ghost who followed the other two out of the womb. The unexpected third. Did he feel it that day in the hospital? As the third (whichever one it was) began its slippery, slow crawl from Kaarina, did Grigoriy *sense* something brooding, something building, something overblown?

"Grigoriy! The boys are here!"

Kaarina from downstairs.

*The boys are here! THE BOYS ARE HERE AND WE DON'T KNOW WHO THE MURDERER WAS AND NOW EVERY-THING IS HEADING TOWARD A BAD END!*

Grigoriy smiled in the glass. He had to. He couldn't stand this negative thinking. It wasn't his way. His way was to pour vodka shots, to make jokes, to perform for his sons and his daughter, to make them laugh. His role in this life was to add, not subtract.

Just as he'd added to—no, propelled—the actions his sons had no doubt begun undertaking already.

What would they do? Would they kill the old, rich man? And

if so, would they need Misha to hang so that nobody ever went looking for the old, rich man?

"Coming!" he called, still smiling in the glass. If he didn't know better, he'd say he looked happy. Happy as the day Kaarina gave birth to a litter of sons.

He left the bedroom then and reached the middle of the stairs as Ekaterina opened the front door for Mikhail.

No, not Mikhail. For Pavel. Or was it Barat? It was both, the two surviving brothers, crossing the threshold, entering the family home, but both looking alarmingly like their slain third.

Grigoriy paused. Did they do so purposefully? Was this an homage?

The second of the two carried a small child. Alexander. Grigoriy's grandson. So that must be Pavel and Barat must have been first, deeper into the house now, the brothers like a nightmare now, growing, replicating, filling the house.

Grigoriy needed to talk to them. But first, Vada, at the threshold, looking up the steps, her partial smile frozen, it seemed, as she had noticed the odd look on her father-in-law's face. Did she suspect something of her husband? Grigoriy thought maybe she did. And if she was suspecting, this meant even she did not know the plans of his sons. If they did discover that the old man did it, would they take him to the authorities like Grigoriy asked?

Or did they now walk the first floor of the home in which they were raised, the blood of the murderer beneath their fingernails?

"Grigoriy," Vada said, nodding. But it felt more like she was asking.

*Grigoriy? What should we do? Mikhail is dead and the balance has been disrupted. What should we, the remaining family, do?*

"Potatoes," Ekaterina said, beaming. She was very proud of the way she made potatoes. Rosemary and thyme. Garlic and sea salt.

Behind Vada, Annushka came. Grigoriy studied her face for

traces of concern. Did she know more than Vada? Barat had looser lips than Pavel.

Annushka didn't look up, and Grigoriy was grateful for that and the gratitude delivered him a small slice of calm. Maybe he was seeing things in people's faces. Maybe he was making things up. Maybe the blood-sniffer Misha deserved to die.

Grigoriy descended the remainder of the stairs.

Pavel exited the washroom just as Grigoriy took the hall to the kitchen. Grigoriy reached for the sleeve of his shirt. He would pull his son back to the foyer and demand he be told what the plan was, and exactly how culpable Grigoriy himself was if, as the case was, the brothers had already eschewed their father's wishes and murdered the man instead of bringing him to Getz.

But his son stepped into the kitchen just out of reach, and Grigoriy's fingertips brushed the sleeve, leaving his hand open for the drink Ekaterina handed to him with a smile.

"Come, Father," his daughter said. "Time to eat."

And beyond her, the family seated at the small kitchen table. Barat and Annushka. Pavel, Vada, and Alexander. Ekaterina quickly joined them, taking the penultimate empty chair. And Grigoriy, eyeing his family, thought:

*Mikhail was the third born, the ghost from the womb, the one born to haunt.*

And his magnificent wife, Kaarina, smiled his way, a fragment of happiness, despite having lost a son. Two remained! Here, in this house, identical sons, seated across the table, and Kaarina's expression silently said that, despite the questions of the cosmos, despite the planets hugging the sun for fear of abandonment, for fear of being sent alone into cold, endless outer space, sitting down to dinner with family still mattered.

# EIGHTEEN

Egorov was home.

The brothers saw the light traveling from room to room as they slid soundlessly through the gate.

They wore the same clothes they'd worn the night before, the same clothes they would wear every time they entered this home.

"The next time he goes upstairs," Barat said, "we go in through the bay window."

Pavel did not respond and in not doing so assented.

But Old Man Egorov took time moving about the rooms on the first floor. And the brothers stood near enough the kitchen windows to see the man slurping raw tuna alone at a large table. The lantern flame waved, creating movement in the black of the man's eyes so that, at times, he looked like he had the eyes of a goat, an abomination seated at the table, slurping fish not from a can but from a river brown with mud.

The man muttered to himself and ran his wrinkled fingers through his hair when he needed to dry them off. His robes sat like folds of fat about him and the Swarovski, ever present, had been laid upon its own chair, as if Egorov had one friend and one friend alone.

At length, he rose. He took the Swarovski and the lantern and left the remaining fish on the table. The kitchen was inhaled by darkness as the light entered the main hall of the first floor. Through the Fedorov glass, the brothers heard the old man muttering. He spoke of the poor, of the ugly, of the stupid, of the damned. He spoke of himself as a cat surrounded by rats, a world of mice and rats. And he spoke, too, of cardinals he'd seen earlier out his window.

"Red birds or blood? Red birds or blood?"

The light migrated up the steps at last, a small fire in an old, empty stable. And the horses that neighed here were the creaking boards and the clacking of that cane, so clear through the Fedorov glass.

The brothers made to move to the side of the house at the same time. Pavel reached the window first and took a special wrench to the hinges. He unfastened them quickly.

The brothers climbed through the open pane and replaced it quietly behind them. They'd felt a pianoforte in this room before and Barat walked to it now. As he did, Pavel got as far from the doorjamb as he could. There he crouched behind a chair draped in canvas cloth.

Barat pulled the cloth back from the keyboard. He looked up to the ceiling and heard the subtle creak of the old man leaning on his cane.

Then he flattened his fingers to the keys.

"Eh?"

Egorov, upstairs. Alarmed.

The creaking became a thunder as the old man barreled his way to the head of the stairs.

"Thieves!"

Barat stepped to the center of the room, kept his arms at his sides, and recalled Mikhail as best he could. He thought of his brother the way he looked as he read. The flat expression of one engrossed.

Heavy thuds on the steps. Egorov had kicked something over.

"Thieves of me!" he cried.

The light was visible now in the music room, if any room in this home could be so named.

Barat saw the man's face, surrounded by darkness, his hair long earthworms dangling from his rotting scalp. Fish guts remained on his lips. He lapped them up as he moved.

But Egorov stopped before he reached the doorway.

"Christ," he said. "Not true!"

Barat did not move. He stood in the scant light, the ghost of his fallen brother, felled by the very beast in the hall. Egorov came forth.

"Does a ghost scatter like a rat?" His lips folded down in a scowl, his nostrils flared, almost as wide as his eyes. The Swarovski clacked into the room, its echo amplified by the near emptiness.

He held Barat's gaze, the gaze of the man he had left on a lampless street, left to leak blood in the gutter.

"Scatter, rat! *Scatter!*"

Barat held his ground, his expression unchanging. The brothers had long mastered silent communication; perhaps as far back as the womb. And now, here, his features flickering in Egorov's flame, Barat spoke to the man without words, his eyes telling the story, telling the old man that vengeance was upon him. Barat spoke without speaking: death would not come quickly, as the hatemonger slept; it would not come by way of a slick slit across the wrinkled thing's throat.

And whatever was coming for Egorov needed no cane.

"*Scatter!*" Egorov shouted.

Barat raised an open palm. In the far darkness of the room, Pavel knocked on the wall.

Egorov turned quickly, eyes bulging. "Guilt like rats in the sewers of my veins. *You will not have it!*"

He rushed from the room, too fast for his weakened body, and fell upon the threshold, fell to the hall floor. He moved quickly, though, to look over his shoulder, to see Pavel—no, Mikhail!— standing in that threshold, only partially visible in the light from the lantern beside him.

Egorov rolled to his back and pushed himself toward the foot of the stairs.

Pavel approached.

Egorov breathed heavily, labored, shaking his face *no*.

"Dormouse or deed, dormouse or deed. Scurrying about my home. What have I done worse than anyone? Yet they come, they need, they feed off my crumbs. Dormouse or deed, dormouse or deed. You do not scatter!"

He lifted an arm to shield what might come.

When nothing did, he lowered it again.

"Eh?"

Nobody in the hall. Nobody at the threshold of the music room.

He pulled himself forward and crawled wormlike back to the lantern that had fallen with him. The light in hand again, he got to his knees. The robes bunched like rolls of snakes on the hardwood floor.

"Eh? Dormouse? Eh?"

He raised the light higher and saw no shape, no silhouette, no specter.

He placed a hand on the ground, on what felt like the cold leg of a ghost.

Egorov recoiled, then saw it was no leg but the Swarovski, his only friend, unrecognizable in the state he was in.

Breathing too hard, he lifted the cane and used it again to stand.

"Scattered," he said. And he listened for movement from within his home.

Egorov remained that way, standing, silent, his eyes darting about the entrance of the music room, long enough for the sun to begin to show through the drapes over the windows.

Then he took the stairs, stopping at each to listen.

Up, this way, he went. And by the time he reached the top, the sun was high enough that he no longer needed the lantern.

But still, he held it tight.

And he listened.

And at the top of the steps, looking down to the first floor, he said: "Scattered. Scared of me. Scattered scared."

But still, he listened.

Then he blew out the flame and entered his bedroom and sat upon the edge of his bed.

But he did not lie down. He did not sleep.

He sat in the dim suite, tapping the tip of the cane to the rhythm of his beating heart, and he listened.

"Deed," he said. "No dormouse, but deed. Well, come for me, deed. Come. For I will commit another in your honor. I will commit again! Eh? Hide in the house, come out to play. But play nice! Ha. I will kill you twice. I will kill your ghost."

# NINETEEN

"You're not getting enough sleep," Annushka said. It was rare for her to advise anyone, even her husband, Barat. Part of their dynamic was the party, the endless flow of energy, the permission, each to each, to sleep as little or as much as they desired.

"I'm not tired," Barat said. He yawned.

Annushka hadn't gotten over the fact her husband looked so much like his deceased brother these days (the haircut, the posture, the way he sat), let alone the idea he was possibly drinking himself to death in grief. Or was it something else that occupied her husband's evenings?

"You look like you're sleeping as we speak," she said. "And it's no good to fool yourself about it. Rest and water, you know as well as I do."

It was their private mantra. Anything, they said, could be fixed with rest and water. And so everything, thus far, had been.

"Barat," Annushka said, crossing the room and wrapping her

arms around his waist. "Where are you going these late nights? You don't smell of booze when you return."

"I don't?"

The truth was, Pavel and Barat carried with them a pint, for sipping twice before entering their respective homes.

"Not entirely," Annushka said. "I know the way you smell, and the sparkle in your eye, when you've really done it right."

"We're not looking to do it up," Barat said. "We're just . . ."

Annushka imagined many ways for his sentence to end but was surprised with the way he ended it.

"We're only happy to have one another."

"I understand," she said. Then she held his gaze a moment before unfastening her arms. "Go see your brother," she said. But Barat heard it as *Go be your brother* and for a moment believed she knew what he was up to.

Then she stepped away from him but not without a smile, permission again, always between them, to head into the night and to attack this tragedy any way he and Pavel deemed necessary.

Outside their flat door, just two steps into the hall, Barat began the transition from himself to Mikhail. In walk, in posture, in visage. And by the time he reached the street below, he'd reached a mirror, unseen glass on the sidewalk, as another Mikhail was waiting for him, the pair of images prepared, again, to haunt.

# TWENTY

Egorov entered his home at half past midnight, but he was not alone. With him was a lithe man, clearly inebriated, evidenced by the volume of the man's every move and every word. The man, Oleg, wore a shabby brown suit too small for himself, giving him the appearance of a thespian; to which his unshaven face and theatrical expressions only added. The man was happy, this much was obvious. The sort who drank not to escape but to celebrate.

"Cold in here!" Oleg said, sipping from the same bottle he'd sipped from all night. "Colder than it is outside!"

Egorov, holding the lantern, was nothing more than a mask floating in the dark.

"You've got those robes on," Oleg said. "So you probably don't notice. But you ought to be careful. One could get sick in here."

"Sick," Egorov said. "Sick indeed. But is it sickness of mind you speak of? Tell! Do you insinuate I have lost my mind in here?"

Oleg snorted two syllables of laughter. "We all lose our minds somewhere!"

Egorov pointed at the man with the Swarovski. "But most don't know it at the time, eh?"

"That's right! And that's why I like you, Mister. You don't shy away from talking about matters of the mind."

"Matters of the mind . . ." Egorov echoed, his voice like creaking wood. "Mind your matters, Oleg! Your bottle is about to fall."

Oleg grabbed the bottle's neck just before it slipped to the floor.

"Wine or wisdom?" Egorov said. "Which nearly slipped from your grasp? And if not for me, here to warn you, would you have known either were gone? Eh?"

Oleg sipped.

"I woulda had no idea."

"None!" Egorov laughed, triumphant.

But his laughter ended quickly. As if he'd remembered there was no reason to laugh.

He held the lantern out, illuminating farther into the house.

"Is your mind on something in this house, Mr. Egorov?" Oleg asked.

Egorov turned to him.

"You came for the guitar," he said. "Wouldn't you like to see it?"

Oleg nodded. "Oh, yes. Absolutely. My sister has been telling me for a long time that I ought to play for people. She believes I could make a lot of money doing just that."

"Yes, yes, so you told me. Come then . . . come see the guitar."

"I suppose I'll have to play it," Oleg said. "But as I told you, I've got a nip of the stage fright. Public, you know."

"But what could be more private than a home?" Egorov waved the lantern toward the deeper house again, creating the illusion of a doorway of light, a passage to rooms and halls thus far unseen. Egorov led the way. The long hair hanging from his scalp like yarn hanging loose over a cracked basket. The two walked many halls, past many rooms.

"In there," Egorov said. "You'll find the guitar."

"Oh? Is this a game?" Oleg said. "I gotta find it, eh?"

Egorov only held the lantern over the threshold.

Oleg entered.

"Deeper," Egorov said. "Yes, yes. Deeper into the room."

As Oleg searched, Egorov took a step, and the lantern's light reached the very bottom of the guitar. Splintered wood and broken strings.

"What's wrong with it?" Oleg asked.

Egorov held the lantern high, eyeing the room as though searching for a person. He moved swiftly to the guitar and tapped it with the tip of the Swarovski.

"Natural or not, natural or not," he said, still scanning the darkness. It seemed he looked everywhere at once.

"Popped some strings," Oleg said. "That kind of thing happens all the time if you leave an instrument unplayed long enough. They get angry, they do."

Egorov nearly knocked Oleg over as he barreled toward objects draped in cloth.

"Someone's fiddled with the guitar," he said. "Someone's been fiddling."

He reached for canvas covering an object as tall as himself. But he stopped.

"Do you hear scurrying?" he said.

"Mice?"

"I didn't ask that," Egorov said. "Scurrying of any kind."

Oleg tilted an ear to the hall they'd come from.

"Maybe I ought to get along," he said. "Seems I've walked into a drama."

"Play the guitar," Egorov said. "Perhaps the music will drive the vermin out."

"Vermin?"

"Vermin or villain, bedbugs or beliefs . . ."

"You got bugs here, Mister? My brother-in-law works as an exterminator. He might be able—"

"Exterminator?" Now Egorov did look Oleg flush in the eye. "Yes, yes. I *do* need something exterminated. But is it memories or mice . . . memories or mice . . ."

Oleg looked to the hall. "Is the door just that way?"

But Egorov was not listening.

"Faint fancies," he said, flashing the lantern at the corners of the room.

Oleg picked up the guitar at last. He strummed a chord and another string broke. And another.

"Ah," he said. "And how much are you asking for this again?"

When he looked up, he saw Egorov held a small knife in one hand, the Swarovski, missing its top, gripped in the other. The lantern sat upon a school desk half covered in canvas.

"School is but a memory," Egorov said. "And can be stored in a home unseen. All lessons, all learned. Unseen."

Oleg dropped the guitar and shouted.

"A ghost!"

He pointed, not at the knife in the old man's hand, but past it.

Egorov spun, crazed, and saw the ghost of Mikhail unmoving at the far end of the room.

Mikhail raised a hand, a finger, and Oleg darted into the darkness of the hall.

"*You*," Egorov said. He held the knife high.

But Mikhail did not move.

Egorov licked the tip of his nose.

"And what would you do but haunt?"

He turned his back on the ghost and found Mikhail inches from his eyes.

Egorov shouted his fear.

Mikhail grabbed the wrist that held the knife.

Egorov, white as the canvas upon the desk, pulled his robed wrist free and, using the remaining length of the Swarovski, hurried from the room, leaving the lantern behind.

The brothers listened to his blind flailing.

"No, Vision!" Egorov cried. "Once you could read and you read an advertisement. Once you could write and you wrote me you were coming. Once you could lift your hands to your throat as I opened it. Now you are only memory, you are only *vision*! Yet, you touch. You touch! And my deeds have become flesh! And my deeds can touch me too!"

# TWENTY-ONE

Egorov woke in total darkness, all the darkness of the world, within this space and without, all of it separated only by the wood walls of his home.

He opened his eyes and stared long into the black beyond the foot of his bed.

"I see you there," Egorov said.

Small feet pattered out in the hall.

"Mice," Egorov said. But he did not take his eyes from the darkness.

He reached for the lantern upon his night table and found only empty space.

"Eh?"

He reached farther, as far as he was able, but there was no lantern.

"*Thief.*"

But the word felt small compared to the one in his head and heart:

*Ghost.*

Was someone there? In the dark? The ghost of the man he killed? The ghost who was getting closer each night?

The ghost who had touched him, made contact?

"*Dead!*" the old man shouted.

He slammed a hand upon the mattress.

"Eh?"

He felt beside him in bed. He felt fur, bones.

Egorov leapt from the bed, his weak legs unable to sustain the sudden movement, sending him to his knees on the hardwood floor.

"Vermin or dead men? Vermin or the dead?"

Egorov slid across the floor, seeking blindly the lantern. Surely it had fallen. Surely he'd find the glass pieces of its shatter.

"You will not guilt me!" And his laughter was hyenas in the dark desert at night.

But his laughter was false.

"You will not scare me!"

He searched the base of the night table. He reached, flailing, under the bed. He found nothing.

On his knees again, he gripped the edge of his bed and stared into the darkness he'd woke to find.

"Do not speak," Egorov said to the darkness. "Do not speak and thus break me."

His fingers upon the bed met with fur and bones again.

"Memories or mice . . ."

He reached for it, whatever he'd slept with, and returned with handfuls of rats.

"Vermin! My bed infested! Who put such there? No doubt you who stole my lantern, leaving me blind, *but not unseen!*"

He threw rats from his bed. Threw rats into the darkness.

"Playing with vermin in bed! *Playing with vermin in bed!*"

Egorov gripped a singularly large rat, its fur and skin bulging from his closed fist. He slid away from the bed, still on his knees, and reached beyond the night table, finding not only the Swarovski, intact, but the giddiness of the upper hand.

It sounded in his voice.

"Lantern, be lost! It's the darkness I love!"

He rose with the cane.

"Be gone! Meek spirit! Be ghosted!"

Out of his bedroom he went, with assurance now, waving the rat before him, out to the railing protecting him from falling to the first floor. There he kept close to the wood, until he reached the top of the stairs and, by way of the Swarovski, made his way down in the dark.

"I am awake, ghost! Are you? Or do you sleep eternal, eh?"

At the foot of the stairs, he moved the way a man who knows his own darkness does. Through the hall without touching either wall, until he entered, at last, the kitchen. He took the only plate from the sink and set it upon the long wood table before slamming the rodent upon it.

Back to the sink, shouting to that which haunted him, Egorov removed the only fork and knife in his home and returned to the table with both.

He sat upon the only chair in the room.

"Dinner for one," he said, wide-eyed, in the dark. "But no dinner for thee, ghost, never again."

He lifted the fork and knife and jabbed the prongs into the belly of the dead rodent before slicing it open with the blade. Egorov licked his lips as he pulled forth the fork, fur and more, and jammed all into his mouth at once.

His throat already slick with rat, yet he still spoke to that which haunted him.

"Dinner for one!"

He swallowed.

The second piece included bone, but Egorov did not spit it up. He crushed the small pieces with his teeth, sure for the ghost to hear him eat.

"I dine myself! I dine as one!"

He sliced the rat wider, then sawed off its head.

"The skull, you see! The head of a rat! Once a deed looked back at me! Now I eat inspired!"

In the dark, alone, Egorov stuffed the rat's head into his mouth, eyes, nose, ears. He crunched it all between his teeth and felt the eyes burst in his cheeks. He licked his lips, licked the tip of his nose.

"Haunt or holiday, eh? Haunt or holiday *meal*."

He got up and fumbled back to the sink. With ratty palms, he scooped filthy water to his mouth.

"Be gone! You fail! You do not give me guilt! You do not scare!"

He hurried back to the table and, no longer using utensils, squashed the remainder of the rat in his mouth.

Mouth full, he said, "Are you watching, ghost? Do you see who still lives and who has died? Do you see there is no revenge, none can match what I've done to thee?"

He coughed as he choked, attempting to bring the body of the rat back up, then swallowed what remained whole.

"I lick my plate clean!"

The feet, the ass, the tail. Egorov slurped the latter like a noodle, eyes wide and unfocused, still searching for shifts in shadow, for evidence of that which delivered the rats to his bed.

When the tip of the tail had been slurped down his throat, he rushed to the sink to wash the animal down.

"I lick my plate innocent! I lick my plate clean!"

Egorov returned to the table, lifted the plate, and licked it clean.

"Eh? Ghost? *Eh?*"

He stood then in silence. Eyeing the darkness intense.

"Memories or mice, memories or mice . . . tonight, both. Dinner for one. I dine on you, ghost. I dine."

He stood still, minutes more, before burping, then taking hold of the Swarovski and clacking his way through the kitchen, down a cave-black hall, to a cupboard that smelled of oil. From it, he removed a second lantern and lit it.

His ghost stood at the far end of the hall.

The ghost's mouth was open, but Egorov did not beg for quiet.

He cocked an ear in its direction.

"Yes?" he said. "And what? What more can you *do* than haunt?"

But the ghost did not speak.

Egorov smiled.

"No," he said. "No words from thee." Then, "You have lost this round, ghost. Vanish into this night. Come another."

Egorov clacked up the hall but came to an awkward stop.

"Ah, the burning in my belly . . ."

He fell to his knees at the foot of the stairs. He groaned.

"Oh . . . ghost . . . do not touch me . . ."

He fell to his side on the hardwood floor.

". . . do not touch, ghost . . . come another . . . come another . . ."

His head to the floor, his hands upon his robed belly, his voice grew weak.

Egorov groaned. Quieter.

Quieter.

Until, sweating, groaning, crying . . .

. . . he slept.

# TWENTY-TWO

The man Misha only wanted to talk about death. Whether or not someone was present, he prattled on, alone in his cell in the dark stone hall of the station. The other prisoners shouted for him to stop, but some had given up and endured his descriptions of a moon made of maggots, floating bone spheres, symbols of life and . . .

"Death!" Misha said. The word thrilled him every time he spoke it. "Death is my maiden, my *ship*, you see. I sail her from shore. I do not live; I die."

Getz sat on a short stool across the cell. Only Misha's cell was illuminated, but Getz was not here to ask questions. Rather, he was thinking what might be done with the man all of Little Russia wanted hanged, the man who probably did not do any of the terrible things he claimed to have done.

"I'm her first mate, Inspector. I was born on the plank. Did you know? My mother was sentenced to walk that plank, full with me. But before leaping into the cold, sharked waters, she perched and pushed myself out onto the wood. The water bag splashed below, but not me. I settled square on the plank. I remember seeing Mother's face framed by all that blue sky. She had wilderness in her eyes, Inspector. She was not afraid! She winked my way. It was the first expression I witnessed. Mother winked my way then leapt into the open mouth of a shark that had leapt from the water to snag her. He must've been satisfied, that shark, must've been amazed, having no idea he'd found a woman who worshipped death. I killed that man and left him in that gutter, Inspector. Why do you look at me as if I hadn't? Please don't muddy this up. Not for you, not for me. I'm on the boat, now, as we speak. You're in here, too, but you have this idea you are living and not yet dying. Am I wrong? You call swinging with women living and maybe it is. I made love to a woman of ninety-two when I was but twenty. She was my first. Inspector! I've never had anything like it since. I killed that man and let him bleed out in the gutter because sometimes death needs to flow. I respect all speeds and styles. Me? I'm ready. I would be hanged tonight. I killed that man, that triplet. I saw his brothers when they were in here, you know, and I get it now. Three of them. One gone. Makes me jealous. Can't get closer to dying while still living than being one of three and seeing one die. Big stuff, there. The death of a triplet. Why don't you read a book, Inspector? Or write one. Write it about *Misha*. I gave them a gift! Killing that brother proved the other two still live. Now they can say they're living and dying at once, and that's not something many of us can say. Have you ever sniffed a crime scene, Inspector? You must. Get on your hands and knees and smell the street, the parlor, the pub. You ever taste blood? I bet those brothers are tasting blood right now. A metallic tinge in their throats, the blood still pouring forth from their third, filling them till their bellies are red. Why look at me like you're unsure about what you'll do with me? You know what to do with me and I say *do it*. If you choose not to hang me, I'll make a run for it and someone will put a musket ball in my back and that'll be all. And won't that run be forever? Those few steps I take, won't they be forever in the mind of the musket man? I killed that brother, Inspector. Little Russia wants me hanged. Let's hang me! I'd like for a sketch artist to render me swinging from the rope if you don't mind. I'd like that. If you could find someone to draw me and place the drawing in a drawer forever, so I'd know I was swinging like that, my time of dying, hanging forever in the dark. Don't you dare take this away from me! I would be so hurt. You would hurt me. I'd make a run and if I somehow survived the run, I'll kill again. And again. I've already killed every single person who's ever died. So you can close all your cases and string me up. Slip that black rope around my neck and let me go go *go*. I'd like it if a child, someone like me, someone who saw his mother leap from the plank into the mouth of a great white, I'd like that child to open the drawer and think, *Oh what do we have here, eh?* And I want that picture of me hanging to go up in his bedroom, so he sees it each night before dying. Can you feel the winds of the open ebony sea? Inspector? That's me, at the wheel, saying Blood Ho! There is blood and the smell of blood and, for those brothers, the taste of it, always, forever in their mouths. I know why they wanted to show themselves to me. Do you? They worship death too. They're just as proud of it as I am. Oh, you had no idea the kind of man you nabbed when you nabbed me, Inspector! You had no idea you'd apprehended the first mate, he who licks clean the deck, lapping up the blood of all who've died at the ebony sea: me!"

The words angered Getz as he lowered his head to his hands.

What to do about this man Misha? This madman who had now confessed to all of death over all of time?

"Hey," Misha said. "Maybe I could be their new third. Maybe I could be a triplet. Three brothers behind the wheel at sea."

"What do you mean?" Getz asked.

"Maybe I can be their ghost."

"Their brother was slain."

"Yes! But have they let him become a ghost yet? Or do they feel responsible to play the part for him? Do they feel responsible as two, to do the work of three?"

# TWENTY-THREE

Egorov woke and groaned at the foot of the stairs.

"You think you're the only man I killed, ghost? Eh? You think you're the only ghost that haunts this house?"

His cane was no longer by his side.

"This house was haunted long before you came, ghost. This house is teeming with pests . . . and poltergeists! Poltergeists and pests. They chitter in every room, they chitter in the floors. If you haunt me, ghost, who haunts you?"

His voice gargled with the pain in his belly.

"I've killed forty and one, ghost. Do you vie for room? Ha. There is no room for you here, ghost. Leave me my cane and scatter. Like the dead rats in my bed above, you cannot stop me. Do not touch me, ghost! I will touch *you* and take you into the kitchen to eat."

He planted his hands on the first step and pulled himself onto it.

"Ah, I can make it up, see. Won't take but a minute to live my life my way, even as you will never live again. Do you see, ghost? Or do you see only red revenge?"

He pulled himself up the second step and lay on his side there.
He moaned. A hand to his robed belly.

"What's the difference at what pace I move? Eh? You think I'll stop killing without my cane? You think I can't slither upon the stones of the city as young love festers beside the river? You've done me good, ghost. Now those I encounter will kneel to assist me. Now I am a reason to be approached. They will feel proud as they offer help to the old man. And when they reach to help, I will lift the knife to their bellies and I will spit into their faces and I will say it was you, ghost, who brought them to me."

He pulled himself up to the third step. To the fourth.

"Twenty-one steps in all, ghost. And I'm already a bit of the way there."

Up to the fifth, sixth, seventh.

He was moaning less now. Rubbing his belly less now.

"Do you know numbers, ghost? Do you know I am a third of the way up to my bed and that there are dozens just like you in these floors, these walls, this home? Do you know how long it took you to die, how many seconds, the blood that spilled from your neck at the slice of my cane? Take the cane, ghost. A keepsake from me to thee. It's more yours than it is mine!"

Up to the eighth. The ninth.

"Getting there, getting there. And will there be a wedding there? Ghost and roach!"

The tenth, the eleventh.

"Over halfway now, ghost. Numbers assist in this way. Just as men and women will assist me, the fallen man, whence I arrive at the river at night with no cane, the old man in robes, with no way of standing, his legs so weak, but with strong arms indeed! *Slice.* Children, too, ghost. Yes, yes, numbers. Your age is not the lowest of the lot. Does that sadden? Does that stink? Come, give me my cane. A fair fight is what I ask for. It was fair once for us, only you were too happy to see unhappiness on its way."

Twelve, thirteen, fourteen.

Egorov rested. He no longer moaned for what he'd eaten but grunted for the effort of climbing.

"Do I die on my stairs? I once imagined so. Me falling, yes, shoved by the ghostly hands of the dead, my neck cracking midway, my feeble legs following like the tentacles of the jellyfish I once gleefully stepped on as a boy. Me, once a boy, ghost? Oh, yes! Just as you were, so recent. You had barely shed thy boy skin when I met thee, when I saw you coming, on your way to my house to purchase a guitar so you could strum sweet chords and find within them meaning. Ha! But I could not wait, see? I grew impatient and, knowing your route, the route you would take, I hid under the awning of a shoe cobbler, as yet listening for your shoes. You didn't know my face when I approached and asked you for direction. You willingly turned to show me the way. You expressed elation at soon owning the guitar you were on your way to get! But would you have killed me, ghost? For the guitar? Many have been killed for less. But see, now I have no choice but *wait*. Now I can do nothing but lie here on my fourteenth step. That's two-thirds the way, ghost. But two-thirds the way to what? To peace? To quiet? To sleep? Or perhaps to the ordinary. My routine. For there is only one thing worse to rob of a man than his life and that is his routine. By taking the Swarovski you have taken my freedom, have you not? How shall I get up and down the stairs? How shall I eat? Perhaps you will supply me with rats."

He climbed to the fifteenth, the sixteenth steps. He grunted, wheezed, cried out when his hands slipped and he almost fell back, all the way back, to the beginning.

"You lurk in my house like a bat. You flutter about through the walls, you do. No wolf or rats to scare you off. Not even the man who slit your neck as you pointed the way, up the street, assisting me after all! Ha! Oh, how death seems to follow assistance. Have you noted? Have you recorded such a pattern? Or do you only fly—bat!—from one to two to three to four, believing trivialities like music to have meaning? Bat or bad? Bad or bat? Have you determined yet, ghost?"

The seventeenth step now.

"So I won't perish on these steps after all."

The eighteenth. The nineteenth.

"So close am I now. Two steps from the top. And I wonder about meaning and meaningless yet. I wonder if your presence is proof of everlasting hope or evidence of a broken mind. Is my mind broken? Ha! Here I still speak as I climb the last two steps. You see? Numbers, ghost. Now that I know so little remains, I've discovered strength in small numbers. But where was this strength when I began? I'm slithering up the last step now, my fingers splintered, a belly full of rat. And my mind . . . uncertain if you are here at all, if you are true, and what it means for me if you are not."

At the top, he did not stop. He slid toward his bedroom, the robes flat to the floor.

"Scant light through the drapes shows me the rats have scattered. Or were they never here at all? I see a clear path to my bed. Will you help me up to bed, ghost? Will you assist me? I'm just an old man. An old man in need. Come closer, come."

The bedroom was clean of dead rats.

"Were they not dead, then? Were they perhaps ghosts? But the one I dined on was surely real."

He was close to the bed, close enough to tug on the hanging blanket, pulling himself closer still.

"Good night, sweet ghost. For I have made it to bed on my own."

But when he reached for the edge of the mattress, the blanket sailed down to meet him, and with it a hundred rats, still living, moving in a blur, running the length of his arms and body.

Egorov screamed and slapped everywhere at once, no way of knowing Pavel and Barat stood just inside the secret door, the Fedorov glass between them.

"*Stop!*" Egorov shouted, slapping everywhere at once. "*Stop this now! Leave me, ghost! Leave me to my routine! You will not guilt me! YOU WILL NOT DRIVE ME MAD!*"

# TWENTY-FOUR

Annushka entered V's Pub to find Vada already seated, half-way through a drink. At the sight of Annushka, Vada gestured for her waiter, who brought forth a second drink seconds after Annushka removed her coat and sat down.

"Now we do as they do?" Annushka asked. "Strange pubs at night?"

"I don't know what they do. Do you claim to?"

"No. Where's the boy?"

"With Kaarina and Grigoriy."

Annushka nodded. She lifted her drink.

"Cheers, then. To not knowing where our husbands are."

They drank together.

"Where do they go?" Vada asked. But she knew Annushka didn't know.

"I figured it was somewhere like this," Annushka said. She seemed lighter than Vada. Perhaps it was the lack of a child that made a missing husband less worrisome.

"They've been gone two nights now. No word. No note."

"None here, either."

"Do you think they found who they believe actually murdered Mikhail?"

"Yes. I do. Either that or they're in jail themselves."

"No, Getz would've told us so."

They drank again.

"So what do we do?" Annushka asked. "Investigate on our own?"

"I don't want Alexander being raised without his father. See?"

"Of course."

"And whatever they're doing, it must be dangerous."

"The secrecy."

"Oh, dammit, they've always been so secret. Even worse so when there were three. Forever these inside jokes, unspoken conversations. I couldn't stand it then and I can't stand it now."

"It's terrible. But hey, we knew what we were getting into. Don't you remember the first time you met all three at once?"

"Of course. It was at the house. Dinner with Kaarina and Grigoriy. Ekaterina was there too. I remember wondering how she could've gone through such a thing, being raised with triplets. The bond."

"There were times I believed Barat was speaking to his brothers when he was talking in his sleep."

"I know what you mean."

"There were even pauses for a brother or two to respond."

"Yes. It's scared Alexander before."

They drank.

"So how do we discover if they are safe?"

"We talk to Getz," Annushka said.

But Vada had clearly been considering this option already.

"Or are you afraid," Annushka said, "of stepping on their toes?"

"A little, I am."

"Barat acts inappropriately all the time. But this is real danger."

"But they are of sane mind. Different than us. But sane."

"Sometimes too sane. Yes. Do you fear getting in the way of something that is just?"

"What if they are behaving justly?"

"That's fine. I'd like to know though. Would make my nights easier."

They drank.

"Getz," Vada said.

"For all we know he's already looking for them."

"Why do you say that?"

Annushka shrugged. "If the man in prison is not the man who killed Mikhail, surely some variety of the truth must have come out by now, yes?"

"You would hope so."

"I wouldn't be surprised if Getz has already spoken to our husbands."

"We should speak to him then."

The women held a glance for a minute. A silent communication of their own.

"At some point, enough will have been enough," Vada said.

"I agree. When is that point? Two more nights?"

"One. If they don't come home tonight, we speak with Getz tomorrow. We speak with Grigoriy too."

"Why do you say only Grigoriy? Why not Kaarina?"

Vada sipped.

"Because he always knows. Grigoriy is like that. If the triplets had a fourth, it'd be Grigoriy. Not that he could ever keep up with them, but like he was the driver of the carriage they were all speaking silently within."

"Tomorrow then," Annushka said.

"Why are you so sure they won't return tonight?" Vada asked, an edge to her voice.

But Annushka only smiled. "Can't you feel it? Whatever they've decided to do, whatever they've begun, it's reaching its height soon."

"Nonsense. How can we know something like that? We can't."

"We can't *know* it," Annushka said. "But we can feel it. You can't feel the swelling? I mean, isn't that why we're here? Women's intuition? Best friends know? The silent communication amongst twins and triplets, those born and bonded at the same time? We have bonds too. Be light, Vada. Whatever our husbands are doing, whether it's dangerous or not, they're close to achieving what they set out to do. And the time it would take us to find them will be the same time they need to wrap it up. You see? So maybe we sit still, or maybe we don't. But I don't think there's going to be any stopping them now."

# TWENTY-FIVE

Egorov woke to find the cane leaning against his night table, well in reach of his bloated hand.

"Aye," Egorov said, his room not much brighter than it was at night, the drapes keeping most the daylight at bay. "You want to play nice, eh? Or maybe you want me to walk through my home, walk into a trap."

He stared long at the open door beyond the foot of his bed. Had he left the door open last night? When he pulled himself to bed, when the rats attacked him, when he woke and climbed, at last . . .

"Am I alone?" he asked. For the stillness suggested he was.

He slid to the end of his bed and looked to the floor.

"No rats today, ghost. Do they only come out at night? Do you?"

Aching, he swung his legs over the side of the mattress. His bare feet touched the wood. He gripped the cane.

He hadn't changed out of his robes, and so the cloth stuck to him, his body coated in dried sweat. Tapping the floor once, Egorov prepared to exit his bedroom.

Outside his door, at the top of the stairs, only a pair of eyes showed. So slight was the vision that, at first, the old man assumed it was another rat. He lifted his cane to demand it scatter, but the fair hair above the eyes told him who it was.

"Ghost," Egorov said.

He came to a standing.

The Swarovski clacked as he limped, slowly, across the room, across the threshold, to the rail that guarded the fall to the first floor.

There was nobody there.

"My eyes are playing fool with me. No ghost. Maybe never."

At the washroom, he set the cane against the sink and set to cleaning his hands. The water came thick and brown.

In the glass, he looked afraid.

"Does a dead man blow darker bubbles than the living? When he falls into the lake, does the dead man blow gray bubbles?"

Behind him, in the glass, the tip of a boot showing in the doorway. Someone standing in the hall.

Egorov removed the handle from the cane.

"Does a dead man's laughter come covered in dirt? When the dead laugh, do they sprinkle dirt where they stand?"

He inched toward the open door.

"Do the sick and dying think dirty thoughts? Are their thoughts buried in the dirt? Do they hear dirty sounds? Do you hear blood flowing through the earth, dead man?"

He'd reached the open door. His eyes widened upon the toe of the boot.

"Memories or mice, memories or mice . . ."

Egorov fell hard to his knees and stuck the knife head into the toe of the boot.

"And now, ghost?"

But there was no satisfaction, no sound or sight of a wounded ghost.

The knife stuck out of the leather like a steel flower.

"Oh, mine! My own boot, it is!"

Through his open bedroom door, in the scant light, before his bed, the ghost stood.

Egorov, shaken, wiped his face with cold fingers, as though capable of dousing insanity's heat.

Still on his knees, he waddled back, deeper into the washroom. He closed the door. On hands and knees on the filthy floor.

Using the Swarovski with one hand and the sink with other, Egorov tried to stand, but the sink broke free of the wall and crashed upon his already weak legs.

He shouted and swung his cane, as if to strike whoever did this to him. But there was no ghost in this room.

"My legs! I see my ruin before my eyes!"

Out in the hall, the creaking of the floors. Against the washroom window, a tapping.

"Everywhere," Egorov said, gripping his cane, the sink still upon his legs. "He is everywhere I go, everywhere I think!"

He fell to his back, still gripping his cane. He closed his eyes.

"Guilt or ghouls? Goblins or guilt? Do you stand there in reality, or does my reality no longer stand? Do the dead blow black bubbles? Do the dead laugh black dirt? Tell me, ghost. Am I dirty? Am I dying? Am I haunted in truth? Or have I gone mad . . . driven myself mad . . . madness or matter . . . matter or mad . . . a family within me, mother and man, children with siblings, mother and man, all of them mad, around the round table, feasting, gone mad . . ."

# TWENTY-SIX

Kaarina sat across from Grigoriy, gauging his reaction to everything Ekaterina told them. Inspector Getz didn't believe the man Misha was responsible for the death of her son. That was his official take now. Okay. This was almost too much to bear. Kaarina had tried to accept that Misha *was*. Worse yet: it was the certainty in her husband, his lack of surprise at this official information, that worried at her.

Had Grigoriy already come to this firm conclusion? Of course he and Pavel and Barat had discussed this the night of the funeral. But did Grigoriy *know*? And if so . . . how? Wouldn't Grigoriy need to know who the murderer was to know that Misha was not?

"He wants me to track down Pavel and Barat," Ekaterina said. "As if I should be doing his job!"

"But isn't his job to track down the man who murdered Mikhail?" Kaarina asked. "Not your brothers?"

"You're not listening, Mother. Getz believes your other sons are seeking revenge, in some capacity. I mean, when's the last time you saw them! Does anyone know if Vada or Annushka know where they are?"

"You didn't go to them first?" Kaarina asked. All the while, watching Grigoriy, whose eyes were upon the empty plate before him, as if suddenly empty plates were his life's study.

"Of course not," Ekaterina said. "I came to you. And to Father. Father? Are you listening to me?"

Grigoriy nodded. But he did not look her way.

"Good," Ekaterina said. "Because something must be done. I don't care if that vermin dies by hanging, but I do mind that my remaining brothers do not."

"Grigoriy?" Kaarina asked at last. "Do you know anything about this?"

Grigoriy looked to her then, and in his eyes she saw he knew all this and more.

"Where are they, Grigoriy? Are they near, far? Is it in Little Russia? Where are they, Grigoriy? Tell us. Now."

"Father! What do you know?" Ekaterina said.

Grigoriy pushed back from the table and stood, as he was wont to do when he was determined to speak the final words on a matter.

"They are in a nice part of town, Kaarina. They are in the wealthiest neighborhood in Little Russia. They are in an enormous home. And the justice we all seek is in their hands." Then, "I know this from a man named Molotov, who confided in me a suspicion. Then, later, when I was concerned, he gave me a name. And by that name, I found an address. So, yes, Kaarina, I know things."

Grigoriy wiped his hands clean of dinner and made to leave the room.

"Grigoriy Kuznetsov," Kaarina said. "You return to this table."

"Father? Where are you going?"

"I am going to bed," Grigoriy said, already up the hall. "For I am not jury. I am not judge. But perhaps I have played my part in justice."

"Father," Ekaterina said. "What is this address?"

Grigoriy reentered the kitchen and looked at his daughter the way he did to let her know that even he would not go to this address, this home, the place of this man.

"No," Grigoriy said. Then, to his wife, "*No.*"

Kaarina rose to slap him but stopped. They stared at each other, husband and wife, and, like their sons, they spoke without speaking, exchanging a single word that explained why Grigoriy's *no* must remain firm and why a *yes* would change nothing. In that unspoken word existed all possible realties, and the result of each, the same. In that unspoken word slept all memories of having raised their sons, the unassailable truth that, their mother and father be damned, the brothers lived outside the rules of any society, the brothers lived alone on an unknown island, the brothers had their *ways;* ways that would not be shaken, altered, amended, or stopped by any amount of interference from their parents.

And Kaarina and Grigoriy knew this to be fact.

That word:

*Triplets.*

## TWENTY-SEVEN

"Is a ghost a bit like a brother?" Egorov said, spit upon his lips, spit pooling in the folds of his robes as the coach rocked upon the cobblestones. "The dead . . . brother to the living. Some might say twin. Aye. My ghost is the dead brother of his living self then, eh? Wretched thing imagines he's still alive. Looks at me as if he were. Does he not know it matters not who stole that life; you have no rights in death? No right to touch the living! Stop, I say."

"Eh?" the coachman said, craning his neck to get a look through the white drapes. The old man hadn't looked good when he flagged down the coach. In fact, Erik the coachman thought Egorov was drunk-sick, then determined the rich fool was likely mad.

But what might bring a man as wealthy as this to go mad? Erik wondered. Why, the old man had offered "four times the fare" if the coachman promised to "only ride" about the outskirts of Little Russia and greater Samhattan, until Egorov "was ready to go home again." His words! The old man was certainly afraid of something. But parting with his money, it was not.

"Not you!" Egorov said, though he muttered the words more to himself than to the coachman. "You go on forever, you do not stop, not even for the dead, brother to the living, twins, as shadow is to that which accepts the sun. Oh, the look in the eye of my ghost! He wants me dead, eh? Aye. He wants an even game." The coach hit a hole in the road and Egorov's head hit the white silk coffin-like roof of the coach. "I do not blame me, but him! Monster that he is! Does he not know? You, ghost! You are the monster! You do not belong! Go, go, ghost, go, go away, ghost, go. What can you do but look and poke and threaten with rats?"

"Rats?" Erik asked. He couldn't quite hear the old man, but certain words leapt from the open-curtained window as if directed at himself. "Rats, you say? We can stop, sir, if you need to rid the coach of rats!"

"Go away, ghost, go! You pitter and you patter and you don't even matter and despite my hatred you stay. Go away! Quit the charade. You may be brother to the living, but you are no brother to me. Haunt another."

Egorov rocked to and fro, sliding on the coach bench until he was seated on the floor. There, his robes gathered the dry mud and crumbs of previous riders.

The coach traveled harder, having reached the thick stones of Ninth Street. Egorov lay upon his back, the cane gripped to his chest. He closed his eyes, then opened them, in rhythm with the rocking of the road.

"What is that? That creaking, that cracking? Are the wheels of this coach near breaking? Or is it my mind; fissures I hear? Oh, ghost, leave me be! Only through grief can a man be undone by the likes of you, and I feel no grief at your passing. *Flee!* Go to the world you belong to now. Where you can play a guitar in tune. Do you follow me, eh? Are you here in this coach? Do you ride beside the coachman, eyes ahead, do you tell him where to go? Does the coachman deliver you to me, *with* me, the haunter and the haunted as one? Brothers, we!"

"Only a mile more of this uneven road," Erik said, the reins clasped tight in his red hands. "You can take a nap if you'd like, Mr. Egorov! It sounds like you might be interested in some rest!"

But Egorov did not hear him. He lay upon his back as the coach moved uphill. He stared at the white roof, where the silk bunched in folds, moving fluidly with the bumpy terrain, so that the face of the ghost showed in the fabric, then vanished, then showed again.

"Aye," Egorov said, angling the Swarovski to the roof. "There you are, ghost, beside me. Like a lover, like a friend, like a twin; death be thy brother, still living. So come to my house, then, for there is no use in my resisting. Come to my house and haunt the halls and haunt the kitchen and haunt the man who took your life, too soon. I have done nothing worse than any other man, nothing worse than you. I feel no grief, ghost, I feel no guilt. Aye, but I will remove you a second time."

Egorov pulled the handle from his cane just as the coach hit another dip in the dirt. For this, his hand swung back, slicing his own cheek, so that blood came fast. When, an hour later, the coach stopped at 33 Vasiliev Court, and Erik stepped down from the box and opened the door for the old man, he howled.

There, on the floor, lay Egorov. And his wide, monstrous eyes peered out of a mask of dried blood.

"Home," Egorov said. "Just in time for a haunting."

# TWENTY-EIGHT

"Do you know *The Ninth Wave*?" Misha asked the executioner, there to measure his neck. "Painted but fifty years ago by the great Aivazovsky. It is the color of death painted with the colors of death. You look as if you aren't sure. It's silly, isn't it? Someone like you, someone who has delivered death so many times, you ought to know the colors of death as well as any. Most assume it's all blacks and blues; why, I could paint a canvas opaque and my fellow man will call it *Death*! Though, some might imagine red, no? You might imagine so, though I'm certain the colors you've seen up close are nothing like the descriptions in the books. I know this. *The Ninth Wave* is not black or blue, of course, but rather green, purple, yellow, white. The lowering sun above the largest wave, the wave that follows the smaller ones, the biggest wave of all. See? Death, too, is the largest, every time it happens. There is no single death any larger or smaller than any other and there is no ninth wave any large or smaller than another. For, who measures? What footing would there be to take measurements?

Ha. Imagine you, executioner, imagine you standing on the ocean, that tape in hand. It's a sight, no? A fun one. And just as the ninth wave begins, so do you begin to sink. So: only an artist can tell us, though even Aivazovsky couldn't have been expected to paint every ninth wave that ever was. I suppose if the sea were frozen somehow, froze every time a ninth wave emerged, then we could line them up and talk size, but then who would know the density of each, the true width? For how far wide does a wave go? How much of the surface of the sea is yet part of that bit that peaks, that wave? Aye, *The Ninth Wave* is the colors of death. There aren't many! But they are more than black and blue. You have some purple in your shirt, some yellow in your hair. Some green in your eyes and some white in your beard. You, sir, are the Ninth Wave, mine, come to measure me for death. But are you any larger or smaller than any other executioner who has undertaken the task before you? Aren't you only as large as you are in the eyes of he to whom you deliver death?"

The executioner looked over his shoulder to the warden. The warden's stone face told the man in purple what he needed to know. This man Misha had been talking like this since he arrived.

"Glad I can be of service," the executioner told Misha. Then he wished he hadn't.

"I implore you to seek out *The Ninth Wave*," Misha said. "It'll articulate what I'm failing to explain. And when you look at the painting, note the majesty with which Death comes. First in small increments, or, in my case, first in interest, Inspector Getz and citywide, Little Russia. Then, now, by the Ninth Wave, that interest peaks, so that I shall be swallowed whole as if by a shark! My mother was swallowed by a shark. Have I told you so? Leapt directly into the open mouth of a shark. Mother knew *The Ninth Wave*. She rode it, though I know nothing more of her: she leapt moments after I was born. What do you think, Executioner? Do you think Mother saw her Ninth Wave coming? Do you think she spied it from the plank upon which I was born? I think she did. I believe she counted the very waves and winked at me as the eighth crashed against the boat's port side. She gave herself a second to breathe in the sea air before leaping into the shark's maw, that giant fish stuck inside that Ninth Wave just as this mosquito is stuck inside the curls of your arm hair, here."

The executioner brought a hand to his arm and pulled forth the dead bug.

"You see?" Misha said, smiling. "Here you have the measuring tape pinched to the exact size of my neck, and even you do not know the death you harbor. Why, Executioner, you have death all over you. In your hair, in your heart, in your eyes. You, Executioner, deliver death daily; certainly as often as you are asked. A veritable coachman, you! And might I wonder aloud: is it a little over a week, each delivery? Eight days between? Ha! Yes, Executioner, you are the deliverer, you are the sea. You are the Ninth Wave."

# TWENTY-NINE

Egorov woke under the bushes, under the stars, beside a long-abandoned pond that was more a grave for dead water than it had ever been a thing to encourage life. He didn't recall being walked to his door by the coachman. Nor did he remember entering his home and hurrying to the back, not wanting to be *in* his home, sensing a showdown within.

It was dark. The moon was big. Egorov noticed none of this. All he saw was the silhouette of the ghost in an upstairs bedroom window. Its back, he thought, was to the glass.

"Ah!"

He sat up, the Swarovski beside him.

Was the ghost unaware of Egorov's location? Did it think it had the upper hand?

Egorov thought: a chance, perhaps, to do the haunting.

He struggled to his feet, his eyes ever on the back of the ghost in the high window. "I will strangle you, ghost, from behind. For, if you can touch my arm, why can't I touch your neck? I'll hang you from the very window by which you stand."

The Swarovski clacked against the brick steps of the backyard path, long overgrown. Through brush as tall as himself, he approached a back door. Beside it, a weathered shack.

Therein lay tools. And more.

"Sit still, ghost. Stay awhile. For it's taken longer than it ought, but I've found the fortitude to kill you twice over."

In the high window, the ghost still stood.

Egorov opened the shack door and felt about for rope. He wondered, briefly, if the ghost, who had proven capable of traveling fast, were not within the dark hollow of the toolshed. He looked up to the glass. There the dead man still stood.

"Ah, shack, empty of ghost then, eh? Better be. I'm no longer the frightened old man who weeps. You have made a killer of me yet. Ha!"

He found the rope then and slung it over one shoulder.

Up in the window, the ghost still stood.

But now . . . some movement; a tilt of the head. As if the ghost were listening for Egorov's return.

"Can't find me, eh? A little hide-and-seek, then."

He moved quickly but quietly to the home's back door. In the kitchen, he lit a fresh lantern.

"You hide, ghost," he said. "I seek."

He walked the halls of his home with renewed vigor, but still: quiet, quiet.

Up the steps with surprising agility, feeling youthful, empowered, the rope's end dragged some way behind, thudding softly with each step to the top.

"Sit still," he said, eyeing the unused room he knew the ghost now occupied. He went into his bedroom instead, and through the passage in the wall he believed even the ghost knew nothing about, he continued to a second, winding, passage, a second false wall, one that would deliver him to where his ghost idled, positioning himself directly behind the awful thing.

"Do not scatter," he said. "Fine memories these will be."

He brought his ringed fingers to the false wall and pressed, only a crack, thereby showing him—yes!—the ghost still standing in the otherwise empty room.

Egorov blew out the lantern. He eyed the few moonlit steps between himself and the ghost. He gripped the Swarovski.

"How many quiet clacks to cross a room?"

He considered. He weighed. He watched. He set the cane inside the secret passage and emerged, rope in both hands. His weak legs felt strong enough, now, today: they would carry him as they once did, long ago, as he crouched in the alleys of Little Russia, eyeing his stainless prey.

He licked his lips and the tip of his nose.

"To kill twice over is to kill brothers, is it not? The dead being twin to the living!"

His legs shook but he did not care. His knees were near to giving out, but he did not stop.

Egorov moved snakelike in the dark.

The ghost, surprised, shouted, as the rope came quickly around his neck.

*"Be gone, my ghost! And with you my guilt!"*

He felt the vigor of youth in his hands.

"Twice over, twice over! You die! Twins! The dead and the living! Two ghosts now, ha! Twice you!"

Egorov dragged the ghost to the glass.

"Now you will hang, just as a man shall hang for my deed done to thee!"

A second set of hands gripped Egorov's shoulders.

"And whose fingers are these?" Egorov said. "How many hands has a ghost?"

The fresh hands moved to his neck. He released the rope.

Flat to the wall, Egorov saw not a living man, but a *second* ghost, so that both stood in the darkness of the bedroom before him.

"Impossible, you!" he cried. "Not true!" And here his legs grew weak again. "I have killed you twice over! Now there are two ghosts for my deeds! Twins in death now, the deceased and the dead!"

One ghost stood with the rope now loose around its neck as the other held the old man to the wall.

Then . . . the second ghost released him. And Egorov fell hard to the hardwood floor.

"*My cane!*" Egorov shouted. "*I need my cane!*"

He crawled for the passage and rose halfway, nearly falling again before finding the handle of the Swarovski still there behind the false wall.

"Two ghosts!" He cried. "Mouse, no: *mice.*"

He fled, then, through the passage, not stopping to close it behind him, the clacking of his cane loud upon the winding stairs that delivered him down to the first floor.

"Two ghosts! I am but an old man! I've shed my youth, my youth is another. And who can be blamed for the deeds of this other, younger man, ghost? And if your second now commits a crime, if he kills me yet, will he be to blame . . . or will you? And will either of you be . . . any better . . . than me?"

# THIRTY

Kaarina sat in the cellar, unsure where anybody in her family was. She'd called upon Ekaterina, but Ekaterina was not home. She'd called upon Pavel and Vada, but they were not home. Nobody had asked her to watch little Alexander, so were they out as a family? Annushka and Barat weren't home either.

Kaarina was fearful of what any member of her family might be doing; might do.

And where was Grigoriy? Her bedrock husband who was as foolish as he was formidable? What horrible decisions had Grigoriy made without consulting her, without letting her in on his plan?

She wept. Not only for Mikhail, for whom she believed she had not yet wept enough, but for all of them, the family, cracked in half by the deed of one man, and not the man Misha, who was sentenced to death.

She should tell the papers, she decided. That was it. Because if there was one reason everyone was quiet it was that nobody wanted to stop the remaining brothers from carrying out whatever plan they'd made. But what plan was that? And how foolish to allow a plan born of grief to be carried out?

She went to the small cellar table against the dirt wall. There, a bottle of vodka seemed to wink her way. It was Grigoriy's way to drink with their sons, to pour shot after shot until raging laughter and debate erupted. Kaarina took drink far less often. But she was no stranger to vodka.

She poured a shot and drank it without declaration.

Yes, the papers needed to know.

Misha was not the man.

Before allowing herself to refute this sudden decision, she found herself on the street, a singular destination in mind. This was calming: it felt to Kaarina as though she'd been suspended in chaos for days.

The man Misha was not to blame for the death of Mikhail. Kaarina believed that now. Her family was out playing American frontier on the streets of Little Russia and the only way she saw fit to stop this was by exposing some truth. Truth, Kaarina thought, always led somewhere good. In the end. Even Getz's hand would be forced: he would not have to take the heat for clearing the name of a man the entire city wanted dead.

Still, despite the drive in her step, she did not feel entirely good about this decision. It felt like a gamble, and Kaarina was not one to take chances. She didn't know the entire story, for starters. She didn't know for sure if Ekaterina, Vada, and Annushka knew any more than she did.

But the numbers were simply not adding up. And the absence of Pavel and Barat told all she needed to know:

They had found the real killer.

Hurrying now, she looked the people she passed in the eye and she wondered, *Does he think Misha is guilty? Does she?*

It seemed *everyone* believed Misha deserved to die. For this, Kaarina moved quickly.

She had never been to the offices of any newspaper before. She did not know what it entailed to tell the truth to the largest voice in Little Russia, and perhaps Samhattan.

Would she need proof of her claim? All she had were half headlines in her head:

*MISHA DID NOT DO IT!*

*MISHA CONFESSED BECAUSE HE WANTS TO DIE!*

*THE REMAINING KUZNETSOV BROTHERS FOUND THE REAL KILLER!*

She stopped walking. She couldn't tell them this. Of course not! This was a terrible idea! What if Pavel and Barat had already done something to the right man? What if she was dooming her family rather than saving them?

Yet . . . there might be a way. A less exact way.

For example: what if she were to simply tell of strong suspicions that Misha is not the murderer the city believes him to be? Would the suspicions of a lone mother be enough for a printed word? And would that printed word then be enough to cause her sons to retreat, would it bring them back home, where Grigoriy might line up shots and joke thunder with their sons about the time they almost killed a murderer rather than allowing the police to do their job?

She set out again, despite these warring voices, this feeling she was unsure what to do.

"The mother," she said. "I don't need to know the story. *I* am the story."

She walked fast, crossing the thin stone bridge over the flowing river. Oh, to see Pavel or Barat right now; to slap them both across the face. To tell them to go to their rooms, to grieve like good boys and to quit this frontier justice they read about in their magazines for boys!

Where was the paper? Oh! Ahead. Yes. Ahead and a turn and another turn and ahead again. Then Kaarina would be inside the building, in the presence of people who would, at first, find her uninteresting, a simple grieving mother, until she told them what she believed.

What her whole family believed.

It struck her:

"Leave out any word of any other killer."

*This* she felt good about.

She was there, at the door, too quickly. She looked once over her shoulder, perhaps allowing her family, any member, to show up just in time, to tell her she needn't do it this way. Pavel and Barat will stop on their own!

But, ah, too late; nobody emerged from the throng.

Kaarina entered the building.

"Hello," she said to the first person she saw. But this person was not a reporter and told her so. Neither was the next. Nor the next.

The fourth person, a woman named Golubev, was.

"I am the mother of Mikhail Kuznetsov. The triplet who has been slain. And I do not believe the man Misha committed the crime."

The reporter Golubev's face went from humoring to sympathetic to fascinated.

And Kaarina was led deeper, much deeper, into the building.

# THIRTY-ONE

Egorov sat at the desk in the library, whittling the wood with the knife from the handle of his cane. The front of the desk was pressed against the door so that the old man sat only the length of the tabletop and the width of the door from the hall beyond.

"Two ghosts, aye," he said, his eyes wide and focused on the door as though watching the entire story play out through the wood, through the hall, through everything. "Killed twice over, aye. Such a thing, such a thing. And here I was wont to believe death was death but no! Death leads to ghosts and ghosts might die as well. What say we kill the two remaining, eh? Then four? From there, eight, and from there I do not want to imagine. Aye. Once was I could murder in the streets unawares; nobody looks for those who walk the streets alone. Yet, this one . . . this one . . . He has me scared, barricaded, I am, here in my own home. This was once a place for one, me, Egorov, now a place for three, or three dozen if you number the deeds, the ghosts that haven't shown like this one. What do I hear? Scurrying? The boots of two ghosts or the heavy legs of spiders? Spiders or sins, crawling up my walls. A window behind me is all my escape, eh? And escape I ought to, never to return. Leave the old home, *forget it*! And leave in it all I've done. No room for furniture in here as I sit upon my murders, I sleep upon my deeds. Guilt? 'Tis for the less intelligent, those who believe in balance, those who believe at all. Ha! I've murdered thirty, nay, forty-one. What might come if I were to kill both ghosts in this house, two shades of one man, one man I knew the route of, he on his way to my home, me unable to resist, thirsty for the neck of him still? Too much! No room to walk from one end of the home to the other, there being ghosts and deeds blocking all passage, specters in every space. But here? Here I am alone. In here, I am alone."

On the tabletop, where he'd been whittling, now a portrait of himself, rendered by him.

Egorov gasped.

"Do I appear so afraid? Once I was the strongest of my class. Once I ran miles to their halves. Once my peers challenged me in pubs and I, arms of muscle, legs of strength, defeated all. Ha! Once was I feared nothing. As a ghost fears nothing, eh? For what do we fear but death or its kin on the way? Once was I leapt from cliffs into deep blue waters. Once was I ran the stone streets of this city for laughs. Once was I felt indomitable in the presence of . . ."

He jammed the knife tip into the wood.

"Had I friends? Or were they simply those in my life I did not kill?"

He did not wipe away the tears. But some came.

"Do you hear me weep, O ghost, O ghosts? Is this what you've come to do? To make a man cry who was once so full of cheer? Aye. Perhaps I've always been crying. Perhaps I was never happy in the way you were, ghost, when you were your brother, aye, the living. When you walked a street with a mind to purchase a guitar and found violence on the way. Violence or music, music or murder? I have moved to the rhythms of violence for as long as I can remember, even—yes!—even as I leapt from the cliffs, thoughts of breaking into pieces on the seafloor, thoughts of no water to catch me!"

Behind him, the window slid open, but Egorov did not hear it. He kept his wide, wet eyes on the portrait he'd carved in the desk.

"Seems I've killed the right man if such a man would become such a ghost! And you, my brother, my face in the wood, you are here to tell me, a friend at last, to tell me that fear is not weak, after all, aye? That being afraid is being smart about those around you and knowing who might die easiest and who might become a rotten ghost!"

A hand upon Egorov's shoulder and the old man spun quickly with the knife held high.

Wide-eyed and clear of head, he saw no one. But the window stood open.

"Who's in here? Eh? Who has snuck into my library to look at my portrait in wood? Am I alone after all? Has a wind pushed the glass my way?"

He was up then, Swarovski in hand, to the window in seconds.

"Who's here? Two ghosts in the yard? Come to drive an old man mad? Show yourselves, two ghosts in the yard! Let me kill you thrice over!"

But no ghosts were seen.

Swarovski in hand, he turned to see the desk was back where it belonged and the door was full open, revealing the dark hall beyond.

Egorov stared, immobile with fright. His wide eyes took in the impossible newness of the library door and the open maw of the abyss.

He did not speak, not even to mutter to himself, as he stepped once, toward the hall, the cane giving a single shy clack. Then a second step, as if the old man had no choice now but to agree to the invite the ghost had sent him. *Come,* the hall said, *it's time for us to finish what we've begun. You turned your back on a room and when you looked again the room had been altered. You will sleep, tonight, perhaps, and wake to find you are rearranged, that your thoughts no longer represent what they once did, that there is such a thing as truth and the horror that accompanies it is guilt.*

Egorov entered the hall. He heard nothing, no movement, but knew the ghosts were waiting. Through the darkness, his darkness! he went, the Swarovski like a distant bell now. Dinner? Perhaps. Maybe Egorov as the dish for the two ghosts who would not leave him alone, would never leave him alone, would torment him forever anon.

He paused at the foot of the stairs. He licked the tip of his nose. He looked up. No light. No sign of the ghosts. But he knew they were here. They were waiting for him in the house, his house! Where?

"Up there?" he said. "I go *not* up there."

The Swarovski sang as Egorov left the stairs, a bear through the blackness, the cane like hooves, like claws, like the patter of rodent feet.

Room to room he went, eyeing the different darknesses, waiting for the ghosts to murder him back.

All night like this, until the sun came up, Egorov walked the halls and opened the doors and entered the rooms of his home, without mutterings, without declarations, almost without thought. And though he did not find the ghosts that haunted him, he knew they were there, that when he saw the library door had been opened, and when he took his first step, he had commenced a long walk, one that might last the rest of his life. Perhaps they were there now, at the end of his life, the pair of them, lying on their backs in his—his!—casket. Maybe, when the men nailed shut the box, Egorov would discover he was not alone, even there, the end of this long walk, in his coffin, in his box, in the dirt, underground.

Yes, even there, the ghosts would not leave him alone.

But the old man could not turn from their invitation, and so he walked until fatigue took him, until he simply could walk no more, as the sun was well up in Little Russia, though the drapes kept most of it away, and Old Man Egorov fell to his knees in the music room, then rolled to his side and closed his eyes.

But not his mind. And while he did not dream, while he was unable to sink deep enough to dream, there they stood anyway, one ghost for each closed eyelid, the two of them looking back at him, standing in the open ebony hall off the library door, still inviting, still saying, *Come out, come out, Old Man Egorov, come out and find us, meet us, for the end of our war.*

# THIRTY-TWO

Egorov sat in the one fine chair in all the house, situated in the center of what might've been the dining room had he ever purchased a table or cooked food or had guests.

He sat in the near dark, the lantern off, gripping the Swarovski.

"Come now, ghosts. Haunt me."

But he need not have invited.

Stepping into the doorway to the dining room was the cut of his ghost, the shape of the slain man, Mikhail.

"Ah! So you listen! A trained ghost is hardly a haunting, and I'll take it at this stage of the game."

The ghost did not move, did not speak, did not allow Egorov the certainty that anybody or anything was actually there.

"Come, then, haunt me! Come groan through my home and my head. Sit upon my shoulders, the weight of my deeds, weigh me down to the floor. Send me rats, foe. Send me dinner for one!"

But the ghost did not move.

Egorov eyed the darkness to his right and left.

"And where is your second, eh? The second ghost of thee? Where is he hidden in all this house?"

The ghost did not move.

"I saw a flock today, mine ghosts, through the windows, a host of people traveling light-footed to the sight of a hanging. Yet, you find me sour for having murdered alone. I saw a flock today, ghosts of mine, with the thrill of fresh blood in their eyes. Fathers and mothers. Children in tow! Yet I am the monster who lives in the dark. Is it not clear to you the blind hollow from which people choose good and bad? Is it not obvious to you too? Haunt me! For the deed and the deeds I have done. And done you! But do not think me bad, ghosts of mine, for I am no worse than the flock who waddle like pigeons to the piece of bread hanging from the executioner's rope!"

The ghost did not move. Or was he not there? Egorov stared long at the shape, gripping his cane, twisting the handle so the crystal tip spun slowly upon the floor, like the top spun by a child, a wealthy child, already with thoughts of murder on his mind.

"Haunt me dearly and haunt me dead. Come into my home and be everywhere at once. Stand over me as I sleep. Yes, I slayed you in the street, ghost! And I slayed you once more upstairs! Ha! Do you think you will win this round three? Or will there be three of you in the end? Triplets who haunt me dead. Oh, how much haunting triplets might do, one ghost, two ghosts, three ghosts, you! Come, come, but beware! No flock is coming to watch you swing. No. Your deaths will be done in the dark. The flock want pageantry, action, no standing still on the threshold of rooms once occupied by me and me alone. Yet, my deeds have lain here too. And they patter upon four legs, each of them, all. You see, ghosts, I am but hungry for things you were not. You chose music, I chose murder. But whose song is better? Here you can no longer play at all! And here I can kill again, a third time now, giving you the triplet perhaps you deserve. What say you, ghost in my door . . . will you haunt me now? Will you haunt me dearly, haunt me dead?"

Egorov bent at the waist and lit the lantern.

"Show yourself, ghost! Show me the details by which a third shall be made!"

But it was not the ghost who stood in the door. Nor was it the second.

"Egorov?" Inspector Getz said. "Is that your name?"

Egorov stared back at the man with wide eyes. He recognized the police in him immediately.

"No!" Egorov said, removing the handle from the cane. "But who drew you to me? Certainly it wasn't I, clean as I am on the streets. And surely it wasn't you, randomly sniffing for crime."

"The father of the slain."

"Father!" Egorov said. "A louse! But what a father, eh? Come, Inspector, come help me up from my chair. I will not put up a fuss. You are much stronger than I. I could not make it if I ran. You heard me speaking of my deeds and so you, the biggest mouse of all, have arrived to eat me, the biggest crumb. Come help . . . a little assistance and I will not resist you at all."

He licked the tip of his nose.

Getz crossed the room and reached for the hand extended him.

"No!" the voice of one of the ghosts cried, erupting from the darkness behind Egorov. But the old man moved quickly and had the Swarovski knife raised high.

Getz saw the lantern light reflected in the blade, saw his own eyes there too.

But the ghost got to Egorov first, knocking the old man's arm askew. And the ghost turned to Getz and spoke.

"Leave," it said.

Egorov moved quickly and stuck the blade deep into the waist of the ghost.

"A third!" Egorov cried. "A third time you die! Now will you haunt me in threes?"

Getz ran to the ghost as the ghost dropped. And the second ghost came fast into the room.

And a third? A man larger than the ghosts but with echoes of their features upon his face. Or maybe, Egorov thought, even as this older man stuck his own knife into Egorov's heart, maybe this man was the father of the man who once lived, the fool who went to purchase a guitar and whose ghost had finally had its revenge.

"Grigoriy!" Getz cried.

But it was too late. Grigoriy had stabbed the old man a second time, a third.

He went to his sons, one crouched beside the other, both dressed as the third.

Getz removed a newspaper from his coat and used it to dry the blood spreading at the stuck brother's waist.

Egorov fell from the one fine chair, fell to his forehead on the floor.

But his eyes still saw and his ears still heard and as Getz cursed frontier justice, even as he mended the wound of the ghost, Egorov read the headline upon the paper being used to mend.

## MOTHER OF TRIPLETS SAYS IT'S THE WRONG MAN SET TO HANG

"Eh?" Egorov said.

The lantern light revealed a few words of the article itself too. The man to be hanged, possibly already hanging now, had been charged with murdering one of three triplets. The mother of three did not believe the sentenced should die.

"Eh?" Egorov said, his eyes widening in death, his breath coming in shorter and shorter waves. "Triplets?"

He looked to the two ghosts and saw the ghosts looked back. But the image of them, their identical image, became red, as blood in Egorov's eyes streaked down his nose to his lips, and the entire world, his world, became blood, blood red, until it seemed no vermin could breathe, no memories or mice might survive.

# THIRTY-THREE

Ekaterina, Vada, and Annushka sat upon the front steps, watching the people pass. They knew from what the people told them that Kaarina had gone to the papers and attempted a last-minute stave-off: she did not believe the murderer of her son had been brought to justice. They also knew the man Kaarina was trying to save was unsavable. And judging by the number of people heading east, it was going to be a memorable event in Little Russia.

But the three couldn't bring themselves to join. Alexander was asleep inside the house, sleeping on Grandmother and Grandfather's bed. Despite the high sun, the day felt very dark, as if the three women were seated on steps inside a home without lanterns.

From the throng, Kaarina stepped toward them. Ekaterina stood and went to her mother and asked where she had been. Kaarina told them of her time in the newspaper offices and how she then spoke with Getz, imploring him to find this other man in time. But this thread was cut short, as Grigoriy and his sons emerged from that same throng, the father's arms slung over the shoulders of both.

The brothers were dressed just like Mikhail once dressed. Their hair was cut the same.

From inside, two little hands pushed open the front door and Alexander came onto the porch. He looked to his father.

But which of them was it?

"What's happened?" Kaarina asked, hysteria in her voice.

Grigoriy's visage did little to dispel her horror.

"The monster has been haunted dead," Grigoriy told her, then told everyone. "The man who took Mikhail's life has been slain."

Kaarina looked to the blood on Grigoriy's cuff.

One of the brothers stepped to Annushka, the other to Vada.

"I am Pavel," Pavel said. He nodded Vada's way and Annushka hugged Barat. But even as they embraced she punched his chest, his shoulders, for the scare he had put her through.

Pavel lifted Alexander off the porch.

Vada made to speak and Pavel said, "We have gotten through it. Losing our third."

People passed in smaller numbers now, the majority of the crowd having made it to the gallows already. But those who still came did so with eagerness and energy. And in their eyes, Pavel and Barat saw something similar to what they'd seen in the eyes of the man who had been jailed for killing Mikhail: worship. They recalled again the blood mask coating the face of Old Man Egorov and how the killer had died on the floor. How long would the old man lie that way, his forehead to the ground, his face bright red, in his own darkness and filth? How long before Getz sent someone to clean him up?

But also: how long before someone else entered that home and turned quickly at the sound of something clacking, bringing to mind the crystal tip of an expensive cane, as the ghost who haunted the home traveled on weak legs?

How long before somebody entering that house understood they were haunted?

"The state wants him dead," Kaarina said. "There is nothing to be done."

Grigoriy said, "He is the opposite of the man who stole Mikhail. For here we find nobility and reverence in innocence, and behind us only evasion of guilt."

# THIRTY-FOUR

"Oh, blessed me, standing in the very spot I've imagined every moment of every day of my life. Whether awake or sleeping, I have seen myself standing still, roped or not, as Death rode her blue horse my way. Oh, blessed me! I've had my last meal of beans and rice and I've had my last rites read by the very Father Khan who must be out there in the crowd. So many faces come to see Death on her blue horse rushing my way! And how will she receive me? Open arms? Eyes wide? A smile? Or will she not even look at me, myself being one of ten thousand deaths to occur at the same time, that of the bumble bee, the maple tree, the dog, only mine is scheduled and so I must be less of a burden to her. Oh, the housekeeping poor Death must endure! For that, I admire her, as long ago I agreed to be first mate upon her ship, to sail her through ebony waters under an ebony sky if only I should get to ride her blue horse when my time came to meet her! Oh, my Ninth Wave has come. Thank you, Samhattan, for refusing to take this moment from me, despite what I hear the papers were saying. Can you imagine? Me *not* the killer? But I so obviously am! Just look at the crowd who has come to see me taken away upon my Ninth Wave! Look at Death reflected in all their eyes, ten thousand renderings of a hanging man, his soul turned to dust in Little Russia. Oh, I can hardly speak her name without excitement, without arousal! I can hardly make sense of the fortune I've experienced, finding myself standing exactly where I've always wanted to be. Do you see how perfect the platform is I stand upon? How perfect the plank? I could easily kick it out from under me before the executioner does, but I will not rob him of his duty. You see? A man must have duty, purpose, and mine has been to sing the praises of Death—hail, Death!—even as so many fear her and avoid her and look down their noses at her ways. They are here now, see? And so I have done my duty, I have turned thousands on to Death, I have plucked Death's reputation from the teeth of ignorance and have shed light, the very sun!—daylight!—upon it! You see, people? Death rides toward me now! Upon my Ninth Wave. Oh! I see her in the distance, even as the executioner stands beside me, prepared to pull the lever that will drop the door and send me hanging, broken bones, broken neck, twisting, under this bright midday sun, as I am cast in ten thousand drawings and sealed in ten thousand drawers that I may hang forever in the darkness of domesticity. Oh! Father Khan! I see you! Inspector Getz! There you are! You both wring your hands but fret not, Death is nothing to be sad for! Death is a most beautiful thing, riding the most beautiful horse, upon the largest wave, through this throng of ten thousand, all here to witness her ways. Stand tall with me, friends, people, stand tall as you can, get onto the tips of your toes and look! *Look!* She rides! This way! *My* way! I hear her horse above your voices, I hear the hooves above your impatient claps! I want to meet her, too, I am with you, impatient people, I am with you too! Make way for Death, people, *make way*! Come to me, Death, come to me, sister!

For I am your brother, standing here upon this platform, seconds from falling into the open maw of your arms. The Ninth Wave comes, sister, traveling enormous now through the ten thousand strong who have come to worship you too. Come, sister! And call me brother! You and I are twins, dear Death, siblings the same who have talked long by way of unspoken communiqué, who can look at each other across a crowd and understand all! We are brothers, dear Death, we are sisters, dear Death, and the blue horse shall ride the Ninth Wave onto this platform, where the wet hooves and heavy wave shall send the trapdoor plummeting below, sending me hanging along with it! And will you watch, dear Death? Or will your eyes already be onto the next, perhaps even somebody from this crowd, someone too old to make it to the end of the day? Such housekeeping, dear sister, dear brother, dear Death. I am so happy to meet you, I cannot stop smiling. I am so proud to number myself amongst your ward. Come for me, dear Death! I love you! At last we meet, as the executioner's hands are upon the lever and he pulls! Dear Death! Do you see me? Did you hear the platform drop? Did you hear the gasp of ten thousand at the sight of my sudden hanging? Did you hear the cries of joy, of rage, of revenge? Oh, love the ten thousand, for they will ride your horse one day too. But today this ride is mine. I love you, dear sister, dear brother, dear Death! I love you. Take me, now, from this broken body, this broken neck, this ebony rope. Do you see the executioner eyeing me? Oh, look! He eyes me through the holes in his mask. You must know him well. What is he thinking, what do you say? Do you think he notices we look alike, dear Death? Do you think he can tell we are brother and sister? Do you think the executioner, the man who has stood next to you more times than any of this ten thousand, do you think he can tell we are twins, that we have spoken without words our entire lives, that we need one another to be whole, that we are the same, you and I? Do you think he recognizes that he is our third? Oh, I love you, dear Death. Take me. Take me in. By this rope, this black rope, growing warmer now, softer to me now, soft around my neck; not so much rope anymore, but yarn; yes, hung by ebony yarn; warm to the neck, warm to the skin; hung by a spinning black yarn."

# AFTERWORD AND
# ACKNOWLEDGMENTS

*A Traveling Title, a City, a Friend*

I didn't have the title yet when I met Ryan Lewis. I didn't have many things.

I had other titles, including *Goblin*, the book that was sent Ryan's way by the radiant lawyer Wayne Alexander. I had *Inspection* and *Unbury Carol*, too. I had *Bird Box* and *Bring Me the Map* and *Decorum at the Deathbed* and more. But *Spin a Black Yarn* wouldn't come up for another couple years, as we worked on getting *Bird Box* into some kind of shape to shop. I don't love words like *shop* and *pitch*. I even feel a little weird including them anywhere in the pages of the book you now hold. But that's kinda the point of this afterword/acknowledgment: the uncanny similarities between myself and Ryan Lewis, manager extraordinaire, down to the words we like using when we talk books, business, life. And we talk a lot. It's probably been an average of five days a week for fourteen years now.

Wow.

And . . .

*Awesome.*

So, okay, a couple years into working together I told him I'd written a few novellas and titled the batch *Spin a Black Yarn* and we both thought, okay, good title, and that's another book we'll have to one day rewrite, too. But what I didn't know then was I hadn't written a book. I'd written some stories that would end up in various places. *Nurse Ellen* would later become *Black Mad Wheel*, released as a full novel. *Fafa Dillinger's Box* (a story of how for each of us there is a box, buried somewhere, containing the worst we're capable of, and who wouldn't be tempted to search for their own?) was published in *A Little Red Book of Requests* by Borderlands Press. *Merry Impresario* (mean Merry!) was in that batch too. It's about a conservative gang of townsfolk who gotta track down an open casket they kicked out into the ocean some days prior, trying to dispose of the eccentric Merry Impresario. *The Last Labor of Lucio* takes place in the year 3001 and shows us the very last group of people (five of 'em) who believe in Jesus Christ, though the religion itself is so diseased and close to death its final stalwarts can't quite remember their savior's name. Geez Kiste means a lot to them, but they aren't sure why anymore. And *Ghastle and Yule* (the story of two warring horror filmmakers obsessed with each other's films and successes) was published as a Kindle Single.

It's this last one that kept the title alive, one might say, as I'd seen the disconnected group of stories going their separate ways just as friends do when they grow up. I needed a publisher name for the Kindle Single, so I pretended it was published by a house called Spinablackyarn Press.

And that, at the time, was that.

What Ryan and I didn't know then was that I'd sorta hinted at what was to come by using the title in a business sense (faux business or not). Still, over the next few years, as I regularly wrote short stories, I started to see them all as a potential book, a single volume, one day to be called (sure, why not) *Spin a Black Yarn*. And so, the title traveled, now a vague overarching umbrella, a vat into which I could drop each new short as they came. This was a great arrangement, right? With each, the nebulous book got bigger. It was the kind of thing you checked at year's end: *How big is* Spin a Black Yarn *now? Thirty stories? Forty?* For someone who likes to keep tabs on how much he's writing, it always felt like a bonus, that ballooning collection.

Yet, the title wasn't done traveling. Nor should it have been.

Am I telling too much? Do notes like these revoke mystique? Or do they add some, by presenting the truth of the matter, the curtain aside, the process?

It's difficult for me to articulate what a match was made when Wayne Alexander sent Ryan Lewis *Goblin* those fourteen years ago. One way of understanding it, for me, is that Ryan and his wife had their first child shortly after we met. I've watched their son (now sons) grow up in the time we've worked together. And when we met, I may have had some things that are very important (enthusiasm, drive, madness, laughter), but I didn't have anything else. No home. No car. No bank account. I had the aforementioned titles in a stack of rough drafts. And Ryan? He had clients. But no novelists. We were the same age and we'd come from far ends of the country (Ryan in California, me in Michigan), yet (and we couldn't have known this at the time) we were coming from almost the exact same place. By the time we met, we already had the root tenets of what would become a shared philosophy in place: *burn no bridges, leave ego out of all collaborative endeavors, momentum above strategy*. He was just starting a family and I was living in a friend's hallway, spending as much time at the bar as I did any other place on Earth (these were magnificent days, and I do have a novel about that period, another title: *The Two Drunk Pool Players*). But wherever we were and whatever we had, it felt like something bigger than either of us happened the first time we talked. In those early days, Ryan started saying we were going to get *Bird Box* published and we were going to get it optioned for film. How did he know this? It didn't matter. No more than how I "knew" the books would one day be read. But it wasn't just Ryan's confidence that thrilled me; it was his levelheadedness. The steadiness with which he talked about these things. He spoke of dreams and the actualization of dreams like someone who handled them all day. I felt I hadn't only met a manager, I'd met a like-minded life coach who was able to put into words something I only felt.

This was beyond "a good match." This was kismet territory.

Ryan and I have a thinking that goes something like this: rather than "don't get excited till the check is cashed," why not celebrate that a thing *might* happen? Then, if it doesn't, you still had a celebration. And if it does happen? Well, holy shit, you get to celebrate *twice*.

We've got a lot of stuff like this. Good-luck charms, even though I'm just superstitious enough not to say those out loud.

They can be found in these pages either way.

And speaking of luck, and the good kind, Ryan was right. About *Bird Box* the book and *Bird Box* the movie. And it was only natural, following the success of the movie and us having other stories, that Ryan proposed the idea we start a production company and act as producers for all film stuff to follow.

Fingers crossed. Eyes crossed.

This was a big step.

Now, me, being someone who not long ago kept what money he had in a hardcover copy of *The Witches of Eastwick*, I was a little scared of entering the "business" side. Would I make sense there? Would I sink? Would I get bit? But, see, it wasn't *me* setting out to do this. It was *us*. And if there's one thing Ryan and I are, it's a team.

So . . . this production company needed a name.

Well . . .

. . . how about . . . Spin a Black Yarn?

And why not? First a collection. Sort of. Then a faux publishing house. Then an imaginary collection of gathered short stories. And now?

A partnership. Complete with a logo that means something to us.

And so we embarked under this new name. And our roles have grown just as our knowledge has.

Yet . . .

That title.

It's just . . .

What can I say? I'm a man of words. Chances are you, holding this book, and *because* you're holding this book, are also a word person.

So, production company or not . . .

Was there still a book to be named? A traveling title to be used?

Yes. I knew there was. I just didn't know where yet.

The first time I visited Samhattan was in the short story "The Givens Sensor Board," published by Max Booth (who is also managed by Ryan Lewis now) in *Lost Signals*. It's the story of a bad man, a mailman who haunted a semi-industrial city prior to the story's start. The story opens on Randy Scotts' burial, and the teenager manning the cemetery at night (the cemetery that resides in the middle of the city like a hubcap) has to check the newfangled Givens Sensor Board to make sure there's no life left in that grave. Well, what would *you* do if you discovered a serial killer had been buried alive?

Samhattan spoke to me, and speaks to me now, in a different way than Goblin does. In Goblin, there's enough color to fill a child's crayon box. Despite the endless rain. But Samhattan is gray, white, semi-industrial, a city as big as Goblin, maybe, but most would choose the latter for a day trip (Goblin has a way of drawing obsessives, after all). But this uncharacteristically spartan setting gave me a stage for any number of ne'er-do-wells to roam. Ben Evans was up next, as he dug up his recently deceased parents and used their bodies as the stars of the movie he refused to quit making in "A Ben Evans Film." By then, I was getting to know Samhattan. A couple more mentions in a couple more stories, and it started to feel like I had a grip. And when Daphne came to town, the seven-foot deranged and denim-clad madwoman, I finally understood Samhattan whole.

I'd finally found the place where you'd spin a black yarn.

In Goblin, that yarn would get wet. And in Chaps, they'd call it *thread*. But Samhattan was just cold enough to give me a serial killer who resisted his urges all his life, and brothers who would stage a faux haunting to drive the murderer of their third brother mad. It also felt like a touchstone, how all hometowns are, a place where a character might've been born before taking a shuttle to Jupiter, seeking cosmic thrills even as he sought to avoid a blooming guilt. Samhattan was unquestionably the kind of place Doug and Judy Barman would be forced to watch their true nature circling them in cold, dark fragments. Yes, as Misha so enthusiastically declares in *Egorov*, black yarn feels more like a necktie than a noose in Samhattan, even as it delivers death. Some Samhattanites *want* this darkness. Here was a place where people like Daphne Vann, Randy Scotts, Ben Evans, and Old Man Egorov could prowl the streets, day or night, some with the strength to resist, others having made cold decisions, determined to see them play out.

I told Ryan I'd found it. I was ecstatic.

The title had a home.

And now, as we move ahead with the production company, as

we learn, as we try, as we celebrate, I know the book you hold is an ode to Ryan Lewis, and working with Ryan, and finding in our talks, now more than ever, those same mindful tenets.

There's no bitterness in Ryan Lewis.

There's no spite.

It's momentum over strategy, spirit over sales. An amazing coupling of acumen and heart.

My favorite duo.

How could I have known when Wayne Alexander sent Ryan Lewis *Goblin* so long ago, he wasn't matching a writer with a manager but putting together ... friends?

Something beyond friends too:

It's not every day, or even every decade, you meet someone who shares the unspoken core beliefs, a person who believes the things that matter are the same things that matter to you.

As the dedication says, this book is for Ryan.

I already called him halfway through this afterword to tell him what the afterword is about. See? It's what we do. Because no matter how many books you write, no matter how many successes you have, no matter the workload and no matter how many frustrating steps are taken ... it all comes down to finding that place where you can spin a black yarn.

Ryan and I found it.

Fingers crossed. Eyes crossed.

We found it.

And now some thanks:

To Wayne Alexander for thinking Ryan and I might make a good team.

To Kristin Nelson for once telling me she thought the title was better than just a name for a nonexistent publishing house.

To Tricia Narwani for seeing in Samhattan not one book but two. And hopefully more to come.

To the Del Rey team for putting these traveling titles on the shelves of bookstores and libraries.

To Allison for being an indefatigable optimist.

To Wow Town: Let's do a theatrical reading for this book in a house or a hotel. Each of these stories *could* work in individual rooms if we want it. Shawn Hasbro in bed. Egorov in the kitchen. Doug and Judy in the tube. Think: painting the walls of a room like the storms of Jupiter. And just down the hall? A pink room. Where Stephanie's horrifying reality waits.

And, always, to Dave Simmer. Thank you for handing me the knitting needles.

And Ryan?

Let's roll. Like we have.

Eyes crossed.

Let's roll.

And you know what? *A Return to Goblin* sounds like a good idea too.

—Josh Malerman
Michigan
October 2022

JOSH MALERMAN is a *New York Times* bestselling author and one of two singer-songwriters for the rock band The High Strung. His debut novel, *Bird Box*, is the inspiration for the hit Netflix film of the same name. His other novels include *Unbury Carol, Inspection, A House at the Bottom of a Lake, Daphne*, and *Malorie*, the sequel to *Bird Box*. Malerman lives in Michigan with his fiancée, the artist-musician Allison Laakko.

joshmalerman.com
Twitter: @JoshMalerman
Facebook: facebook.com/JoshMalerman
Instagram: @joshmalerman